RIVERS *of* GOLD

RIVERS
of
GOLD

TRACIE PETERSON

BETHANYHOUSE
MINNEAPOLIS, MINNESOTA

Rivers of Gold
Copyright © 2002
Tracie Peterson

Cover design by Jenny Parker

Published by Bethany House Publishers
A Ministry of Bethany Fellowship International
11400 Hampshire Avenue South
Bloomington, Minnesota 55438
www.bethanyhouse.com

Printed in the United States of America by
Bethany Press International, Bloomington, Minnesota 55438

Library of Congress Cataloging-in-Publication Data

Peterson, Tracie.
    Rivers of gold / by Tracie Peterson.
        p.   cm. — (Yukon quest ; 3)
    ISBN 0-7642-2380-1 (pbk.)
    1. Survival after airplane accidents, shipwrecks, etc.—Fiction. 2. Women pioneers—Fiction. 3. Botanists—Fiction. 4. Alaska—Fiction I. Title.
    PS3566.E7717 R58   2002
    813'.54—dc21   2001005674

With special thanks to

Cheryl Thompson,
Administrative Assistant,
Dawson City Museum.

BOOKS *by* TRACIE PETERSON

Controlling Interests
Entangled
Framed
The Long-Awaited Child
A Slender Thread
Tidings of Peace

WESTWARD CHRONICLES

A Shelter of Hope
Hidden in a Whisper
A Veiled Reflection

RIBBONS OF STEEL*

Distant Dreams
A Hope Beyond
A Promise for Tomorrow

RIBBONS WEST*

Westward the Dream
Separate Roads
Ties That Bind

SHANNON SAGA†

City of Angels
Angels Flight

YUKON QUEST

Treasures of the North
Ashes and Ice
Rivers of Gold

*with Judith Pella   †with James Scott Bell

TRACIE PETERSON is an award-winning speaker and writer who has authored over forty-five books, both historical and contemporary fiction. *Angels Flight,* a recent collaboration with James Scott Bell, highlights the courtrooms of 1903 Los Angeles. Tracie and her family make their home in Montana.

Visit Tracie's Web site at: *www.traciepeterson.com.*

Part One

OCTOBER 1898

It is of the Lord's mercies
that we are not consumed, because his
compassions fail not.

LAMENTATIONS 3:22

⊣ CHAPTER ONE ⊢

MIRANDA COLTON floated in a sea of warmth, the sensation unlike any she had ever known. *Maybe I've died*, she thought. *Maybe I've died and this is heaven.* She attempted to open her eyes to confirm her thoughts, but her eyelids were too heavy.

Drifting in and out of a hazy sleep, Miranda knew nothing but the comfort and assurance that all was well. There was no sense of panic. No fear of the unknown. Her spirit rested in complete peace.

In her dreams, she saw herself as a young child, happily playing in fields of flowers, the mist of the ocean upon her skin, the salty taste upon her lips. She lifted her face to the sun and felt the delicious warmth engulf her. She would like to stay here forever. Safe and warm. Happily contented among the green grasses and colorful flowers. At times, a delicate aroma wafted through the air, delighting her further with the luscious scent of roses, honeysuckle, and lilacs.

Then voices called to her. Miranda didn't recognize the language, but somehow she knew the words were being spoken to her. She struggled to listen—to understand. With great difficulty she opened her eyes and stared into the brown, well-worn face of an old woman.

Miranda felt no sense of recollection at the sight of the serious countenance before her. The woman was clearly a stranger, yet she seemed so concerned, so gentle. A momentary tremble of fear seized Miranda's heart, but the woman's tender touch made her realize the old woman was no threat to her well-being.

"You wake up now," the woman said in a thick, almost guttural tongue.

Miranda opened her mouth to reply, but no words came out. Her mouth felt as if it were stuffed with cotton. Closing her eyes, she heard the woman call to her again.

"No sleep. You make too much sleep. You wake up now."

The command did little good. Miranda had no energy for the task.

She felt the woman swab her face with a cool cloth. The woman gently urged, "You wake up. You no die."

Die? Miranda wondered at the word as she listened to the woman chatter on. Wasn't she already dead? She couldn't remember what had happened to her, but she was certain that it had been a very difficult journey. It didn't startle her to think of dying or even of being dead. She merely wondered why she couldn't wake up. Weren't you supposed to see pearly gates and hosts of angels after death? Nowhere in her church upbringing could she remember anything about brown-faced women escorting a person to their reward.

The woman forced water into Miranda's mouth. The cold liquid felt marvelous as it trickled down her throat, dissolving the cotton taste. *How very pleasant,* Miranda thought.

"How is she?" a masculine voice questioned in a decidedly English accent.

Miranda started to open her eyes, certain that she was about to meet God. Funny, she had never thought of him as an Englishman. She hesitated a moment. Didn't the Bible say that you would die if you saw God's face?

Then it came to her. *If this is God, then I'm already dead and it won't matter.* She opened her eyes, prepared to meet her maker. Instead, she met the compassionate gaze of dark brown eyes. The man had a gentleness about him as he leaned over her to touch her forehead.

"I say, seems the fever is gone. You'll soon be right as rain." His dark brown mustache twitched ever so slightly as he offered her a smile.

"What?" Miranda barely croaked the word out.

The man patted her on the head as if she were a small child. "Nellie will fix you right up. You'll see. She's quite gifted in the ways of healing."

Miranda wanted to question the man but had no energy to do so. She watched in silence as he turned to the woman. His alabaster skin was quite the contrast to the older woman's native complexion. His dark hair had a haphazard lay to it. Perhaps he had just awakened, or perhaps he wasn't given to worrying over appearances.

"I've prepared the herbs you asked for, Nellie. That should help considerably. Shall I put a pot of water on to boil?"

The old woman nodded and followed the man. Miranda wanted to call out to them and beg them not to leave her, but again her voice failed her. She tried to remember what had happened to her. *How did I get here?* But even as she worked at the foggy memories, Miranda knew only one thing for certain. This wasn't heaven—she wasn't dead.

Thomas Edward Davenport, Teddy to his friends, turned from the ancient Indian woman and went back to his worktable. He had hoped to have a better showing for a summer's worth of work, but after categorizing the plants and herbs he'd gathered, Teddy was rather disappointed. He would spend the winter recording and cataloging his finds for the botanical research book he intended to produce. This was his life's work—work that had brought him to the vast regions of the Canadian provinces. Leaving his beloved England behind had been a difficult task, but after the death of his mother, Teddy had no real reason to remain. His father had died years before, succumbing to a terrible round of influenza. And while English soil might hold the bodies of his dearly departed parents, Teddy knew their souls were safely in heaven with God.

He glanced across the cabin room and watched Nellie spooning tea into the young woman's mouth. Teddy couldn't help but wonder about the woman. Local natives had brought the half-drowned creature to his door, knowing Nellie had a gift for healing. Teddy could hardly turn the unconscious woman away, but the interruption was most unwelcome. He had no time for diversions. His work would suffer—had already suffered—because of this stranger's arrival.

Teddy toyed with a bit of dried alpine geranium. *Who is she?* he wondered. No doubt she was one of the thousands who had come north with their hearts set on gold. So many parties had been lost upon the wild and reckless waters of the Yukon. The shores along the lakes and rivers were littered with the sad reminders of the invasion from the south. Teddy wished with all his heart that the strangers would all return to wherever they had come from. In the five years he'd been at work in the Yukon, he'd known a tranquil and graceful land. That tranquility, however, was greatly diminished in the wake of the Klondike gold rush.

"She sleep again, but not so long, I think," Nellie said, coming to the table where Teddy worked only halfheartedly. "I think she much better."

Teddy nodded. "Yes, I believe you are right."

"I make you supper," Nellie said and walked back to the stove without another word.

Teddy required the old woman's presence, because without her he simply lost track of time and forgot to eat or sometimes to sleep. His work consumed him. It was a thing of great interest and passion, but it was also a challenge that he could not seem to shake. His father had always loved plant life and his desire to come to North America for the research of Canadian vegetation was a dream Teddy intended to see through to fruition. It was a sort of legacy Teddy would leave in honor of his father.

Albert Davenport had been very much a dreamer. Teddy's mother had found his love of plants annoying, for it had taken them from her beloved estate outside of London and plunged them into the heart of Cornwall. Eugenia Davenport would endure her husband's sojourns to the country for a time, but then, after no more than a month, she would announce her return to London. Declaring she would simply perish from the isolation of the country, Eugenia cut everyone's stay short, for her husband was not inclined to remain in the country without her.

Teddy had adored his mother, for she was a loving parent, but he'd also resented the pain she caused his father. Albert's dreams were unimportant to her, but not to Teddy. He had vowed to his father, even as he lay dying, that he would see to fruition his father's dream of creating a great book of botanical study on the Canadian landscape. That vow had become a driving force in Teddy's life, and he was bound and determined to see it through.

Perhaps that was why the presence of this woman bothered him so greatly. He didn't want this stranger to become a deterrent to his work, as his mother had been to his father.

Teddy glanced back across the room to where the young woman slept. She had been in his cabin for over three weeks. Off and on she would awaken and then fall back to sleep. Nellie said her lungs had been full of lake water, and at first, the old woman hadn't believed the stranger would live. Teddy had prayed for the injured woman, knowing that there were some things only God could heal. Within a fortnight, Nellie announced her belief that the woman would recover. It would take time for a full recovery, however. Time Teddy wasn't entirely sure he could offer.

It was already October and the snows had set in. Normally he would already be heading back to his hotel room in Dawson. But he could hardly pick up and leave this complication. The woman couldn't be left behind—but neither could she be moved.

Teddy pushed up his sleeves and leaned forward on the table. What was he to do? The woman needed him. She was helpless, and although Nellie felt confident of her recovery, Teddy couldn't help but wonder what he was to do with her once she regained her health.

A knock on the cabin door brought Teddy out of his thoughts. What new interruption awaited him? Nellie padded across the room, a slight limp noticeable as she walked. He had once asked her about the limp and she'd told him a horrific tale of having been caught in a trap when she'd been young. The incident had left her both scarred and crippled. Teddy offered her his condolences, and Nellie had merely shrugged, saying, "It not your trap did this."

Nellie opened the door and stood back to look at Teddy. Teddy didn't recognize the man at the door. The stranger pushed back his fur parka and brushed crusty ice from his beard.

"I wonder if I might warm up for a spell," the man questioned.

Teddy nodded. "Come in. I'm about to take supper."

"I'm much obliged," the man said. "The name's Buckley. J. D. Buckley."

"Thomas Davenport," Teddy replied. Nellie closed the door behind the man and waited to take his coat. "Feel free to warm up at the stove or the fireplace," Teddy added.

"It's not too bad out there today," Buckley stated. "I've seen worse, but I'm glad to be inside for a spell."

Teddy nodded. He didn't usually get visitors and that was the way he liked it. Though centrally located for his work, his cabin was well off the beaten path. There had been an increase in traffic since the gold rush pandemonium, but his

TRACIE PETERSON

area hadn't yielded much in the way of profitable dust. For this, he was most grateful.

"If I might ask," Teddy began, "how did you find yourself in this part of the country?"

The man rubbed his hands together. "Well, to tell you the truth, I got lost. I ain't been up in these parts long, and I guess I took a wrong turn. I was following the Yukon River, then moved inland for a ways in order to follow an easier path. I thought I'd stayed with the Yukon, but now I see I didn't."

"You most likely took the fork for the Indian River. It runs off the Yukon, and if you walk too far inland and aren't familiar with the lay of the land, it's easy enough to get way-laid. Especially as you fork off from the Indian River and follow some of the lesser creeks and streams, which surely you must have done to wind up here."

"Can you point me in the direction of Dawson?"

"That I can, but the hour is much too late to travel." Teddy knew, regrettably, that he had no choice but to offer the man lodging. It was a sort of code in the north. You dealt kindly with strangers, otherwise it could cost someone their life. Especially when the weather turned cold and unforgiving. "You're welcome to lay your blanket by the stove. I can't offer you much in the way of privacy or space, but it will be considerably warmer than a tent in the woods."

"That's mighty kind of you, Mr. Davenport."

"Think nothing of it."

Nellie dished up a thick elk stew and placed the wooden bowls on the table. "You eat now."

Teddy pushed his work aside and motioned to the man. "Please pardon my poor manners. Pull up a chair and join

20

me. Nellie will bring us tea and biscuits as well."

"Sounds good. I'm afraid I ain't had a hot meal in some time."

Teddy frowned. "Have you been lost all that long?"

The man took out a handkerchief and blew his nose loudly. Bits of ice loosened from his mustache and beard, seeming to soften the stranger's appearance. "I ain't been lost all that time, but to tell the truth, my partners and me had a falling out. I got the sled and a few other supplies, but not much in the way of food."

"Have you dogs for the sled?"

The man laughed. "Nope, been pulling the heavy thing myself. My partners kept the dogs, knowing they'd fetch a good price in Dawson. Fact is, I really have no need for the sled. You wouldn't be of a mind to trade me for some food, now, would you?"

Teddy rubbed his chin. The stubble reminded him he'd not shaved that morning. "I just might be able to help you out. I have a guest staying with me who is quite weak. It might be a good thing to have a sled to carry her in when I make my way to Dawson."

"I'd surely be obliged."

"Then consider it a deal. We'll arrange a pack for you and load it with a variety of food. I'll be closing out the cabin and heading to Dawson myself as soon as my guest can travel, so I'll give you what I can."

The man nodded and dug into the stew without another word. Teddy cleared his throat and asked, "Do you mind if I offer up thanks?"

The man looked rather sheepish and put down his spoon. "Like I said, I ain't ate a hot meal in a while. Weren't no disrespect intended to the Almighty."

Teddy bowed his head. "For that which you have provided, oh God, we thank you. Bless us now as we share this meal. May you ever be the unseen guest at my table. Amen."

"Amen," Buckley said, barely waiting long enough to utter the word before shoveling another spoonful of stew into his mouth.

Teddy glanced across the room to where Nellie ministered to the sick woman. He had thought of giving her a name. Always calling her "the woman" seemed so impersonal and somehow unkind. But since he'd spent his life's work attaching the proper name to plants, he didn't feel right in simply attaching a random moniker to the stranger.

"So what brings you out here, mister? Gold?"

Teddy returned his gaze to the man and noticed that he looked around the room with an unguarded interest. "No, I'm afraid not. I've no interest in rivers of gold unless they hold some new botanical specimens."

"Botanical what?"

"Specimens. I am conducting research on the vegetation of the region. I'm chronicling it for a book."

"So you're an educated fellow?"

Teddy smiled. "I suppose you might call me that. I've a deep love of learning."

"Ain't had much time for such things myself. My pa didn't hold much respect for learnin' in a school. He said life was a better teacher."

Nellie brought them tea and a platter of biscuits. Without a word she placed the food on the table.

"Could you spare another bowl?" Buckley questioned, raising the empty bowl.

"Certainly. Nellie, please give the man another portion."

The old woman nodded and took the bowl. She seemed none too pleased to deal with the stranger. She hadn't cared for white men when Teddy approached her village some five years earlier. She had seen the damage done by the prospectors and others who had come north for their own greedy reasons. This was prior to the rush, and now that hundreds poured into her land on a daily basis, her feelings were only confirmed.

Teddy had won her over by first winning over her son Little Charley, so called not because of his physical size but to distinguish him from Big Charley, his father. Unable to speak their native language, Teddy had been greatly relieved to find many of the natives spoke a fair amount of English. Teddy explained his situation and offered to hire on several of the English-speaking natives to guide him and assist him in identifying the vegetation they found.

Five years of honorable relations had forged a bond between Teddy and Nellie. She now stayed with him from the breakup of the ice until the first heavy snows. She seemed to know when Teddy would return without his even telling her. The day or so before he was ready to head out, Nellie would be packed and ready to leave the cabin. Then when he returned in May, he would find her already sweeping out the musty cabin. They had a companionable relationship, and Teddy knew that part of this was due to his contentment with solitude, as well as his respect for the land.

Nellie put the refilled bowl in front of the stranger, then left the men to their meal. Teddy wondered if Nellie sensed something dangerous about the man. He eyed Buckley with a steady gaze, hoping that, should the man be more than he appeared, God would give Teddy clarity to know the truth. But Buckley had eyes only for the meal and scarcely drew a breath while devouring the stew.

Well, God always has a purpose for allowing circumstances in our lives, Teddy thought. He hadn't yet figured out the reason for the unconscious woman's appearance or the stranger's, but Teddy was content to leave the matter to God. Leaving the details of life to his heavenly Father left Teddy free to concentrate on what really mattered. Not that the woman didn't intrigue him, but he couldn't afford to let himself get carried away. His work came first. His work would honor his father and bring glory to God.

—[CHAPTER  TWO]—

"IT JUST DOESN'T seem like Christmas should be only days away," Karen Ivankov said as she hung up a pair of her husband's trousers to dry. "I figured we'd be in a cabin by now."

Grace Colton, now swollen in the latter months of pregnancy, nodded. Her brown eyes were edged with dark circles. "I'd hoped so as well. I hate the thought of bringing a baby into this world with nothing more than a tent to offer for a home."

Karen's strawberry blond hair curled tight from the humidity of the washtub. She pushed back an errant strand, regretting that she hadn't taken the time to pin it up. The heat felt good, however, and Karen cared little for her appearance, given their setting. Living through the Yukon winter in a tent hardly allowed for niceties such as fancy hairstyles and pretty clothes. In this country everything needed to be functional and useful. Otherwise it was just extra baggage.

Her husband, Adrik, had tried hard to find them a home. He'd hoped to stake a claim and build them a house, but the pickings were slim and most of the good land was taken. Those who wanted to sell out and leave before the winter charged exorbitant prices. One man sold his claim, complete with cabin, for thirty thousand dollars before catching the last boat out of Dawson. For a family who had barely managed to hang on to the smallest amount of money, thirty thousand dollars was nothing more than a dream.

"We'll just have to make the best of it," Karen finally replied. "I know Adrik doesn't want us here any more than we want to be here."

"Of course not," Grace agreed.

"Don't worry, Grace," thirteen-year-old Leah Barringer encouraged. "We can make things real nice for you and the baby. You'll see. Jacob said he'd build you a cradle. He remembers when Pa made one."

"Your brother has his hands full, chopping enough wood to keep us warm," Grace said with a smile. "But I appreciate the thought."

"At least it's warmed up some," Leah offered. "It's not nearly as cold as it was in November."

"That's for sure. I hope I never see forty below again," Karen commented. "A person can hardly move away from the stove for fear of their blood freezing in their veins."

"Yes, it's much warmer now. I heard Adrik say this morning that it was clear up to five degrees above zero," Grace said, turning her attention back to her sewing.

"A veritable heat wave," Karen said, laughing. She wrung

out the last of the laundry and hung it over the line. "We'll just pull together. I know this isn't what any of us imagined, but since Christmas is nearly upon us, we should plan for some sort of celebration."

"The Catholic church needs folks to sing in the choir for the midnight mass on Christmas Eve," Leah offered.

"We aren't Catholic."

Leah looked to Karen and shrugged. "It doesn't matter. They said they'd take anybody they could get. Apparently the other churches help them out on Christmas Eve, then the Catholics come and help out on Christmas Day with our church. I guess they just want it to sound pretty for Jesus' birthday."

To Karen, the idea didn't seem like such a bad one. It was a pleasant thought to imagine churches joining together to offer each other support in spite of their differences. "I suppose we could go sing with them on Christmas Eve. I'll speak to Adrik about it."

"Jacob won't want to go. He can't sing. He says that Ma and I were the only ones who were blessed with that talent. He and Pa couldn't carry a tune no matter how hard they tried."

Karen noted the twinge of sorrow in Leah's voice. Her mother had died prior to the family's coming north, and her father was believed to have died in an avalanche near Sheep Camp. The child had no one, save her brother, Jacob, to call family. Karen loved the girl, however. Her brother, too. Karen had become a surrogate big sister and mother all rolled into one. She had made a promise to herself and to God that she would care for these children until they were grown and able to care for themselves. It seemed a companionable arrangement, and they offered each other comfort in the wake of each tragedy.

And the entourage had known their share of sorrow. Karen had come to Alaska in hopes of finding her missionary father. He had died before they could be reunited. Grace had lost her sister-in-law, Miranda, during a storm on Lake Laberge. This had also been a huge blow to the morale of the party—especially to Adrik's friend Crispin Thibault, who fancied himself in love with Miranda. Crispin had long since parted their company—seeking his solace in a bottle of whiskey rather than God. He was one more casualty of the gold rush as far as Karen was concerned.

The frozen north was well known for exacting its toll. Families all around them had suffered loss. Babies and children died from malnutrition and exposure to the cold. Women died in childbirth, and men were often injured while working to mine their claims. Death was everywhere. It was the one thing that truly bound them all together—even more so than the gold.

"Isn't there some sort of town Christmas party planned?" Grace questioned. "I heard one of the nurses talking about it when I was over to the hospital the other day."

"Yes, there are plans for quite a shindig," Karen replied. "I suppose that will be the best we will have for a celebration. There's hardly opportunity or means to exchange gifts and certainly no room to put up a tree in here."

She looked around the room. The eighteen-by-twenty-foot tent had seemed so big when Adrik had managed to trade their smaller two tents for this one. Now, the walls seemed to have moved closer together. They had five people living in a space hardly big enough for two. Karen was most anxious to put an end to the adventure.

"So did you get a chance to talk to Father Judge?" Karen asked Grace. Grace had gone to the Roman Catholic hospital to inquire as to the expense for having her baby delivered there by a doctor.

"For all the good it did. He told me it would be one thousand dollars for my hospital and doctor's fees."

"A thousand?" Karen asked in disbelief. "That's outrageous. How in the world can he expect us to come up with that much money?"

"We can't," Grace replied sadly. "Apparently the hospitals are poorly equipped for women's needs. The nurse there suggested I talk to a midwife. So I spoke to a woman who lives just over the river. She can come to the tent and deliver the baby and will only charge me a hundred dollars."

Karen's emotions got the best of her. "Prices are so inflated a person can scarcely stand in one place without being charged for it. If we weren't squatting on this land now, we'd be paying through the nose for rent."

"Don't forget what Adrik said," Leah offered. "Nobody much cares that we're here right now. The town offers folks more interest because of gambling and drinking. But if they find gold over here or if someone decides it's worth something, then we'll be in trouble." She had quoted Adrik almost verbatim.

"Still, we need the town to survive. We can hardly head out into the Klondike with Grace due to have a baby any day. That would be totally senseless. It's bad enough that we're as far away as we are, especially with the river standing between us. Come spring, there will no doubt be problems," Karen muttered.

"We couldn't very well afford any of the sites in town. Not that much of anything decent was available," Grace offered.

Karen sighed and reached up to tie back her hair. "It's all about money—the love of it is destroying the heart and soul of the people who crave it."

"Still, we can hardly exist without it," Grace said, adding, "even if it is hard to come by."

"We'll just have to get the money," Leah said as if by saying the words the money might magically appear.

"Well, I was waiting to share this news until later, but I might as well tell you now. I heard about a job," Karen announced. "They need a cook at one of the restaurants. They're willing to pay $150 a month."

"To cook?" Grace questioned, looking up. "Are you sure about that amount?"

"Very sure. It was only to be one hundred dollars, but that was if I needed room and board. I convinced them that I didn't, but that I did need the extra cash. We settled on fifty dollars more, and I've agreed to take the position."

"What did Adrik say?" Grace asked, looking to Leah as if she might have the answer. The child in turn looked to Karen.

"He doesn't know about it—yet. I figured I'd tell him after I hear what news he comes back with this time. If he still hasn't managed to find us a cabin, then I'll tell him. We're running out of money, so someone has to do something. Besides, this is a good amount of guaranteed money. He may well change his mind and want us to stay here."

"We have plenty of food," Leah offered.

"Yes, but that won't last forever. Besides it's mostly dried goods. Our canned goods are running low and we haven't had fresh fruits or vegetables in forever," Karen replied. "And even though Adrik and Jacob managed to shoot an elk and a moose, there are so many other supplies we need. Soap, for one, and that costs a small fortune. I think the job is exactly what we need to help us fill our purses again. I can cook fairly well, and it's not like I'd be doing the job forever."

"I suppose not," Grace said, "but I can't imagine that Adrik will like the idea."

Karen thought of her bear of a husband. His large frame often caused folks to shy away, thus, they never learned of his gentle nature. Karen knew her husband wouldn't like the idea of her having to work to keep their heads above water. Especially when the jobs he'd managed to find while searching for a claim or housing offered so little pay. The real money was in the saloons and gambling houses, and Adrik refused to work for either of those. Karen wholeheartedly supported his conviction.

"He'll just have to get used to the idea. My mind is made up," Karen said firmly. "He knows I'm pigheaded. He knew it when he married me. It comes with the red hair and Irish heritage." She laughed at this, but a part of her was edgy and nervous at the thought of facing Adrik with the news.

———

In the weeks that followed Miranda's return to consciousness, she gradually regained her physical strength. The old Indian woman she'd seen in her dreams proved to be a real person—so, too, the handsome man. Her surroundings were unimpressive. A crude log cabin with two rooms kept out most of the wind, but not the cold. A large cooking stove and small fireplace offered the main sources of heat, with a smaller stove in the solitary bedroom on the back of the house. It was in this room that the handsome man spent his nights.

Teddy was most unusual, Miranda had decided. It was evident he loved his work and God, but he seemed interested in little else. He worked until the late hours of the night before retiring and was almost always up and working again before Miranda would rise for the day.

Day. Now, that was a word Miranda thought rather a misnomer. There was no day or very little of it, for darkness surrounded them most of the time. Miranda thought she might go mad at times. The hours of hazy gray light were so few—only four or five at best. How she missed the sunshine and beauty of her San Francisco home. Even a foggy day there would be better than the muted light of the Yukon.

"How are you feeling today?" Teddy asked, barely looking up from the notes he was making as he crossed the room.

Miranda had taken her breakfast at the table and was still seated there, contemplating the dark. "I'm feeling much better, thank you."

"I'm glad to hear that. Nellie's returning to her family."

The words came out without any indication of concern. Miranda looked up, rather stunned. "Leaving? When?"

Teddy shrugged. "Today or tomorrow. She would have returned a long time ago, but . . ."

"But for me. I'm sorry to have been a burden on everyone. I'm so very grateful for all that you've done. Nellie, too." Miranda had shared her gratitude many times, but each time Nellie had only nodded and Teddy had actually seemed embarrassed—just as he did now.

Teddy turned away from her, but not before Miranda saw his cheeks flush.

"Yes, well. I must return to work. If we're going to be stranded here, I must accomplish as much as possible."

"But when will we go to Dawson? I need to find out if my friends survived the storm." Miranda couldn't really re-member much of what had happened on that fateful day, but she did recall the rolling black clouds and rain. She had a vague memory of being tossed about on the deck of their scow, but little else until waking up in Teddy's cabin. Had she not been told that she'd most likely been thrown overboard on Lake Laberge, Miranda would have had no idea of what had happened. It simply didn't register in her memory.

Teddy put his journal aside and threw more wood into the stove. He dropped several pieces and awkwardly bent to pick them up. "I . . . well, that is to say . . ."

He turned and met her gaze. Gold-colored spectacles framed his dark brown eyes. Miranda had noticed he only wore them when he was busy with his writing. No doubt the dark wreaked havoc with his sight.

Teddy turned toward the window, as if surveying the weather conditions. "I suppose we'll be able to head out soon. I'll ask Nellie to send her son Little Charley over. I'll talk to him about helping us with the sleds."

"The snows are very deep, aren't they?" Miranda asked. She had peered from the doorway on more than one occa-sion and had been stunned to see the snow-covered land-scape. Her hometown of San Francisco didn't get much snow—certainly nothing like this.

"That's why we'll go by sled," Teddy replied, turning to

pull his coat from a hook near the door. "I must see to something. I'll be back."

Taking up a lantern, he hurried out before Miranda could make any comment. He was such a nervous sort. Miranda wasn't entirely sure if it was simply his nature or if she caused him this discomfort.

Getting up from the table, Miranda went to the stove and warmed her hands. She couldn't help but wonder about Grace and Karen and the others. She prayed they were safe. Prayed they'd not be worried overmuch about her. Teddy said it was nearly Christmas, and last Miranda could remember it had been September.

"They have no way of knowing I'm safe," she whispered. "They probably have given me up for dead." It sorrowed her to imagine them weeping over her when she was safe and sound. It sorrowed her even more to imagine they'd not made it through the storm. If she'd been thrown overboard, there was a good chance they had been lost, as well.

Dread washed over her in waves and continued with each new revelation. Mr. Davenport had said that Nellie was leaving. That would mean she'd be alone with a man. A man she scarcely knew. It certainly wasn't appropriate, yet there seemed to be no choice in the matter.

Thinking of Teddy Davenport only complicated things. His nervousness around her amused Miranda, while at the same time his lack of interest in sharing conversation or even a meal left her lonely and frustrated. He was unlike any man she'd ever known. He seemed to care whether she recovered, but he wanted very little to do with her otherwise.

Miranda supposed that should comfort her mind about the upcoming departure of Nellie. But it didn't. Instead, it only added to her worry. What if the man was only acting this way because Nellie was around? True, she was an Indian and most whites held little respect for the natives, but it was very possible it was her presence in the house, sleeping on the pallet at the foot of Miranda's bed, that kept Mr. Davenport silent and subdued.

Picking at the worn wool skirt she wore, Miranda could only pray for comfort. "God, please give me hope. Please watch over me and strengthen me so I can go to Dawson and find my family and friends. And please, God, please let them all be safe and well." She thought again of the man who'd offered her a place in his cabin. "Thank you, Lord, for Mr. Davenport's kindness. Please, please, let his heart be fixed on you. Don't let him hurt me." But even as she prayed, Miranda felt the words were almost ridiculous. Teddy Davenport had proved to be no threat to her well-being. Perhaps she was borrowing trouble by even concerning herself with the matter.

With little else that she could do, Miranda curled up on her bed and dozed in the warmth of the heavy quilts. Her dreams were interrupted, however, when Teddy came bursting through the door.

"You'll never believe what I just found!" He panted and his breath came out in little white clouds that faded in the warmth of the room. He stomped his snowy boots and held up a small branch of dried, dead leaves.

"It's a *Salix hookeriana.* They're supposed to be limited to the Alaskan Territory."

"I beg your pardon?" Miranda questioned and got to her feet. She'd never seen Mr. Davenport more animated. "A *Salix* what?"

"*Hookeriana*," he declared. "A Hooker willow. William Jackson Hooker discovered them and wrote about this species as being isolated to Alaskan plant life—but here it is in the Yukon. He was wrong! This will certainly validate my work."

Miranda sunk back to the bed. She looked to the man and tried to gather some excitement for his find, but her heart was still racing from the shock.

"I suppose I am very happy for you, Mr. Davenport," she finally offered.

"And well you should be. This is most sensational."

Teddy appeared mindless of the snow from his boots melting into puddles on the floor. He crossed the room, took down a book, and without even bothering to shed his coat, went to the stove where he kept his ink ready for use.

"I might never have found it but for your arrival and our late departure. A rare specimen, indeed," he declared, then turned his full attention to the branch.

"Glad I could be of help," Miranda muttered and shook her head. The man was truly a rare specimen himself.

—|CHAPTER THREE|—

"WELL, I'LL BE!" declared Adrik Ivankov. He slapped his right thigh and let out a loud and hearty laugh. "If it ain't Gumption Lindquist."

An old man with a full head of snowy white hair looked up from his plate of food. His thick and equally white mustache twitched in amusement. "Ja, dat be me."

"I figured you for grizzly food by now," Adrik said, pulling Karen along with him. "Gump, I want you to meet my wife. You always said I'd never get married unless I found a woman uglier than me. I just wanted to show you how wrong you were. I got the cream of the crop."

"Ja, dat you did," the Swede said, putting aside his plate. He got to his feet and without warning, pulled Karen into a welcoming embrace. "She looks like good stock. You done well for yourself, boy."

"Karen, this old reprobate is Gumption Lindquist. Gump to his friends."

Gump released Karen and nodded. "Ja, you call me Gump."

Karen smiled at the old man. He looked much like many of the other miners, well-worn and weathered, yet he had a contentment about him that others seemed to lack. "Gumption is such a unique name for someone to call their child."

Gump's smile broadened, revealing a full set of perfectly matched teeth. "My folks, they had six boys before I come along. Not a one of them was amountin' to much, so my father, he say, 'Let's call this one Gumption. I've always wanted one of the boys to have some, might as well give it to this one in a name.'"

Adrik reached out and reclaimed his wife. "Too bad they missed again with you."

Gump laughed and picked his plate back up. "Ja, they didn't think much of me leavin' the farm to come north when I was a boy."

"So were you living in America?" Karen asked.

"Ja, I was born in Sweden but grew up in Kansas. We had a farm."

"Gump came north way back when he was just seventeen," Adrik told her. "Of course, I wasn't born yet, but my father was. He and Gump were good friends. They used to fish together."

"Ja, dat's right." The old man shoveled a huge hunk of moose tongue into his mouth and smiled as if he'd died and gone to heaven.

Karen looked to her husband. "I wish Grace would have

felt like coming tonight. This looks like quite the celebration."

"It's a good one, by golly," Gump replied. "I remember last year. I had Christmas dinner with some of the fellas who were working claims near to mine. We had quite the time, not near so good as this, but nearly."

Karen heard the makeshift band strike up a Christmas carol. It echoed across the main room of the log house. Donated by one of the local families, the cabin was about twenty-by-twenty and was decorated from top to bottom with whatever could be found. Greenery, guns, and even a Union Jack flag had been nailed to the wall to lend itself to the occasion.

"So, Gump, did you strike it rich?"

"Nah, I find a bit now and then. Usually enough to keep me interested," the man said in between bites of food. " 'Course, with the cold you have to wait. I light a few fires and dig up some ground. Come spring I'll go through it, all righty."

"Do you know anyone who's selling out for a cheap price? Even a fractional claim?" Adrik asked.

"Nah. Most folks are hunkered down for the vinter."

Karen liked the man's singsong cadence of speech. His intonations went up and down like a child's seesaw.

"I was afraid of that," Adrik said, frowning. "I'd heard someone mention the government was changing the rules on claims. Guess we'll have to check into it. We've not had much luck in securing a claim or a house. We're living in a tent across the river, about a mile or so from town. There's five of us, soon to be six. My wife's friend is expecting a baby soon."

"It's not a good time to be havin' a baby."

Karen tried not to let the old man's tone frighten her. She knew well enough the odds were against them. The bitter cold and lack of money did nothing to reassure her that things would be all right.

"Vait a minute," Gump said suddenly. "I know a man who says he vants to hire folks to help him. Maybe he vould hire you on and give you a place to live."

"Does he have a cabin?" Adrik questioned.

"Ja, a good big one, with two, maybe three rooms. He had him some friends vorkin' with him, but they go home before vinter. He been out there all by himself, and I know he could use the help."

"Well, I'd like to talk to him," Adrik said, looking to Karen. "We'd be happy to work for the man. Karen is a good cook and fine housekeeper."

"Not that he'd know," Karen threw in. "We haven't lived in a house since we married."

Gump laughed. "By golly, we go ask him tomorrow. He didn't come tonight or we could ask him now."

"That's all right. It'll wait until tomorrow," Adrik answered.

For the first time in a long while, Karen heard hope in her husband's voice. She knew he worried incessantly about his little band of travelers. He and Jacob had taken odd jobs from time to time—sometimes splitting wood or helping with construction. But more often than not, there was nothing to do—not that would earn them any money.

Karen thought at least a dozen times to tell Adrik about the new job she'd taken. He wouldn't be happy, however, and because of this she delayed. She didn't want to upset him. Now that he had prospects of a place to live and a real job,

Karen figured she'd just wait until they knew something for sure. For the time, she'd just enjoy the holidays and the party that the people of Dawson had put together.

The celebration was a kind of combination for Christmas and Boxing Day. The party lasted well into the night and by the time they'd stuffed themselves with moose and mince pies, plum pudding, and cakes, it was nearly one o'clock in the morning.

Jacob had taken Leah back to the tent hours earlier, and now as Karen and Adrik made their way from the happy celebration, Karen couldn't help but feel a sense of desire to keep her husband to herself for just a little longer.

"I wish we didn't have to go back—just yet. I kind of like being alone with you."

Adrik looked at her and grinned. "Why, Mrs. Ivankov, behave yourself."

Overhead the northern lights danced and crackled. No matter how many times she saw it, Karen could never get used to the wonder of this cosmic show. Red and green ribbons of light danced on the cold night air. The colors changed, and white, almost as bright as sunlight for just a moment, burst through and streaked the skies. This was followed by blue and then green.

"I've never seen anything so beautiful!" Karen declared.

Adrik pulled her into his arms. "Nor have I."

She looked up and found his gazed fixed on her. "I meant the skies. The aurora."

"I didn't." His voice was low and husky. Karen hardly noticed the sub-zero temperatures around them.

"I love you, Adrik." She thought for a moment of telling him about her job but knew it would ruin the moment.

"Please never forget how very much I love you."

He lowered his lips to hers for the briefest kiss, then pulled away. "We'd best get home or we just might freeze this way."

Karen giggled. "Can't you see the story in the *Klondike Nugget*? Husband and wife found frozen together."

"It wouldn't be the first time, sadly enough. When I think of all the folks who've been lost on the trail north . . . Well, it's enough to discourage a man." Adrik held her close and moved them toward home. "I'll be gone several days as I travel to speak with the man about the cabin," he said, changing the subject. "Maybe even weeks. Gump can put me up. Will you be all right?"

"I'm sure we will. We're not that far from help if we need it. Plus, we have those two other families living nearby. If I need anything I can always call on them."

"I know, but I just want reassurance. I figure to take Jacob with me. He wants to ask about his pa around the claims."

"He just isn't ready to let go of the hope that Bill is still alive." Karen felt sorry for the boy. Leah had handled her father's death better than her older brother. Jacob seemed driven to confirm his father's existence or death, while Leah was content to relegate it to the past.

"I wish we could be certain of what happened to Bill, but so many people have lost loved ones. The lists held by the Mounties go on and on. Folks get lost on the trail, freeze under an avalanche, or drown in the rapids."

"Or during a lake storm, like Miranda."

"Exactly. This territory is unforgiving—and is not in the leastwise interested in whether it hurts your feelings. It's more likely to claim a life than to spare it. My guess is that both Bill and Miranda have been sharing the Lord's table in heaven."

They were nearing the tent and Karen couldn't help but pause. "Adrik, I know God has blessed us and will show us where to go—where to settle. My biggest concern right now is for Grace. It's not going to be easy to have a baby out here—in the dead of winter."

"I thought she arranged to have the baby at the hospital in town."

"She would have, but the priest told her it would cost a thousand dollars."

"That's robbery. I thought they were doing God's work."

Karen smiled. "Well, apparently God's work costs more up on the Klondike."

"Everything costs more here. I just hope Grace can nurse that baby without any trouble. What little fresh cow's milk can be had is sixteen dollars a gallon, and canned milk is running out fast."

"I'm sure we'll get by," Karen told him, looping her arm through his. But in truth, she worried about such things as well. Perhaps if she told him about the job, he'd relax and accept that God had provided them a way to at least have money to buy the essentials they needed.

"Come on, let's get inside. The temperature's already dropped considerably. Gump says it's going way down—maybe even as low as sixty below."

Karen shivered just at the prospect of such an unreasonable temperature. "I doubt I'll ever be warm again."

Adrik laughed. "I'll keep you warm. Once we get

snuggled into my sleeping bag, there won't be room for the cold to bother us."

"Won't be room for you to breathe either."

"Then I'll hold my breath. Being that close to you leaves me breathless anyway."

———

Sometimes when Miranda first woke up, she could almost believe that she was safely back at home in San Francisco. At those times, like now, she would purposefully keep her eyes closed tight and imagine that when she opened them she'd see the white fluttering curtains that graced her bedroom window at home. She could almost smell her mother's cooking. Oatmeal and sausages. Coffee and tea.

She liked to pretend what she would do that day. Thoughts of long strolls in the park or shopping for fresh fish at the wharf seemed most appealing. Funny how she had taken all that for granted.

"Oh, bother!" Teddy declared from across the room.

Miranda realized the poor man was struggling to fix his own breakfast again. Smiling, she eased out from the bed, fully dressed albeit wrinkled. She used her fingers to get the better part of the tangles out of her hair. Mr. Davenport had seemed completely oblivious to her needs. A blizzard had kept them locked inside the cabin after Nellie had gone back to her village. There had been no sign of Little Charley and the dog sleds, but in this weather, Miranda hadn't really expected them.

She quickly plaited her hair and tied it with a worn piece of rawhide. "Can I help?" she asked, coming to kitchen area.

"I would be very grateful if you would take this matter

over," Teddy replied as he gestured toward a pan full of oat-meal, which was running over onto the tiny stovetop.

Miranda wanted to laugh, but the situation was such that she didn't. She merely took the task in hand. "How much oatmeal did you put into the pan?"

"I don't know. I filled it halfway and then stirred water in until it was filled."

Miranda kept her head down so that he couldn't see her smile. "That's way too much oatmeal. You only need a cup or so to make enough for both of us."

"I can see that now. At least the coffee is passable. Strong, but passable."

"Good. Now why don't you set the table, and I'll have this mess under control in just a minute."

Teddy nodded and went quietly to the task of pulling down bowls from the cupboard. It was in moments like this that Miranda liked Mr. Davenport very much. But other times she didn't know what to make of him. He seemed so closed off—so antisocial. He constantly buried his nose in his books and writings, and whenever Miranda tried to talk to him, he only grunted and murmured unintelligible answers.

This, added to the fact that he had no apparent under-standing of time, left Miranda frustrated with the man. She'd asked him several times when they might find their way to Dawson. He'd only shrugged and suggested they were at the mercy of the weather and the natives. Without the sled dogs and help of his friends they were stranded, because Teddy had no way to pack his supplies and books back to Dawson.

Miranda cleared away the excess oatmeal, salvaging what she could for their meal. She turned to bring the pan to the table when she smelled the unmistakable odor of something burning.

She stopped and sniffed the air. Turning, she looked once again to the stove to make certain she'd not missed some of the oatmeal in her cleanup and was surprised to see the smoke wasn't coming from atop the stove, but rather the oven door showed the telltale sign of black wisps.

"Mr. Davenport," Miranda questioned, turning back to Teddy. "Have you something in the oven?"

"Oh, dear," he muttered, dashing across the room and sending Miranda sprawling backward onto the floor. Oatmeal flew from the pan and landed everywhere, including on Miranda's only skirt and blouse.

Teddy, meanwhile, reached into the oven, showing at least the presence of mind to use a potholder, and pulled out a pan of charred remains that Miranda supposed to be biscuits.

Thinking it all rather amusing in spite of, or perhaps because of, the oatmeal that oozed down her cheek and blouse, Miranda began to giggle—quietly at first, and then louder. Teddy caught sight of her and shook his head.

"This isn't funny. Just look at this mess. Look at yourself."

"I am." Miranda wiped away the tears that had trickled down her cheeks. "That's why I'm laughing."

Teddy cocked his head to one side and then tossed the pan into the sink. "Well, I see nothing funny about this. Our breakfast is either burned or splattered across the floor."

Miranda shook off her mirth and got to her feet, no thanks to Teddy offering any help. "My mother always said, 'When bad times come we can either laugh at them or cry.'"

"That makes no sense. Was your mother quite all right in the head?"

Miranda picked up the pan. "I assure you, my mother was quite sane. She was also very content with life because she tried never to let problems overwhelm her. I wish I could be more like her."

"I'm not entirely certain that would be to your benefit."

Miranda smiled and began wiping up the oatmeal. "Well, I know for certain that it would greatly benefit us both to stop taking things so seriously. Who knows, Mr. Davenport. You might actually have some fun."

———

As Teddy added wood to the fireplace and prepared to retire for the night, he thought of Miranda's words and shook his head. His mother had always been one for having fun. As a young boy, Teddy had enjoyed her zest for living. Where his father would have been content to sit in his solarium cultivating a new type of rose, Eugenia Davenport was one for cultivating life.

It had been his mother who had taught Teddy to ride and hunt, his mother who had taken him to the museum and opera. She had spent hours teaching him about art and the pleasure that could be had in a single painting.

His mother had loved people with a great passion, and her enthusiasm was contagious. Teddy remembered as a boy being allowed to join his mother for luncheons and afternoon teas. The food was always an adventure of flavors served on the finest china. And it was his mother's laughter that rang out most clearly in his memory—laughter not so very much different than that of Miranda Colton.

The flames greedily consumed the dried logs, crackling and popping. Teddy's memories intertwined with the present.

His mother and Miranda Colton were very much alike. They both had a flair for living that seemed to overwhelm their environment. Teddy was more like his father. He enjoyed the quietness and solitude of introspection. He preferred a good book or time spent with his plants, to conversation and revelry.

He thought of his father succumbing to an ailment the doctors were never quite sure how to diagnose. Cancer seemed the most likely culprit, but there was nothing that could have been done on any account. His father simply wasted away, day after day. His dreams of travel to North America dying with him.

"I won't disappoint you, Father," Teddy whispered, staring into the fire as if he could see the image of Albert Davenport in the flames. "I'll stay the course."

He heard Miranda sigh in her sleep and felt a foreign sensation creep up his spine. She was a lovely woman—gentle and spirited and lovely—in spite of the lack of amenities with which to care for herself.

Eugenia Davenport had also been a lovely woman—and she had broken his father's heart. Teddy squared his shoulders and firmed his resolve. He wouldn't fall victim to the same temptations as his father. He wouldn't allow a woman to put an end to his dreams.

⊣ CHAPTER FOUR ⊢

"PLEASE UNDERSTAND," Miranda began. "I don't mean to be a bother, but I'm most desperate to get to Dawson City. Is there no way we can get a message to your native friends?"

Teddy looked up, distraught to have been drawn once again from his work. "Do explain to me, Miss Colton, how we might send this message."

Miranda crossed her arms. He noted the determined look in her eye. She was a pretty young woman, probably at least five years his junior. *Her eyes are most appealing*, he thought, noticing the way she watched him with unyielding interest. He remembered his determination from the night before and shook off his thoughts of admiration.

"Please understand me, Mr. Davenport. I realize the situation is difficult, but might we simply hike out? You could leave your things here until your friends could bring the sleds. I'm completely well now, and I know you might not believe this, but I'm fully capable of hiking long distances."

"Leave my things here?" he said, hardly concerning himself with anything else she'd said. The very thought of it was absurd. The woman simply didn't have any understanding of his work or its importance—just like his mother, who couldn't understand when Teddy took up his father's torch, determined to pick up where his father left off. "I can't just leave my things here."

"And I can't just stay here all winter. I want to know what happened to my friends. I need to know whether they made it or not. Your plants will still be here in the weeks to come."

"And if your friends are in Dawson, they will still be there as well," Teddy countered. "There's no chance they could make their way out if they've not already taken their leave. At least it's highly improbable. Certainly, there are ways, as in any situation. Dog sled teams can be hired and such. Walking out is possible, but very dangerous and highly unlikely unless, of course, your friends are native to the area and quite used to the harsh elem—"

"Oh, you are impossible!" Miranda stomped her foot and moved to her corner of the cabin.

Teddy looked at her in surprise. He'd merely tried to explain the situation. There was no call for her to get so angry. He waited, thinking she might begin again. When she remained silent, he breathed a sigh of relief. Maybe she'd leave him alone now and let him work. He picked up a piece of charcoal and began to sketch the outline of a dried subalpine buttercup.

Ranunculus eschscholtzii, he wrote in small charcoal lettering. *Petals—five, colored a brilliant yellow.* He went to work sketching the petals of the flower.

"Why can't you try to understand my position?"

Bother! She is back. Teddy looked up, hoping his expression betrayed his frustration. Slowly he took off the gold-framed spectacles he used for his closeup work. "Miss Davenport, I have a feeling you will endeavor to explain it, so I might as well hear you out." He put his elbows on the table and leaned his head against his hand.

Miranda took the chair opposite him and folded her hands as if he might be about to serve tea. Teddy was more frustrated at the interruptions than angry. After all, she did cook a nice meal and her mannerisms were not at all unpleasant—except for this incessant nagging. He hated to continue conjuring up the likeness of his mother, but Miranda's attitude was very much like hers. They were both very likable, but not entirely thoughtful.

"My friends most likely believe me dead. Imagine their pain and suffering. It's inhumane to sit here and let them assume the worst. What if they've written to my mother and father?

"I'm not without regard for the work you're doing here, Mr. Davenport. In fact, I highly respect it. I love books, and I well imagine that your book will be quite fascinating and accurate. I'll probably be determined to purchase a copy— not only because of having known you, but also because of the topic. Even so, you must understand my position."

Her expression bore evidence to the pain in her heart. Teddy lost himself for a moment in her huge brown eyes. Her eyes were just about the same light nutty color as the cone of the Canadian spruce. If he'd saved a specimen he could show her. He looked around the room for a moment, and then realized she'd fallen silent.

Looking back to her, Teddy offered an apologetic smile. "I say, please continue."

"Why should I? You don't care. All you can think about is your own need."

"Until recently, that was my main concentration, I must admit. However, with your arrival, I found my plans very much altered. You cannot, with any reasonable truth, suggest otherwise."

Miranda leaned forward, causing Teddy to pull back ever so slightly. The young woman made him nervous. He'd never been around many women other than his mother or servants. This woman had the ability to rattle his thoughts and leave him struggling for words.

"I wasn't suggesting that your life hadn't been altered by my arrival. I am very sorry you were delayed. But I'm even sorrier that you continue our delay." She got to her feet and put her hands on her hips. "Look, if you haven't any desire to take me to Dawson, then perhaps I'll set out on my own. I have the things Nellie left me and I'll just follow the river. It can't be that hard."

Teddy actually smiled at this. She no doubt assumed he'd find such a suggestion threatening. "You cannot be serious. The temperature is forty below, and the river is some distance from here. The creek will do you little good because it branches off in several directions—none of which lead to Dawson, which I might add is a good three days journey from here. Not to mention we are enjoying only about four hours of daylight, and most of that is spent under heavy clouds and snow."

"I don't care. My friends and family mean too much to me."

She turned to go to her bed. Teddy watched as she began pulling together the things Nellie had given her. She laced on the thick elk-skin boots Nellie had crafted while tending to Miranda. Next, she pulled on a fur-lined cloak, also crafted by the old Indian woman. Somewhat amused by her show of independence, Teddy secured his glasses on his nose and began to study the petals of the buttercup in more detail.

Maybe her persistence at gathering her meager belongings would wear Miss Colton out and leave her willing to forego her adventure. Not that he truly believed she'd step foot outside the door.

Teddy lost himself in thoughts of his drawing and the work at hand. There was no sense in worrying over his guest. She would settle herself down and realize the sensibility in waiting until help came their way. Perhaps she'd even put on a pot of tea. It wasn't until he heard the door to the cabin open and felt the cold rush of arctic air that Teddy realized he'd underestimated Miranda Colton.

Miranda slammed the door to the cabin, hoping it jarred Mr. Davenport's teeth right out of his head. The man was insufferable. He kept his nose buried in his notes and drawings from morning light until dark. Even then, he would often take up a lantern and work until the allotted supply of oil was gone.

Stepping off the small porch, Miranda felt an alarming sense of folly when her booted feet sunk into snow that came up over her knees. And this was in the area that Teddy had managed to clear away prior to the last big snow. How deep must it be in other areas?

Miranda pulled her fur hat down, trying desperately to ward off the frigid temperatures. Her eyes were crusting with ice as she blinked against the painfully cold air.

"Oh, God," she murmured as she pushed out across the once shoveled path. "I need your help. I have to get to Dawson. I have to know if Grace is safe." The frigid temperatures slowed her steps. She was so poorly prepared. Even without Teddy there to tell her so, Miranda knew she would be dead before she ever reached Dawson.

"What do I do, God?" she whispered, burying her face into the fur lining of her cloak. She was grateful Nellie had left her such a fine gift. She only wished the fur extended to cover her entire body.

A twig snapped and Miranda froze in her steps at the sound, her heart racing. Could it be wolves? She'd heard horror stories of wolves that attacked humans and fed off their bones while the person was still alive. Swallowing hard, she turned and strained to see into the darkening woods. If she were to be attacked, she would meet her assailant head on.

She let out a long breath when Teddy's bundled figure emerged from the shadows. "Why are you following me?"

"Because someone has to," he replied. "Stop this nonsense and come back to the cabin. You're lost already. At this rate you'll end up in Whitehorse before you ever see Dawson. Now come along. Much longer out here and we'll both pay the price."

Miranda knew it was hopeless to argue. Her lungs already hurt from the frigid air. "Very well, Mr. Davenport. As it appears I have no other choice, I will do as you suggest."

"This truly wasn't necessary," he said as they made their way back. "You may believe me to be heartless and completely void of understanding, but I know very well that your need is great."

"You certainly don't act like it," she said, struggling to keep up. Stubbing her toe against a buried rock or branch, Miranda cried out and would have fallen face first in the snow, if not for Teddy.

Steadying her with one hand, he reached out and took her bundled things with the other. "I say, we'll both be ready for a spot of tea when we get back inside."

Miranda felt completely humiliated. It had been purely childish and even selfish to take this action.

Once back in the cabin, Miranda warmed her hands by the fire. Her gloves had helped to keep the cold at bay, but her fingers were numb, as were her toes.

"I fail to see what you thought that would prove."

Miranda looked up to see Teddy watching her most intently. "I thought it would prove my willingness to risk my life in order to ease the concern of my friends."

"But if you had died on the way it would have proven nothing—especially if your friends think you already dead. You see, the logical thing—"

"Oh, please don't give me your analytical review of the matter," Miranda said, closing her eyes in exasperation. "My heart has no understanding of it and it is my heart that urges me to find my friends. Can't you see that?" She opened her eyes and looked at him. His expression seemed to suggest that he could not comprehend her meaning.

"Oh, just forget about it. I don't expect you to understand." She turned back to the stove.

"I am not without concern for your emotions," Teddy countered. "But I am a man of logic, and that logic tells me that we dare not attempt the wilderness on our own. I've stayed alive up here by listening to the advice of those who know better. You'd do well to follow my example."

Miranda knew the truth in his words, but she didn't want to admit it. A tear trailed down her cheek as she realized she might well be stranded until spring. She turned away so that Teddy wouldn't see her cry. No sense in bothering him with her sorrow.

"I'm sure you know best, Mr. Davenport," she finally said. "I'll try my best to understand."

"Perhaps you should take some of your own advice and not take this situation so seriously."

Miranda realized he was using her words against her. She turned, hands on her hips. "Mr. Davenport, laughing over spilled oatmeal is one thing, but my dear sweet mother may very well be inconsolable over the loss of her only daughter. My friends may be suffering guilt and pain over their belief that they've played a part in my death. I cannot help but take this situation seriously."

Teddy gave a halfhearted smile, causing him to look youthful and vulnerable. Miranda almost felt sorry for him. His gentle spirit was no match for her temper. Calming a bit, Miranda drew a deep breath. "I know there is nothing to be done. I will try to be useful, instead of antagonistic."

After arranging her meager belongings under the bed, Miranda stretched out atop the bed and tried not to think of home. She tried her best to put aside thoughts of how sad Christmas must have been for her parents. She tried not to worry over whether or not Grace had given birth. *I might as well be stranded on the moon for all the good it does me. Never mind that we are less than one hundred miles from Dawson. Never mind that it's already January of a new year and I have no idea where any of my friends and family are.*

She thought for a moment of Crispin Thibault. Both he and Mr. Davenport bore themselves with a sort of European flair—that flavor of aristocracy that Americans always seemed so desperate to emulate. But where Mr. Davenport was driven and passionate about his work, Crispin had been a free spirit—simply living to experience life. He hardly cared where they went or when they might arrive. Crispin was the kind of man who would be just as content to get in the boat and let the river take him where it would. Mr. Davenport, on the other hand, would go no place unless it merited him to do so. They were completely opposite—and in more ways than one, for Miranda knew that Mr. Davenport was a godly man. He prayed and read Scriptures to her every day. He also talked of God on occasion, but for the most part dedicated himself to his work.

"I am taking the liberty to reheat the leftover portion of our luncheon stew," Teddy said, jarring Miranda from her thoughts.

Miranda shook her head and sat up. The man had a penchant for destroying meals. "I'll heat it," she said getting to her feet. Reluctantly, Miranda crossed the room and took the pot from Teddy's hands.

"I'm happy to help."

Miranda looked at him and forced herself to smile. He was trying to make up for his attitude and lack of interest in her situation. "I suppose you could slice the bread."

"I believe I can handle that," he said, heading to the counter.

Miranda worked in silence for several moments. Teddy Davenport was such an unusual man. She found herself wishing she knew more about him. "Tell me about your homeland, Mr. Davenport."

"It's certainly different from this place," he answered. "We would never have to endure cold like this. In fact, it rarely snowed."

"What part of England are you from?"

"Well, actually, my parents owned two estates. One was very close to London. My mother's people were from the area, and she loved the city. London, of course, is quite fascinating. There are many fine places to go—museums, shops, and such."

"But you didn't care for it as much as the other place?" Miranda questioned, feeling certain her guess was true.

Teddy smiled. "You are very astute. My favorite place was by far and away the estate of my father's people. It was in Cornwall, not far from the coast. It was quite lovely there year round. We had magnificent gardens and my father was good to train me in every area of horticulture."

"Do you still live there? I mean, when you aren't in Canada." She was amazed that he had shared so much information with her.

"I do," Teddy admitted. He took the bread to the table.

"Do you have caretakers who tend it while you're away?"

"Of course. They tend it while I'm in residence as well."

"You must be very wealthy." Miranda never heard his response, however, for without warning, the front door blasted open and Miranda reached out to take hold of Teddy's arm as if for protection. She ducked behind him when two bulky figures entered the room.

Teddy stood frozen in place, and Miranda wasn't sure if he was more concerned with his visitors or her actions. It took a great deal of willpower to let go of his arm and step back. Watching the figures shake themselves of their ice-crusted blankets, Miranda wasn't at all surprised to see that their visitors were Indian.

"Little Charley!"

Her heart skipped a beat. Could it be? Had help arrived? Were they truly going to leave this place and make their way to Dawson?

Teddy turned to her and smiled. "It would appear that, even if my knowledge of your need is less than what you desire, God has heard your prayers. Little Charley has come to take us to Dawson."

⊣ CHAPTER FIVE ⊢

IT HAD BEEN MORE than two weeks since Adrik and Jacob had gone off with Gump Lindquist, and frankly, Leah Barringer was starting to worry. She knew her brother was quite capable of taking care of himself, but the separation was maddening. She couldn't seem to convince Jacob that searching for their father was a waste of time. He had no doubt died in the Palm Sunday avalanche the previous year. She could accept it. Why couldn't he?

Stirring a pot of beans, Leah heard Grace stir from her bed across the room. The tent allowed for very little privacy. Adrik had stretched a rope across the area where Grace and Leah shared a crude bed. Karen had draped a blanket over the rope to partition the room off for the sake of changing clothes and such, but it also blocked what precious heat could be had.

Leah glanced over and saw Grace struggling to sit up. Karen had long since left for her job at the Sourdough Café, leaving the two women to entertain themselves for the day. Leah knew there was washing to tend to as well as bread to make, so keeping busy wouldn't be difficult.

"I've got some prunes and oatmeal ready for breakfast," she called to Grace. "And I've already put the beans on for our supper. By the time they've cooked all day with bacon, they should taste pretty good."

"Leah," Grace barely whispered the name. "Leah, something is happening."

Leah put down the spoon and came to the bed. "What's the matter?"

Grace looked up, her eyes filled with pain and fear. "It's the baby. The baby is coming."

Leah had watched her mother die in childbirth, there was no way she wanted to be left alone with another woman who might well do the same. "I'll have to get help." She looked around the tent as if the answer might well be at hand.

Grace reached out and gripped her arm. "Remember where the midwife lives? Just down by the river. You'll have to go and bring her back."

Leah nodded. "Will you be all right while I'm gone? I mean, it's still dark, and Karen's already gone to work."

Grace released her hold. "I'll be fine." She clutched her abdomen. "Just hurry."

Leah ran for her coat and boots. "I'll be as fast as I can."

Once outside the tent, Leah quickly realized her main adversary was the weather. Heavy snow made the going difficult. She held a lantern in front of her as she stumbled again and again, wishing silently that she owned snowshoes for such occasions. Assessing the situation momentarily, Leah tried to reason out what was to be done.

"Help me, Father God," she prayed aloud. The wind bit into her face, stinging painfully as it pelted her with ice and snow. The path seemed to obliterate before her very eyes. "I don't know which way to go."

After a search that seemed to take forever, Leah stumbled down what she hoped was the path to the river. If she was on the right path, she knew she would soon be approaching the small bridge she could cross over to reach the Dawson side. The midwife lived in a small cabin behind one of the more popular saloons. Leah hated to go there alone, but there wasn't any chance of a proper companion—save God.

The snow seemed to ease up a bit, but the darkness was just as maddening. The lantern did very little to aid her. Leah slipped and felt the rock solid ice against her knee. She struggled to keep from dropping the lantern as she got back to her feet. Moving even more cautiously now, Leah continued to pray. She hated the darkness. It was frightening and so filled with death and dying. Karen had brought home a copy of the town paper that told of an entire family that had been found frozen to death in their tent. There were other deaths listed as well. Miners who hadn't been able to endure the harsh cold of winter. Babies and children who were no match for the elements. The horror of such tragedies frightened Leah more than she wanted to admit.

The north had already claimed her father's life. Would it also claim hers?

Leah finally reached the river and breathed a sigh of relief. She had only to cross the bridge and then make her way to the midwife's cabin. It shouldn't be that hard, she reasoned. The snow was lessening, and the glow of light from the windows in town could now been seen through the flurry of white. God had heard her prayers. Everything would be all right.

But it wasn't all right. After Leah had pounded on the midwife's door for over ten minutes, a woman bearing heavy makeup and a haggard look impatiently opened the door and told Leah there would be no help—the midwife had taken ill and lay on her deathbed.

"I have to have help," Leah declared. "My friend is having a baby. She's all alone."

"Women been doing that for years, sweetie," the older woman told her. "Just grab yourself a pair of scissors and a ball of string. Boil some water for cleaning up afterwards and warm some blankets by the stove. Nature will do the rest."

Leah felt her stomach lurch. "But what if there are problems?"

The woman shrugged. "Honey, I can't help you there. Get her to the hospital or get yourself another midwife." She closed the door, leaving Leah to stand alone.

Leah thought of Grace all alone and knew she couldn't leave her without someone to help. Still, she didn't know what to do. *Karen will know*, Leah thought. *Karen will know exactly what to do.*

Leah turned in the direction of the Sourdough Café. She pulled her coat tighter and hugged the lamp as close as she could. She knew it was risky to take the shortcut behind the saloon, but time was of the essence. She picked up her pace, feeling the hair on the back of her neck begin to prickle. She saw things in the shadows. Her breath came in strained pants as she pressed toward the street.

Coming out onto the main thoroughfare, Leah slowed her steps and her breathing. *I'm being such a goose,* she thought. *I'm scared of my own shadow.*

At the Sourdough, things only worsened. Karen had gone off with the owner's wife and daughter to retrieve several crates of dried fruit. The man who told her this had no idea how long she would be.

"Please tell her she's needed at home," Leah said, realizing she had to get back to the tent. Grace might very well be giving birth any moment.

"I'll tell her, but she's needed here, too," the man replied gruffly.

"Yes, but her friend is having a baby. That must be more important than cooking."

The man grunted something unintelligible and continued sweeping the wood floor. Exasperated from her lack of success, Leah bolstered her courage and headed back to the tent. She had just rounded the corner of the Klondike Gold Saloon when she tripped and fell face first to the ground.

Though she had somehow managed to keep the lantern from breaking, Leah wasn't entirely sure the same could be said for herself. She felt as though the wind had been knocked right out of her. Easing up on her hands, Leah could barely stifle a scream. The rock she had presumed she had tripped over was no rock at all, but rather the extended leg of a man—a man who appeared to be dead.

Leah picked herself up and pulled the lamp close. She gasped at the ghostly figure. "Crispin!"

She placed the lantern down beside him and reached up with her gloved hands to pat his frozen face. "Oh, Crispin, please be alive."

The man opened his eyes ever so slowly. A grin spread across his face. "I know you."

His breath reeked of whiskey. Leah frowned. He wasn't dead, but he was drunk. "Crispin, you'll die if you stay here. Come with me. I need you."

He blinked hard several times, then struggled to get to his feet. Leah helped him stand, forgetting her fall and the pain it had caused. "Crispin, Grace is having her baby, and I can't find anyone to come and help me."

"I can't help you. I have never done . . . that . . . sort of thing." His speech was slurred, and he began to weave back and forth on his feet.

Leah wasn't entirely sure she could sober him up or get him to understand the seriousness of the situation, but for the moment he was all she had. "Come on, Crispin. I can make you some strong coffee back at our tent. We're just across the river and up the path a ways."

Crispin seemed to forget her mention of the baby and put an arm around Leah's shoulder. "Are you having a party? I could use a drink."

"Yes," Leah said, pulling him toward the bridge. "I'm having a party."

How she ever managed to get back to the tent was a miracle to Leah Barringer. She struggled against the ever-increasing snow, and as the wind picked up to howl a blizzard in their path, Leah found herself half carrying the drunken man.

She almost expected to find Grace dead upon her return. She'd been able to push aside the images of her mother only by focusing on the task to retrieve the midwife. But now those images came back in a rush. She could see it all as if it were only yesterday. How very pale her mother had been just before closing her eyes in death.

Leah felt tears come to her eyes. It made a painful prickling as the wind crusted the liquid to ice. Fighting to control her emotions, Leah knew a tremendous amount of relief when she reached the tent.

"Come on, Crispin, let's get you inside."

"For the party?" he questioned.

"Yes."

Inside, Leah found Grace still very much alive. "Where's the midwife?" she asked as she realized the stranger standing next to Leah was no woman.

"She's taken sick and may not even live," Leah answered. "I found Crispin on the street and brought him back with me." She looked at the staggering man and then returned her gaze to Grace's worried expression. "I'm hoping he can be of help."

"He looks to be drunk."

"He is," Leah admitted. "But I hope to fix that with some food and strong coffee."

"We need someone to help," Grace said nervously. "I don't know how much time we have before the baby will come."

"I know. I went to the Sourdough to find Karen, but she wasn't there. She'd gone with the owner's wife to get something. I told them to send her home as soon as she got back."

Grace nodded and seemed to relax a bit. "That's good. Karen will know what to do."

"That's how I had it figured."

Leah worked over the stove to fix a pot of coffee. She noticed that Crispin hardly seemed to care that there was no real party. He had plopped down at the table and was now asleep.

When the coffee was ready, Leah brought a steaming mug to Crispin, along with a hunk of bread. "Crispin, wake up. I have something for you to eat."

He didn't rally and for a moment Leah again feared he had died.

"Crispin!"

He moaned and struggled to raise his head. "Why are you yelling at me? Why did you bring me here? There's no party."

Leah sat the cup down rather hard, sloshing some of the contents onto the table. "I brought you here to help me. You have to sober up now. Grace is going to have a baby, and Karen isn't here to help me." The wind howled loudly, shaking the tent and causing Leah to fear for the first time that Karen might well be stuck in town until the worst of the blizzard passed.

Blinking back tears, Leah tried to compose herself. She didn't vocalize her fears, but a quick glance to where Grace lay writhing in pain told her she didn't have to. Who was she fooling by trying to appear ever so strong and controlled? Grace knew very well how serious the situation was, and Crispin was too drunk to care.

With all the strength of her thirteen and a half years, Leah reached her hand into the black curls of Crispin's hair and yanked his head up and back. "You listen to me, Crispin Thibault. I need you, and I need you sober. You drink this coffee and eat what I give you, and I don't want to hear any kind of protest. Understand?"

He looked at her oddly for a moment, then smiled. "I believe I do."

"Good," she said, letting go her hold. "I'll bring you more coffee after you've finished this cup."

Grace screamed out against the pain. Leah's blood chilled her veins. A dull ache started somewhere at the base of her neck and edged its way up her head. She thought of her mother—saw her lying pale, almost colorless against the white sheet of her bed.

Leaving her memories behind, Leah picked up the coffee pot and slammed it down in front of Crispin. "You'd better drink fast."

—[C H A P T E R   S I X]—

MIRANDA SAW HER first glimpse of Dawson amidst a heavy snow. Buried under a mound of covers, she stayed warm enough in the lead sled, while Teddy rode in the sled behind her. The town looked surprisingly big. Miranda wasn't exactly sure what she had expected of Dawson, but after months in the wilderness, any collection of buildings and people seemed like heaven.

Sitting a little straighter, Miranda realized she had no idea what she should do. She didn't know where her friends might have gone. She had no idea if they had even made it this far. Frowning to herself, Miranda watched the rhythmic movement of the sled dogs. They seemed to pull the weight so easily. At first Miranda had felt sorry for them, but watching them work, she realized the dogs seemed to enjoy their task. Teddy had told her they were born and bred for this work,

71

but until she'd witnessed it firsthand, Miranda had doubted the truth of that.

Little Charley brought the dogs to a halt in front of the Dawson Lucky Day Hotel. Miranda pushed back the blankets and struggled to climb out of the sled basket, but Little Charley quickly reached down and lifted her up without a word. After placing her on the boardwalk outside the hotel, he turned to unload the rest of the sled.

"Thank you," Miranda said, turning to see where Teddy might be. The falling snow seemed to lighten a bit, but the entire town was covered in a fresh blanket of white. Teddy stood a few feet away, surveying the town as if looking for something in particular.

"What is it?" she asked coming up beside him. "Is something wrong?"

Teddy looked over and smiled. "Not at all. I was merely reacquainting myself with this soiled dove."

"Why do you call Dawson that?"

"Because that's what she is. She was once pure and un-spoiled, and now every man who can make his way north has come to use and abuse her. She looks good in snow, how-ever. Almost clean again."

Miranda had no way of knowing whether this was true or not. "I suppose I can understand. Look, Mr. Davenport, I have no idea what I should do." She hoped he might have some suggestions. "I don't know how to find my friends."

"I can well understand your concerns. My suggestion would be that once we've checked into the hotel, you might make your way to the claim registrar's office. It's my under-standing that everyone who seeks gold must secure their claim with the local authorities."

Miranda barely heard his words. She was still contemplating his statement about checking into the hotel. "I have no money. I can't very well check into the hotel. If I could find my friends right away, I could stay with them."

"The wind is picking up and the temperatures are dropping. It's hardly the right time for a search. Just come along with me and I'll see you receive a room. I know the management here, it won't be a problem." He smiled pleasantly, but it did nothing to ease her concern.

"But I can't pay for it," Miranda protested. "A place like this is no doubt expensive. Everything up here has been far more costly." She looked to the etched-glass doors of the hotel. "I'm sure they'll want the money up front. Besides, they might not even have room."

"It's not a problem, I assure you. I stay here every winter. I have an adjoining room where I usually set up my workroom. If the hotel is booked up, I can simply arrange my things in my room and you can stay as long as you need."

Miranda felt an overwhelming sense of gratitude. For all her anger and frustration with the seemingly indifferent Mr. Davenport, she realized he wasn't without mercy. "It would only be until I could find out what happened to my friends."

"Of course. Let's get inside." Teddy hardly seemed to concern himself with the matter. He turned away to direct Little Charley and the other man. "Bring my things into the lobby. I'll direct you from there."

Miranda followed the men inside, anxious to begin the business of locating her friends. A warm waft of air touched her cheeks as she crossed the threshold. *Oh, to be warm again,* she thought, sighing. She moved across the marble entry floor to a large, inviting fireplace. A heavy oak mantel framed a hearth trimmed in Delft tiles of blue and white. Miranda pulled off heavy fur mittens and held her hands out to the flames. She glanced behind her where she heard Teddy instructing the hotel clerk to bring them supper.

Miranda's stomach rumbled loudly. It'd been a long time since they'd shared their cold lunch of jerky and biscuits on the trail. Teddy motioned toward the stairs and Little Charley nodded and began to ascend with one of Teddy's heavy crates. The other man picked up another crate, while Teddy took up a third.

"Miss Colton, if you'll follow me, I'll show you to your room."

Miranda came alongside without a second thought. "I know it's dark, but I thought perhaps I should go check the recorder's office. What do you think?"

"I think you should eat a hearty meal and rest for the evening. Tomorrow will be soon enough to begin your search. If they're here, they aren't going anywhere tonight."

"I suppose you're right."

Miranda climbed the carpeted stairs, gently touching the polished wood banister. The hotel was more beautiful than she could have imagined. How in the world had such elegance come so far north? She marveled at the plush opulence. It was as if someone had taken the finest hotel in San Francisco and transplanted it to Dawson.

Mr. Davenport and his men seemed to take it all in stride. Apparently they'd seen the hotel many times before and the effect had worn off. Of course, she reasoned, Mr. Davenport had come from a well-to-do English family. He'd told her briefly of stately gardens where he'd learned a love of vegetation. It was really all she knew of Teddy Davenport. Funny how a person could share such close quarters with someone for months and still not know anything about them.

Reluctantly, Miranda pulled her skirt up a bit and continued her climb. Her legs felt leaden. She had lost so much of her strength by having nothing to do but sit around the cabin with Mr. Davenport. Teddy, on the other hand, hoisted the crate as though he worked days at the freight dock. His strength came as a surprise to Miranda, who had thought him a dandy at worst and a gentleman of leisure at best.

Yawning, she kept a silent vigil behind the men. In the morning she would have to get a telegram off to her parents. She worried that they had been notified of the accident. She'd been practically frantic over the thought of their suffering such news. She'd labored with images of her mother for weeks. When she closed her eyes at night, she could almost see her mother wandering around the house, crying in her grief. Miranda had to let them know she was alive and well.

"Well, here we are," Teddy grunted under the weight of his crate. He gently lowered the box as if it contained his most valuable possession. And in truth, Miranda knew that, to Teddy, those bits of dried vegetation and notes were his most valued articles.

Teddy procured a key from his coat pocket while Little Charley eyed Miranda. She felt her cheeks grow hot under his scrutiny and lowered her gaze to the floor.

"Just put those inside," Teddy instructed. He glanced to Miranda and reached out to offer her something. "This is the key to the room next door." He motioned to the right and Miranda realized he intended her to admit herself.

Without waiting for any other comment, Miranda took the key and opened the door. The room was grander than any she'd ever known. The brass bed had been done up in a heavy coverlet of brocaded burgundy and navy. Brass sconces on either side of the bed held thick white candles.

Without warning the side door opened and Mr. Davenport popped into the room. "I say, looks just as I left it."

"It's a lovely room. Much nicer than anything I expected to see in Dawson," Miranda admitted.

"Well, to be honest, it is one of the finer accommodations in the hotel. I stay here regularly, and these are my private rooms."

"I see. Are you sure you can spare the room?" she questioned. "I mean, I plan only to be here as long as it takes to find my friends or to make other arrangements."

"Nonsense," Teddy assured. "The room is no problem. I've set my things up in the sitting room and Mr. Ambrose, the manager here, will have the staff put in another bed."

"I've taken your bed? That hardly seems right. Perhaps they could move me to another room."

Teddy shook his head. "There are no other rooms available at present. Please do not concern yourself. I wouldn't have extended the offer if it were a bother. Now, do get your things settled and we'll have supper."

"I'm afraid, I have very little to settle, as you probably remember." Miranda dropped her own bundle of meager belongings on the bed.

"I'd nearly forgotten," Teddy said, frowning. "We should look into purchasing you a wardrobe."

"No!" Miranda exclaimed. "You've done enough. And don't forget, I have plenty of things, clothing especially, with my friends."

"That hardly helps you in this setting. We'll figure out what to do after supper."

"I would like to wash up," Miranda said, looking around the room.

"Of course. I'll send someone with towels and hot water. There's a bath down the hall, but in the winter it is sometimes less than congenial."

"Thank you. The water and towels will be more than enough."

———

"I suppose after tonight," Miranda began, "we'll see little of each other."

Teddy looked up rather surprised. He'd seemed distracted throughout the meal, but he now gave her his full attention.

"Why would you say that?"

"I'll be searching for my friends, and you have your work to see to."

"Yes, well, it may take some time for you to locate your friends. This area is more far-reaching than it seems. The claims of gold have been staked along nearly every river and creek in the area. There are hundreds of miles to cover in order to check each and every one. If your friends have failed to file a claim, or if perhaps they are working for someone else, there will be no record of them in the claims office. Short of finding someone who knows them or remembers them . . . well, it might be quite a task. I didn't want to say anything for fear of discouraging you."

Miranda hadn't considered that it would be that hard. She hadn't figured the town to be much bigger than the other stops along the way, and she certainly hadn't thought the claims to be so far-reaching.

"I suppose I didn't consider the situation in an accurate light. But then again, I had no idea I would encounter such a place."

"Of course, who's to say that God hasn't already straightened this crooked path out for you?"

Miranda nodded. Her hope was fixed on God. For the past months she had prayed and prayed for His deliverance and guidance. "I'm counting on God for just that, Mr. Davenport." And she knew in her heart it was true. For after all, what possible alternative did she have?

"The town isn't safe for you to journey too far alone," he continued. "It might be wise to check in with the officials."

"I plan to." Miranda toyed with her silverware for a moment, then cut into the thick steak on her plate. "This is quite delicious. I don't remember the last time I had a steak."

"I'm glad you're enjoying it. I wasn't sure you'd care for the flavor of moose."

"Moose?" She eyed her plate. "This is moose?"

"Indeed. It's rather an acquired taste unless it's prepared exactly right. We have a marvelous chef here at the hotel, and when he is able to get the right ingredients, he does a wonderful job."

"The entire dinner has been perfect," Miranda said, taking another bite of the meat. This time she focused on the flavor. She decided it was still quite delicious, in spite of knowing its origins.

Later that night, as she slipped beneath the thick wool blankets and heavy brocade cover, Miranda realized she'd not given any further thought to Teddy's sleeping arrangements.

She thought to double check and make sure he had a bed in which to sleep, but even as she considered approaching their adjoining door, she held back.

It was hardly appropriate for her to go to him. He was a grown man and fully capable of seeing to his own needs. She thought of him, determined and focused on his work. He was probably bent over some piece of dried greenery even now.

Miranda smiled to herself and snuggled down deeper in the covers. A spirit of hope washed over her, energizing her and making sleep seem impossible. For all her exhaustion earlier, now she felt as if she could run a race.

She longed to find Grace and Karen. She longed to let them know she was alive and well. But then the reoccurring horror of knowing that they might well have died in the storm crept into her conscious mind.

What if they had all perished in the storm?

She shuddered. "Oh, God, please let them all be well and safe. Let me find them and rejoin them. Let me return to my parents and ease their worry."

But even as the words were out of her mouth, Miranda felt a strange aching in her heart. To return to her friends and family meant she would have to part company with Mr. Davenport.

"I'm being silly," she quietly whispered into the darkness. "Of course we'll part company. We are nothing to one another. We were thrown together for the sole purpose of. . . ." Her mind was incapable of completing the sentence. Why had they been thrown together? Was there some other plan for them?

Miranda thought of Teddy as a brotherly sort. He wasn't exactly like her own brother, Peter, but he was caring and kind. He didn't look at her like Crispin Thibault had. Crispin's lingering gazes had always warmed her and left her a little jittery inside. Teddy's glances did nothing but . . .

But what?

Miranda hugged her pillow. *This is so nonsensical,* she thought. *What's wrong with me anyway? Mr. Davenport is nothing more than a kindly benefactor. As soon as I find Grace, I'll be gone. I'll probably never see him again.*

The thought made the dull ache more intense. Could it be she'd come to care for Mr. Davenport? Care for him in such a manner that leaving his company could actually cause her grief?

The winds picked up outside and made a mournful whine. Miranda had heard it said that the dark northern winters could cause a madness to settle upon a person. It caused all manner of trouble. Some people went screaming into the night and were never seen again. Some retreated to the silent darkness of their cabins and weren't found again until spring.

Maybe her strange feelings in regard to Mr. Davenport were nothing more than a part of this winter madness—a sort of northern plague that would pass with the coming of the summer light. Maybe.

—[C H A P T E R   S E V E N]—

LEAH AND CRISPIN looked down on the wrinkled baby boy
with expressions of awe. Grace smiled at her two champions.
Had it not been for their devotion and determination, she
and the baby might well be dead.

"He's so tiny, Grace," Leah said, shaking her head. "I
didn't know he'd be so little."

"He's perfectly normal in size," Crispin stated. The haggard look on his face and dark circles around his eyes caused
Grace to worry over his health. She wondered if it was the
first time he'd been sober in quite some time.

"Mr. Thibault, we have quite despaired of ever knowing
your fate. Have you come back to us now?"

Crispin seemed to suddenly realize not only the hour and
setting, but also his state of sobriety. He reached for his coat
and pulled it on without ceremony. "I have not come back. I

was merely taken in hand by this lovely lady." He smiled sadly at Leah. "I'm glad I could be of help, but I must go. I have places to be and the hour is late."

"Crispin, don't leave. Karen hasn't come home, and what if I need someone?" Leah questioned.

Grace heard the concern in the child's voice, while noting at the same time the determination in Crispin's expression. "Perhaps Mr. Thibault has other obligations," Grace said softly. She pulled her son closer to keep him from chilling. The baby slept as though completely disinterested in his surroundings.

"I do indeed," Crispin said, giving the ladies a slight bow. "I bid you farewell for a time."

Leah walked to where Crispin's fur hat had been carelessly left to dry. "Here. Don't forget your hat. You might need it."

He smiled at her as he took the hat. Grace couldn't help but wonder what had transpired between Leah and Crispin prior to their arrival at her bedside. Crispin reached out and took hold of Leah's hand. Bending, he kissed her fingers.

"Parting is indeed a bittersweet sorrow."

"You don't have to go," Leah said matter-of-factly.

"Ah, but I do. You'll understand better as time goes by. Now stay here and care for our little mother and her babe. I'm sure Karen will return after the storm abates."

"But you shouldn't go out in it either," Leah protested.

"I'll be perfectly fine," he assured them and then, without further ado, was gone.

Leah's eyes filled with tears and Grace reached out her hand. "Come here," she said softly. "Come sit with me and Andy."

Leah sniffled. "Andy? You've named him already?"

"I've thought for a long time of what I would call him, if I had a son. I love the name Andrew, and if you remember your Bible stories, you'll know that Peter and Andrew were brothers who were called by Christ to become disciples. I figured with his father's name being Peter, Andrew was a most appropriate name. They just go together, don't you think?"

Leah wiped at her eyes and nodded. "He is a beautiful baby, Grace. I was so scared he wouldn't be born."

Grace squeezed her hand. "I know your mother died in childbirth. I'm sorry you had to bear this."

"I just kept thinking about Mama." The tears fell in earnest now. Suddenly it seemed that the intensity of the day had finally caught up with Leah. She sobbed into her hands and buried her face against the side of Grace's cover.

Stroking the child's head, Grace tried to think of some words of comfort. It seemed only a short time ago that she herself had been young like this—young and innocent and so very carefree. Grace thought of her home in Chicago. Of the finery and blessings they'd enjoyed. She had never known what it was to really need or want something. How very different things were now.

She let Leah cry, thinking it was probably a cleansing help to the girl. So often people buried their feelings inside and never allowed them to come out, never let their souls be cleaned and refreshed by the rain of their tears.

How very often I've tried to refrain from tears, she thought. *I've tried to feel nothing but the determined hope that God would somehow make everything right, when down deep inside I hurt so very bad.* Grace thought of Peter and looked to the baby who now slept wrapped safely in her arms. Would Peter care that he had a son? Would he forgive her the anger of the past and come to realize the importance of putting his trust in God?

Surely it was better that she remain here, separated from her husband, to raise her son in the presence of God-fearing people who cared about them both, rather than return to a loveless marriage—a union that promised all parties nothing but pain and sorrow.

Grace continued to stroke Leah's hair, even as her own tears fell. *Father, I know you have a plan in all of this. I know your love is there for me—for Andrew. But, God, it hurts so much to know that Peter is far away from us, to know that he doesn't care for your Word, or for you.* Grace cried softly while Leah's sobs still filled the room.

Andrew stirred and began to fuss. As he cried louder, Grace and Leah both looked at each other and then to the baby. Grace began to smile. A fine trio they were with their tears.

"He's probably hungry," Grace surmised. "The midwife told me he would probably want to nurse first thing."

"Is there anything I can do? Is there anything you need?" Leah asked, drying her eyes.

Grace untied the neck of her nightgown with her free hand. "No, nothing. God has seen to making this quite a self-sufficient matter." She positioned the crying baby to her breast and watched as he began rooting. She startled when he latched on and began to suck.

Leah laughed. "He must be pretty hungry. You must be hungry too. I'll fix you some food."

Grace nodded. She was feeling both hungry and weary. When Leah had gone to the stove, Grace returned her gaze to the dark-haired baby. How wondrous and awesome to hold something so tiny, so alive, and know that it came about because of the love she shared with her husband. God had given her a son—a son who would no doubt be very much like his father.

As if to concur, Andy opened his eyes and looked up at her. Grace couldn't help smiling. She saw the future in her son's eyes. She saw the hope that she and Peter could one day be united again in love.

"Oh, let it be, dear Father," she whispered.

To their surprise, not more than an hour after his departure, Crispin Thibault returned to their tent. He brought with him a none-to-pleased local doctor. The man grunted a greeting to Grace and Leah, then immediately took the baby in hand to examine him.

"I thought you might both rest better if a doctor were to declare everything well done," Crispin announced.

Leah pulled the blanket across the roping to afford Grace and the doctor some privacy. She turned to Crispin and smiled. "Will you stay?" she asked hopefully.

"No." His voice was flat and void of emotion. "I can't."

"Because of Miranda?"

Crispin looked blankly at Leah for a moment. "Yes."

"It hurts a lot to lose someone you love. I know because I've lost both my ma and pa. I was really scared to be here with Grace, and I know I couldn't have done it without you. See, my mama died trying to have a baby. I was scared Grace would die, too."

"Yes, well," Crispin stammered in obvious discomfort, "it's all behind us now."

"But it's not," Leah said, putting her hand on his arm. "You won't stay with us because of Miranda's death. You blame yourself, but it isn't your fault."

"You have no idea what you're talking about." His voice took on a gruff edge. "I need to go. The snow has abated, and no doubt Karen will return."

"Please, Crispin, don't go. I know how you feel inside, but the whiskey won't help."

"You talk as one who knows, and yet you're a child."

"My mama said whiskey was nothing more than a crutch some folks used to help them hobble down the road to hell."

Crispin actually smiled at this. "I suppose her to be correct in that statement."

"She said God was the only one who could ease our sufferings."

He frowned again. "I see God as a crutch used by mere mortals to raise them higher to some supposed glory."

"I don't mind leaning on God as a crutch," Leah declared boldly. "I'd sure enough rather lean on God than a bottle."

"That's your choice. Now leave me to mine."

Crispin turned to go, but Leah held fast to his arm. "You can't just ignore God or your need for Him. My mama always said that without God we'll never be happy. You do want to be happy again, don't you, Crispin?"

He looked down at her, his dark gaze penetrating. "I will never be happy again. Not with God. Not without Him."

He jerked away from her hold and left without even waiting to hear of Grace's condition. Leah felt a strange desire to run after Crispin. She had admired the man from their first meeting, and when she'd learned that he didn't believe in God, she felt that perhaps it was her duty to set him straight.

But that chance never came, at least not until tonight. As hard as it was to see him leave, Leah thanked God for the opportunity to finally talk to him—no matter how fruitless her words seemed.

"Mrs. Colton is to have complete bed rest for two weeks," the doctor said as he came from behind the blanket. "She's clearly not a well woman. This pregnancy has weakened her considerably."

Leah nodded. "I'll see to it that she rests."

"She needs to eat plenty of meat," he stated as he pulled on his gloves. "Have you meat?"

Leah nodded again. "Adrik shot an elk. We have plenty of food. I'll see to it that she eats."

"Good. The baby is small, but time will tell."

"What do you mean?" Leah questioned.

"I mean," the doctor said, "he will need much care in order to thrive. It's nearly thirty below outside. You're going to have to keep him warm and well fed. If the mother doesn't make enough milk, you'll have to supplement his diet with canned or fresh milk—whatever you can lay your hand to. If that can't be found, fix him a little sugar water and find a bottle with which to feed him in between nursings."

Leah nodded, fearful that the baby might die. She wanted to ask the doctor of the possibility, but her mouth wouldn't form the words.

"Lastly, I would make a place for the child between you both. He'll need the warmth of your bodies to survive. This tent is no place for a newborn, but if you take precautions, he might well live."

He left in the same quick manner as Crispin had, leaving Leah to stare after him in stunned silence. She had figured now that the baby had been born, and had even cried and nursed, that he would be just fine. She hadn't even considered that he could die.

She pushed back the curtain and looked to Grace. "I suppose," she said, seeing the understanding in Grace's expression, "you heard what the doctor said?"

"I heard him," Grace replied.

Leah reached out and took hold of Grace's hand. "I'll do whatever I can to help you. We'll see to it that Andy makes good progress. You, too. You'll rest and take care of Andy, and I'll bring you meals and take care of everything else."

Grace bit her lower lip and tears came to her eyes once again. "He must live," she finally whispered.

"He will," Leah said, promising in her heart that if she could make it so, it would be.

That night, even though she worried because Karen had never returned to the tent, Leah crawled into bed beside Grace and helped her to nestle Andrew between them. The baby slept without concern for his surroundings, and Leah thought it rather a blessing that he should know so little. The dangers were something she'd just as soon not know about—for knowing only made surviving the night all that much harder.

Leah thought of Crispin and worried about him drinking the night away in one of the many saloons. She wondered, as Grace's even breathing indicated sleep, if he would get drunk and pass out in the snow as he had when she'd come upon him only that morning.

"God, please take care of Crispin," she prayed in a hushed whisper. "Let him know how much you love him. Let him come to understand that you really do exist—that you really do care."

⊣ CHAPTER EIGHT ⊢

KAREN DIDN'T KNOW when she'd been so tired. Even climbing the Chilkoot Pass hadn't been as exhausting as working for nearly eighteen hours without a break. First she'd gone to help unload supplies from storage, and then she'd found herself out in the blizzard bringing in wood from the stacked pile behind the café.

After that she waited tables, washed dishes, and was eventually allowed to cook—the job she'd been hired to do in the first place. They'd been so shorthanded that everyone had been forced to pitch in and do a little bit of everything.

Yawning, Karen pushed back the outside tent flap and unfastened the ties of the inner flap. A lantern burned on the stove, but other than that the room was dark and quiet. Grace and Leah had no doubt gone to bed. Yawning again, Karen blew out the lantern and found her way to her own bed. Adrik had built a frame of ropes, and together they'd sewn canvas from their makeshift sail into mattress coverings. These they stuffed with pine boughs and anything else they could find to make a soft resting place.

Sinking into the bed, Karen managed only to kick her boots off before pulling the covers high. Within a moment she was fast asleep.

Strange thoughts and sounds drifted in and out of her dreams. Karen thought at one point that a baby was crying. But her eyes were much too heavy to open and investigate, and her mind was cloudy with thick fog of sleep.

It wasn't until morning, when she heard Leah moving about the tent, that Karen forced herself to wake up. She didn't have to report to work until noon and had thought to spend a few extra hours asleep, but the cry of a baby pierced the silence and caused her to bolt upright in bed.

"What's that?" she asked, throwing back the covers. "Grace, are you all right?"

Leah laughed. "Grace had her baby."

Karen looked to the wide-eyed child and shook her head. "You're just kidding me, aren't you?"

Leah took hold of her hand and pulled her to the blanket partition. "See for yourself."

Karen looked behind the covers to find Grace smiling at her from a propped up position. The nursing baby seemed completely oblivious to her intrusion.

"I don't believe it."

"Neither did we," Grace replied. "At least not at first."

"Why didn't you come get me?" Karen asked, looking to Leah for an answer.

"I did. I went first to get the midwife, but she was on her

deathbed. So then I went to find you, but the man at the café said you were off helping get supplies. He promised he'd tell you to come home when you got back, but he wasn't happy about it."

"Apparently his displeasure kept him from telling me the truth," Karen stated, angry that she had been deceived.

"I found Crispin on my way back," Leah said, then frowned. "He was drunk, but I sobered him up, and he helped me deliver the baby."

"They did a perfect job and it saved me one hundred dollars," Grace said, shifting the baby.

Karen was still in a state of disbelief. "So is it a boy or a girl?"

"A boy," Grace answered. The expression on her face caused Karen's heart to ache for her friend. No doubt Grace was thinking of Peter and his long absence.

"What have you named him?"

"Andrew. But we call him Andy. Seems like a better fit," Grace replied.

"Crispin paid for a doctor to come and check on Grace and the baby," Leah said authoritatively. "The doctor said they both need rest and lots of good food."

"And no doubt a warm cabin," Karen threw in. Why couldn't they have found a home first thing? She couldn't help but wonder what plan God had for them and why it included Grace giving birth to her son in a chilly tent.

"We were worried about you," Grace stated, looking rather worried. "Are you all right?"

Karen saw the look of loving concern in her friend's eyes. "I'm fine. The blizzard seemed to drive folks in to the café rather than keep them away. We had a bevy of folks from the hotels, and those that didn't come to take a meal at the café sent someone to bring a meal back to them. We were working all day and night."

"I'll fix you some breakfast," Leah said, pushing back the blanket partition. "You just sit down and rest."

Karen smiled appreciatively and took a chair beside Grace's bed. "She's been such a help."

"That she has. She never balked at the work of helping me with Andrew's delivery. She and Crispin worked as a remarkable team."

Karen looked around the tent. "Where is Crispin?"

"He left," Grace admitted. "He left even before the doctor finished his examination. He looked awful."

Karen nodded. Adrik had told her on more than one occasion that he had seen Crispin drunk. The news positively broke Karen's heart. Crispin had cared so very much for Miranda Colton, and he just couldn't seem to let go of feeling responsible for her loss.

"I hope he's all right. Adrik should try to talk to him again."

"Leah did her best to reason with him. I figured if anyone had a chance of getting through to him, it would be her. But Crispin just bolted."

Karen watched as Grace gently lifted her son to her shoulder. Patting him firmly, she burped him, then looked questioningly at Karen. "Would you care to hold him?"

The longing in Karen's heart for a child surfaced all at once. "I would love to." She reached out and took the baby in her arms. He was so small, yet so perfect.

Andrew Colton looked up to Karen with wide blue eyes.

His dark brown hair reminded Karen of Grace. "He favors you."

"He looks like Peter, too," Grace assured. "I see it in his nose and mouth." She lowered her face. "I'd give anything to have him here."

Karen cuddled the baby close and nodded. "I know you would. We'll get word to him, one way or another. We'll tell him about his son and we'll pray that he comes."

Grace lifted her face. "But I want him to come for more than the baby's sake. I want him to come because he's come to love God and he knows what's right. And I want him to come because he loves me."

Karen looked at Grace and saw the sadness in her expression. "I know he loves you."

Andrew closed his eyes while Karen gently rocked him in her arms. How wonderful he felt in her embrace. She couldn't help but feel a touch of envy. Here Grace was years her junior and she was already a mother. Karen gently handed the sleeping boy back to his mother. She smiled with an assurance she didn't feel. "I know we'll find Peter, and I know he loves you."

"I just about have the flapjacks ready," Leah called out.

A rustling at the door flap and the stomping of boots brought the attention of all three women to the front of the tent.

"You'd better throw some more of those on the stove," Adrik Ivankov's booming voice rang out.

"Adrik!" Karen exclaimed and jumped to her feet. She threw herself into her husband's ice-encrusted arms.

Adrik hugged her tight and kissed her soundly. Karen thrilled to his touch, feeling a wave of longing rush over her.

They'd had so little privacy since they got married. There was rarely any opportunity for intimacy between them.

Jacob stumbled in behind Adrik. "I'm starving."

"You're always starving," Leah called out.

Karen pulled away from her husband and laughed. "Oh, it's so good to have you both back. I have wonderful news for you."

"We have some pretty good news ourselves," Adrik said, pulling off his heavy coat.

"Well, I can't imagine it can top this," Karen said, motioning to Grace. "Grace has a new son."

Adrik beamed a smile. "Congratulations, little mother."

Grace nodded. "Thank you. This is Andrew Michael Colton." She held the sleeping baby up ever so slightly.

"He's a beaut," Adrik declared.

"Leah helped deliver him," Karen told her husband. "Along with Crispin."

Adrik frowned. "Crispin?"

"I found Crispin nearly passed out in the snow," Leah said matter-of-factly. "I made him come back here with me."

"I would have paid good money to see that," Adrik said, laughing.

Jacob patted his sister on the shoulder. "She can be real pushy when she wants something."

"Well, in this case, I'm glad she was," Grace added. "She sobered him up and he helped with delivering the baby."

"Where is he now?" Adrik asked, looking around the room.

"He wouldn't stay," Leah replied. She turned her attention back to the stove. "I tried to talk to him, but he was just too sad."

"Sad?" Adrik questioned.

She nodded. "Yes. Sad about Miranda. He seems to have lost all hope and purpose."

"I wouldn't be surprised if you aren't right on that matter," Adrik said, looking to Karen. "I can well imagine how I'd feel if I lost Karen."

Karen reached out to hold his hand. "I don't even want to think of how things would be if you weren't here. I worried about you the whole time you were gone. I'd pray and pray and then worry that I needed to pray some more."

"Well, we do have good news," Jacob said, seeming to suddenly remember. "Tell 'em, Adrik."

Adrik looked at Karen. "Gump said he'd like to hire us on to work his claim. Even though there isn't as much to do this time of the year, he'd like us to come just the same. Said he'd split whatever we found fifty-fifty. We aren't going to get a better offer than that. His cabin is small, but it should be sufficient. We can add onto it when the weather warms up." Adrik puffed out his chest as though quite pleased with himself. "I told him I'd come back here and pack everybody up and be there within the week."

Karen's mouth dropped open. "What? Just like that?"

"Just like what?" Adrik seemed genuinely surprised.

"We can't just up and leave. Grace just had the baby. She can't possibly travel."

"We can arrange for her. She could stay here in town for a spell, and then we could come back and get her. Look, I borrowed Gump's dogs and sled. I can't keep him waiting longer than the week. It takes two days just to get to where his claim is on Hunker Creek."

"But I thought you went to check out another claim.

Didn't Gump suggest some friend of his might need help?"

"Gump's friend didn't need the hands, but Gump did. We started talking on the trip out there, and Gump talked about how hard it is to work a claim by himself. He wants to give it one big go in the spring and then pack out by fall of next year. He figures if we help him with it, we might all come out on top. After all, most of the claims on Hunker Creek are netting good finds."

"But Adrik, we can't . . . I mean . . ." Karen's voice trailed off. She tried to think of how to tell him about her job. She looked to the others in the room. Leah and Grace seemed to understand, but Jacob just looked on, as if confused by the entire encounter.

Grace nodded to Karen as if to bolster her courage. Karen looked to her husband and decided it was better to just get things out in the open. "I have a job. It pays good money. One hundred and fifty dollars a month, to be exact."

"That *is* a lot of money!" Jacob exclaimed. "What do you have to do for it?"

Adrik took a step back and looked down at his wife. "Yes, what do you have to do?"

Karen felt her cheeks grow hot, but whether from embarrassment at the suggestive tone of her husband or her own anger, she couldn't tell. "Nothing that would shame either one of us. I have a job cooking. It's a good job. I figured we could use the money what with the baby and all. Grace and the baby need four walls and a roof, not a tent."

"And that's exactly what I propose to offer them," Adrik replied.

Karen looked around the room, frustrated to have an audience. That was the biggest problem with their living in a tent. There was never any place for real privacy, and outside was far too cold to take a stroll for something so menial as an argument.

"Adrik, I took the job because I thought it might ease the burden for you and Jacob. The job isn't hard, and I don't mind doing it."

"Well, I do. I don't want my wife supporting me," Adrik said sternly. "I'm the one who took it on to see to your welfare and that of everyone else in this room. I wouldn't have done it if I didn't think myself capable."

"And you are," Karen replied, hoping to soothe his irritated spirit. "I just thought this would free you up to find what you were really searching for."

"I've already found what I'm looking for," Adrik answered. "Gump has been a good friend for a long time. He needs the help and we need what he can offer. It's a good trade, and since there's still plenty of winter left, I don't intend to see you living it out here in a tent."

"But—"

"No, Karen. We're doing this my way. I'm the man of the family." He looked to Grace and nodded. "In Peter Colton's absence, I'm Grace's protector, as well. I know what's best. Grace, do you trust me to provide a place for you and your son?"

Grace looked to Karen and then back to Adrik. "I know you'll do right by us."

Adrik turned to Karen. "Will you trust me?"

Karen knew there was no reason to continue the argument. Adrik's mind was made up, and she wasn't going to change it. "All right," she said reluctantly.

Adrik took hold of her shoulders. "Karen, I've prayed this

through. I know God has provided for us and at the same time, He's provided for Gump. This is all going to work out. You'll see. Gump gave me some money for extra supplies and a bit to tide us over. I'll use the money to secure Grace and the boy, then we'll get whatever else we need and head out. When the weather improves, I'll come back and get Grace and the baby."

And so it was settled. Leah stirred more flapjack batter while Jacob and Adrik went to care for Gump's dog team. Karen went to sit beside Grace, still not entirely certain this solution was for the best.

"I don't want to leave you behind," Karen said in a hushed tone.

Grace patted her hand. "Don't worry. I know that God has this completely in His care. I know Andy and I will be just fine. You go ahead and we'll join you as soon as we can. Just trust Adrik to know what's best. He's a good man."

Karen smiled. "You sound like the teacher now rather than the student."

Grace shook her head. "No, I sound like a lonely wife."

Karen took hold of her hand. "I'm so sorry, dear friend. I know you would much rather be with Peter, safe and warm in some distant home. I should never have brought you north. I should have insisted on having you return to California. I should have bought the ticket myself and put you on the ship."

"No," Grace replied. "I believe God had a purpose in allowing all of this."

"Yes, but if it hadn't been for Mr. Paxton and his unyielding desire to force you into marriage, you might never have had these problems with Peter."

"But for Mr. Paxton, I might never have met Peter. We must remember that, as well."

"I suppose you're right," Karen said, feeling overcome by a sense of defeat. "Sometimes I think this is all a dream and other times, a nightmare."

"At least we have each other," Grace whispered.

"For now. But Adrik will separate us on the morrow."

"I'm confident of our reunion. Andrew and I will join you before you know it. We'll be safe and sound and you may fuss over us as much as you like."

"I hope you're right," Karen replied, looking across the tent at all their worldly possessions. Things weren't nearly as important as the people in her life. They never had been, but now more than ever, Karen sensed the emptiness of their humble dwelling. Would things ever return to normal? *At this point*, Karen thought, *I can't even say that I know what normal is anymore.*

⊣ CHAPTER NINE ⊢

"WESLEY TELLS ME it's possible to get as far north as Lake Lindeman, even in the dead of winter," Peter Colton told his mother and father as they concluded breakfast. He'd waited for just the right moment to break the news that he'd soon be headed to Alaska.

"Does Captain Oakes tell you how to go about doing this?" Ephraim Colton asked his son.

Peter pushed back from the table and nodded. "Wes says he can take me as far as Skagway. From there I'll take the train as far north as I can and hike out from there. The biggest problem will be the cost of supplies, but I'm working on that."

"I wish you didn't have to go," Ephraim stated. He pushed around the food on his plate before focusing on Peter. "I won't rest as long as I know you're in danger."

"The danger should be minimal, Father. After all, there are far more settlements and conveniences now. The Mounties have worked hard to maintain law and order, so even the criminal problems have been reduced."

"Still, it's hard to know you'll be so far away," Ephraim murmured.

Peter knew that since his father had suffered a heart attack, he'd been far more concerned about Peter sticking close to home. It was as if the older man feared his death might yet come from the attack, leaving Abigail without someone at her side to help with the arrangements.

"I have to go," Peter finally said. "If I leave right away, I can be there when the first thaw allows travel on the lakes."

"If you leave now, when do you imagine you might find Miranda and bring her home?" Abigail questioned.

Peter looked to his mother and smiled. "I would guess late May at the earliest. If I can get to Dawson right away, say by early June, I can head home with Miranda by the end of the month. That should see us home by August at the latest."

"My poor Miranda. I fear for her having to live these long cold months alone," Peter's mother sniffed.

Peter knew the separation had been hard on his parents. It had been only compounded by the knowledge that Grace was dead. They all mourned that loss and shared their sorrows daily. Peter knew it was impossible to wish or pray his wife back to life, but he couldn't help but turn his eyes heavenward, hoping against hope that God might somehow reverse the order of the past. It seemed like only yesterday word had come from the Mountie station at Whitehorse. His wife was dead, one more victim of the Yukon gold rush. His sister was left alone, and it was his duty to bring her home safe and sound.

"We'll soon have her home, Mother. I'll see to it," Peter promised.

"I had some good news from Mr. Hamilton," Ephraim said, changing the subject.

"And what does our good lawyer tell us these days?"

Ephraim smiled. "He believes it will only be a short time before our assets are returned to us. With Martin's death and the questionable legality of the contract between us, Hamilton feels confident Colton Shipping will soon be back in family hands."

"That is good news," Peter replied. He had missed being the captain of his own ship, *Merry Maid*. "Perhaps if the details are worked out soon enough I might sail myself to Skagway. Perhaps even take a load of goods and reap a profit." But even as the thought crossed his mind, Peter couldn't help but remember Wes's prediction that the high-profit days of the Seattle-to-Skagway route were quickly coming to an end.

"It's always possible," Ephraim said thoughtfully. "You do realize the trade is slacking off."

"I was just remembering that," Peter said, smiling. "Funny that you should be on top of that, as well."

"Not funny at all, considering it's my business to know." Ephraim then turned a loving look on his son. "I know I've not always been a wise businessman. I know my choices have often been made because of ease or even the liberty involved. That is in the past, however. In coming back to an understanding of what God would have of me as a man and provider, I realize that I must also be a good steward of that with which He has blessed me."

Peter understood his father's heart entirely. Following his own will had brought him nothing but misery. Turning his thoughts to God and leaning on His ways had brought about the only peace Peter had known since losing Grace.

Peter looked to his parents. "I thought I was doing a good thing when I took control of the family business. I figured it to be an act of love, but now I see it was a deception of selfishness. I wanted to be important—indispensable."

"But, son, you already were," Ephraim said, shaking his head. "You were all we could have hoped for in a child. As you grew into manhood, you were protective and loving with your sister, and you were astute and conscientious regarding the business. The fault is on my part, if there is any to be had. I tired of the burden. I'm tired even now, which is why I plan to sign the business over to you in full, once we resolve the legal circumstances, of course."

Peter would have thrilled to hear those words only a year ago. But now they rang hollow. Grace was gone. So, too, was his chance for real happiness. He would never love another woman. Grace had made her way into his heart, and her memory refused to leave him in peace.

Peter tried hard to push aside the thoughts that Grace had died believing the worst of him. She had thought him to be a heartless cad—ruthless in his decisions and indifferent to her needs. At least, that's what Peter imagined she thought. And that hurt him more than anything else, except her actual absence. It was difficult, if not impossible, to remember that he had purposefully caused her pain.

" . . . that's all I ask."

Peter realized his father had been speaking, but he'd not heard a word. "I'm sorry. What did you just say? I'm afraid my mind was a million miles away."

Ephraim reached over and gently touched his son's shoulder. "I said, it is my desire that your mother and I be allowed to live here, comfortably with your sister. Otherwise, you may do as you choose with the business and its profits."

"But of course you may live here. I would fight every court in the country to see to it that you remained in the home you love. Look, I don't wish for us to discuss any more about the shipping business," Peter said, getting to his feet. "I'm going to start putting together my plans for going north. I have a good understanding of what I need and how much money it will take. There's one benefit that the north can offer, and that is the tired souls who are giving up their dreams of gold. They will have all the supplies and tools that I'll need. And they'll be willing to sell them at a much discounted price."

Abigail dabbed her eyes and looked away. "But what if something happens to you? You could just as easily be lost on the same lake that claimed your wife."

Peter went to his mother and hugged her close. "God is with me, Mother. No matter the outcome, I am His now. I am His and He will guide me. If and when He chooses to take me from this earth, please know that I am ready and willing to face Him."

"I might know it in my heart, but I would still miss you—need you," Abigail replied, lifting her gaze to meet Peter's.

Peter leaned down and kissed his mother's forehead. "Please don't fret, for nothing will ever truly separate us."

Just then a knock sounded at the front door. Peter exchanged a look of curiosity with his parents. "Who could that be?" He gave his mother's arm a gentle pat before heading to the door.

Peter's heavy booted steps echoed in the empty hallway. The house seemed so quiet without Miranda and Grace. Sometimes he ached to hear their girlish chatter. Sometimes the silence of the house threatened to encase him like an empty tomb.

Opening the door, Peter met the gaze of a small, simply-dressed woman. She looked to be in her fifties and there was a certain air of refinement about her. Gazing into her eyes, however, Peter saw a haunting reminder of his wife.

"I'm Myrtle Hawkins," the woman announced. "Grace's mother. Are you Peter?"

Peter felt the wind go out from him. "Yes," he managed to say.

"I recognized you from Grace's descriptions. You are a fine, handsome man," Myrtle said with a sober smile.

"I . . . ah . . . I don't know what to say," Peter replied. He had written to Myrtle months ago to tell her of Grace's death. He hadn't told of their separation or of the problems they were having. He hadn't even related the issues of Martin Paxton's continued harangue. Peter had thought to save Grace's mother from all of that, and because he had never figured to have to face her, he felt certain it was the right thing to do. Now, however, he felt like a fraud.

Myrtle reached out and took hold of his hand. "Peter, my daughter loved you very much. You needn't say anything more."

Her words only convicted him that much more. "I must say," Peter began, "I never expected to meet you. Welcome to San Francisco." He stepped back from the door and added,

"Won't you please come in?" He looked past her to where a hired carriage waited at the curb. "Do you have baggage?"

"Yes, but I needn't impose on you," Myrtle replied. "I had thought perhaps you could escort me to a decent hotel."

"Nonsense. You'll stay with us. I'll get your things."

Peter quickly retrieved the bags and paid the driver. A rush of thoughts consumed his attention. Why was she here? What could she possibly want with him? What could he possibly do to ease her suffering when his own was still so raw and fresh?

"Come inside," Peter said as he climbed the steps. "I'll introduce you to my mother and father."

"Peter, before we join the others, I must tell you something. In private," she added.

Peter put her things down inside the door and waited until she'd joined him in the entryway. Dreading what she might have to tell him, Peter braced himself as Myrtle Hawkins unfastened the buttons of her traveling coat.

"I've come because I received some news from my late husband's lawyer," Myrtle said as she paused to look Peter in the eye. "News that will profoundly change your life."

‑| C H A P T E R T E N |‑

TEDDY ARRANGED HIS office as best he could. Working and sleeping in the same room had reduced his level of comfort, but he felt confident that he had no other choice. The hotel was full and Miranda needed his help. He couldn't just leave her to venture into the unknown.

It was strange how she'd managed to worm her way into his daily thoughts. Teddy had never been one given to daydreams, but of late, he found Miranda's sweet face ever coming to mind.

Looking over the variety of specimen bottles and crates, Teddy knew he'd have to abandon thoughts of the brown-haired beauty or fall hopelessly behind in his work. This had never been a problem in the past—when little could distract him from his botanical research.

"Lord," he prayed, "I cannot say I understand my state of

mind. It seems an oddity to me at best and a fearful thing at worst. Please steady me to complete the work you've given me to do."

Teddy looked to the door that adjoined his room to Miranda's. He wondered if she was there just now. He wondered what she was doing and how she planned to go about searching for her friends. She was a delicate and lovely flower— petite and gentle, but with a fiery sting when angered. He didn't like to think of her alone on the streets, for he knew full well how some would be inclined to take advantage of her.

Crossing to the window, Teddy noted the skies were clearing. A light snow still fell, but the winds had calmed. Perhaps Miranda would choose this time to go scouting for her friends. Perhaps he should offer to help. Once again, he looked to the tables of work behind him.

"I must stop this nonsense. I have become flighty." He reached for his coat and pulled a list of needed supplies from the table. "I might as well occupy myself by attending to this first thing. Perhaps then my mind will be fixed for work."

But even as he rechecked his list, he found himself adding things for Miranda—a dress, new boots, stockings, and other such things that might be pleasing to her. She had told him not to worry about her, but Teddy didn't want her going about looking like a street urchin.

"Maybe something red," he murmured. "Something the color of the mountain ash berries."

Heading to the hardware store, Teddy tried to bring his thoughts into order. He knew it would do more harm than good to continue focusing on Miss Colton. She was a pleasant enough woman, but he had work to do. *I must stop this nonsense and turn my attention to the task at hand,* he told himself.

Squaring his shoulders, Teddy was determined to purchase the things he needed, and then return to the hotel and spend the day buried in his work. Maybe he wouldn't worry about getting Miranda a dress. After all, he didn't even know her size. And maybe she didn't like red. Tucking his face down into his coat, he put Miranda from his mind.

The ring of the bell on the door of MacCarthy's Hardware seemed to jolt Teddy's senses. He looked up, but not in time to avoid stepping headlong into the chest of a broad-shouldered man.

"Oh, please pardon me," Teddy said, stepping back.

"No problem, friend."

Teddy sized up the large man and smiled. "I'm afraid my mind was elsewhere."

The big man laughed. "Mine's somewhere to the south where the winds blow warmer and the fishing is easy. Unfortunately, that's a long way from this place."

Teddy returned his thoughts to his list just as a young man joined them. "Adrik, they don't have any sleds they can sell."

Teddy looked up. "Sleds? Did you say you were looking for a sled?"

The big man nodded. "That's right. Do you know where we might buy one?"

"I have one," Teddy replied. "Oh, where are my manners, the name is Davenport. Thomas Davenport."

"Adrik Ivankov is my name," the big man said, extending his hand. "And this here is Jacob Barringer."

Teddy nodded. "I have a sled, and since I'll be staying

throughout the winter, I'll have no need of it. You're welcome to purchase it."

"What kind of price are you asking?"

Teddy looked around the small confines of the hardware store. "Well, I'd not considered the price." He chuckled. "But then again, I hadn't considered selling the sled until just now."

"Well, we aren't wealthy by any means. Fact is, I'm taking part of my party out to a friend's claim and leaving part of it here. My wife's friend just had a baby, and there's no sense in risking their lives until things warm up a bit. Still, I need two sleds. I can work in a trade—chop wood or build just about anything you need."

Teddy shook his head. "I'm afraid I have little need of either of those things. I'm staying at the hotel across the street."

"We have a lot of extra meat," the young man offered. "We shot us an elk and a moose not too long ago."

"Fresh meat could be a real bonus. I would imagine the hotel might well be glad to get it," Teddy said rather absent-mindedly. "All right, I'll trade you meat for the sled."

"How much do you reckon would be a fair amount for the sled?" The big man asked.

Again Teddy felt perplexed. He'd never dealt in such matters and the consideration of a fair trade was completely beyond his interest. "Why don't you give me what you believe to be fair. I'll trust the good Lord to watch over my end of the deal," Teddy finally said.

"Well, He watches over every deal I make." The big man smiled. "I'll tell you what. The boy and I will go load up the meat and bring it around within the hour. We're in a bit of a hurry, so why don't you show us where you'd like to meet."

Teddy motioned them to follow. "As I said, I'm just there across the street. Come along and I'll show you the sled. That way you can better judge for yourself a fair trade."

The men followed Teddy down the walk and across the frozen snow and mud of Second Avenue. Teddy heard them commenting on the blessing of running across this stranger, but thought little of himself as their rescuer. He was glad to unload the sled. It was of little use to him. Come spring he'd simply hire someone to pack him out to the cabin on horseback.

"We're heading out to Hunker Creek," the big man told him. "Have a friend with a claim there. This is certainly going to be an answer to prayer."

"Well, here we are, gentlemen," Teddy said, stopping behind a small storage shed. The alleyway behind the hotel was covered in undisturbed snow and the wind had blown drifts across the doors to the shed. Teddy used his booted foot to push aside a good portion of the drift before pulling a key from his pants pocket.

"This should do the trick," he said, unlocking the shed. Dim light filtered into the confines of the dark storage room. A variety of supplies and other articles were stacked atop each other. Teddy's sled was just inside, due to the fact they'd only just arrived.

The big man pulled the sled out into the alleyway and nodded. "It's a fine, sturdy piece," he commented, looking it over for any defect.

Teddy pulled out his pocket watch and popped open the cover. It was nearly lunchtime. How had he managed to waste half a day? He began to make a mental calculation of his morning activities, not clearly hearing what the big man told him.

"If that meets with your approval."

"What?" Teddy questioned. "I'm afraid I was a bit adrift."

The big man laughed. "No problem. I merely said the sled is worth a good portion of meat. I'll bring it by here right away. Can you meet us here in an hour and make the trade?"

"Certainly," Teddy replied.

He waited until the men had headed off at a trotting pace before wrestling the sled back into the shed. He fiddled around with the lock, finally mastering it. Securing the door before heading back around the side of the hotel, Teddy considered what he should do now. The day was clearly getting away from him and he still had to come back to deal with the man who wanted his sled. He might as well purchase the supplies and then head back to the hotel for a bite of lunch. It would no doubt be time to meet the man after that. After he squared things away with the sled, he could certainly set about organizing his work.

Once again he crossed the street, anxious to purchase his supplies and get back to his room. There was a great deal of work yet to be done, work that would no doubt keep him busy until spring.

"Teddy Davenport, is that you?" an older man called as Teddy once again approached the hardware store.

Teddy looked up and met the approaching man somewhat apprehensively. "Lawrence Montgomery?" The man's face was buried behind a thick fur cap.

"That's right. I say, what are you about this day?"

"I was going to purchase some supplies. I'm working

rather diligently to catalog my newest findings."

"Still working on the book, eh?"

Teddy nodded. "Most assuredly."

"Well, that's fine. Just fine. Say, you wouldn't be interested in having a spot of lunch with me, would you?"

"I shouldn't. I truly have a great deal of work to do." Teddy had never really cared for Montgomery's company. They had little in common, save England. Montgomery had been a member of Her Majesty's Navy and he never failed to bore Teddy with tedious stories of life aboard ship. Teddy wouldn't have minded hearing about the foreign ports, but Montgomery was far more consumed with naval life than the scenery he'd experienced.

"Just a cup of tea, then?"

Teddy knew the man was lonely for company, but he really didn't want to lose anymore time. "Perhaps we could meet later today. I simply must get back to work at this time."

"Then it will have to be another day," Montgomery said, "for I'm off to meet with the Arctic Brotherhood after lunch. We're discussing the possibility of building a new hall. You really should join us."

"Perhaps at the next meeting," Teddy promised. He knew the organization to be one of good charity and good times, but the meetings were generally not to his liking.

Turning to head back to the hotel, Teddy had barely crossed the street when he realized he'd completely forgotten about making his purchases at the hardware store. With a sigh, he rubbed his gloved hands together and made his way back to the store. He doubted he had any chance of making this day a productive one. The best he could hope for was a time of peace and quiet in the afternoon. Of course, there was also the matter of selling his sled. Pulling his watch once again, Teddy noted the time. He didn't want to make an enemy of the big man by failing to show up at the appointed time.

"Mr. Davenport," the clerk called out from behind the counter. "Good to have you back in town. What can I do for you today?"

Teddy closed the case on the watch and thought for a moment. *Oh, bother.* Now what had he done with his list?

⊣ CHAPTER ELEVEN ⊢

MIRANDA LOOKED OUT the window of the hotel. Happily she found that the wind had abated, as well as the falling snow. The street below was covered with a thick layer of white powder, but already there were dozens of people forging a new path through the pristine blanket.

"This ought to be as good a time as any to go in search of the registration office," Miranda said, letting the curtain fall back into place.

Gathering her coat, Miranda slipped into the hall. She glanced briefly at Teddy's door, wondering if he was hard at work inside. She thought to let him know that she was leaving for a while, but remembering how irritated he became with interruptions, Miranda decided against it. She owed him no explanation.

After getting directions to the recorder's office, she

rushed in the direction indicated. Miranda was eager to learn the whereabouts of her friends. She had prayed fervently for their safety and could only trust that God had kept them from the same fate she'd suffered.

"I'm looking for my friends and family," she told the official once she'd managed to work her way through the gathering of men.

An older man with a thick bushy mustache of red and gray, looked at her as if to consider the validity of her statement. "You ain't one of them gals from Paradise Alley, are ya?"

"I'm afraid I'm not familiar with that particular place. I'm from San Francisco."

The men around her laughed while the older man looked at her sternly. "Paradise Alley is the entertainment center for men who are looking for female companionship. I'm just askin' if you're one them kind of gals."

Miranda felt her cheeks grow hot. "I should say not. I was coming north when we encountered a storm on one of the lakes. I was swept overboard and it's been many months since I've seen or heard anything of what became of my friends and family. I'm staying over at the Dawson Lucky Day Hotel."

The man nodded as if he'd known the truth all along. Apparently this was enough to satisfy his curiosity. "So what's the name?"

"I believe the claim would be under Ivankov. Adrik Ivankov."

"Hmmm, name don't ring a bell, but let me look through the records."

Miranda waited patiently while the man searched his

ledgers. "Nope, don't see no Ivankovs listed here. I have an Ivanovich. Would that work?"

He suggested the name as though Miranda were picking out colors for new draperies. "No," she answered. "How about Colton? Do you have any listing for Colton?"

"That spelled with an E-N or O-N?"

"O-N."

The man flipped through the pages and ran his finger down a long, hand-printed list. "I got a Benjamin Colton marked down on the Little Skookum. Would that be them?"

Miranda shook her head. "No."

"Maybe this here Ben Colton would know about your Coltons."

"No, I don't think so. You see, that's my family name and I've never known us to have a Benjamin in the family."

The man rubbed his chin. "Well, guess I can't offer you much help."

"Do you have any other suggestions for locating folks in this area? If my friends haven't filed a claim, is there any other way I can learn if they made it this far?"

"You could check in with the Mounties. They're trying to keep tabs on the folks comin' and goin'. They might have something for you."

Miranda thanked the man and walked back outside. The air was crisp, almost painful to breathe. The frosty cold filled her lungs, causing her to bury her face against the lining of her collar. Looking up and then down the street in hopes of seeing someone familiar, Miranda tried not to succumb to the feeling of overwhelming hopelessness.

What if they were all killed on the lake? What if I'm the only one who survived? Oh, God, please don't let that be the truth of it. I can't imagine never seeing them again.

Of course, it was possible that upon arriving in Dawson and believing Miranda dead, they could have returned to San Francisco, or at least Grace might have returned. But Grace had said it wasn't her home and she couldn't go there without Peter.

Thoughts of her brother gave Miranda an idea. Perhaps she could telegraph Peter in Skagway. Of course, he might have gone back to San Francisco by now, but he also might have stayed. But where could she send the message to be delivered? She had no idea where Peter might have gone. The sensible thing to do seemed to be to send her parents a wire and make sure they knew she wasn't dead. From there, maybe they could get word to her about Peter. The only problem was it cost money to send a telegram—money she didn't have.

Perhaps I could ask for a loan from Teddy, she thought. He had certainly offered her plenty of other things—a room, clothes, food. Surely he wouldn't begrudge her a telegram to her family.

Spotting a Mountie, Miranda crossed the street. "Sir," she addressed, "can you tell me where I might send a telegram? I need to contact my parents in California."

"I'm sorry, miss. There aren't telegraph connections for that kind of contact. Your best bet would be to post them a letter. I can direct you to the postal office."

"How long will it take a letter to reach them?" Miranda asked, her heart sinking with every new discovery.

"It could be months. The mail is taken out on dog sled and sometimes it's very reliable and other times it's less than so." He smiled apologetically. "I wish I could be more encouraging."

Miranda nodded. So much for sending a telegram. In a spirit of complete dejection, she shuffled through the icy snow and made her way back down the street. Shivering from the cold, Miranda decided to take a shortcut through the alleyway. She could see the top of the hotel at the end of the narrow path and felt confident she could reach it more quickly by this route.

She'd not gone ten steps, however, when a bearded man popped around the corner from the opposite direction. She bristled, knowing that it had been foolish to get off the main street. What if the man meant her harm?

She sized him up. Although dressed in a heavy coat and hat, Miranda thought the man looked rather thin and gaunt. He looked at her for a moment, then raised a bottle and took a long drink. Lowering the bottle, he looked at her again and took several steps forward. The shock was clearly written in his expression.

Miranda studied him. Her momentary fear passed as she recognized something familiar about the man. The light was fading from the skies, however, and the shadows could have been playing games with her. Moving a step closer she called out, "Crispin, is that you?"

The man dropped the bottle at this and began backing away. "No!"

"Crispin, wait. Where are you going?" she called out. "Where are the others?"

The man fell backward over a barrel, but quickly regained his feet and shook his head. "Leave me be. Go away!" he shouted.

He turned and fled, disappearing almost as quickly as he'd appeared. Miranda hurried after him, but it was to no avail. She came out of the alley near the hotel and looked in both directions.

"Crispin!" she called. The word echoed back at her.

He had simply vanished, as if he'd never been there at all. She rushed to where the alley intersected a narrow passage between buildings and looked first one direction and then the other. He wasn't there. Perhaps the whole incident had been nothing but a figment of her imagination. Perhaps she longed so much to find her loved ones that her mind had begun conjuring them up.

"Oh, Father God," she whispered. "I cannot begin to understand what just happened. Surely if that man was Crispin Thibault, he would have come to me in greeting. Surely he would have taken me to my friends. What do I do now?"

She continued down the alley, feeling nothing but dumbfounded of the strange meeting. The sight of Teddy at the storage shed behind the hotel did little to lift her spirits.

"I say, what are you doing here?" he questioned as she drew near.

"I was just coming from the deed office. No one has heard of my friends. I thought to send a telegram to my parents, but a Mountie told me there are no such services here in Dawson." Miranda felt tears come to her eyes. "And just now, I thought I saw one of the gentlemen from my party, but he ran off in a fit of fear." Tears stung her eyes against the cold air.

Teddy put the key to the shed in his coat pocket, and then extended his arm. "Now, now. You mustn't cry. The air is much too cold and your eyes will positively freeze. Look, I've had a bit of luck in ridding myself of the sled. I made a rather nice trade for some elk and moose meat. What say we get the cook to fix us some of it for our supper? We can dine and discuss what you must do next."

Miranda was surprised at his generous offer of time. "What about your work?"

Teddy looked to the skies overhead. "I'll simply work into the night. Come along."

Miranda didn't know what else she could do. Reluctantly she reached out and took hold of Teddy's arm. "I'm completely confused," she told him, looking up into his warm brown eyes. She saw his expression soften. "I'm so alone."

"Nonsense," he replied, patting her arm with his gloved hand. "You have me. I shall help you in whatever manner presents itself to me."

Miranda turned to Teddy, captured by his gallant concern for her well-being, and felt that she was losing her heart to his quiet, gentle ways. Though she felt so vulnerable—so lost—he was like a refuge in the cleft of the rock. A shelter from a certain, otherwise unbearable, storm.

—[CHAPTER TWELVE]—

TEDDY FELT A STRANGE fluttering and warmth in his chest. He typically didn't concern himself with the emotions of others—in fact, it wasn't something he'd really ever done before now. His mother had been a very loving woman whose strength and independence he had greatly admired. His father, a refined Englishman, was soft-spoken and gentle of spirit. Teddy had never had cause to deal with such depth of feeling—until now.

"I am sorry about your friend," Teddy said as he guided Miranda into the hotel. "But you truly shouldn't let his reaction upset you."

"Why do you say that? I've been gone for months," Miranda replied indignantly. She pulled away from him and shook her head. "They believe me to be dead. He acted as though I were a ghost."

"But they'll know the truth of it in the end." Teddy thought his argument to be perfectly reasonable. Miranda's expression suggested otherwise.

Taking hold of her well-worn skirt, Miranda crossed the lobby in obvious displeasure. Teddy could scarcely believe her reaction. What had he said that was wrong? He rethought his words as he followed her up the stairs.

"Miss Colton, I say, you surely misunderstand me."

"I understand that you believe my concern to be silly and unwarranted."

"I never said it was silly," Teddy replied, trying hard to remember any comment that might have given her this impression.

"You act as though it's nothing more than a simple misunderstanding," Miranda countered as she topped the stairs. She turned, pulling her wool bonnet from her head. "You suggest that the truth will come out in the end. Well, let me explain something to you, Mr. Davenport. My friends believe the end has already come and gone. They believe me to be dead in Lake Laberge."

Teddy nodded, trying hard to guard his words. "Yes . . ." he began hesitantly, "but you're not."

"Exactly!" She made the declaration and lifted her chin defiantly.

Teddy watched Miranda stalk down the hallway toward her room. He went over every piece of information, each comment he had shared. But her actions and attitude simply did not follow any rational response. Why was she so angry with him? Only moments ago she had been tearful.

"Miss Colton," Teddy called as he followed after her, "I must be allowed to say something—to explain . . ."

Miranda turned, her eyes narrowing. "To explain why you are so heartless?"

"Me? Heartless? I assure you that is hardly the case. I am trying my best to offer you comfort by presenting a reasonable explanation. Your friends cannot leave Dawson, short of heading out on dog sled. That is highly unlikely, as there isn't a sled to be bought in town. A man told me that just this morning, when I sold him my sled."

"What could that possibly have to do with any of this?"

"Just this," Teddy said, hoping she'd hear with her logic and not her emotions. "If that was your friend—the man you saw earlier—he won't be leaving Dawson until spring thaw. That won't come until May. That gives you months to track down your friends."

"I hardly have months, Mr. Davenport. I cannot expect to go on living here without a job. I have no clothes to speak of, no money for personal items, and I cannot pay for the room in which I'm sleeping."

"But the money is immaterial," Teddy assured her. Finally he felt confident of the subject matter. "I've given you the room without requirement of pay. I've offered to buy you new clothes, and I'd be happy to give you cash for your personal needs."

But instead of making her happy, Teddy could see that this announcement only intensified her irritation. "I'm not your responsibility," Miranda said firmly. "I'm not about to allow a strange man to keep me, almost as if I were his . . . his . . . mistress."

Teddy felt his cheeks grow hot. He was unaccustomed to women speaking in such a manner. He was befuddled. First Miranda had been upset because she found her friend and lost him. Then she was upset about being without money or clothes. And when Teddy offered to help, she was angry about that as well.

"I *never* suggested that I expect anything in return, Miss Colton," Teddy finally managed to say. "I don't know where you could possibly get such an idea."

Miranda put her hand on her hips. "I'm a woman and you're a man. You're keeping me in a hotel, in an adjoining room to your own sleeping quarters. You pay for my meals and now you offer to put clothes on my back. What will people think?"

"Well, I really don't care what people think. We know what the truth of it is. I don't think of you as a woman," Teddy said, suddenly halting, realizing his blunder the minute he'd spoken. Not only was it the wrong thing to say, it was a lie. He was only too aware of Miranda as a woman.

"You are without a doubt the most insensitive and simpleminded man in all creation," Miranda proclaimed. "You don't understand anything unless it grows out of the ground and can be pressed into your books for further study. In fact, I'm beginning to think you are incapable of understanding anything not associated with vegetation. I believe, Mr. Davenport, it very well may be possible that your brain is composed of nothing but mulch and compost. Good day!"

Abruptly she turned and opened her door without even looking back at him. When she slammed the door behind her, Teddy knew it had been done for his benefit.

"Mulch? Compost?" He shook his head and pulled the room key from his pants pocket. Women were queer creatures. So temperamental and emotional.

With a slow shake of his head, Teddy opened the door to

his room and stared in stunned amazement. The room, which that morning had been in perfect order, now lay in complete disarray. Books, plants, jars, and clothes were scattered about the room like children's toys in a messy nursery. Months of work had been destroyed, completely obliterated in this attack on his personal belongings.

Teddy walked in, not even bothering to close the door. He picked up one of his journals and dusted the flaked pieces of dried *Calypso bulbosa*—fairy slipper—from the leather cover.

Who could have done such a thing? He wondered at the destruction, barely able to comprehend the situation. No corner of the room was untouched. The bed had been torn apart, the bedding left to lie on the floor, mattress hanging off on one side.

Teddy began picking things up without any real thought or order. He was standing there rather dumbly, his arms full of this and that, when Miranda Colton knocked on his open door.

He looked up to catch her expression of disbelief. "Who did this?" she questioned.

"I don't know."

"Why would they do this?" she asked, stepping into the room.

"Again, I cannot say."

He shook his head and looked back at the disarray. "I had nothing of value here—not in a monetary sense. However, in the sense of work and months of searching—these possessions are invaluable."

"I'm so sorry, Teddy." Miranda's soft-spoken tone soothed his frayed nerves. "Not only for this, but for the way

I acted. I know you were only trying to help me, and I wasn't very kind. I'm sorry."

"No, I'm the one to apologize. You must understand— I've not had much experience with the fairer gender. I suppose myself to be rather remiss in dealing with the emotions and even the physical needs of women." Teddy moved to place the armload of materials on the table.

"Is there anything I can do?" Miranda asked, coming to stand beside him. "I could help you clean this up."

"The work will be extensive. I can't just tear into it. I'll have to take it a little at a time. It will be rather painstaking."

"I don't mind. I owe you much."

He turned and caught the compassion in her expression. How was it that she could be so sympathetic and concerned, when he had obviously hurt her deeply only moments ago?

"You owe me nothing. The law of the north is to do unto your neighbor as you would have done to you. The law of God's Word is to love your neighbor as yourself. I would have wanted someone to help me, had I washed ashore in the same condition."

"Yes, but I haven't acted very grateful. I really would like to help you here. But first, perhaps we should ask to speak with the management. I think the owner should know of this."

"He already does," Teddy replied. "I am he."

"You own this hotel? Why didn't you tell me?"

Teddy shrugged. "It never seemed important. When the rush first came on, I used funds from my parents' estate and built the nicest place I could."

"Well, at least that explains why you had no trouble putting me up," Miranda said smiling. "You are quite the man of many surprises, Mr. Davenport."

He looked away. "I could have done without this surprise." He thought of her offer and realized that, in the destruction of all that he held dear, he needed her. He needed her comfort, her gentle nature, and her companionship.

"I will allow you to help, but only if I may pay you a salary." He held up his hand to ward off any protests. "I will deduct the price of the room if that makes you feel better, but I would have to pay someone—so it might as well be you."

"But I would do the job without charge," Miranda replied, coming to stand in front of him. "Teddy, you've already done so much for me."

"Then allow me to continue. You have no other alternative, unless you would like to become a saloon dancer or scarlet woman. And while your appearance would definitely put the others to shame, such an occupation would never befit you. Let me pay you to be my assistant. But I will warn you—I'm an absolute bear to work for. The work will be tedious and the hours long. We've much to accomplish in order to right this wrong."

"Very well, Teddy. I will allow you to furnish my room and board and whatever else you feel fair. In return, however, I will work the same hours you work. So, if you plan to labor into the wee hours of the morning, I'll be right there at your side."

He smiled to himself and bent down to pick up a dried sample of fireweed in order to keep her from seeing his face. The idea of having Miranda at his side was most appealing. He'd grown very accustomed to her company, and though he didn't understand her emotional outbursts, he was drawn to her presence like no other.

He straightened and held up the plant. The fuchsia color had faded a bit since he'd picked it for his collection, but it was lovely nevertheless.

"Do you know what this is?" he asked, holding up the flower.

Miranda shook her head. "I haven't a clue."

"It's *Epilobium angustifolium,* commonly called fireweed or blooming Sally. It's generally considered to be a nuisance to those who garden. Some even call it a weed." He twirled the piece in his finger a moment, and then handed it to Miranda. "I've collected many of them in my explorations of the land, but I thought this one to be an exceptionally nice example."

"It is lovely—weed or no," Miranda said, taking the flower.

"I thought so as well."

"How shall I preserve it for your work?"

He nodded toward the table. "We shall gather the samples and lay them out atop the table. As we gather them, I'll try to categorize them again. It's not going to be easy."

"Well, as you said earlier, there's no place to go short of mushing out on a dog sled, and since you've sold your sled ... well, that pretty much means we are here until spring."

"I suppose you're right," he replied.

———

After they had worked in companionable silence for several hours, Miranda felt a gnawing in her stomach and suggested they stop for a bite of supper. "I'm quite famished and I know I could work better on a full stomach."

"I suppose it would be best," Teddy said, pulling off his gold-rimmed glasses. He carefully folded the glasses and put them in his pocket. "I traded the sled for a large quantity of meat, so we're bound to have a pleasant supper."

Miranda stretched, glad for the rest. Her back ached from the constant bending to retrieve pieces of vegetation. How Teddy could identify each piece and correspond it to a place on the table was beyond Miranda. Most of the plants looked quite the same, especially the leaves.

"If you don't mind, I'd like to freshen up a bit," Miranda told him. "I won't be but a minute. I just want to wash up and fix my hair."

"Your hair looks lovely," Teddy said, then instantly appeared embarrassed by his outburst. As if to cover up his mistake, he continued. "I suppose I haven't told you this before, but the color reminds me of the bark of the mountain maple. The brown species—not the gray."

Miranda reached her hand to her hair. "I'm betting a few more years like this one and it will be all gray."

"I think not. You've many years before that will come about," Teddy replied.

"Well, just so long as the mountain maple is of sturdy stock," Miranda said, moving toward the door. "My people are all from sturdy stock. We are fighters, and I won't have it said that I resemble anything less than a strong specimen."

"Indeed, you are that," Teddy said, his voice dropping to a husky, barely audible tone.

Miranda smiled to herself. He wasn't such an unlikable sort. Just quaint and unique in his compliments. She'd had her hair praised and admired before, but never had anyone compared it to the bark of a tree. Coming from anyone else, it might have seemed insulting. Coming from Thomas Davenport, it almost seemed a term of endearment.

Part Two

MARCH 1899

And he hath put a new song in my mouth,
even praise unto our God:
many shall see it, and fear,
and shall trust in the Lord.

PSALM 40:3

—{ CHAPTER THIRTEEN }—

PETER SAT ALONGSIDE his father in the law office of Mathias Hamilton. The news was all good, and Peter knew the blessing had come from God.

"The judge has agreed that the contract was not issued in a legal manner. The fraudulent manner in which Mr. Paxton conducted his business and the disregard for your son's legal partnership in the business has rendered the judgment in your favor."

Peter breathed a sigh of relief. He had fully planned to leave the month before, but the lawyer had deemed it necessary to keep Peter close at hand. Now, at last, he would be free to go north and find his sister. Already his mind raced with plans.

"I have also seen to that other matter," Hamilton continued, addressing Peter. "I have looked over the trust papers given to you by your mother-in-law. Everything is in order."

Peter could scarcely believe the news Myrtle Hawkins had brought him. Paxton had thought he could ruin Hawkins through his bank account, but her husband had been too wise for that. Knowing the ruthlessness of Martin Paxton, Frederick had secured most of his fortune in an irrevocable trust for Grace.

When Paxton discovered the truth—that Grace was the one who would hold the purse strings—he had forced Frederick into compliance, threatening to share the story of his adulterous affair. Poor Frederick Hawkins had had no choice but to give in. The last thing he wanted to do was alienate the affection of his wife and only child. What Frederick Hawkins had thought would offer his daughter protection from Paxton's evil schemes was instead the very thing that drove him to pursue her. The trust would be hers upon her twenty-first birthday, and was the real reason Paxton had pushed for marriage prior to her coming into her majority. He was determined to ruin Hawkins in any way he could, and all because Hawkins had broken Martin's mother's heart through their illicit affair.

Of course, Peter now felt, in the aftermath of knowing the truth of Paxton's actions, that he could understand—at least in part—what had driven the man. Had anyone tried to dally with his mother, he would have had similar desires to see that person ruined.

"In light of the information you've given me, in regard to your wife's death," Hamilton continued, "I shall send a post to the authorities in Canada and see what we can do to receive confirmation. After her death is confirmed, we can proceed on arranging the affairs of the trust."

Peter nodded, not wanting to talk about Grace's death. He didn't want to deal with any aspect of the situation that would remind him of his loss. Standing, he extended his hand and firmly shook the hand of Mathias Hamilton. "Thank you for your time."

Ephraim Colton did likewise and added, "You will see to transferring the company entirely to my son?"

"The matter is already being tended to," Hamilton assured them.

Peter and his father hailed a cab outside the law office and made the journey home. "I know Mother's spirits will be lifted by this news," Peter said.

"Indeed. Although she doesn't care as much for the business as she does for having the matter resolved and behind us."

"She worries about you—about your health."

Ephraim sighed and settled back against the leather seat. "I know she does, but in truth, none of us know how much time we have on this earth. We're here for a short time, the Bible says. We must make every effort to live our lives in a manner pleasing to God and to be a blessing to others for His glory."

Peter found his father's words to be inspiring. "I agree. That's why I'll head north at the end of the week. It's time I found Miranda and brought her home. By the time I arrive in Skagway, it should be close to spring thaw."

"I know it would comfort your mother to know what has become of her," Ephraim agreed. "She has worried incessantly about her all winter. She felt remiss in having encouraged her to go north with Grace, yet . . ."

"Give it no other thought," Peter interjected. "I believe

God has had His hand in all of this from the beginning. I didn't always feel that way, but I most certainly do now. I know God has a plan for my life and a purpose that only I can fulfill. It's no less for Miranda or you—or Grace."

He felt the bittersweet sorrow of her memory come over him. He could almost see her dark brown eyes and smell her sweet fragrance. What was it—apple blossoms and roses?

His father's touch brought his senses back to the present. "Son, I know your heart is heavy. I loved her, too, you know."

Peter met his father's gaze. "I know."

"We are better for having had her in our lives. But let us not lessen that experience by focusing on the pain. Grace would never want us to live in a manner that would suggest that God is anything other than just and loving. She would want us to move forward in love for each other and for the God she so dearly loved."

"I know you're right, but sometimes it's just so hard." He paused. "I reach for her in the night and she's not there. I think I hear her come into the room and turn to find that it's only the wind."

Ephraim nodded. "It's not easy, but in time the pain will lessen."

"I'd like to believe that," Peter said, "but I doubt it could possibly be true. Still, I'm willing to leave it in God's hands. After all, there are few other choices."

"Especially choices that would honor Grace's memory and be in keeping with God's desire for your life."

The cab stopped in front of their townhouse, interrupting the moment. Peter paid the driver, and then helped his father from the steps. He looked up at the house, noting that it no longer felt like a home to him. Leaving San Francisco seemed the only hope of maintaining his sanity. He'd been happy here with Grace, despite the arguments and the painful words between them. Words he'd spoken in anger. Words that had driven her away.

"Come on, son. Let's tell your mother the good news."

Ephraim headed up the steps of the walkway, and reluctantly Peter followed.

———

Peter lightly fingered the pink silk gown that he'd given Grace shortly after their marriage. She had looked radiant in the dress, but then, she'd looked radiant in most anything she wore. Caressing the gown to his face, he breathed in her perfume—now faded and barely distinguishable.

"Oh, Grace. Why did I have to wait until it was too late to know what I had in you?"

"Peter?" Myrtle called from behind the closed bedroom door.

Putting the dress aside, Peter went to the door. Opening it, he found his mother-in-law looking rather expectant. "Yes, Myrtle?"

"I wondered if we might have a moment to speak together. I don't want to take you away from anything important."

"No, that's all right. I wasn't doing anything that can't wait until later. What did you want to talk to me about?" He stepped back to allow her to enter the room.

Myrtle walked past him, then turned and smiled. "Peter, your mother tells me that you're heading north by the end of the week."

"Yes, that's correct." He motioned to a chair. "Won't you sit down?"

Myrtle nodded and took a seat. Her black gown, a constant reminder of her widowhood and Grace's death, swished in gentle whispers as she straightened her skirts. Peter pulled up another chair from the opposite side of the room and sat down across from Myrtle.

"I figure to leave by Friday. I want to be north as soon as possible and find my sister."

"I pray God will grant you His favor in your search. I plan to leave by the end of the week, myself. I wondered if you would be so kind as to escort me to the train station on the day after tomorrow."

"I would be happy to do that," Peter replied. He had a hard time looking at Myrtle, especially at her eyes. She reminded him so much of Grace that it hurt. He had to look away.

"Do you suppose you will learn anything more of Grace?"

Her question pierced his heart. "I don't know. I don't expect to be shown a grave or anything like that. I don't imagine they would be able to ... to ..." He couldn't say the words.

Myrtle nodded. "No, I don't imagine they would have recovered her body." She folded her hands in her lap and looked down. "I just wondered if you thought there might be some further word on her. Maybe Miss Pierce would be able to share something more."

"It's possible. I'm sure if anyone would be able to give us further insight, Karen would be the one. Miranda, however, was also very close to Grace. She loved her like a sister, and they'd grown quite close." Peter hesitated before suggesting,

"Why don't you stay here while I'm gone? I know my mother and father would love to have you here."

"No, I would rather go back to my aunt's place. She's old and needs the help. Besides, there is something renewing and invigorating in living in such a simple rural setting after having lived in Chicago."

"I'm sure that is true."

"I only ask that you keep in touch," Myrtle said rather sadly. "I don't wish to lose contact with you simply because Grace is gone."

"And you won't. I've already spoken to my lawyer. I am arranging to set up an account for you with the money Grace inherited. I want you to have whatever you need."

Myrtle's face reddened a bit and tears came to her eyes. "You are a good son-in-law, but really, you mustn't worry about me. I'm set well enough with my aunt."

"I insist. I'm not sure how long it will take to resolve, but should you need anything prior to that, please don't hesitate to contact us. I'll leave an account with my parents. Just let them know what you need, and we'll do our best to see to it."

"Oh, Peter, you are truly as remarkable and generous as Grace told me."

"I wish I'd been as generous of spirit with Grace. I'm ashamed to say that I wronged her terribly, Myrtle. I didn't tell you everything that transpired between us, but our marriage was not as pleasant or loving as it could have been. I'm afraid that before I knew God I was rather ruthless at times."

Myrtle wiped her eyes and smiled. "Marriage is hard work—for everyone. I remember times when I wanted nothing more than to throttle Frederick. He would speak to me as if I were a child without good sense."

"I know I did that to Grace on more than one occasion. I have a bad temper."

"Surely no worse than my Frederick." Myrtle reached out and took hold of Peter's hand. "She loved you—be certain of that. Her letters said that and so much more."

Peter's heart flooded with gratitude. "Thank you for saying so. It helps. I hate to think of Grace's last thoughts of me being how truly awful I was and how sorry she was for having married me."

"Then rest your mind and put your worries aside. She told me of difficult moments, but she always stressed that her love for you was stronger than anything that could possibly go wrong."

Peter gripped her hand gently. "We should have had this talk a long time ago."

"I didn't realize how much you were hurting until I came here. Watching you has shown me proof of your deep abiding love for my daughter. How I wish things could have been different." Myrtle's voice was tinged with regret. "I just wanted you to know that I understand. I miss her and Frederick more than I can say, but God alone will ease the pain—in His time."

"I only wish I had known what a priceless gem I had in her, before it was too late. When I come back from the Yukon, maybe I'll take some of her money and erect a monument to her in the cemetery."

"Why not put the money to some better use, something that would bring glory to God and make Grace proud?"

"Such as?" Peter questioned.

"I don't know. Pray about it, and perhaps God will give

you a mission," Myrtle said, getting to her feet.

Peter immediately stood and embraced the older woman. "Myrtle, you were a godsend. You've given me comfort as no one else possibly could. When I return, I shall visit you in Wyoming."

"I would like that," she said, pulling away. "I would like that very much."

─┤ C H A P T E R   F O U R T E E N ├─

MONTHS OF WORKING with Teddy had given Miranda quite an education. She could now identify many flowers and dried leaves without having to ask Teddy for assistance. She had also come to realize that her frantic concern for locating her friends was lessening in the wake of her pleasure in Teddy's company. She'd become rather lackadaisical in her inquiries.

Truth be told, there were many days when she never even left the hotel room. She labored with Teddy, helping him catch up his research to at least the point where he'd left off when they'd come to Dawson in January. Now, with March winds alternating between freezing them to the bone and teasing them with a touch of spring, Miranda knew she needed to rededicate herself to the pursuit of locating her friends. However, Teddy was more adamant in their work than ever before. The summer would mean he could be back in the fields, and if his work from the previous year went uncompleted, he'd have to delay his trip.

As she poured over Teddy's journals and ledgers, Miranda wondered what course of action she should take. She had inquired around town about her friends when the opportunity presented itself. Many people knew of large, burly miners whose description fit that of Adrik Ivankov, but no one could tell her for sure that the men were one and the same.

At the same time, Miranda was torn by the thought of Teddy leaving for the wilderness. She tried to tell herself that it was only because they'd become such close companions in their work, but in her heart she knew it was more than that.

"I believe that," Teddy said, coming into the room unannounced, "if we persevere, we may well have this work completed by the end of next month. That will work in perfect accord with my return to the cabin."

It was almost as if he'd read her very thoughts. Miranda straightened from where she'd been bent over his books. She decided it would be best to broach the subject of what was to become of her once he was gone.

"Teddy, what am I to do if I cannot locate my friends?"

He looked at her rather blankly for a moment. It almost seemed to Miranda that he'd not given the possibility even a moment's thought.

"Why, I suppose you might stay here," he said, then turned to hang his coat on the peg by the door.

"I can't very well do that without a job," Miranda chided. "I could return home. After all, it's important to me that my family knows I'm safe."

Teddy looked at her for a moment. Miranda held his

gaze, watching him search her face as if looking for something. "Passage would be expensive," he finally said. He walked to the window and pulled aside the sheer curtain. The skies were staying light for more hours of the day, and Miranda was grateful for this.

"I think it would be wiser to locate your friends rather than just leave. After all, they must be somewhere in the area."

"I've not seen Crispin again, and he was in the area as well," Miranda replied.

"Yes, but that could have been a man who just favored your friend. You said yourself that you couldn't be sure."

Miranda nodded and walked to the stack of drawings Teddy had asked her to file. Bringing them back to the table, she began to sort through them. Paintbrush, shooting stars, larkspur, and subalpine buttercups graced the pages of stiff paper. Teddy Davenport was quite an artist. The flowers, rendered only in charcoal and pencil, were detailed and labeled in such a way that they allowed for easy reference for anyone who wanted to study the species more closely.

Realizing Teddy had joined her at the table, Miranda looked up. "I know it could have been a complete stranger," she finally said. "It seems likely that it was, but I have to make a decision before you head out."

"You could come with me. I won't be staying at the cabin the entire time. I'll be traveling the area, in fact." His voice took on an excited tone. "Yes, that's it. You could accompany me. If your friends are not evident come the thaw, you could travel with me and look for them as I take collections of the vegetation."

"I suppose that's a possibility," Miranda replied

thoughtfully. She looked up and caught the animation in his expression. "Are you certain it wouldn't be a hindrance? After all, you mentioned more than once that my arrival to your cabin had seriously altered your schedule and routine. And now you've had to endure my company here in Dawson as well."

"I'd hardly say that I've had to endure your company. You've been a tremendous help to me. I'd not have this work done by now if not for your help."

"It's been a great deal of fun," Miranda said, surprised by her declaration. "I've really enjoyed the education. I've always loved to learn, although my family never encouraged formal education past the normal schooling for girls. I often thought it would be fun to attend a university, but my brother was against the idea, feeling it wasn't proper. He prefers to see me at home." She smiled and rearranged the papers in her hands. "But that's unimportant. What I wanted to say to you was that I've also enjoyed feeling useful."

"Well, you've certainly been that and more."

Miranda looked into Teddy's eyes, lost in the warmth of his gaze, and the words she'd thought to say froze on her lips. Realizing he was now only inches away, she felt suddenly shy, almost nervous.

"I'm sorry that I ever said you had altered or interfered with my schedule," Teddy said, his voice dropping. "I never meant to hurt your feelings or give you the impression that you had caused me any grief. Your help has allowed me to reclaim the time lost to me because of the vandalism to my room."

Miranda licked her lips and struggled to form the words to reply. "I ... I'm ... glad to know ... I mean, I'm glad I didn't cause you any real problem."

She felt her knees grow weak. Why hadn't she realized how handsome he was before now? She had known him to be attractive, even found his appearance to be quite nice, but he'd never affected her like this before. Now she could see every detail of his face—the furrows in his forehead from the long hours of concentration over his work, the fullness of his lips. He needed a shave, and she was sorely tempted to reach up and run her fingers over the stubble on his chin.

Like a child caught with her hand in the cookie jar, Miranda felt her face grow hot as they locked gazes once again.

"Miranda," he whispered in almost a reverent tone.

When she leaned forward, Miranda had no intention of initiating a kiss—yet that was what she did. Putting her hands on his shoulders, she stretched up on her tiptoes and kissed him lightly upon the lips.

He did nothing, and when Miranda pulled away, she put her hand to her mouth. "Oh, please forgive me." She hurried for the door, completely embarrassed at what she'd done. "I'm sorry. I didn't—I mean I shouldn't have—" She opened the door and turned to see him standing there still stunned by her actions. "That was a mistake—it won't happen again."

She hurried out of the room, not even bothering to close the door behind her. She ran for the comfort of her room, frightened by the emotions raging through her. Closing the door, she leaned against it, panting, struggling to draw a decent breath.

"Why did I do that?" she whispered.

Her stomach did flips, her emotions alternating between giddy and terrified. "I kissed him," she said aloud to the room, as if it might offer her some comment. "How could I have acted so wantonly?"

Shame flooded her soul. "Oh, forgive me, God. I never meant to be so forward. Mr. Davenport has done nothing but be the perfect gentleman. He's helped me every step of the way, providing for my needs, and I repay him by this. I'm so sorry."

She began to pace the room, the heavy navy wool of her skirt flaring out around her as she moved. He'd bought her the skirt, as well as the cotton blouse she wore. He'd bought her other things as well—shoes, boots, undergarments. At the thought of the latter Miranda felt her cheeks grow even hotter.

I've ruined everything, she thought. *I acted on impulse and now look where it's taken me. I deserve for Teddy to march over here and throw me out.*

As if on cue, a loud knocking sounded at her door. Miranda froze in place. "Who . . . is . . . it?" she stammered.

"Open the door, Miranda."

It was Teddy. He'd come to reprimand her and to ask her to leave. Gathering her courage, Miranda went to the door and opened it. Before she could offer another word of apology or even a plea to be given a second chance, Teddy swept her into his arms and kissed her ardently on the mouth. His lips lingered for more than a moment and Miranda lost herself in reckless abandonment. If this was good-bye, then she'd go out in style.

Releasing her rather abruptly, Teddy stepped back. His eyes were ablaze with passion. "I don't want it to be a mistake," he said, his voice husky and very different from the businesslike manner in which he usually communicated.

———

Grace Colton sat nursing her son after a long day of washing out linens and towels. Adrik had secured her a place with a local dentist, Dr. Brummel, and his wife, Georgia. As soon as she recovered from Andy's birth, Grace had gone to work for the couple doing housekeeping and laundry, along with some cooking. Her efforts were rewarded with room and board for herself and Andy and a small amount of pocket money.

She had very little time off, but that didn't matter to Grace. In fact, she preferred things that way. When working, she didn't have time to dwell on Peter. Not that she could ever put him totally from her mind. Looking down upon her brown-haired son, she knew she would be forever reminded of her husband—no matter his decision regarding their marriage.

Andy cooed as if knowing her thoughts. He pulled away from her breast and laughed, his tiny hand reaching up to take hold of her unpinned hair.

"Oh, my sweet boy," she whispered. "You are my very life. God was so good to give you to me."

She shifted him into an upright position and adjusted the neck of her nightgown. How she cherished these quiet moments in the late evening. This was her time with Andy. Hers alone. Had Peter been a part of their life, he would have shared in the time, and then he would have seen for himself how very special their relationship might be.

"Oh, Andy," Grace said sighing, "I wish your papa could know about you—see you. If he were here right now, I know he would adore you."

Andy made gurgling noises as Grace began patting his back in order to burp him. She rocked back and forth in her chair, humming to herself in rhythm. Andy's eyelids grew heavy, and after burping him, Grace lifted him to her shoulder and pulled his hand-knit blanket around him.

"Thank you, God," she prayed as Andy fell asleep—his face nuzzled against her neck. "Thank you for this child and for the protection afforded me by Dr. Brummel and his wife."

She rocked in the silence for several minutes, enjoying the simple pleasure that the moment afforded her. It was hard to imagine, given the peace she felt, that the entire world outside her window could be so caught up in the pursuit for gold.

There had been numerous claim jumping incidents and even deaths related to misunderstandings. Grace had found it far easier to remain in the safety of the Brummel house, rather than risk her life on the streets. She'd only gone out twice, and both times were to venture no farther than the corner dry goods store.

Each trip had been marked by an unusual event. The first one had brought her face to face with a group of "scarlet women," as Mrs. Brummel called the local prostitutes. The day had been warmer than most and Grace had decided the short outing would be good for both her and Andy. But babies were a fairly rare sight in the town, and Andy brought much unwelcome attention—especially by a group of prostitutes who had wandered over from Paradise Alley.

Grace had been rather uncertain as to how she should handle the moment. The girls, heavily painted and gaudily dressed, had each wanted to hold Andy. They cooed over him, reaching out to touch the pure and innocent child. Grace pitied them and allowed them their moment of pleasure.

One woman, not so much older than herself, held Andy longer than the others. She gently stroked his cheek and spoke in low, soft whispers. Grace couldn't hear what she said, but when the woman returned Andy to her arms, Grace saw tears in the prostitute's eyes.

The moment had moved Grace beyond words. She was certain she would always remember the woman's face and wonder what problems had brought her to such a sorry life. Was there a baby in her past—perhaps a child who had died or had been taken from her? The very thought left Grace deeply saddened.

The next time Grace ventured out, she had gone alone. This time the store was filled with raucous miners, and an argument ensued about which creek was bearing the best show of gold. Before Grace knew what was happening, the men had separated into two groups, and Grace found herself positioned between the two as she stood at the counter preparing to pay for her goods.

In the next moment, one of the men took a swing at another and Grace was pushed to the floor. As she looked up she was shocked to see the store owner bring down a large wooden mallet on the counter.

"You are a disgrace to mankind," the owner told the men as the sound of the mallet strike echoed in the small confines of the store. He came around the counter and helped Grace from the floor and then unfolded his handkerchief and laid it out flat on the counter.

"You all owe this lady an apology. A pinch a piece ought to say it well enough."

Grace watched as each of the hardened sourdoughs ambled up, muttered their regrets, and deposited a pinch of gold dust on the cloth. By the time they'd finished she had fifty dollars worth of gold to her name.

After that she had decided it would be best not to risk another trip. Andy needed her—she was all he had until Peter could be found. Of course, she knew Karen and Adrik would happily provide for the child, but they were two days away down on Hunker Creek. Only that morning she had penned Karen a letter, telling her how much she longed for their company and hoped the time would soon present itself for her and Andy to join the others.

With Andy asleep, Grace put him in her bed and rolled thick blankets in a circle around him. He needed her warmth for the cold nights, but she didn't want to risk rolling over on him. Mrs. Brummel had suggested the arrangement and had even rearranged the room to place the small bed up against the wall so that Grace needn't fear Andy rolling out once he became more mobile.

Yawning, Grace sat down to complete her final task for the night. She turned up the lamp just a bit in order to see better. Taking up a pencil and paper, she began writing a letter to Peter. In the letter she told of Andy's birth. She hadn't had the courage to do so until now. The baby was two months old, and she needed to let Peter know of Andy's existence.

What she dreaded most was that Peter would come to her only because of Andrew. She didn't want her husband to journey to the Yukon out of a sense of obligation or duty.

She wanted him to come because he loved her and wanted her to be his wife. If he found out about Andy, how could she ever be sure of the reasons behind his return? She had prayed about the matter more than once, knowing it was only fair that Peter should know about his son's birth. She even wondered if God might use Andy to show Peter how important his marriage vows were—that his promise to God and Grace were the very foundation for the family he was called to lead. At the same time, however, she truly regretted having to break the news to him via a letter. She had thought to take a ship back to California, come summer, but now she wasn't so sure.

The letter she'd written to Peter's parents after Miranda's death gave him every indication of her whereabouts. It hurt her that they had made no contact. She had made it clear that their party had intended to winter in Dawson City. She had assured Peter and his family that she could receive mail at "general delivery" in town. But no letter had ever come, and in the months since Miranda's death, Grace had worried that maybe there would never be a letter from her husband.

"Lord, I don't want him to come only because of Andrew," she whispered, her tears falling upon the paper. "I want Peter to love me and to love you. I want Peter to come to me . . . but only if it's forever."

┤CHAPTER FIFTEEN├

"THAT LEG LOOKS INFECTED, Gump," Karen said as she assessed the week-old ax wound.

"Ja, I think you might be right."

"Adrik, I think you're going to have to take Gump to the doctor in Dawson before this gets much worse. It's already showing signs of proud flesh."

"You think it's that bad?" Adrik came over and upon seeing the swollen, red wound let out a whistle. "Gump, you should have told me it had festered."

"I figured it'd get better," the old man said, his voice betraying the pain he felt as Karen sopped at the wound with alcohol.

"Well, it hasn't. I guess we're going to have to make a trip to Dawson and get you squared away."

"You could also pick up Grace and the baby, couldn't

you?" Karen questioned. While she enjoyed Leah's company in the small cabin, she longed for another woman to talk to. Especially one she knew as well as Grace. Grace was like her own daughter in so many ways.

"I suppose we could arrange for that as well," Adrik replied. "It's warming up a little at a time. Probably won't have any more of those forty-below temperatures."

"I hope you're right. Anyway, I miss her a great deal and hate to think of her being all alone with Andy in Dawson." Karen had only heard from Grace a few times. One letter had come just a few days ago, brought in by one of their neighbors who'd taken a two-week furlough in Dawson while his partner kept the claim.

"If you take me to Dawson," Gump said, "who vill be here to care for the place?"

"I'll be here," Karen replied. "As much as I'd like to see civilization again, I'm just as happy to stay here. Leah and Jacob and I can take care of things while you're gone."

"I don't like the idea of leaving you," Adrik said.

"We'll be fine, Adrik," Jacob Barringer promised. "I've cut enough wood to keep warm until May and you won't be gone that long." He laughed good-naturedly. "And if you are, well, I'll just cut more wood."

"Not that there's a lot left. Some of the areas are positively stripped of vegetation," Karen said as she wrapped Gump's leg with a makeshift bandage. "There, that will have to do until you can see the doctor." She gently helped him get his boot on. "Try not to walk around too much. I'm afraid you'll make it bleed again."

"A man's no good if he can't be helpin' out," Gump replied.

"You'll be no good at all if that poison gets into your bloodstream and kills you," Adrik told the man sternly. He looked at his watch and then to Karen. "It's too late to leave now. We'll head out first thing in the morning."

Karen knew Adrik was just as worried about the old man as she was. Gump had been good to them, and she'd grown to love the old man's stories. Of course, it would have been better had the cabin been bigger. Adrik had helped the matter by fashioning some collapsible beds. They folded up when not in use, which allowed them extra living space during the day and early evening. Still, the cabin was barely twenty-by-twelve feet, and at times Karen could swear the walls were closing in.

Turning from Gump, Karen focused her attention on helping Leah with supper. A large piece of elk roasted on a spit over the fire in Gump's hearth. The delicious aroma almost made Karen forget that she was sick and tired of elk. But she longed for fried chicken and creamy mashed potatoes. And she would have walked a mile for a piece of Aunt Doris's strawberry cream pie. She would have walked two miles in the snow for a glass of fresh, cold milk.

Leah sat near the fire faithfully turning the roast, and she smiled when Karen offered to take over. "At least it's warm here."

"Sometimes I doubt we shall ever be warm again, but Gump assures me the air heats right up in the middle of summer."

"And the sun stays up for hours and hours. I think that's so wonderful," Leah said, her voice edged with girlish wonder. "I think it's amazing how God gives the north so much light in the summer, to make up for not having much in the winter. It's like a little present."

Karen chuckled at the analogy. "I suppose you could say that."

"But I also like the northern lights," Leah continued. "They put on just about the prettiest show I've ever seen. God made that, too, didn't He?"

"You can be sure He did," Adrik answered for Karen. "There are a great many wonders in this world, and all of them come compliments of the Almighty. Why, you should have heard Karen's papa talk about God's glorious creation. When he was preaching the Gospel, he used nature and the beauty of the land to show the glory of God to the folks who were listening."

"Maybe that's why the natives liked him so much," Leah suggested.

"I know it was an important part," Adrik said, nodding. "Mr. Pierce always said in order to get people to take an interest in what you had to say, you had to meet them where they lived."

"What's that mean?" Leah questioned.

"It means," Karen interjected, "that most folks only take an interest in what's most important to them. If you want people to listen to what you have to say, you have to show them how it pertains to them—why it should matter to them."

"Exactly. You also give them examples they can relate to," Adrik added. "Mr. Pierce lived among the natives, especially the Tlingit. He lived as they lived and ate what they ate. He worked alongside them and never complained or judged them. He showed the love of Jesus in human form. He was one of the most godly men I've ever known."

Karen wiped a tear from her eye and turned back to the roast. "I think our supper is just about ready. Leah, did you get the bread sliced?"

"Yes, ma'am. I'll put it on the table." She got up and went to the cupboard.

Karen smiled at her husband. "Thank you for the nice things you said about my father. Sometimes I miss him and Mother so much. It still makes me sad to think of how I came north to find him, only to lose him."

"He's not lost to you," Adrik said, reaching out to take hold of her. The roast was forgotten as he embraced her. "He's waiting in heaven with your mother. You'll see them again."

"I know, but I made the trip and then . . ."

"And then you found me," Adrik said firmly, tilting her chin upward to meet his gaze. "And I found you, and now my life is so much better. I'm blessed and whole."

Karen looked into the longing expression of her husband. She knew how much he desired for them to have time alone. He'd promised her he'd build them a private room as soon as the weather warmed.

"I'm blessed as well," she whispered. "Blessed beyond all my expectations."

―――――――

The next morning, Adrik kissed Karen soundly and waved good-bye as the dogs pulled the sled down the trail. She hated to see him go. What if something happened to them on the trail? What if wolves or a rogue bear that had awakened early from its hibernation attacked them?

Karen knew it was senseless to worry. "*Worry is a sin,*"

her mother had told her when she was young. It was like saying that God wasn't able to see to her needs.

Karen and the children busied themselves for the rest of the day with cleaning the cabin. They were all restless. The old timers called it cabin fever. But whatever it was, Karen longed for an end to it. She couldn't help but believe things would have been better if she had a home of her own—with real beds and walls. She wondered if she had what it would take to spend the rest of her life in Alaska or the Yukon. The uncertainty concerned her, at times to the point of making her fretful. Adrik would never be suited to life in the southern states. He had made that quite clear, and Karen worried that she might fail him in her longing for what once had been.

By dinnertime they were all exhausted and quite ready to settle down to warmed elk hash and canned peaches. Karen always tried to dole their food out in a responsible way. She wanted them to have variety, but too much variety would cause them to forfeit their supply. There was no way of telling how long it would be before they could buy additional food items. And then there was no way of telling how much the food might cost.

They were just finishing up the supper dishes when a knock sounded on the cabin door. Karen looked to Jacob, who immediately went for the rifle. He nodded his readiness and stood behind the door as Karen opened it.

Steadying her nerves, Karen opened the door. An unknown man loomed in the doorway. His gaze fixed on Karen, his eyes narrowing. She smelled whiskey on him almost immediately.

"Howdy, ma'am."

"Hello." Her tone was clearly cautious.

The man scratched his beard and pushed back his hat. "Well, ma'am, I was wonderin' if your menfolk are around."

"They are," Karen said, counting Jacob as man enough for the moment.

"Can I talk to them?" His gaze devoured her, making Karen feel extremely uncomfortable.

"No, I'm afraid not. They're busy right now."

The man stepped forward and looked into the cabin. "I don't see anybody but you and the girl."

Jacob stepped out from behind the door. "The lady said they're busy." The rifle did not go unnoticed by the man. He stepped back immediately and nodded.

"I was hopin' to talk to them about takin' some mail into town for me. I heard a rumor they was headin' into Dawson."

Karen stiffened. The man had probably been watching the cabin and knew Adrik and Gump had already taken off, but she felt inclined to pretend they hadn't. "You might catch them down at the creek," Karen said, feeling the moment merited the lie. Besides, she hadn't said *which* creek they might be by.

The man cleared his throat and spit on the ground outside the door. "Guess I could go lookin' for them."

Karen began to close the door. "That would be best."

"Or I could just wait here for them. Maybe beg a cup of coffee."

"No, I'm sorry. That wouldn't be possible. You might try the next camp if you're looking for coffee. I'm afraid we're completely out." At least that wasn't a lie. It was at the top of the list of items for Adrik to bring back from Dawson.

The man shrugged but refused to go. Karen continued to

close the door. "I'm sorry, but the room is growing chilly." She closed the door in his face and quickly latched it.

She turned to Jacob and shook her head. In a hushed voice she said, "I don't like this one bit."

"Me neither. I'll make sure the shutters are closed tight and barred. You might want to put something in front of the door."

"Do you think he'll try to hurt us?" Leah asked fearfully.

"I hope not," Karen replied. "We must pray for God's protection." She glanced back at the closed door, grateful for the thickness of the roughhewn wood. Gump, being of good Swedish stock and familiar with cold weather, had made the entire cabin with thick walls and few windows. There had been a time Karen might have taken a great displeasure with this, but now she was quite grateful.

"I think we'd best load the other gun. Just in case." Jacob's voice wavered slightly as he spoke.

Karen looked at him and nodded. "Might as well be prepared." But she didn't feel at all prepared. She felt very vulnerable and frightened. *Oh, Lord, please shelter us from whatever harm that man intends. You know what he was up to, even if we don't. Please thwart any evil that might be planned against us. And please bring Adrik back quickly.*

A crash sounded as Jacob dropped the box of ammunition, causing Karen to jump a foot. She looked to the young man and tried her best to smile. She read the worry in his eyes, however, and knew she couldn't fool him. She might be able to convince Leah that things were all right, but Jacob was old enough to know better.

"Sorry," he said, picking up the bullets.

Leah walked over to Karen and wrapped her arms around

her. "I'm scared," she whispered. "I didn't like that man at all. What if he comes back here tonight?"

"We'll be ready for him," Jacob stated firmly. "I'll keep watch. You two can sleep and toward morning you can take over for me. Then come daylight we can talk to the Jones brothers at the next claim and tell them what happened. Adrik figures them for good folk—Gump, too."

"Maybe we should go there now," Leah said, looking hopefully to her brother.

"No," he said and resumed loading the Winchester for Karen. "He might be out there hoping we'll do exactly that."

Karen trembled at the thought and Leah held her all the more tightly. "I wish Adrik were here," Leah barely breathed.

Karen nodded. "I wish he were, too."

———

Jacob Barringer sat alone in the silence of the night, his rifle across his lap as he sat poised—watching, waiting. Come what may, he was ready. At least he hoped he was. He didn't know what to make of the stranger who'd frightened them all.

He hadn't seen Karen so shaken since their store in Dyea had burned down. Jacob tried not to let the man's appearance bother him. He tried not to imagine that the stranger was out there in the darkness, plotting and planning against them.

What had he wanted? Had he known all along that the menfolk were gone, with the exception of Jacob? Jacob would never have admitted it to Karen or Leah, but at the moment, he didn't feel that much like a man. He wanted to prove himself to be brave and capable, but frankly the idea of having to shoot someone—possibly kill him—was something Jacob didn't stomach well.

He supposed he wasn't intended to like the idea of shooting someone, but he'd seen so much destruction and death on his way to the Yukon that even the idea of dealing with one more confrontation was more than Jacob wanted to face.

What he did want was to leave the Yukon. He'd denied the discouraging truth long enough, but now he resolved to accept that his father had died in the Palm Sunday avalanche on the Chilkoot Trail. If his father were alive, he'd be here in the heart of it all—working his knuckles raw as he tried to find gold. If his father were alive, he would have at least sent word back to Karen at the store.

No, his father was dead. Jacob had to accept the truth, no matter how hard or painful. But with that acceptance, came another overwhelming truth. He was responsible for Leah. He needed a good job and he needed to provide her with a real home. The only trouble was, he didn't see how he could do both. He wanted to go to work for Peter Colton. He'd gotten to know Peter fairly well during their days in Skagway, when Jacob would meet up with him on the docks before transporting the goods to the store. Peter had promised Jacob he could have a job with Colton Shipping anytime he wanted one.

The real problem was Leah. He didn't want to leave her again. She'd been truly hurt when he'd left her to head north. They'd only talked about it once or twice, but he knew she had felt abandoned. How would it be if he took a job that kept him far away from her for long periods of time? And where would she stay? Karen had offered them both a home for as long as they needed it, but Jacob couldn't very well expect Karen and Adrik to give up their future to care for Leah forever.

Yet he'd seen how Leah and Karen interacted. Karen had become a mother to Leah, and Adrik had filled in the place of a father. It seemed right for her to be a part of their family. Leah would be all right with Karen and Adrik, especially if Jacob promised to come and see her from time to time. If he worked for Peter's shipping company he could no doubt do just that. Maybe he'd mention it to Karen tomorrow—see what her thoughts were on the matter.

The crux of all his problems was this: He didn't want to disappoint Leah. Not after all she had been through. He didn't want to hurt her, and he didn't want to make a mistake where she was concerned. God had given him a responsibility. And God would expect him to take the matter seriously and to make plans for their future—plans that would benefit them both.

A scratching noise at the door caused Jacob to jump to his feet. As silently as he could manage, Jacob moved to the door. He listened, waiting for something more.

The unmistakable sounds of movement on the other side of the door caused the hair on the back of Jacob's neck to stand up. His chest rose and fell in rapid, shallow breaths. Perspiration beaded on his forehead, even though the cabin was quite chilly.

Anxious to make sure the rifle was loaded, Jacob cocked the lever just enough to expose the breech. The sight of the cartridge reassured him. Next he checked the magazine. Finding it loaded with extra cartridges, Jacob let out the breath he'd been holding.

A loud thump sounded against the door. Jacob jumped

back. He glanced over his shoulder to make sure the noise hadn't disturbed Karen or Leah. There was no sign of either one of them stirring.

Jacob didn't know how long he stood fixed and rigid at the door. After a good deal of time had passed, however, and no further noises sounded from outside, he decided to open the door and check outside.

The rush of cold air momentarily surprised Jacob. He glanced again over his shoulder to see if Karen or Leah had stirred, then focused his attention outside. Hearing a sound to his right, Jacob strained to see in the dark. As he leveled his rifle he saw the unmistakable outline of a bear. Cautiously, Jacob backed up and closed the door. There was no sense in shooting the poor animal and waking the entire valley. No doubt the bear had awakened early from its hibernating and was simply looking for food. Relief washed over him.

Yawning, Jacob realized how tired he was. A quick check of the clock on the mantel revealed that he still had a good two hours before dawn.

"Help me to stay alert, God," he whispered the prayer. "And give me the wisdom to know what to do." He paused and glanced again to the bunks where Karen and Leah slept before adding, "And the strength to do it."

—│ CHAPTER SIXTEEN │—

"THERE'S COME A message for you, Mrs. Colton," Dr. Brummel stated, handing Grace a folded piece of paper. "Seems your friends are in town and are prepared to transport you and little Andy back to their cabin."

Grace looked up from the ironing she was doing. She'd worked all morning to wash and iron the sheets, and she was on her last one. A thread of joy wound about her heart at the thought that Karen and Adrik were in town.

Taking up the paper, she read the note. "It looks like Adrik had to bring that nice Mr. Lindquist in to the hospital. I do hope it isn't serious." She looked to Dr. Brummel as if for some insight to the man's condition.

"I couldn't say. I was only there to pick up some laudanum for a patient."

"I see. Well," Grace said, her tone quite animated, "I suppose I should pack my things."

"We're going to miss having you here, Mrs. Colton."

"Now, why will we be missing Grace?" the dentist's wife asked as she came into the room.

Grace turned to face the woman. "My friends have come to take me to their claim site."

"Why, it still gets down to forty-below some nights. You can't be traveling with a baby in that kind of weather," Georgia Brummel complained.

"I'm sure my friends have made provision," Grace answered. Already she was packing her things in a carpetbag. "I'm sure we'll be just fine."

Georgia looked at Grace as if ascertaining whether she could change her mind. Finally she relented. "Very well. I'll pack you some things for the trip."

"Thank you, Mrs. Brummel. I do appreciate all you have done for me. I only hope I can one day repay you for your kindness."

"Nonsense," Dr. Brummel declared, "you've worked harder than any house girl we've ever had—and we've had plenty. Why, down in Sacramento, where we hail from, we had a new girl almost every week some months."

"He's right," Mrs. Brummel sniffed. "No one was ever as good to us as you are."

Grace looked at them both. "No one outside of my family and Karen Ivankov has ever been as good to me as you've been. Andy and I might have died were it not for you. We surely couldn't have made the trip before now. Thank you so much for all you've done for us." She reached out and hugged them in unison.

Dr. Brummel reddened in the face and stepped back. "I . . . uh . . . I'll take you and Andy over to the hospital when you're ready."

Grace nodded and hurried to gather her things. Andy slept peacefully, even when she bundled him into the warm beaver-skin bunting she'd made for him only days earlier. Pulling on her own coat and a fur cape given to her by Mrs. Brummel, Grace felt a bittersweet emotion in her departure. Though she missed Karen and longed for her company as much as she could anyone's, Grace knew she would miss Dr. Brummel and his wife. She would also miss being in a real house with wooden floors and rugs and curtains at the windows. She knew from Karen's letters that the accommodations at Gump's claim were desperately short of womanly touches.

"I guess I'm ready," Grace finally said, carrying the sleeping baby in her arms.

"I'll get your bag," Dr. Brummel offered and disappeared into Grace's room.

"I've packed a box of things for you," Georgia said. "Some things to eat along the way and a few items to remember us by."

"I won't forget you," Grace said. "And when I come back to Dawson, I will visit."

"Oh, do. And bring Andy as well."

Grace nodded. "You can be sure I will."

Grace allowed Dr. Brummel to carry everything but the baby and followed him out into the frigid morning. The walk to the hospital wasn't far, but even that short distance could freeze the lungs of a man—or woman. Grace had already secured Andy inside her cape, but now she buried her face down deep in order to keep from breathing the raw, painful air.

She hastened her steps to keep up with Dr. Brummel and felt great relief when the hospital came in sight. She felt a giddiness at the prospect of seeing her friends again. She was especially anxious for Karen to see the baby.

"Adrik!" she called as soon as she caught sight of the man.

Adrik turned and smiled as Grace came through the hospital doors. "Why, hello there, little mother. How does it go with you?"

"Wonderful!" Grace tried not to sound too exuberant. She didn't want to hurt Dr. Brummel's feelings, so she quickly added, "The Brummels have been so good to us. They have taken such good care of Andy and me."

"I knew they would," Adrik replied, nodding slightly to the older man. "They're good people. I wouldn't have left you with them if they hadn't come highly recommended."

"Well, it's me and the missus who are grateful," Brummel interjected. "Grace has been a great help. Georgia sometimes suffers great bouts of depression, but she wasn't upset even once while Grace was here."

"Oh," Grace lamented, "you don't think my leaving will cause her to become ill, do you?"

"My dear, you mustn't worry," Dr. Brummel reassured. "She'll be fine. I'll see to it. Now that I know she does better with the company of a good friend, I'll endeavor to find someone else to be a companion. No more of those bitter old women who clean house like prisoners forced to work against their will. No, I will find another sweet young woman such as yourself. Maybe even one with a child."

"I'll pray for her," Grace offered. "It's easy to fall into despair in such a cold and lonely place. Andy has helped me a great deal." She lifted the baby to her shoulder. "He's given me a will to live life anew."

Adrik put his arm around Grace's shoulder. "This little gal has a way of praying that goes right from her mouth to God's ear. If she's praying for your wife, then you can be sure things will come around right."

They bid Dr. Brummel good-bye and waited in the hospital corridor for Gump to reappear. When he did, he looked none too happy.

"Fool doctors are always trying to find vays to drain a man of every cent."

"What's wrong, Gump?"

"Oh, dat doctor vants to keep me here. Says my leg might be needin' surgery."

"Well, you ought to do what the doctor says," Grace said softly.

Gump eyed her suspiciously. "Who are you?"

"I'm Grace Colton," she replied.

"She's the one we've come to take back with us," Adrik added. "And I agree with her completely. You ought to do what the doctor says."

"Vell, I am," Gump muttered. "But I told him I von't be stayin' here, so I'm supposed to come back in two veeks if it's not any better."

Adrik nodded. "That sounds reasonable enough."

"Ja, I think it vill be better," Gump replied. "Either that or I take the leg off and get a new one." He smiled as if he'd made some great joke.

They headed toward the door, but Gump put his hand

on Adrik's arm. "I vant to go to the recorder's office."

"Sure, Gump, but why?" Adrik questioned.

"I got me some business."

Adrik looked to Grace. "Will that be all right with you?"

"Certainly, Adrik. Andy and I are more than happy to comply with whatever plans you have."

Adrik smiled. "Well, you'd best bundle up, then. It's not warmed up enough out there so as a man can even breathe decent. I sure wouldn't want you comin' down sick. Karen would never let me hear the end of it."

The bottle slipped from Miranda's hand, crashing to the floor in a loud, disheartening sound, shattering into hundreds of tiny pieces.

"Oh, bother," she sighed, taking up Teddy's favorite saying. In a hurry to clean up the mess before Teddy returned, Miranda failed to give proper attention to the task. Without warning, her hand sliced across one of the larger pieces of glass, ripping a long cut on the side of her palm.

Stunned, Miranda stared at her wounded hand for a moment. Blood poured from the cut, spilling out onto the floor at an alarming rate. Her breathing quickened and a light-headed feeling washed over her.

"Oh my." It was all she could manage to say, and so she repeated it several times.

Humming a tune, Teddy walked in completely preoccupied. "I say, the cost of . . ." He fell silent at the sight of Miranda.

Seeing the way his expression changed to worry, Miranda hoped to reassure him that everything was all right. "I've made a mess," she tried to explain, her heart racing.

Teddy seemed to quickly assess the situation. He pulled a handkerchief from his pocket, taking long strides to cross the room as he did. Kneeling, he gently wrapped the cloth around her hand. His touch was so tender and gentle that Miranda very nearly forgot there was a problem.

"What happened?"

"I . . . I . . . dropped the bottle. Oh my." She gazed into his eyes. He looked almost frightened. Again, she felt the need to reassure him. "I'm so . . . so . . . sorry. You mustn't worry. I don't want to be a bother." Her voice sounded foreign, almost childlike to her own ears.

Teddy firmly held her wounded hand. "No bother at all," he said, helping her up by cupping her elbow. "Let's have a look at it in the light."

The cloth was already soaked a bright red when Teddy pulled it away from her hand. The wound was deep. Miranda could see that much.

"It will have to be stitched, I'm afraid," Teddy told her. "Let me find a better bandage and we'll go straightaway to the doctor." He looked around the room.

"Don't worry. I'll be fine." But in truth, Miranda wasn't sure about that at all. She felt dizzy and sick from the sight of so much blood. Her hand didn't really hurt all that much. Certainly it didn't hurt as much as the time she'd let the knife slip when peeling potatoes. That wound hadn't required stitches, but this one was clearly deeper.

"I'm not worried," Teddy said, coming back with the case that he'd pulled off a pillow. "This ought to do."

Miranda let him wrap her hand with the pillowcase, then

waited as he retrieved her coat. She felt numb, almost sense-less.

When Teddy returned he was already wearing his own coat and gloves. "Come along," he said, putting the coat around her shoulders.

As he half dragged, half carried her down the hall, Miranda's mind raced in a million different directions. *Who will clean up the mess?* she worried. *What if I get blood on this lovely hall runner? Will it hurt terribly to have stitches put in?*

Teddy led her down the stairs and to the front desk. "I'm going to take Miss Colton to Dr. Hauge's. She's broken a jar in the workroom and cut her hand. Would you get someone to clean up the mess?"

"Sure, Mr. Davenport," the clerk replied.

Miranda thought the man very kind as he offered her a smile.

"Hope you'll be feelin' better, miss."

"I'm fine, really. Thank you for your concern," Miranda replied. The man nodded at her with a look that suggested he didn't believe her.

Teddy helped her to secure her hooded coat. He carefully maneuvered her hand through the sleeve and then did up the buttons for her. Miranda felt rather flustered at his nearness. Her nerves were making her jittery, and she couldn't help but give a little giggle.

"I feel like I'm five years old. Silly glass and silly me for getting cut."

"Never mind that," Teddy said very softly. He put his arm around her. "Lean on me if you feel the need."

What a strange suggestion, Miranda thought. *Of course I don't need to lean on him. That would be entirely unseemly.*

But in the next few steps, she wasn't at all convinced of the impropriety. Miranda felt as though she were floating. A weakness drained her legs of strength, and she found that all she desired was a chair and a warm fire. She felt so cold, and they hadn't even been outside for more than a minute.

"Oh, bother!" Teddy said as he came to a stop in front of the doctor's office. "He's gone to tend someone on a claim. Let's just go to the hospital and be done with it. We're bound to find a doctor there."

Miranda had no argument for him. She wasn't even sure at this point how much longer she could maintain consciousness. She felt strange and a peculiar heat seemed to penetrate her face and neck. Leaning against Teddy, she tried her best to keep up.

"Teddy," she whispered. "I don't feel at all well."

He stopped and, without giving her a chance to protest, lifted Miranda in his arms. "It's the loss of blood and the pain. You're going into shock. Stay awake, Miranda. Talk to me."

She looked into his eyes and lost herself for a moment. My, but he was handsome. If she died now, in his arms, she would at least know the contentment of being near him.

"Talk to me, Miranda," he ordered.

"I don't know what to say." She smiled weakly.

Teddy crossed the street and continued down the way to the hospital. "Tell me about San Francisco. Does it get this cold there?"

Miranda shook her head. "Oh no. Never."

"I wouldn't have thought so. Are the summers hot?"

"No, they're never hot. They're so very lovely. The flowers bloom all up and down our street." She tucked her head down against Teddy's neck. He smelled wonderful. She wondered what the scent might be. In fact, she hadn't noticed it when they'd been working.

"You smell good," she whispered. "Like spices and flowers."

"You're becoming delirious," he said with a laugh.

"I like spices and flowers," she countered, not at all sure why he would laugh. "I like you, too." Shadows in her mind beckoned her to rest. She could almost see their dark fingers motioning her to follow deeper into the black recesses of her mind.

"I'm honored and deeply touched," he replied, then added, "I like you, too, Miranda."

She smiled. He was such a pleasant man when he wanted to be.

They arrived at the hospital and once inside, Teddy set her down on the bench in the hall. "Stay here. I'll find the doctor." He studied her for a moment. "Maybe I shouldn't leave you alone."

"Nonsense," she managed to say, forcing herself to sound alert. "I'll be fine."

"If you're sure. I'll only be a moment."

Miranda nodded and leaned back against the wall and closed her eyes. She wanted so much to be a good patient for her worried friend. Opening her eyes, Miranda looked down the hall in the direction Teddy had taken. He had gone through one of the open doorways, but Miranda couldn't be sure which one.

Then her gaze caught something unexpected. A large, broad-shouldered man appeared at the other end of the corridor. She heard him laugh and recognized the sound. Struggling against her weakness, Miranda jumped to her feet and called out. "Adrik!"

The word barely made a sound in her throat, and then darkness consumed her and Miranda fell to the ground. *Not now*, she thought. *I can't faint now.* But it was too late. Certain that she'd finally seen another of her traveling companions, Miranda slipped into unconsciousness.

———

The recorder's office was surprisingly void of traffic. Adrik figured the cold had kept most folks hunkered down in their tents and cabins, or it might have been that a general malaise had settled on the community. At any rate, no one seemed to be too anxious to buy and sell claims if it meant going outside.

So much had changed. Adrik had heard the sad stories of those men who had figured to be able to get a claim for little or nothing. Stake your claim and rake up the gold—that was the battle cry. But it wasn't the reality. Claims had been quickly snatched up, and those who were willing to sell usually demanded a high price to transfer ownership. That, coupled with the Canadian rule against the selling of fractional claims, had left a lot of people without a chance to seek their dreams.

"Come with me." Gump motioned Adrik to follow him into the office. "It's too cold out here for you, much less that little lady and baby."

Adrik took the bundled baby from Grace, then helped her from the sled basket. As the trio followed the limping old man into the office, Adrik was anxious to see what business he had to tend to.

Adrik was more surprised than anyone when the old man requested that his claim deed be rewritten to add a partner.

"I vant Adrik Ivankov here to be my partner." The clerk looked to Adrik and then proceeded with the paperwork.

"Why are you doing this, Gump?"

"I vant to," the old man said. Then sobering a bit, he frowned. "I von't be much good to you for a time. Maybe not for a long, long time. You and Jacob will have to do most of the digging by yourselves."

"But we don't mind. I never expected you to give up half your claim," Adrik said. "You could be out a small fortune by doing this."

"Or you could be out a lot of hard vork for nothin', I'm thinkin'. I vant to do it this vay. Besides, somethin' could happen to me. Then the claim vould go back to the government. I'd rather give you the gold." Gump's singsong cadence was stronger when his emotions ran high. Adrik saw the determination in the set of the old man's jaw and decided not to challenge his decision.

Once the matter was settled to Gump's satisfaction, the foursome returned to the sled and were finally on their way back to the cabin. Adrik couldn't imagine why the old man had offered up half his claim. Sure, Gump was a bit incapacitated for the time, but there wasn't a whole lot they would be able to do until the weather warmed up, anyway. Maybe the situation with Gump's leg was more serious than he was letting on. Maybe the doctor had told Gump he could die. That idea bothered Adrik greatly. He wished fervently that he could make life easier for the old man.

I'd like to send him back to Kansas a rich, comfortable man, Adrik thought. *I'd like to see him retire from working so hard and just enjoy his old age.* But of course, that wasn't likely to happen. Gump's attitude and spirit was much the same as Adrik's. They'd probably die working.

Thinking of work, Adrik began to plan for the claim. There was gold to be had, but it would come only after a great deal of hard work was given in trade. Panning and sluicing, spending hours in the cold water washing the creek gravel—it was enough to drive a man quite insane and crush his dream of riches. Many folks believed the gold to be buried some fifteen feet below the surface. To dig down that far required hours and hours of backbreaking work—all in the hope that they could break through the frozen barriers of muck and rock and find the mother lode.

After a few feet of muck, there generally was a frozen layer of gravel, and sometimes, if a man had sunk the shaft in the right place, he hit pay dirt just under this. Gump had insisted that they'd strike it rich if only they kept digging, instead of panning. Most miners used a ground fire to thaw the surface, but that was time consuming and not always very effective—the digging went horribly slow. Steam boilers were making the job a lot easier for some miners who could afford the expense. Though Adrik wished they had a steam machine to thaw the ground, he knew they didn't have the money for anything extra.

He considered how he might rig up his own steam machine. He had a metal washtub they could use to heat water, but that wouldn't solve the problem of capturing the steam and focusing it into the ground. Adrik had studied the setup from a drawing at the mercantile. The display showed how a steam boiler could be fixed near the site, with pipes coming out one end for the steam and a chimney of sorts to vent the firebox. The pipes went into the ground where they would pump hot steam and thaw the frozen muck. Adrik wasn't sure that the time spent would produce a steamer that worked, but he decided to discuss it with Gump when they got back to the claim.

Adrik's attention turned to Grace and the baby, snuggled deep in a pile of blankets and furs, along with Gump. The body heat of the two adults would no doubt keep the baby plenty warm, but Adrik had other worries concerning their safety. He'd heard wolves howling along the trail on their way into Dawson, and he wanted no part of having to fight off a pack to keep his friends alive.

Then there were the two-legged wolves. Men who pretended to be sheep but were really vicious animals who would eat you alive. Trouble had been a natural companion to the gold rush. The Northwest Mounted Police, the pride of the Yukon, had done a wonderful job of controlling things in the area, but there would always be problems so long as there was a profit to be made from stirring up trouble. Adrik could only pray he was doing the right thing. He'd never considered becoming a part of the stampede. In fact, he thought those poor souls who pinned their hopes to gold instead of God to be misguided. The word gold was just one letter more than God, and Adrik had always figured the *L* to stand for *Lies*.

Much of the gold rush had been built on lies told by one man and passed on by another. People lied about what gold they found, and they lied about what they didn't find. They lied about their pasts and preyed upon others who'd believe their lies for the future. It was a kind of sickness born out of sin.

But as for me and my house, Adrik thought, remembering the Bible verse, *we will serve the Lord.* But here he was in the center of the rush, making his own scars upon the land, seeking his own methods to find the gold.

But I'm doing this for Gump and for the others, he told himself as he urged the dogs to pick up the pace. Self-examination questioned that declaration, however. Was he really doing this for the others? Or was there some small dream of gold in the back of his own mind?

─┤ CHAPTER SEVENTEEN ├─

"BUT YOU DON'T UNDERSTAND," Miranda moaned. "I saw one of my friends."

"It's all right, Miranda," Teddy encouraged, "you probably just thought you saw him. I say, you lost a lot of blood. There's no telling how it played with your mind."

"I'm not crazy," Miranda said, growing angry. "I'm telling you, I saw him. He was standing down at the end of the corridor."

"The same corridor where I found you on the floor?"

Miranda turned away. "Never mind. I don't expect you to understand. You didn't understand the first time—the time I saw Crispin."

"Was this Crispin the same man you saw here at the hospital?" Teddy asked, gently.

"No, I . . ."

"Well, let's get this over with," the doctor said coming into the room. He didn't even bother to introduce himself, and Miranda thought him very rude.

Taking hold of her hand, he unwound the cloth and studied the wound for a moment. "Um, yes. I see," he murmured.

Miranda felt a wave of nausea as she caught sight of her bloody hand. Leaning back, she found Teddy there to support her. She looked to him, hoping he could somehow give her the courage she lacked.

"It will be fine. You'll see," he whispered.

"Will it hurt?" she asked.

"Most likely," the doctor said without emotion. He began to wash to wound, mindless of the pain.

"Talk to me, Miranda. Tell me about your friends," Teddy encouraged. "Don't think about what the doctor is doing."

"That's easier said than done," Miranda declared, wincing at the pain. "Must you be so rough?" she asked the doctor indignantly.

The man looked at her as though stunned by her words. "If I don't clean it out, miss, you'll most likely get an infection."

"I don't mind the cleaning, it's the way you attack the job as though you're gutting and cleaning a rabbit."

The doctor paused and actually smiled at her rebuke. "I do apologize. It's been a rather hectic day. I shall attempt to limit the pain I cause you."

"Thank you," Miranda replied, turning to Teddy as the doctor took up a needle and thread. "Adrik is the man who let me come on the trip. He and Karen got married in White-horse. Karen . . ." She closed her eyes as the doctor pierced her skin. Tears came unbidden to her eyes.

"Go on, Miranda, tell me about your friends," Teddy prodded.

She opened her eyes and licked her lips. "Karen was the nanny to my sister-in-law, Grace. You remember, Grace is married to my brother . . . my brother . . . Peter." She felt a strange warmth creeping up her neck, flushing her face and making it difficult to focus.

"I'm here," Teddy whispered. "Don't be afraid. I'll see to it that you're all right."

His words were comforting, and Miranda tried hard to keep them in her mind as she faded in and out of consciousness.

"There. All done. You are free to leave," the doctor said, wrapping a bandage around her hand.

"Thank you," Miranda murmured, leaning her head against Teddy. She felt so weak.

"Mrs. Colton, you will need to do as little as possible with your hand. I have made several stitches," the balding, heavyset man continued. "You must keep your hand immobile." He turned to Teddy. "You must see to it that your wife keeps the hand dry, clean, and covered. We don't want to risk infection."

Teddy didn't bother to correct the doctor regarding their martial status, and Miranda thought it rather odd. Perhaps he was caught up in his concern over her wound. She had no more time to consider it, however, for Teddy was reaching out and helping her to stand.

"I'll see to it that the wound is well cared for. When should we return?" Teddy questioned.

"Two weeks."

The doctor turned to go, but Miranda called out, "Wait!" The man turned, a brow raising. "What is it?"

"Did you see a big man at the end of the hallway?" she asked. "It would have been earlier, prior to my arrival. I saw him there and believe him to be a friend of mine."

The doctor looked to Teddy, who merely shrugged. "She's been separated from her friends and family and has been searching Dawson for them."

"I saw no one fitting the description. Perhaps the loss of blood gave you hallucinations," the doctor replied, then left without another word. The brief moment of kindness he'd offered her earlier seemed all but forgotten.

"I say, not much of a bedside manner."

"I know what I saw," Miranda said, feeling suddenly very weak. "I know it was Adrik."

"If it was, then he'll be around in town somewhere. We'll find him."

"The doctor thinks I'm crazy."

"Nonsense, he merely suggested that you might have . . . well, that is to say . . ." Teddy looked uncomfortably to her, as if expecting Miranda to rescue him from having to say anything more.

Miranda leaned heavily on Teddy, realizing she was completely spent by the entire affair. Perhaps Teddy was right. Maybe she had conjured up Adrik from the recesses of her subconscious mind. She longed to find her friends again and the long months of isolation and winter darkness had left her very discouraged. If not for her work with Teddy, she might have lost her mind to be sure.

"Oh, just take me home, Teddy."

Outside in the long corridor, Miranda caught sight of

another doctor. Her hope surged anew. Surely it couldn't hurt to ask him if he knew Adrik, she thought. "Excuse me, Doctor," she said as Teddy started to walk toward the man.

The bearded man looked up from the chart he'd been reading. "Yes?"

"I saw a very large man—down there—earlier. Maybe an hour ago. He was very tall and broad shouldered. He had a beard."

"Oh yes." The man nodded. "I saw him, too. He came in with a friend of his who has an ulcerated leg."

Miranda let out an audible sigh. "I knew it. Did you get his name? I'm looking for my friend, and I thought it might be him."

"No, I'm sure I don't know the man's name. The patient was called Lindon or Lindberg—or maybe it was Lindquist. Yes, I believe it was Lindquist."

Miranda frowned. "I don't know any Lindquists. My friend's name is Adrik. Adrik Ivankov."

"That name sounds familiar," Teddy said, looking at her oddly.

"Well, it should, I have been talking about him—along with all my friends—ever since I woke up in your cabin," Miranda countered. "You're certain you don't know the name of his friend?" she questioned the doctor again.

"No, I'm sorry. The man was only here a short while. He brought in his friend and then left to retrieve supplies. They were heading back to their claim, as I recall. I was called in to offer an opinion on the leg, but nothing more. The man wasn't even my patient."

Miranda nodded. "I understand. Thank you." She turned to Teddy, more drained and discouraged by the man's answers than by her wounded hand. "He's probably gone by now. That was some time ago, at least an hour. No doubt they've headed back to their claim." She felt as though her world were crumbling all over again.

"Please take me back to the hotel."

Teddy gave her a look of compassion. "Indeed. I shall take you back and see to it that you are put to bed. I'll bring one of the housekeepers to sit by your bed, as it would hardly be appropriate for me to care for you."

Miranda barely heard his words. She was certain she had seen Adrik, and the fact that no one else seemed to understand or know where she might find him was more than she could bear.

When they returned to the hotel, Teddy arranged Miranda's bed while the housekeeper he sent for stood by to assure propriety. Then he left the room while the girl helped Miranda change her clothes.

His staff had done a marvelous job of cleaning up his workroom. There was no telltale sign of the glass or the blood. He'd have to offer them a bonus for their good work.

Taking out his spectacles, Teddy bent over one of his journals and studied the drawing he'd made. *Epilobium augustifolium.* His gaze fell on the second part of the name. *Augustifolium.* The name made him think of Miranda's friend. What had she called him?

Adrik? Yes, Adrik Ivankov. The name sounded familiar to him, but for the life of him, Teddy couldn't remember where he'd heard it. Perhaps he was simply recalling the memory of Miranda speaking the name so often—but he didn't think so.

The name seemed to attach itself to a vague memory of the same type of large man Miranda had described to the doctor.

"I have Miss Colton all tucked in," the house girl said, opening the adjoining door. "She asked me to keep the door open between the rooms."

Teddy was surprised but pleased with this news. He hated that propriety wouldn't allow him to tend to Miranda as he had back in his cabin. Of course, Nellie had been the one to actually care for her at that time, but he had been able to look in on her at his leisure. And for some reason, that was very important to him.

"I've arranged lunch," Teddy called in to the next room just as a knock sounded at the door. "That should be it now." He opened the door and a young man of about sixteen or seventeen stood holding a tray laden with food.

It was the boy, however, and not the food that caught Teddy's interest. The boy looked familiar, yet Teddy was quite sure they'd never met.

"Do come in. You may leave the tray on the table over there," he instructed the boy.

As the youth entered the room and passed by Teddy, the memory suddenly came to him. The boy reminded Teddy of the young man who'd accompanied the buyer of his sled. The big man with the beard.

The big man . . .

Teddy felt the wind go out of him. Adrik Ivankov. The man who'd bought his sled had introduced himself as Adrik Ivankov. Of course! Teddy looked to the open door adjoining his room to Miranda's. He should tell her, of course, but then what? He had no idea where the man had headed after purchasing the sled. He only recalled that the man and the boy had planned to depart immediately.

He supposed he could tell Miranda that much. But what if she hated him for failing to recognize Adrik? Granted, it had been a simple and innocent mistake, but she had been sharing information about her friends and family for months. Teddy simply hadn't bothered to listen carefully. He'd been too caught up in cataloging his plants and creating the book of his dreams—of his father's dreams.

"Do you need anything else, Mr. Davenport?" the boy asked.

Teddy shook his head, tossed the boy a coin, and glanced again toward Miranda's room. What could he say to her? He could tell her that he was a thoughtless oaf—a man given to his own selfish interests. But, of course, she already knew that.

And he could hardly say, "Sorry, old girl, I was just remembering that I had an encounter with your friends when we first arrived in Dawson City. Pity I hadn't paid attention to your stories or descriptions of them."

Teddy turned away from the open door and walked to the window. The hours of light had increased over the months and soon the thaw would be upon them. He would be ready to return to the fields to gather specimens. He had hoped Miranda would accompany him and prayed she would consider making their arrangement a more permanent one.

If I tell her the truth, she'll hate me, he thought. *She'll blame me for letting them get away all those months ago. She'll never speak to me again.*

He looked down on the streets below where a bustle of activity assured him that a change was in the air. The cold had kept people rather immobile for many months. Now whenever the sun was overhead and the weather higher than thirty-below, folks ventured out as if spring had come.

"I can't lose her," he whispered against the glass. "I can't." In that moment he made his decision. He would say nothing. He would keep his secret and pray that Miranda would never learn the truth.

⊣ C H A P T E R   E I G H T E E N ⊢

SKAGWAY HAD COME into its own during Peter's absence.
The sights, sounds, even the smells, were different than the
little mud-flat harbor town he'd known before. Hotels,
stores, gambling halls, and drinking establishments lined the
main thoroughfares and beckoned his company. Church
spires, schools, and a train depot suggested a more civilized
society.

The railroad, now running over White Pass, was rumored
to make it all the way to Lake Bennett by summer. Peter
thought it amazing, given the fact he'd worked on the railroad's inception only last year. The rugged terrain did nothing to welcome a railroad, that much Peter knew firsthand.
They'd been forced to blast rock shelves out from the sides
of the mountain in order to lay track. The work had been per-
ilous and often deadly. Apparently the workers' temperaments

matched that of the land. Stubbornness and pure grit would see the railroad built to Dawson City.

"Mister, want to buy some mining equipment?" a scruffy-looking man asked. "They've found gold in Nome, ya know. If you're headin' out to Nome, you'll need some gear."

Peter smelled the foul odor of the man before he turned to meet his gnarled expression. "I don't think so."

"I got me an outfit I bought off a man who was headed home. I need the money, mister. I can sell it to you for five hundred dollars."

Peter shook his head. "Sorry, I already have the goods I need."

The man spit and wiped brown tobacco juice from his beard with the back of his sleeve. "Ain't going to find a better deal. I'll make you a bargain. Let's say . . . four hundred-thirty."

"No," Peter said more firmly. "Now, if you'll excuse me."

He'd barely taken five steps down the street when yet another man, equally repulsive and odorous, offered to sell Peter a tent.

"I have no need for it, sir," Peter told the man.

The bum smiled, revealing multiple holes where teeth had once been. He scratched his belly, then shrugged. "I got snowshoes and sleds, as well."

"I'm sorry, but I have everything I need." Peter moved on, amazed at the number of people who walked the streets trying to sell him something. By the time he got to Jonas Campbell's house north of the city, he'd been offered everything from fruit to satin slippers.

Knocking on the door, Peter waited for Jonas to appear. It was late enough in the day that Peter was sure he'd find his friend at home, rather than down at the train shops where he worked repairing engines.

"So you found me," Jonas said with a smile as he pulled the door open wide and laughed at the sight of Peter. "I guess my directions were good enough, eh?"

"They were perfect," Peter replied. "I came straightaway without trouble. Unless, of course, you count trouble as being harassed by every other man on the street to buy their goods."

"Those cons are everywhere," Jonas said, ushering Peter into his small house. "They offer to sell you almost anything you can think to ask for. The law tries to keep them under control, but it's more than what this town can handle."

"Didn't seem so bad last year," Peter said, pulling his cap from his head.

Jonas motioned for Peter to take a seat at the roughhewn table. "I got some coffee for us." He poured the steaming liquid and brought the mugs to the table. "Things weren't this bad last year," Jonas admitted as he handed Peter a cup. "But then the height of the gold rush glory was just coming to a peak. Now things are dying down."

"Is the gold played out?"

Jonas shook his head. "No, I don't believe it is, but the people are. The winter wore most of them to the bone. Those that didn't collapse and die vowed never to endure another arctic winter."

Peter took a long drink from his mug. "I can well understand that. Here it is the twenty-fourth of April and it's still incredibly cold outside. Looks like it might even threaten snow."

"Most likely," Jonas replied. "So tell me about this trip of yours. You goin' to take the train north?"

"As far north as it will go."

"Well, it's over the pass, that much I can offer you. They're working on the tracks again, but not making much progress. The snows have kept them pretty buried. They've even broken into two teams—one working from the north and heading south, and the other is heading north from the front of the line. They hope to meet in the middle and have the thing at least as far as Lake Bennett."

"I had heard that destination mentioned. Jonas," Peter said, leaning forward, "what should I do after getting as far as Bennett? Can I hire a boat to take me to Dawson?"

"Oh, yeah, these days—or I should say when the water isn't three feet thick with ice—they run steamers through most areas. It ain't half the trouble it was last year. Why, you had people crashing on the rocks, losing their boats and lives. . . ." Jonas's voice trailed off. "Sorry, Peter. I just remembered about your wife. I do apologize."

"No offense taken. I'm glad they worked to make the route safer. I would pray that no other man be saddled with the pain of losing someone they love."

"Well, I'm sure your sister is glad to have you comin'. I wouldn't want no sister of mine alone and unprotected in Dawson City. That place is just plain wild from what I've heard."

"I've heard the same," Peter said, knowing only too well the horror stories. "That makes it all the more imperative for me to get there as soon as possible."

That night, Peter lay awake for a long time. He thought of the first time he'd come to Alaska. Grace had been aboard his ship, *Merry Maid*. She had been so gentle and soft-spoken—and so terrified. He had known there was trouble in her life, but something about her had drawn him so completely to her. She needed him for protection.

He thought of her first night aboard the ship. He'd unthinkingly assigned her a small, windowless cabin, which she shared with Karen Pierce and Karen's aunt. They didn't seem to have a problem with the lack of windows or fresh air, but Grace had grown ill. She left the cabin against his orders, and when he found her, he nearly scared her half out of her wits.

I spent the rest of our marriage causing her to fear my condemnation, he thought. *I left her with nothing but fear and hurt feelings.* The thought devastated him, and in spite of knowing God forgave him for his past failings, Peter would have given anything on earth to know that Grace had forgiven him as well.

––––––––

"Oh, he's grown three times over," Karen declared as she lifted Andy Colton into her arms. "He looks just like you, Grace."

"He does favor me a bit," Grace replied. "I wish Mother could see him. I know she'd fall positively in love with him."

"Have you had any word from your mother?"

Grace shook her head. "I wrote shortly after the accident. I don't suppose the mail is very reliable up here."

"To be sure," Karen replied. She cuddled Andy on her lap and shared the quiet morning moments with Grace. Everyone else was about their chores, and Adrik had encouraged Grace and Karen to spend the morning together. Karen was grateful for the rest. She hadn't slept well with Adrik away, and waiting for his return had felt like forever.

"So what do you think of our claim?" Karen asked. "Did Adrik tell you that Gump signed half of it over to Adrik?"

"I was there when Gump did the deed. I'm so glad for all of you. Now I won't feel so bad when I go back to California."

"You're going back?" Karen said in disbelief. "I thought you planned to stay up here with us."

"I've given it a lot of thought," Grace told her, "and I've decided to return to California to introduce Andy to Mother and Father Colton and then head to Wyoming, where my mother is living."

"What about Peter?"

Grace shrugged. "I don't know. I wrote him a letter and had thought to mail it before leaving Dawson, but I couldn't bring myself to do it. I kept thinking, 'Why bother?' I mean, it's obvious that Peter could have come north to bring me home, if he cared enough to do so. But apparently he doesn't."

"You don't know that for sure. He might not even realize where you are."

"I left him a letter at the hotel and paid the owner good money to see to it that Peter got it. I told him everything in that letter. How his anger hurt me. How I couldn't bear his ugly words—the words he swore he didn't mean. I also told him how much I loved him." Her expression changed from passive to sorrowed. "If he received that letter . . ."

"*If* he received it," Karen interrupted. "You can't be sure he ever got it. He may not even know where you are. You know it's possible he never returned to the hotel to learn of your whereabouts. He may well have figured you to have returned with his parents to California. He may have gone there himself, not even knowing you were in the Yukon."

"Well, if that's the case, it's even more imperative that I get to California. Besides, this cold climate is no good for Andy. He's not all that strong."

Karen frowned. "Perhaps it wasn't wise to bring you here."

"Nonsense. It would have been just as cold in Dawson," Grace argued.

"Yes, but in Dawson you had doctors at your fingertips. Here, there's no one to help."

"I would have had doctors at my fingertips for two hundred dollars a visit. Did you have any idea they were charging that much money?"

"No, I guess I didn't."

"Dr. Brummel even made that kind of money for his dental work and usually all he did was pull teeth. Look, you're here and I feel confident of your abilities. After all, you were my teacher. You gave me wise counsel and taught me a great deal. If anyone can keep us in health and good spirits, I say it will be you."

Karen felt uncomfortable with her friend and one-time student's adoration. She worried that perhaps by encouraging Grace to join them, out of her own selfish desire, she had somehow risked the lives of both her friend and Andy. Looking down at the happy baby, Karen knew she could never forgive herself if anything happened to him on her account.

Karen handed Andy back to Grace, then went to take her apron from the hook. "So what do you think of the place? It's crowded and dark, but it keeps out the chill."

"Anything would have to be better than the tent," Grace

said, smiling. "I just hate feeling all closed in."

Karen laughed. "Well, after a few weeks here, you may change your mind. Adrik and Gump made the berth bunks. I feel like I'm living in a wooden box, but when you tack a cover up there to totally enclose the bed, it does retain the heat pretty well."

"I was warm enough last night," Grace admitted. "I hope Jacob and Gump didn't mind sharing a bed."

"No, I know they didn't. There were times through the coldest nights when they slept together and Leah slept wedged against the wall with Adrik and me. There wasn't any room to move even an inch, but we kept from freezing."

"Well, Leah and I could sleep together with Andy between us. He'll stay warmer that way, and then Gump and Jacob can each have their own bed."

"That was the plan, but we didn't know you'd be coming in last night and Leah fell asleep in the smallest bunk. It wouldn't have done any good to get her up and rearrange everyone then."

"Oh, I agree," Grace replied. "Although I am happy to learn my permanent place will be the lower bunk instead of the upper. I thought I'd break my neck climbing down this morning."

Karen turned to the stove and checked the cast-iron skillet. She tossed a few droplets of water into the pan to see if it was finally hot enough. The popping and sizzling was all the encouragement she needed.

"I'll fry up some bacon and then put the oatmeal on," she told Grace. "You sit there and relax, and we'll have breakfast on in a moment."

Leah appeared just then. She was bundled from head to

toe and was still shivering from the icy morning air. Carrying a bundle to Karen, she held it up like an offering. "Adrik . . . said to give this . . . to . . . to . . . you." Her teeth chattered as she spoke.

Karen took the bundle and motioned Leah to the stove. "Come warm up, and next time don't stay outside for so long. A half hour in this cold could kill you." She directed Leah to stand near the firebox on the stove. "Gump hasn't stoked up the fireplace yet, so the stove will have to do."

"I could stoke up the fire," Grace offered.

"No, I want you and Andy to rest and warm up from your long trip. Leah will get warm enough right here." Karen unwrapped the bundle to find a half dozen good-sized potatoes. They were a little old, but never had anything looked so good. "Where in the world did he find these at this time of year?"

Leah shrugged. "He didn't say. Just told me to give them to you. Guess he thought they'd be good for breakfast."

"Indeed they will," Karen agreed. "I'll fry them up in the bacon grease."

"Hmmm, I can just taste them now," Leah said, looking rather wistful.

Karen thought it a shame that they all treated food with such enthusiastic, even wanton, behavior. She wasn't at all sure what she might or might not do for a piece of fresh fruit or a nice green salad.

Karen hurried to wash and cut up the potatoes, skins and all. She cooked the bacon and pulled it from the skillet. "I can't believe we're actually having potatoes for our breakfast. This will be wonderful." She dumped the plateful of cut up spuds into the grease and jumped back as fiery droplets spit back at her from the pan.

Just then Gump, Adrik, and Jacob entered. Each man carried an armful of firewood—just a portion of the supply they would need for the day.

"Smells near good enough to eat," Adrik teased.

"Ja, it smells like a good house should," Gump added.

Karen turned and smiled. "I don't know where you managed to lay your hand on potatoes, but I'm eternally grateful."

"I have my ways," Adrik said, depositing his wood beside the fireplace.

"Don't I know it," Karen said, smiling at her husband. "You probably sweet-talked some poor unsuspecting soul just when she was at her most vulnerable."

Adrik grinned roguishly. "My lips are sealed, Mrs. Ivankov. Just be grateful we didn't eat them on the trail, for we were sorely tempted."

A loud commotion from the dog pens caused Adrik to raise his hand for silence. Karen heard the awful racket and trembled. The team was awfully worked up about something, and that usually spelled trouble. Taking up his rifle, Adrik moved to the door. Jacob was right behind him, and Gump followed after the boy. Each man took up his firearm and moved outside with caution.

"What is it?" Grace asked.

"I don't know. What I do know is that I don't intend to wait here," Karen said. "Why don't you put Andy in the play box Adrik fixed for him and we'll investigate."

Karen heard Adrik yell something. "Hurry, Grace. Let's go see. Never mind leaving Andy—just grab that blanket and bring him. Here, we'll wrap it around both of you," she said, helping to maneuver the blanket around Grace's shoulders.

Leah followed close on their heels, still wrapped in her coat. *She's the only sensible one of the group*, Karen thought, as they rounded the edge of the cabin and looked to see what the men had uncovered.

The dogs were still barking up a storm. They'd congregated at the north end of the pen and were jumping at the fence and pouncing upon each other as they howled and carried on.

"What is it?" Karen asked.

Adrik shook his head. "Someone was messing around the shed. They've stolen the sled I bought in Dawson."

"Why would they take the sled and not the dogs?" Leah asked. "The dogs are worth three hundred a piece."

"Ja, she's right," Gump said, making certain the pen gate was secure.

"Why would anyone want that old sled?" Adrik questioned.

Karen was just as perplexed. "Who'd you get it from in Dawson?"

"I bought it off an Englishman—a botanist, to be exact. He was there putting together a book on plants of the Yukon. He didn't need the sled anymore and offered to trade it when he heard me talking in the store about needing one."

"Maybe he stole it from someone else," Leah suggested.

Jacob shook his head. "Nah, he didn't seem the type. He was one of those bookish fellows—the kind that studies all the time. I can't see him stealing a sled from anyone."

"Me neither," Adrik replied.

"Maybe the thief was a friend of the botanist," Karen

suggested. "Maybe there was something of value that had been left on it."

"Can't imagine what it'd be. It was just an old sled."

Karen bit at her lip and rubbed her arms. She'd been foolish to come outside without a coat. "Did the man sell you anything besides the sled?"

"No. The only thing he sold me was this sled—oh, and the sled box. But we're using that for Andy. It's the box I fixed up for him to play in and sleep in during the day."

"Maybe there's something about the box," Karen suggested. "We should go check it out."

"Nah, it's just a wooden box, nothing special."

Grace had already started back to the cabin when Karen turned to follow. She heard Grace scream and feared the thieves had struck again. Adrik came running, whipping past Karen in a flash.

Karen then saw what had caused her friend's dismay. Smoke was pouring out the cabin door. "The potatoes!" she screamed and charged past her husband to enter the cabin.

She could barely see what she was doing, but somehow Karen managed to pull the skillet from the stove. She put the pan in a washtub and hurried outside, nearly knocking Adrik down at the door.

"Silly woman," he said, taking the smoldering tub from her. "You could have died from the smoke."

Karen coughed and sputtered for air. She looked at the charred potatoes and felt tears come to her smoke-filled eyes. "But our potatoes were burning."

"I'd say they're already gone," Adrik replied, this time in a less serious tone.

"No!" Karen declared. "I won't believe it. I was so looking

forward to those potatoes. I won't let them go to waste."

Adrik laughed. "You go right ahead and eat 'em if you want, but as for me, I plan to find something a little less well-done."

Gump chuckled, as did Jacob and Grace. Leah was the only one who offered Karen any real sympathy. She came and put her arm around Karen's shoulder and patted her gently.

"Come on, boys," Adrik called, "let's get the cabin opened up and clear out the smoke. If we stand out here much longer, we'll all be frozen in our tracks."

"Not if we warm ourselves by the potatoes," Grace suggested.

They all broke into peals of laughter, and even Karen had to smile. Gone were her dreams of potatoes fried to a golden brown, a hint of bacon flavoring each morsel. Easy come, easy go. It was the story of gold, be it rock ore or potatoes.

┤CHAPTER NINETEEN├

APRIL 26, 1899, dawned in Dawson City at forty-below. To say it was cold was to come nowhere near describing the painful bite of the northern wind. Very few people moved on the streets below, and those who did brave the cold were bundled like furry snowmen.

The cold seemed to permeate everything. It seeped into the very core and left a person with the desire to do nothing but bury himself under piles of covers. Teddy gave serious thought to making this his last winter in the Yukon. He felt trapped. As surely by his own conscience, as by the cold.

Teddy stood at the frosted window of his hotel room. His thoughts bothered him in a way he didn't want to acknowledge. He was keeping the truth from Miranda.

It wasn't hard to rationalize why he was remaining silent, but it was hard to see how much she longed for some kind of contact with her friends—and do nothing to help. Teddy turned from the window and paced the room. Miranda had gone downstairs to the kitchen to get some hot water for their tea. Teddy had suggested they simply have one of the staff bring it up, but Miranda had wanted the exercise. She was suffering a terrible bout of cabin fever and longed for sunny days and warmth. Teddy didn't blame her. He longed for the same, only he longed for such things with Miranda at his side.

"But surely she'll leave me when she finds her friends," he said aloud. "And how could I fault her for that? She has history with them that she does not share with me."

Teddy's thoughts went back to the day they'd kissed. He'd been so dumbfounded by her initiation of the act that he had initially said nothing—done nothing. Then when she'd fled from the room, looking as though she'd broken all ten commandments at once, he knew he was in love with her. He knew, too, that he wanted to kiss her again, and this time he wanted to be the one to initiate the kiss.

And he had kissed her. The thought of her lips upon his still haunted him. He would have kissed her many times over since that wonderful day, but Miranda had been skittish and shy around him ever since. The only time she'd really seemed her old self was when she'd cut her hand.

Teddy wouldn't have wished her pain for all the world, but he did enjoy her neediness when she was incapable of helping herself. He felt wonderfully necessary in her life when she was ill or injured—though he certainly had no desire for her to spend her days as an invalid. No, he really just wanted her to need him all the time. To need his company—his hospitality—his love.

His earlier fears of Miranda's interfering in his work had faded with the passing of each day. She was nothing like his mother. Eugenia Davenport had cared nothing for her husband's dream while Miranda Colton seemed quite enthusiastic about Teddy's desires. The only problem was that Teddy's enthusiasm for his work was fading in light of the revelation that he had fallen in love.

Already he could envision a future with Miranda working at his side. They'd complete the book and go on a lecture tour discussing the various aspects of Yukon vegetation and forestry. They'd spend quiet evenings in discovery—discovery of books, plants, and each other.

A cloud settled over him, making Teddy feel quite black in his mood. There would be no future with Miranda, however. She would hate him when she knew the truth. Maybe he could still figure out a way to keep her from finding out.

"I must tell her," he declared in defeat. Keeping the truth from her was making him feel quite heartsick. He argued with himself in his dreams from dusk to dawn, and when he would awaken from his restless sleep tormented with guilt, he'd start the whole process all over again with his conscious mind. No, it was best to get the truth out and tell her exactly what had happened and why he'd not told her the truth.

"But the setting should be special," he murmured. "Perhaps then she'd be more inclined to forgive me." *Please let her forgive me.*

An idea came to him to have the cook prepare a special dinner. They could eat privately in the little office downstairs. He'd have it all arranged. There would be candles and beautiful linens and, of course, crystal. He would see to it that the table was perfect.

Teddy began plotting the dinner, deciding on whatever fancy feast his money might buy. He'd heard that Muldoon's Saloon and Restaurant had some pork chops that they were selling for an outrageous sum. Perhaps he could get cook to secure a couple for their meal. They would be tasty with a bit of rosemary, which Teddy could provide from his supplies of herbs. He'd considered it his great fortune to have traded cash for a vast array of herbs from a woman he'd met in British Columbia. The herbs had served him well on many an occasion and would no doubt be just the thing to make their rather bland fare a bit livelier.

"Here we are," Miranda announced, opening the door. She balanced a tray of tea and Swedish cookies on her right hip, looking as if she'd been serving tables her whole life.

"Let me help," Teddy said, going to her. He took the tray and smiled. "What would you think about a surprise?"

"It depends on what the surprise is," Miranda replied. "Cutting my hand was a surprise. Falling overboard on Lake Laberge was a surprise. I'd just as soon know about the arrangement prior to deciding whether I'm for it or against it."

"It's a good surprise," he replied.

Miranda's expression turned to one of excitement. "Have you found my friends?"

Teddy felt bad for having given her false hope. "No, but I think you'll be pleased with my idea, nevertheless."

She lowered her face, and Teddy knew she was struggling to keep him from seeing her disappointment. She'd tried so hard to be stoic—for his sake. He knew he'd been less than comforting when she'd brought up the past and the long separation she'd endured. But in a town with some thirty thousand people, she was expecting the impossible. He had only wanted her to understand the situation and how difficult it was. He didn't want her to feel that she couldn't confide in him, yet sadly, he knew that was how she felt.

"So what did you have in mind?" she asked softly.

Teddy put the tray down and began to pour the tea. "If I told you, it wouldn't be a surprise."

Miranda moved to the table and studied him for a moment. Cocking her head, one brow raised ever so slightly, she questioned him again, "What are you planning?"

"I assure you it is all good. I would never do anything to hurt you." He swallowed hard, and this time it was his turn to look away. Of course, he hadn't meant to hurt her, but by being inattentive and not listening to the names of her friends, he had inadvertently kept Miranda from finding her loved ones months ago. There was no way he could keep that from hurting her.

"So when is this surprise to be unveiled?"

He handed her a cup and saucer. "Tonight. Tonight at seven."

She nodded. "Very well, Teddy Davenport. I shall trust you this once."

Her words went through his heart like a knife. *Oh, please, Lord,* he prayed. *Please let her understand.*

———

The candlelight dinner completely captivated Miranda. She had come to expect certain things from Teddy, and romantic displays didn't fit that list.

Upon his instruction, she had dressed in her finest gown, a pale cream wool trimmed in gold braiding. Teddy had purchased it for her from a local seamstress. The woman had fussed and fawned over Miranda until she thought she might very well faint from exhaustion. The experience, however, had merited her three new gowns, and of all of them, this was the most beautiful and elegant.

"Teddy, what is this all about?" she asked as she unfolded her napkin.

"I thought we deserved a special evening. I had an epiphany of sorts and needed to share it with you. But first, we shall dine on very fine food. I've had cook scouring the city since this afternoon. He's procured for us two very thick pork chops, baked potatoes, applesauce spiced with cloves and nutmeg, and a brandied plum cake, which he assures me will be most rewarding."

Miranda thought the food sounded most delightful. She certainly hadn't gone hungry staying here at the hotel under Teddy's care, but neither did they eat all that well. This was Dawson, after all. They were isolated in the frozen Yukon without hope of major deliveries until spring breakup. Supplies were running low—and the variety was definitely lacking. Spring thaw couldn't come soon enough.

Miranda knew that date was to come upon them within a month or so, as people were already placing bets on when the river's ice would thaw enough to break free. It certainly wasn't going to happen if the days stayed at forty-below, as this one had. But it would come—soon enough.

One of the housekeeping girls acted as their server. She brought the plates, bearing the offering of the beautifully arranged meal, hot from the kitchen.

"Might I offer a prayer?" Teddy asked.

Miranda nodded. "I'd like that."

"Father, we thank you," Teddy prayed, "for this bounty

and for the bounty you will provide on the morrow. We thank you for hearing our prayers and for tenderly caring for us. Amen."

"Amen," Miranda whispered.

They ate in silence for several minutes. Neither one seemed willing to let the food get even marginally cold. The serving girl brought in fresh hot rolls and Miranda nearly swooned when she saw they were accompanied by a small amount of butter.

"I've not tasted butter in ever so long," she said, taking a tiny bit to smear on her roll.

Teddy reached across and slathered the roll more sufficiently. "I'm not that fond of butter, but I know it is a treat for you."

Miranda felt overwhelmed by his kindness. Surely he longed for the comforts of civilization. He was of a fine English family, moneyed and educated. It must have been hard on him to be so isolated from the things he'd grown up with.

"What do you miss most about England?" she asked.

Teddy looked at her thoughtfully for a moment, then he turned his gaze to the ceiling above her head. He looked to be a million miles away.

"I miss the comfort of having everything neatly ordered. There is a settled feeling to the land—a knowledge of whom it has belonged to for centuries. Wherever you look, you have the feeling of a gentleness that cannot be had here." He looked back to smile at Miranda. "If England is a refined and elegant old lady, then the Yukon is her defiant and rebellious grandchild."

"I would love to see England some day," Miranda said softly. "The man I told you about, Crispin Thibault, the one

I thought I saw in the alley, he was from abroad. He told such wonderful stories. He had skied in the Alps and sailed fjords in Scandinavia. He made it all sound so wonderful—so completely amazing. Before I came with my parents to Alaska," she said thoughtfully, "I'd never traveled outside of California. In fact, I'd hardly seen more than San Francisco."

"Perhaps one day you'll visit England. I'd love to have you stay at my estate. I would love to show you all the places I love so much."

Miranda sobered and looked into his dark eyes. She saw something in his expression that wasn't all together clear. There was a certain amount of passion and desire, but there was something else as well—something almost akin to regret.

The dinner passed much too quickly, and once the dishes had been cleared away and fat slices of plum cake had replaced the entrée, Teddy decided to speak more seriously.

"I have something to tell you. I'm not at all sure how you will take it, but I beg you to bear with me and hear me out before you comment."

Miranda felt a tightening in her chest. What was he about to tell her? Had he found out something horrible in regard to her friends? "What is it?" she asked, leaning forward.

"First promise to hear me out."

"I promise," she said without thought. "Now tell me."

"I came to realize the other day, the day you cut your hand, where it was I had heard the name of Adrik Ivankov."

"Is that all? I told you about him—and Karen and Grace and the Barringer children. How could you have not remembered?"

"Because I failed to really listen." He bowed his head momentarily, refusing to meet her gaze. "I was selfishly enveloped in my own affairs. I was focused only on completing my work. You see, this book was very important to my father, and I wanted very much to honor him."

"I don't understand." Miranda had the feeling she wasn't going to like what Teddy had to tell her, but she needed to know the truth.

"When we arrived in Dawson, do you remember that I sold our sled?"

"Yes."

"Well, the man I sold it to was Adrik Ivankov."

"What?" Her voice took on an alarmed tone. "You sold it to him and didn't tell me?"

Teddy pushed back from the table, his face betraying his anguish. "I didn't realize who he was. Please, just hear me out. I hadn't remembered you telling me the man's name."

"But . . ."

He held up his hand. "Please. I didn't know it, or I would have brought him back here and opened the door for the happy reunion. I ran into the man, quite literally, in the mercantile. He said he was looking for a sled, and I told him I had one. He was with a young boy of about sixteen or seventeen."

"Jacob Barringer," Miranda filled in.

"I suppose so. You see, I didn't pay either one of them much attention. Mr. Ivankov talked of his need for the sled and how he was moving his group to one of the creek claim sites. I didn't listen closely enough for the name to register."

"Oh, Teddy, how could you be so unthinking? You had to know I was looking for friends in those circumstances."

His expression contorted in misery. "I know. I've asked myself that at least a thousand times since you spoke his name at the hospital and I realized where I'd heard it."

"But that was over two weeks ago, Teddy. You've known all this time and still said nothing?" Miranda struggled to keep her temper. "Why? You knew how very much I wanted to find him—to find all of them. Why would you do something so selfish?"

"Because I didn't want to lose you," Teddy suddenly blurted out.

Miranda sat back stunned. "What?"

"You heard me. I didn't wish to lose your company. Don't you see, Miranda? I've fallen in love with you."

She felt her breathing quicken to the raging pace of her pulse. "You love me?"

He came to where she sat and got down on one knee. "I love you with all my heart. And the thought of losing you— of having to let you go—nearly breaks me."

Her heart softened toward him. It had never been her nature to hold grudges, and her anger fled in the light of his devotion. She loved him, as well. She'd known it for some time. His love of God made him perfect in her eyes. How could she not forgive him?

"Oh, Teddy, I'm so sorry. I shouldn't have lost my temper."

"I'm the one who is apologizing. Please forgive me. I promise to be more sensitive to your needs. I promise to listen more clearly and to give you all my attention. Please, just please say you'll marry me."

"Marry you?" Her voice left her as her breath caught in her throat. He was proposing marriage!

"I'll make you a good husband. I promise that with God's help, I'll be everything you need me to be."

"Oh, Teddy." She felt tears come to her eyes. "I . . ."

"FIRE!"

The shouts rang clear from the lobby. Teddy jumped to his feet just as the cook burst in on them. "Boss, the whole town's on fire!"

Adrik and Jacob had grown restless waiting for spring thaw. The gravel that Gump had dug up prior to their arrival beckoned them for sluicing and exploration. Adrik knew they couldn't wash the solution in water, as they had to fight the frozen creek just to get enough water to drink and wash with. But Adrik had another plan.

Taking a pick, he worked loose a chunk of gravel and frozen muck and brought it into the cabin. Diligently he and Jacob worked at thawing the mass by putting it in a wash pan near the fireplace. From time to time, one of them would turn the pan to offer heat to the various sides of the pan and, little by little, the mass thawed.

"You beat 'em all, Adrik. Yes, by golly. You beat 'em all."

Picking through the rock and mud, Adrik took Gump's good-natured teasing in stride. He knew Gump was just as interested in what he might find as everyone else. A few flakes of gold encouraged Adrik to keep at it. Gump had said there was enough gold on the claim to keep him comfortable, but they all needed a really strong show of color. And in the twinkling of an eye, that was exactly what they got.

"Gold!" Adrik declared and jumped to his feet. He held up a nugget the size of a peanut. "Look what I've found!"

Gump limped across the room. His leg had healed, but

he still walked with a bit of difficulty. "Are you sure there? It could be fool's gold."

"No, this is the real thing!" Adrik dropped the rock in Gump's hand.

"Ja, it's the real thing all righty."

Karen and Grace moved in closer, while Leah played with Andy. "Is it true?" Karen asked. "Have we struck pay dirt?"

"I think it would be safe to say we're getting closer," Adrik replied, pulling Karen against him in a tight embrace. "I think once the warm weather comes, we're going to strike it rich."

"Ja ha!" Gump let out a yell, then quieted quickly. "No sense in lettin' the whole vorld know just yet."

Adrik shook his head and laughed. He'd never seen the old man so happy. "We're going to make it," he told Gump and the others. "We're going to find the gold!"

⊣[CHAPTER TWENTY]⊢

"OH, TEDDY, this is just awful," Miranda declared, looking at the charred remainders of Front Street. The town had suffered cruelly, the fire razing much of the business district, as well as Paradise Alley.

"What in the world could have happened to the firefighting equipment?" Teddy questioned, not really expecting an answer.

"I'll tell you what happened, mister," a complete stranger interrupted. "The fire department was on strike for more pay. They didn't keep the water heated so when the people tried to use the hoses, it froze in the lines before it could even come out the nozzle. Those hoses burst quicker than a spoiled melon. It's the firemen's fault so many folks are out of business."

"Do you have any room at the hotel, Teddy?" Miranda

asked as her gaze followed hundreds of people who were wandering up and down the street in a daze.

"We have some room, but not nearly enough. We'll do what we can, however. Let's get the word out that we're open to take in those without homes. Let them come and share whatever we can offer."

Miranda smiled. "I'll start spreading the word."

———

From the looks of the crowd that had gathered outside the hotel doorway, Miranda figured the news had traveled rapidly among the citizens of Dawson. Tired and completely worn by the evening's events, Miranda worked until the wee hours of the morning to ensure that everyone at least had a place on the floor to throw down a blanket.

"Come on," Teddy said, pulling her away from the front desk. "We're going to have to get some rest."

"How can we?" Miranda questioned. "There are still so many people outside."

"The hotel staff can take care of them. You've done enough for one night."

"It seems like an entire week has passed instead of one night. If it wasn't for the heavy smell of smoke on the air, I would think it had."

Teddy smiled. "A good night's sleep will help a great deal. Once you are able to rest in your own bed . . ."

"But I can't," Miranda interrupted. "I gave my room to a group of women. I believe there are seven to be exact."

"Seven women are going to sleep in that small room?"

Miranda nodded. "I think they're used to a lot worse."

Teddy seemed to understand. "The soiled doves, eh?"

Miranda smiled. "I knew you'd understand."

"As long as they don't try to conduct business in my establishment. But the real concern, of course, is what you are to do now. I suppose you can sleep in my room, and I can try to find a place elsewhere."

"I had one of the girls move my things into your room, but I don't have to sleep there. I just didn't want to lose track of my belongings."

"If we were married, this wouldn't be a problem at all," Teddy said, a rye smile on his lips.

"Yes, well, we aren't married, and so it presents a problem," Miranda said, feeling the heat come to her cheeks.

"Do you trust me to remedy the situation?"

"What do you mean?"

Teddy shrugged. "Well, I could secure a license and see to our marriage—if you only give me a yes to my proposal."

"What about the sleeping arrangements now?" Miranda asked with a grin.

"I'll take a spot on the floor in the office, but only if you agree to my proposal."

"And if I don't?" She was amused with his teasing tone.

"Then you'll soon learn what it is to sleep eight women to a bed."

Miranda laughed. "Oh, Teddy, you are such a dear."

"Is that a yes?"

She leaned into his arms and wrapped him in her embrace. "Yes. Yes, I will marry you, Thomas Davenport."

"I knew I could wear you down with my genteel charm."

"Actually, I was pretty sure I would marry you that morning you overflowed the pan of oatmeal back at the cabin. I figured anyone that needy..."

"Oh, hush," he said, silencing her with a kiss.

Miranda cherished the moment, wanting nothing more than to go on holding him for a long, long time. She had found the love of her life, even with his absentminded ways. He was hers, and that was all that mattered.

––––––

Teddy and Miranda married in a simple ceremony on the fifth of May. By that time tents had sprung up all along Front Street, even while the blackened debris remained to be hauled away. The saloons and gambling halls were the first to be back in business, with the scarlet women following right behind.

Miranda marveled at the transformation, but no more than she did at the transformation in her own life and that of her husband's demeanor. The once shy, soft-spoken Teddy seemed to take on a manly pride about him. He strutted proudly with Miranda on his arm, never failing to introduce her as his new bride.

For Miranda, the joy of her new marriage was almost more than she could put into words. And she had tried. Writing to her mother and father, she had sought to explain her feelings and decision. She knew Peter would be livid that she'd not consulted him prior to speaking her vows, but she was a grown woman in her majority, and she'd been through enough adventure over the last year to know her heart and mind on the matter.

"Can you take this over to the charity hospital?" Teddy asked as he finished wrapping a bundle of labeled herbs.

Miranda looked up from her letter and nodded. "Of course."

"You might delay in case the doctor has another list. Tell him I will do what I can to secure whatever he needs to help the burn victims."

"It was good of you to help arrange the charity hospital," she said, coming to her husband's side. Kissing him lightly atop his head, she was unprepared for his sudden embrace. He pulled her onto his lap and kissed her passionately upon her mouth.

"I still can't believe you're my wife. The most beautiful woman in all the world and she belongs to me!" He kissed her again, this time a bit more ardently.

Miranda wrapped her arms around Teddy's neck and gave herself over to the emotions that welled up inside her every time he touched her. How she loved this man!

"Ah, you'd better take this and go," Teddy said, pulling away rather suddenly. He nearly pushed Miranda from his lap and then handed her the package. "If you don't go right now, it might very well be hours before I'm prepared to let you leave."

Miranda giggled. "Whatever you say, Teddy dear."

She was still grinning when she descended the stairs, package in hand. She had never known such happiness. *Oh, Father God, you are so good to me. You have blessed me beyond all my expectations and dreams. Thank you for helping me choose this godly man for a husband. Now I can truly thank you for allowing the storm upon Laberge and for my accident. If not for that, I might never have met Teddy.*

Walking the short distance to the hospital, Miranda lifted her face to the noonday sun. The warmth was minimal, but it was wonderful nevertheless. The breakup of the ice on the river was impending, and daily there were reports to relay the situation on the Yukon River. She'd heard it rumored that the government had plans to load the winter garbage atop the ice floes just prior to the breakup and that way, what the river didn't claim as its own, the ice would carry away downstream. Miranda couldn't imagine those folks who lived downstream appreciating the gesture, but she had no say in the matter.

The hospital tent had been purchased by Teddy from a local man. In fact the structure was actually two tents fixed side by side. Miranda entered the structure and found an unoccupied desk and chair at the opening. Beyond this were rows of cots where writhing, pain-filled patients waited for some form of care.

Just then a young man of medium build passed by Miranda. "If you're looking for a patient, just take a walk down the aisle. My bookkeeper has gone off to purchase more bandages."

"Are you the doctor?" Miranda questioned.

The man stopped and turned on his heel. "I am. Is there a problem?"

"Not at all. My husband is Thomas Davenport. He sent this package of herbs for your use."

"Oh, that's a relief," the man said, stepping forward to take the offering. "I'm beyond myself in trying to treat these poor men."

"Teddy, my husband, wondered if you had another list of needs? Herbal or otherwise," she added quickly.

"I do indeed. Let me step over to the other tent and get it."

Miranda nodded and watched as the man hurried from the room. The moans of the men filled her ears, and without knowing why, Miranda turned her attention to the occupants of the tent. Slowly she walked down the aisle, looking first at this one and then that one. She prayed silently for each man, hoping God would be merciful. By the time she reached the patient at the end of the first row, Miranda could not suppress a gasp.

"Crispin?" she whispered his name, but it was enough to make the man open his eyes.

"Miranda," he breathed. "An angel come to take me to my death."

"No," Miranda tried to assure him, "you're not going to die. Not yet."

His eyelids flickered. "Are you really here? You're dead. You can't be here."

"I didn't die, Crispin. I fell overboard but was rescued." She knelt beside his cot and took hold of his bandaged hand. He was burned—badly. And for the first time, she wondered if she'd given him false hope in her statement regarding death.

"You didn't die? But we were certain." His raspy voice struggled to form the words.

"God watched over me and brought me safely to Dawson."

"I'm so glad," Crispin replied.

He closed his eyes, and for a moment Miranda thought perhaps he had passed away. Tears formed in her eyes. How awful to find him like this. "Oh, Crispin, I'm so sorry you've been hurt. Where are the others? Are they here with you?"

He rolled his head slowly from side to side. "No. We separated when we came to this place. I couldn't bear to stay on. I kept thinking of you—how I had failed you."

"Oh, but you didn't. Please don't think such a thing." She kissed his bandaged hand.

Crispin's breathing grew very ragged. Miranda feared he was nearing the end, and she knew that she had to talk to him about Jesus. "Crispin, where are you going?" She hoped he would understand exactly what she was asking him.

He looked at her and shook his head again. "I don't know. Can you show me the way?"

"But of course I can. Jesus said that He is the way, the truth, and the life. You have only to put your trust in Him and repent of your sins. He will do the rest. He will guide your way." She touched his forehead, noting the cold, clammy feel to his skin.

"I'm sorry that I doubted God. I was foolish. I thought I would never need such a thing in my life." He fell silent and once again closed his eyes.

Miranda wiped her tears with her free hand. For several moments she heard only his ragged breathing and the moans of those around her. The smell of death was thick on the air. Why hadn't she noticed it before? Unable to bear the thought, she finally offered, "I can pray with you, Crispin. If you want me to."

"No need," he whispered. " 'Tis done."

"I'm so glad. Now I shall see you again in heaven," Miranda said, trying to keep from sobbing. She couldn't believe the emaciated man, so burned and scarred, was the handsome Crispin Thibault who had wooed her with his charming intellect and stories of faraway places.

Crispin opened his eyes and looked up at her. "Thank you so much for coming. I told God I would be glad to do the right thing—only I didn't know what the right thing might be. I only wanted to go home, but I had no home to go to. I prayed for an angel and here you are."

He wheezed and struggled to breathe. Miranda turned to see if the doctor had returned. She felt frantic to find him. "I'll go for the doctor," she told Crispin.

"No," he whispered. "I shan't be here when he comes." He drew a ragged breath and added, "I have never stopped loving you."

With that he closed his eyes and surrendered his life. Miranda burst into tears and fell across him, knowing now she could do nothing to help him.

"Mrs. Davenport?" the doctor called her name, reaching out to help her to her feet. "Did you know him?"

She nodded, wiping her eyes and trying so very hard to regain control. "He was a friend."

"I'm sorry. Is there anything I can do?"

Miranda nodded. "Yes. Please don't send him away to be buried in some unmarked grave. My husband and I will pay for his burial. Please do what you must, but call the funeral parlor to care for him. I'll make the arrangements."

"All right," the man said sympathetically. "I'll send my man when he returns."

"Thank you. Now if you'll give me your list . . ."

"Oh, of course. Here you are."

Miranda squared her shoulders and pulled her wool cape close. With one last glance at Crispin, she hurried from the tent and nearly ran all the way back to the hotel.

Once inside the sanctuary of Teddy's hotel, Miranda darted up the stairs in an unladylike manner and rushed into their room. The sight of her husband caused her to break into tears anew. "Oh, Teddy. Something awful has happened!" She collapsed in his arms, her tears dampening the front of his shirt.

"What is it?" Teddy asked, his tone betraying his concern. "Are you hurt? Did someone bother you?"

Miranda lifted her face to meet his gaze. "No. No one bothered me. I found my friend Crispin Thibault at the hospital. Oh, Teddy, he'd been horribly burned."

"I'm so sorry." His expression of worry melted in the wake of her declaration. "Is he going to make it?"

"No. He died while I was with him." She sniffed back tears. "He was waiting for someone to come tell him what he needed to do in order to go to heaven. What if I'd not taken the herbs to the doctor? What if I'd come too late?"

"But you didn't, my dearest. Remember, God is never too late. He knew your friend's heart was ready to receive the truth. I'm so proud of you for sharing with him—for helping him in his final moments."

"But imagine all the others, Teddy. What if they're waiting, too? What if they're dying to know the way home, just as Crispin was?"

He nodded. "It's a possibility that we should seek to rectify. No one should die without knowing Jesus Christ and the gift He offers them."

Miranda put her head against his shoulder and let Teddy hold her close once again. No matter what happened, she promised God, she would see to it that each of the injured had a chance to know the truth about salvation. She didn't know how she might accomplish it, but she felt the inspiration of certain purpose course through her veins. She wouldn't let them die without knowing that God loved them and wanted to give them a home in heaven.

─┤ C H A P T E R   T W E N T Y - O N E ├─

THE WARMTH OF MAY brought with it the thaw. The excitement built toward the last of the month when the ice finally began to crack and pop. Then loud moaning and muffled thunder rose from the frozen water, signaling the arrival of spring.

Daily, Miranda walked back and forth from the hotel to the charity hospital. And daily she sat for hours beside the various patients' beds. She listened to their stories, prayed with them, and offered them bits of hope laced with love.

Many of the patients died slow, painful deaths. There was little anyone could do. Some had originally come because of the fire, but after being evaluated it was clear they were dying for other reasons. Scurvy, cirrhosis, malnutrition, and a variety of other desperate conditions claimed more lives than the smoke and burns. They were the downtrodden and poor wretches of society. They were the forgotten of the gold rush—those souls whose lives could offer nothing of value—so no one cared to know where they had gone or what had happened to them along the way.

But Miranda cared. Her heart broke over the neediness of them all. She felt sorrow in their passing and attended their burials faithfully. If they had even the remotest family member still living, Miranda wrote their final letters and promised to mail them. She was an angel of mercy and love—an angel offering a light to guide them home.

"They tell me," Miranda said as she sat by the bed of an elderly man, "that the river is open and new arrivals are expected within the week."

"Tell 'em all to go back where they came from," the old man said. "Tell 'em the abundance of gold is a myth perpetuated by the devil hisself."

Miranda smoothed back the old man's white hair. "They wouldn't listen. You know that." She smiled and tenderly pulled his blanket to just under his chin. "You get some sleep now."

"Will you come again tomorrow?"

"Of course," Miranda whispered, not at all certain that the old man had any tomorrows left.

———

Peter Colton felt a sense of urgency as he stepped down the gangplank of the steamer. It was like a hunger driving him forward. He saw it in the faces of those around him, only they were in search of gold and he was in search of flesh and blood.

Sunlight poured down upon him like golden rain. It

radiated around him, giving him hope. He had to find Miranda. It was all that he could think of. She would be alone and scared, no doubt, and he desired only to offer her comfort and to take her home.

"Lord, please help me to find my sister," he prayed in a hushed breath. All around him the crowds trudged through the muck and mud streets, eagerly chasing after invisible goals. The gold was all they sought. The gold was what they thought they needed.

From the moment he'd first stepped onto the steamer, Peter had heard nothing but tales of getting rich and fat on Yukon gold. He'd heard tales of the Klondike before, but these rivaled most he'd known. The frenzy of the early days, so questionable and uncertain, had been replaced by a passionate confidence that drove men to the gold fields. They were noisy, desperate witnesses to the age-old story of men who would sell their souls for the taste of wealth.

Peter's patience for the entire lot had worn thin. This greed and hunger for power, the desire for overnight fame and fortune, was all such a waste of time and effort. Peter could see that now. In light of his recent inheritance from Grace's estate, Peter knew that the money he'd worked so hard for all his life meant nothing. It was so very unimportant without the woman he loved.

Checking in first one store and then another, Peter asked each clerk or owner if he knew of or had seen Miranda. He produced a picture, several years old, but still bearing a strong resemblance to his beloved sister. When he stopped in at the government house to check with the mounted police, he got his first break.

"I believe I have seen that woman," the sergeant told

Peter. "She looks like the lady who helps at the charity hospital."

"Where would I find that place?"

The sergeant gave Peter directions and wished him well. Peter, excited and grateful for the news, hurried off to his destination without even thinking to thank the man. His long-legged strides seemed slow compared to his usual gait. Peter knew this was only his imagination. He wanted so much to know that Miranda was safe and well. The months and miles that had separated them could no longer stand between them, and Peter thrilled to know he would soon be reunited with his sister.

Coming through the opening to the tent hospital, Peter met the youthful yet haggard man who sat as guard at the door.

"Yes, may I help you?"

"I certainly hope so," Peter replied. "I'm looking for Miranda Colton. She's my sister and I was told I might find her here."

"She was here earlier," the man admitted. "I think she's gone back to the hotel where she lives."

Peter frowned. "Can you direct me?"

The man pointed out the way. "It's just down the street," he said, walking Peter to the door. "The Dawson Lucky Day Hotel. You can see it from here."

Peter nodded and this time remembered to thank the man. He hurried down the street, feeling ever more sure of his reunion. She was really here. She was only a few hundred feet away.

Initially impressed with the elegance and grandeur of the Dawson hotel, Peter sought out the clerk, giving little regard for anything else. He was grateful to know Miranda wasn't staying in some run-down madhouse.

"I'm looking for Miranda Colton. I was told she had a room here."

"Yes, sir, she does."

Peter smiled. "Wonderful. I'd like the room number."

"I'm sorry, I can't give that information to you. Miss Miranda is a proper lady and doesn't receive gentlemen in her quarters unless . . ."

"I'm her brother. She'll receive me," Peter replied, his patience wearing thin.

"Mister, a lot of folks could say they were her brother, but that still doesn't prove it."

"Is there a problem?" a man called from the stairs.

Peter turned to spy the well-dressed, dark-haired man. "Are you the manager here?" he demanded.

"I'm the owner," came the reply. "Thomas Davenport."

Peter eyed Davenport suspiciously. "I'm trying to find Miranda Colton, and if one of you doesn't start talking, I'm going to lose my temper." He approached Davenport in what he hoped was a menacing stance. The man was only an inch or two shorter than Peter's own six foot height, but Peter felt confident he had a good twenty or thirty pounds on the man. Muscled pounds at that.

"I'm afraid I cannot allow you to know her room number. I do not know you and it wouldn't be prudent . . ."

Peter grabbed Davenport by the suit coat and slammed him up against the wall. "I'm Miranda's brother, Peter Colton. If I don't get some answers, I'm going to—"

"Peter!"

Peter looked over his shoulder and saw Miranda staring

at him in disbelief. He slowly loosened his hold on Davenport, surprised by the changes he saw in his sister. Could a year have changed her so much? She looked so much older—wiser. Her brown hair was very simply pinned into a bun at the back of her head and her attire was just as plain and unassuming, but her countenance fairly glowed. She was radiant and lovely. Her cheeks were rosy and her eyes were bright with the joy of living.

Forgetting about Davenport, Peter rushed to Miranda and lifted her into the air. "Oh, but you're a sight for these eyes of mine," he declared. "It was a long and tiring journey, but here you are. I'm so blessed to find you at last."

"Peter, it's so wonderful to see you. How long have you been in Dawson?"

He put her back on the ground and laughed. "I just walked off the boat. I started searching for you from the moment my feet touched the shore. I've come to take you home. How soon can you be ready to leave?"

Miranda looked past Peter, her expression searching for something Peter couldn't quite comprehend. He turned to the Davenport man, then back to his sister. "Well? When can you be ready to leave? I told Mother I'd have you home as soon as possible."

"I'm not leaving, Peter." She walked by him and went to stand with the stranger. "Peter, I'd like you to meet my husband, Thomas Davenport. Teddy to his friends."

Peter felt as though he'd been gut punched. "Husband?"

She smiled and turned an endearing look on Teddy. "Yes, we were married on the fifth of this month. Teddy is a botanist and I've been helping him with his research. He's writing a book describing and detailing the vegetation of the area."

"I can't believe it." Peter felt the heat come to his face. Of all the nonsensical, crazy things for her to have done. No doubt a cold winter of isolation and loneliness had led her to make her choice.

"Oh, Peter, don't be angry with me. I love Teddy dearly, and he's a wonderful, godly man. You'll come to love him as well."

"This is madness. You can't possibly know this man well enough to have married him."

"Peter, if you'll recall, you once told me you fell in love with Grace upon first setting your gaze upon her—how was it you put it?—'angelic features'? You surely haven't been gone so long you don't remember how it feels to first fall in love?"

Peter winced. How could she so flippantly mention his dead wife? Didn't she know the pain he'd suffered because of his actions? "I suppose I didn't think of it like that," he said, at a loss for any other way to explain his thoughts.

Miranda's expression softened. "Please be happy for me, Peter. I'm so very content with my new life. Please don't be angry."

Peter saw her joy and knew he couldn't be upset with her. His chance for true love might be gone forever, but he shouldn't wish it away for Miranda. "I'm not angry, just surprised. I would never have imagined in a hundred years that you would meet and marry that quickly."

Miranda laughed. "Well, neither did I. But Teddy saved my life, and I lost my heart to him."

"Then it would seem I made this trip for naught," Peter said, feeling suddenly dejected. The excitement of the trip north and the anticipation of finding his sister faded in light of this new discovery.

"How can you say that? What about Grace?" Miranda asked, leaving Teddy's side. "What of your wife?"

If he hadn't known better, Peter would have thought she was angry with him. "What of her?" Peter asked softly. His heart felt raw at the very sound of her name.

"What of her? Don't you care about her? Why worry about me when you should be focused on finding her?"

"That's rather impossible, don't you think?" Peter said, feeling defensive.

"Why should it be? I've been searching for her, as well as the Ivankovs, since coming to Dawson. I did manage to run across one of our party, but he died in the hospital just a few days back."

Peter felt confused by her words. "Are you suggesting that it's possible to find Grace? What do you mean? Surely you won't find Grace here."

"Why not? This is where the party was headed. I expect her to be near to this vicinity, even if she's not here in the city. Of course, thirty thousand people venturing in and out of the city makes our work that much harder, but . . ."

Peter shook his head. "This is madness. What are you telling me?"

Miranda looked at him oddly. "I'm saying that Grace is somewhere nearby. She's probably no more than a day or two in any direction."

"But that's impossible. She was lost on Lake Laberge. We received a letter stating this from the Mounties."

Miranda blanched. "No, Peter. I was the one who went overboard on the lake. I was lost in a storm and washed ashore. They don't even know I'm alive, because I've not been able to find them to let them know. Some native people found me and took me to Teddy. He helped nurse me back to health with the aid of a wonderful old Indian woman. As far as I know, because my friend who died just a while back told me so, the rest of the party is fine."

Peter sat down hard on the staircase. He felt dizzy, sickeningly dizzy. "You're saying that Grace is alive?"

Miranda came and sat down beside him. "Teddy, get him some water, please."

Teddy went off to do as she asked while Miranda took Peter's hand in hers. "Peter, I'm so sorry. I didn't realize you'd believed her dead all this time."

He shook his head back and forth, hoping to clear his vision. Tears came unbidden to his eyes. Could it really be true? *Dear God, how many times have I pleaded for it to be true? Have you given me the miracle I asked for?*

Teddy returned and handed Peter the glass of water. Peter drank it down without pause and handed it back to Teddy. "This is so incredible. So wonderful and awful at the same time. If only I'd known she was alive—if only I could have come sooner."

"Peter, there's something else you should know," Miranda said, looking quite serious. "It's probably going to come as quite a shock, but you must hear it from me."

Peter felt his chest tighten. What could she possibly say that was so important in light of the news she'd already given him?

"What is it? Tell me everything."

Miranda took a deep breath. "Not very long before I fell overboard in the storm on Lake Laberge, Grace made an announcement to our group. Peter, Grace was expecting a child."

The news was impossible to comprehend. Peter leaned back against the stairs and stared in dumbfounded silence. A baby? Grace was to have his child? The misery he'd known—the anguish he'd endured—seemed to fall away in light of this latest declaration.

Grace was alive, and he was to be a father.

⊣ C H A P T E R T W E N T Y - T W O ⊢

"THE WAY I SEE IT," Teddy began over breakfast, "we can put out word that Peter is here searching for Grace. As miners come in from their claims and new folks go out to find gold for themselves, we can pass the word."

"That can only help," Miranda agreed. "After all, it will be far easier to locate Grace if we enlist the help of the local folk."

"What about checking with the government?" Peter questioned. "Don't they have to keep records of who has a gold claim?"

Miranda took a sip of tea and nodded. "They do keep records, but I've already checked. I figured the claim would be under Ivankov. I even checked Colton, but there was only one name listed, and it was completely unrelated."

"Since she was already expecting when we parted

company in Skagway," Peter said, "then she would have already delivered the baby. Are there no records for that? Surely she would have gone to the hospital."

"Not in Dawson," Miranda said. "There aren't many facilities that cater to women, but even when they do, they cost more than you could imagine. I heard a woman say the other day that she would have to pay fifteen hundred dollars to have a baby in the hospital. I know from our earlier days on the journey north that we never had enough money for Grace to deliver in a hospital. Now, if they struck it rich upon arriving in Dawson, then perhaps. We can always ask around."

"It was so simple to find you. Why can't it be just as simple to find her?" Peter pushed his food around absentmindedly. Never mind that he was privileged to have some of the first fresh eggs available in Dawson since the onset of winter.

"We'll commit it to prayer," Miranda said. "I've been praying all along, but now that you're here . . . well, maybe that was just what God was waiting for."

Peter suppressed a yawn. Apologizing, he shrugged. "I didn't sleep well last night."

"Of course you didn't," Teddy replied. "I can't say that I would sleep a wink if Miranda were lost to me—no matter how temporary."

"The thing is," Miranda continued, "I feel almost certain the party will return to Dawson for supplies. There's also Queen Victoria's birthday celebration tomorrow. Not many people will miss that, even if there are more Americans in Dawson than territorial folks."

"Do you suppose they'll come for the celebration?" Peter

asked. His tone betrayed his eagerness.

"Up here, folks can't afford to miss out on a good party. The eating is always better, and the company breaks the tedium of the long winter. I think we should position ourselves throughout the town and spread the word," Miranda answered.

"I say!" Teddy exclaimed. "Let's offer a reward. I'll put up the money. Maybe folks will be inclined to dig deep into their memory if something profitable is at stake."

"That's awfully generous of you. I have funds of my own—back in San Francisco. I could easily reimburse you."

"Nonsense. I should have thought to do this earlier. Miranda has been so faithful in her search. I don't know why it didn't come to me before now."

Miranda patted Peter's forearm. "We will do what we can. One way or another, we'll find her. I feel certain of it now that you're here."

Miranda didn't expect Peter's appearance at her door. The hour was late and she figured it to be Teddy, so she opened the door wearing her nightgown and shawl.

"Peter! What are you doing here at this hour?"

"I couldn't sleep. I heard Teddy tell you he'd be late working with the bookkeeper, so I thought maybe we could talk for a minute."

"Sure, come on in."

Miranda closed the book she'd been reading and put it on a small table. She motioned to two chairs on either side of the table. "Have a seat and tell me what's on your mind."

Peter sat quickly and looked at the book Miranda had

been reading. "Botany?" He looked up at her with a quizzical expression.

Miranda grinned and took her own chair. "I figure if I'm to be a help to my husband, I need to understand his line of work. I find it all quite fascinating."

Peter shook his head and smiled. A bit of the haggard look left him and Miranda felt encouraged. She worried about her brother. She knew he had been dealt a terrible shock and she actually feared it might wreak havoc with his mind. Men had gone crazy over things of less consequence. Peter had always prided himself on being the patriarch— even savior—of his family. She was certain this new revelation was a shock.

"So what did you want to talk about?" she asked softly.

"Grace."

Miranda nodded. It was the first time since Peter's arrival that they'd had a chance to be alone. *Peter must have a million questions.* Miranda only hoped she could offer him satisfactory answers.

"Did she hate me after I left?"

Shaking her head, Miranda tried hard to be reassuring. "No. Not once did she ever say anything that would suggest such a thing. Quite the contrary, in fact. She would often cry . . ." her words trailed off.

"Go on, I need to hear it all," Peter urged. "I know the truth isn't always pleasant."

"She cried a great deal after you left. She wouldn't let anyone near her know it firsthand, but we heard her crying and saw her reddened eyes." Miranda lowered her gaze and bit her lip. She knew Peter wanted the truth, but she wanted so much to spare him the pain.

"Grace never stopped loving you," she said finally. "She only wanted you to love her—to love God. She knew you two would be destined for misery if you didn't find the truth of God to be valid for your life."

"I know," Peter replied. "She was a very wise woman."

"She still is," Miranda said. "You have to stop talking about her in the past tense. She's alive. I know she is. I know we will find her, Peter. I feel very confident of this."

"I'd like to have that confidence for myself. It just seems that this is all a very bad dream. A dream sprinkled with teasing clues that refuse to allow me to solve the puzzle."

"I know it's difficult. Here I've been fretting that you and Mother and Father believed me to be dead, and all along you've been mourning the loss of your wife. I'm so sorry."

"I'm the one who's sorry. I've made a mess of things," Peter said, burying his face in his hands. "Tell me about your accident—when you were lost on the lake."

Miranda tried to remember back to those early days. "I really don't know what happened. I know there was a storm, but I don't remember falling overboard. I can't tell you much of what happened in the weeks that followed, either. I simply don't remember.

"I do remember waking up in Teddy's cabin. Nellie, the Indian woman who helped him, cared for me. She was so gentle. I remember she had these pudgy, calloused hands, but she was infinitely tender. It taught me a lot about not judging people by their looks."

"How so?"

Miranda smiled and gazed at the ceiling. "I think I always looked at things—the appearance of things—and judged for myself their value. Not in a malicious manner, mind you, but rather in a way so as to determine if I was safe—if the circumstance was prudent."

"Those are good things," Peter said. "I wish I'd been more cautious about a great many things."

"Sometimes we can be overly cautious. Sometimes we are afraid to live life."

"And sometimes we're not afraid enough."

Just then Teddy returned from his office work. He looked to Miranda and seemed to instantly understand the situation. He motioned to the bedroom door and then to himself as if to suggest he could slip away if she needed him to. Miranda shook her head and motioned him to join them.

"Come sit with us, Teddy."

At this Peter looked up, and there were tears in his eyes. Miranda was nearly undone by their appearance. She had always seen her brother as the strong one, the leader whose confidence was never shaken. Now, here he was, fallen from his pedestal, flesh and blood just like everyone else.

"I'm sorry. I was just leaving," Peter said, getting to his feet.

"Don't leave on my account," Teddy interjected. "We've a holiday tomorrow, remember? We can sleep late if the noise in the town doesn't get us up with the dawn." He smiled, then sobered. "Seriously, if you'd like to stay, I can send for tea."

"No," Peter said, moving toward the door. "What I really need is to spend some time in prayer."

Miranda got up and followed him to the door. "If you need me, I'm here. Please let me be there for you, as you've always been there for me. Being the strong one all the time must be an exhausting endeavor."

Peter smiled sadly. "I believe God has broken me of my craving for control. Now, all I long for is my wife and child."

Miranda closed the door after he'd gone and locked it. Shaking her head, she looked to Teddy for strength and support. "I just don't know if he can bear this."

"He'll have to. Pride is a harsh mistress," he said, coming to wrap her in his embrace. "So, too, is obsession."

Miranda looked up to meet his gaze. Puzzled by his words she asked, "What are you saying?"

"I'm saying, I've long been devoted to an obsessive desire. It almost cost me your love. I've been driven to work on this book—to fulfill my father's dreams. I thought that if I brought this book to life, it would in some small way give life back to my father."

"You loved him very much, didn't you?"

"As much as a boy can love his hero. I adored my mother, for she was fun-loving and sweet and gentle, but my father was the man I wanted to grow up to be. My mother never understood his passion, but I did. Not because it was plants and flowers—but because it was so much a part of him. It was his desire as much as she was."

"Didn't she try to understand?" Miranda questioned.

"I don't know. I think she must have. After all, she would tolerate the trips to Cornwall. But my father was always very much alone in his work. It was one of the reasons I took up the interest. I wanted to be close to him—to let him know that someone understood and cared."

"That's why I want to help you with your research. I know what this project means to you."

"I'm glad you know, because what I want to say—to offer—is given out of my deepest love for you."

"I don't understand, Teddy. What are you talking about?"

"I'm saying that instead of leaving next week for the cabin, we'll stay here and help Peter search for Grace. We'll purchase supplies and horses, and we'll hit the trail and look up and down every creek where they've had even so much as a dusting of gold."

Miranda knew the cost of Teddy's gift. Her heart swelled with joy and love for this man—her husband. That he would sacrifice for her in this manner was all the proof she needed that she had done the right thing in marrying him.

"Oh, Teddy, you are more wonderful than I can find words to say." She wrapped her arms around his neck and pressed his head down. Ardently, she kissed him, pouring out all her emotions in that one action.

He moaned and pulled her tight against him. Miranda felt him sink his hands into her hair. Pulling her head back gently with one hand, he used his free hand to gently touch her cheek. At this, Miranda opened her eyes.

"You may not have the words to say," Teddy said in a low, husky voice, "but I think I understand your meaning just the same."

The celebration started early, as expected, but it didn't awaken Peter. He had been awake for hours. In his mind he kept replaying the news that Miranda had given him. Grace was alive. She hadn't died as he had thought. She'd lived an entire winter in the Yukon. She'd carried his child—alone. Given birth—again alone.

He had no way of knowing if the baby was a boy or a girl, or even if it had lived. The uncertainty threatened his sanity. He had always considered himself a strong, sound-minded man, but now he questioned that.

He tried to pray, but he felt there was a wall between him and God. Why did God seem so far away? Peter had given his trust to Him—claimed Jesus for his Savior. So why did it seem he was standing here alone?

A carnival-like atmosphere was going on outside the hotel, but Peter could barely muster the interest to pull back the drapes and see what was happening. Outside, the entire world seemed to have put on its Sunday best. Women wore ribbons and feathers and gowns more beautiful than he'd seen in some time. The men were equally bedecked in their finest suits or at least their cleanest jeans.

An audience had gathered around one man who was juggling while balancing on a unicycle. Not far from this group, another collection of folks were intrigued by an acrobatic act.

There were barkers calling out their wares. Everything from food to colorful banners declaring best wishes to Queen Victoria could be had for a price. Peter despaired of stepping into the madness in hopes of finding Grace. The crowd was growing by the minute, and it was barely past nine.

"Peter?" Miranda called out as she knocked on his door.

Peter found his sister dressed smartly in a red-and-green plaid skirt and white blouse. Her hair had been perfectly coifed and her face was bright with the radiance of a woman in love. She looked the epitome of a reserved and proper lady. Their parents would be proud to know her manners and upbringing had not been forgotten in the Yukon.

"Are you ready to venture out? There are all sorts of planned events—pie-eating contests, ax throwing, and races, to name a few. People are so happy at the new shipments of food and supplies that, whether the queen had a birthday or not, we'd no doubt have a party."

Peter took up his jacket and pulled it on. "I'm nervous," he admitted. "I'm terrified and excited all at the same time. I've never felt so lost."

Miranda cocked her head to one side and looked at him rather quizzically. "Lost in what way?"

"I tried all night to pray—to seek guidance so that today I might do exactly the right thing. But I feel as if God isn't listening. I just feel . . . alone."

"Oh, Peter, I know how you feel. I went through that myself when I woke up at Teddy's cabin. There I was, with a man who hardly even knew I existed and an old Indian woman who barely spoke my language. I prayed and nothing seemed to make sense. But just when things seemed as lost and hopeless as they could be—God always sent me a sign."

"What kind of sign?"

"It all depended on the situation," Miranda admitted. "But when I felt my lowest—when I gave up and left it in God's hands—things were accomplished."

"So you're telling me to do nothing?"

"Not at all," Miranda said, reaching up to touch Peter lovingly. "I'm saying commit it to the Lord, and be assured that He hears you. Sometimes His ways are obscured and foreign to us—but it doesn't mean He isn't there. It doesn't mean He isn't listening."

"I know you're right. I feel like I have nothing left to give."

Miranda nodded. "When you get to the place where Jesus is all you have," she said with a smile, "you'll find that Jesus is all you need."

Peter pondered her words as they made their way out into the streets. Teddy waited for them at the entryway of the hotel. He beamed Miranda a smile, warming Peter's heart. At least Miranda was happy. He could see that. He couldn't have picked a better mate for her than she'd chosen for herself.

The crowd grew, and by noon Peter was convinced that no fewer than twenty thousand people had flooded the muddy streets. He had asked what seemed like ten thousand of that number if they knew of his wife, but no one seemed to have a clue about the dark-eyed beauty.

"Any news?" Miranda asked, coming with Teddy from across the street.

"No. No one knows her."

"We've not had any better time of it," Miranda said. She came to stand beside Peter while Teddy excused himself to go back to the hotel.

"I'll rejoin you both in about an hour," he told them. "I have an appointment that is of great importance."

Miranda waited until he'd gone before turning to Peter. "He's considering selling the hotel. He's been talking to some of his friends, and they believe the new finds of gold in Nome are going to send most of the people west. They worry that Dawson will dwindle back to nothing."

"Where will you go, then?"

Miranda shrugged. "I don't know. We still have work to do in this area. Teddy's entire focus for the past few years has been to compile this book on the plant life of Canada. He's rearranged his thinking, however, and now he seems more inclined to consider other possibilities."

"Such as?" Peter asked, as a man jostled him from behind. "Hey there, buddy," Peter said, turning to suggest the man go elsewhere with his rowdiness.

"I said you're a liar," the man called out, ignoring Peter. He turned away from Peter to throw a punch.

Peter quickly grabbed hold of his arm. "I'd appreciate it if you did your fighting elsewhere."

"That's it, mister, hold him for me," another man called out, rushing them.

Peter was appalled to see that Miranda stood directly in the line of fire, and rather than concern himself with the man he held, Peter threw himself in front of his sister and took a blow full on the mouth.

Blood spurted out of Peter's mouth, along with a tooth. He reached up in agony as Miranda screamed. The two men, seeing they'd caused a fuss that clearly couldn't benefit them, slipped into the crowd and were gone before Peter could gather his wits.

"Peter, are you all right?"

"I have a horrible pain in my jaw. I think that ninny loosened up every tooth in my mouth."

"Say there, son, I'm a dentist. Why don't you come with me? My office is just a couple of blocks away," a man urged, taking Peter's elbow.

"Yes," Miranda encouraged. "Let's go with him, Peter."

Peter reluctantly allowed himself to be led away. He could hardly think clearly, and his mouth hurt fiercely. A fire had started somewhere in his jaw and had traveled down his neck.

"Come on, right in here," the man said, pointing Peter to his office. The man opened the door and motioned Peter to the dental chair.

"Just sit back and I'll get some water and a bowl so we

can rinse your mouth and see what's what."

The dentist moved quickly around the room, gathering what he needed. He offered Peter a glass of water and a bowl in which he could spit. Peter rinsed his bloody mouth several times, fearing each time that he would spit teeth out with the water.

Finally the dentist went to work. "Ah, it doesn't look too bad. Knocked out one of the back molars and it's bleeding a good bit. Loosened up the others, but they'll firm up again when the swelling goes down and the tissue has a chance to heal." He looked down at Peter. "I'm Dr. Brummel, by the way."

"Peter Colton," Peter managed to say when the dentist took his hands out of his mouth long enough to reach for a clean towel.

"Colton, eh? I know a couple of Coltons. Are you related to a Mrs. Grace Colton?"

Miranda dropped her handbag and stared at the man, while Peter came up out of the chair. "I'm her husband. I'm here looking for her." His hand went to his mouth as pain shot through his jaw. "Do you know where she is?"

"Sit back down, son. You're in no shape to go jumping around. I don't know where Grace is now. She lived with us for a time after her son was born."

"Son?" Dizziness overcame Peter as he sunk into the chair. "I have a son?"

"You sure do. Didn't you know? Well, I guess the mail being what it is, a fellow can't expect to hear anything in a timely manner. Yes, sir, you have a fine boy. She named him Andrew, but we all called him Andy."

Peter didn't even feel the procedure as the doctor

continued to work him over. He had a son. "How long ago did Grace leave you?" Peter asked.

"Well, now, let me think. I believe it was March—might have been April. No, I'm thinking March. She met up with her friend—a right nice fellow name of Ivankov. He'd come to town to bring another friend of his to the hospital and then pick her and the baby up. It was still pretty cold, but they said something about only having a two-day trip by dog sled."

"Two days?" Peter looked to Miranda. "Can we get a map and have Teddy help us draw a perimeter that would mark the distance of two days surrounding Dawson?"

"I know we could. Teddy would be happy to help. He knows the land around here very well. He's already explored a good portion of it."

Peter eased up out of the chair as Dr. Brummel concluded his treatment. "Come back in a week and let me take another look just to make sure everything is doing what it's supposed to be doing."

"What do I owe you?" Peter questioned.

"Not a thing," Brummel replied. "Your wife was a joy to my household. My wife and I very much enjoyed her company and that of the baby."

Peter squared his shoulders. He felt his hope return. God had given him the sign he so desperately needed. Looking to Miranda, he smiled, and she smiled in return. *"Weeping may endure for a night,"* he thought, remembering the scripture, *"but joy cometh in the morning."*

Part Three

AUGUST 1899

I have fought a good fight,
I have finished my course,
I have kept the faith.

II TIMOTHY 4:7

┤CHAPTER TWENTY-THREE├

YUKON SUMMER WAS A SPLENDID thing to be certain, but Peter saw little in the way of the beauty around him. Desperation marred his vision as he traveled with Miranda and Teddy from one creek to another. There were gold mines staked out at hundreds, maybe thousands of locations along creeks and rivers too numerous for Peter to count.

They searched the banks of creeks called Bonanza, Eldorado, Skookum, Nugget, Too Much Gold, and All Gold. Back trails wound their way through defoliated lands where miners had made roughhewn cabins or pitched their tents.

They found men who were worn-out and ready to pack it in and men who were wealthy beyond their wildest dreams. What they didn't find was Grace or any sign of the Ivankov party.

"They have to be close," Miranda told her brother. She

was trying desperately to keep up his spirits. "We've already checked so many different camps, I'm sure we'll find them soon. Teddy says there's a lot of activity on Hunker Creek. We can head there after returning to Dawson for more supplies."

"I'm beginning to think we've made a mistake in searching. Maybe it would have been better to just stay in town and wait for them to come to us. After all, everyone needs fresh supplies from time to time," Peter said, his tone dejected.

"Perhaps, but we've already talked to most of the storekeepers, and they allowed us to put up those flyers you suggested. If any of the party should venture into Dawson, they're certain to spy one of them."

"Maybe, but I just feel like I'm wasting my time out here," Peter said, kicking the dirt. "I'm not finding what I'm searching for any more than most of the rest of those men out there."

"They may never find what they're looking for, Peter, but I feel confident that you will find Grace."

Peter shook his head. "I can't claim your confidence. I wish I could, but it's been months. It's August now. The bugs have been fierce. The nights have grown cold, the sun is waning to the south, and even though there are plenty of hours of light left each day, it's clear that the weather will turn on us in the weeks to come."

"But that's weeks, Peter. You can't give up." She reached out to take hold of his arm. "God is still with you. He hasn't left you to fend alone."

Peter sat down on a rock. "I know that." He stared off in the direction Teddy had gone only moments ago. "How long do you suppose Teddy will be gathering plants?"

"Not long," Miranda said, coming to sit beside him. "Are you that anxious to get back on the trail?"

"I'm anxious to be at the end of the trail. I'm anxious to be done with the search."

Adrik had never seen Gump happier. The gold was proving itself with every new dig into the earth. The panning hadn't been nearly as productive, although it had yielded a little gold flake now and then. No, it had taken the rigged-up steam contraption and thawing of the land to really find the gold. At first, it had taken hours of backbreaking work—steaming, digging, hauling, and then sluicing and sorting—all to find a bit of gold now and then. But finally the gold was coming in more readily than it had before and Gump declared them all rich as kings.

The only problem was that strange things continued to happen around the camp. From time to time Leah or Grace would mention seeing someone darting in and out of the trees just to the back of their camp. Sometimes Adrik would go outside and find the cache door open and the dogs barking up a storm. Other times he would find something else amiss. But always there were footprints in the dirt to suggest the culprit wasn't a four-legged beast.

Because of this, Adrik had taken to keeping a guard on duty twenty-four hours a day. Gump took guard duty during the day while Adrik and Jacob worked. Adrik then went to sleep right after supper and allowed Jacob to take the first watch. Then around two in the morning, Jacob would wake Adrik for his turn. Since posting the men, there had been little disturbance, and that was just how Adrik wanted to keep it—especially now that they had accumulated several thousand dollars in nuggets and gold dust.

"I'm going out," Jacob said, checking the Winchester to make certain it was loaded.

"God be with you," Adrik said, same as every night. "You'd better wear your jacket. Felt like the wind was going to shift. Wouldn't be surprised if we were in for an early cold spell."

Jacob nodded and grabbed his coat on the way out the door.

"Do you think we'll have to continue standing watch until we leave?" Karen asked as she sat down at the table. She took up some mending and began working.

"I think it's probably going to keep us on the safe side of things," Adrik answered. He yawned and stretched. "Well, I think I'll head to bed." He got up, then crossed to where Karen sat.

She lifted her face and smiled. "I'll be glad when all of this is behind us. I miss sharing a bed."

Adrik nodded. The separation hadn't been his favorite development either. But it seemed only prudent to do things this way. Karen had taken to sleeping in the single upper berth, allowing the men to alternate using the lower bunk as they came and went in the night. Gump kept his own upper berth without the need to share it as he had done throughout the previous winter months.

"When are we going to leave?" Leah asked. She came from the kitchen area, where she'd finished cleaning up after supper.

"I don't know, sweetheart," Adrik said smiling. She was such a pretty little thing, and he worried incessantly about keeping her out in the wild among the miners and no-accounts. Karen schooled her every day as best she could, but they had no materials to make the situation very productive. At least the Bible afforded good reading.

"I hope we'll go south before the snows come," she said rather sadly.

Adrik studied her for a moment, not expecting her solemnity. "Why is that?"

"Well, Jacob said that with his share of the gold we'd buy Papa a gravestone. I want to make sure we do that before we lose the money or spend it somewhere else."

Touched by her request, Adrik nodded. "We'll do our best to get back to Skagway before the snow sets in."

"Jacob said we could always hire a dog sled to take us to the train. He said we'd be rich enough to buy tickets for the train and still be able to buy a real nice stone."

"That is an idea," Adrik replied. "I'll sleep on it and see what I come up with."

He slipped off his boots, then crawled into the berth, carefully arranging the blankets that draped out the light. Sometimes the heat made sleeping uncomfortable, but the light made it worse. The sky would be light until nearly midnight, wreaking havoc with their sleep patterns. Gump had made shutters for the few windows, but the light still seemed to permeate the room—peeking in through the door cracks and places where the chinking had fallen out.

Settling against the pillow, Adrik sighed. *Lord*, he began to pray, *I ask that you help me to make the right decisions. I see the needs of my loved ones, and I want to make it right for each one. I want to find Peter Colton for Grace and little Andy. I want to bring Bill Barringer back to life for his children. I want to be alone with my wife for weeks on end, with no one but each other for company.*

The future held many questions and few answers, as far as Adrik was concerned. Gump had already told him of his desire to sell his half of the claim and be out by the end of September. He had plans to head back to his parents' farm. He wanted to see his brothers and find out whether his folks still lived. Adrik couldn't blame him for that. It did pose a problem, however. Should they just sell the entire claim to strangers and take what they could get?

The gold was showing good color. Was it wise to leave now, just when the getting was good? Adrik turned restlessly and sighed again. Sleep would be hard in coming.

Jacob didn't mind standing watch in the evening. The summer sun kept things light for long into his watch, and by the time the skies darkened it was nearly time to wake Adrik for his shift.

The time alone gave him a chance to think things through—to make decisions about his future, and Leah's future, too. He wanted to get back to Colorado before the winter set in. He'd thought about that decision for a long time and knew that he had obligations to see to.

First, he would buy a stone for his father's grave. Then he would take Leah and return to Colorado to buy a stone for their mother's grave. After that, he hadn't figured out what was to be done. While Peter Colton had once offered him a job with his shipping firm, that didn't take care of what to do with Leah. Besides, no one had seen Peter Colton in some time. The offer of a job might not stand at this point.

Walking the perimeter of the claim was easy. It wasn't very big, and because other claims butted up against it, it was within easy walking distance of the neighbors. There were rumors among the creek folk that the Ivankov party had hit it big and thus the reason for the rotating guard duty. Adrik thought it best not to explain that their worries were related to the stolen sled and the unwelcome visits that followed.

Jacob had told Adrik about the stranger who'd come when Adrik had taken Gump to Dawson. The story hadn't set well with the older man. Apparently Karen hadn't told him about it, but then, she'd been caught up in the reunion with Miss Grace. It was after that when Adrik started keeping a closer eye on the strangers who passed through the area. Gold brought out the thieving in men, he'd said, and Jacob could see that it was true. Why, just the day before there'd been a big fight among four brothers across the creek. There had been enough noise to raise the dead before it was all over. And all because the youngest brother felt the other three were cheating him out of his rightful share of gold.

Gold. How he hated the very word.

Jacob had seen his mother, sister, and father suffer because of gold and silver. He wanted to be done with it all— to be rid of such nonsense. He wanted to work at a regular job with regular pay and have a home.

A noise behind the cache caught his attention. Several of the dogs began to bark. Jacob immediately moved to the area, but found nothing amiss. *It might have been a bear*, he told himself.

Like many of their neighbors, Gump and Adrik had built the cache with two purposes in mind. One, the raised platform and enclosed storage area for their bulk food provided protection from wild animals. It also allowed them to store tools and other things that had become too plentiful in a house filled with seven people. Down below, Adrik and Gump had arranged a makeshift pen alongside the support posts for the cache. Here they quartered the dogs, while under the raised platform they found a perfect place to shelter the sled. Jacob felt certain that should anyone try to steal from them, the dogs would be the first to know, and from their apparent irritation, something had caused them to feel threatened.

The dogs quieted momentarily, then began letting up a wild howl, yipping toward the stand of trees behind them.

"Who's there?" Jacob called, leveling the Winchester. "Come out, or I'll start shooting."

"Whoa there, boy. I didn't save your life in Whitehorse just to get myself shot." A figure emerged from the shadows, and Jacob recognized the man as Cec Blackabee. Cec had indeed saved his life. It had been while Jacob was working in Whitehorse at Cec's saloon that Adrik had found him.

"What are you doing sneaking around our cache?" Jacob asked, lowering the rifle. "Don't you know it's foolish to threaten another man's supplies?"

The wiry old man stepped closer and Jacob could see he carried his own rifle and pack. Cec looked thinner to Jacob, maybe even sickly. He had a scruffy look to him that suggested it'd been months since he and a bath had exchanged pleasantries.

"I wasn't so much threatenin' your supplies as trying to reclaim my own," Cec replied.

"What are you talking about?" Jacob asked warily. The

old man was up to something underhanded. He could almost see it in his expression.

Licking his lips, Cec struck a casual stance as he leaned back against the trunk of a tree. "Well, it's like this, son, I came north after you left me. I figured to do me some gold pannin'."

"Thought you said there was more gold in whiskey than panning," Jacob interjected.

"I thought so, too. Maybe still think that, but I had a chance to make it big. Had me a partner who figured we could do well with a claim he'd discovered. He sold me half, and I sold off the bar to pay him his share. Then the double-crosser took off with our supplies. He stole our sled and dogs and left me for dead. If I hadn't been found by a Mountie on patrol, I probably would have froze to death."

"What's that have to do with us?"

The dogs continued to yip and howl at the intrusion, causing Jacob to motion Cec away from the pen. This quieted the dogs a bit. Jacob was surprised their barking hadn't roused Adrik by now. "I don't see what you need with us. Your ex-partner isn't here."

"No, I know that full well," Cec replied. "But he sold off our sled, and you folks ended up with it."

"The sled we bought was stolen . . ." Jacob stopped and looked Cec in the eye. "It was you, wasn't it? You're the one who took it."

"I did it, but it was mine to begin with. He had no right sellin' it off like that. He took all my gear and I figured he might have sold that to you as well."

Jacob shook his head. "No. The sled was all we bought."

"There weren't nothin' else? No sled box?"

Jacob wasn't about to tell Cec that they had a baby inside the house sleeping in the sled box, so he shrugged. "Could be, I don't remember too clearly. Adrik bought a lot of things in Dawson that day."

"Look, boy," Cec said, moving closer. The dogs didn't like the threat to Jacob and picked up barking again. Cec looked around him as if to make certain they were alone. "I'll give you a good amount of money if you'll help me get that sled box back."

"What's so important about it?"

"Call it sentimental value," Cec said, grinning.

"No," Jacob replied. "I don't want anything to do with you, and I certainly don't want anything to do with anything illegal."

"Now, hold off there, boy. Who said it were illegal?"

Jacob backed up a step in order to be able to better maneuver his rifle. "If it's not illegal, you won't mind coming inside to tell Adrik and Gump your story."

"We don't need to go bringin' them in on this. I thought you and me were friends. After all, I saved your life."

Jacob nodded. "Yeah, but Adrik paid you for your trouble."

"Look, I can make it worth your time if you just help me out."

"The truth, Cec. I want the truth."

The old man scratched his jaw and spit. "Well, guess it does no harm to tell you. That box held some important papers—a claim deed and a map. I need them."

"I never saw anything like that. The man who sold us the sled must have taken them out first," Jacob replied.

"Jacob! Jacob, what's going on out there?"

Jacob breathed a sigh of relief and turned toward the cabin. It was Adrik. "I'm out back, Adrik. Come quick."

Cec pushed Jacob forward, causing him to fall flat on his face. By the time he got to his feet, the older man was gone and Adrik was rounding the corner of the cabin.

"What's got those dogs all riled?"

"Cec Blackabee," Jacob answered. "Remember him? He's the guy who saved my life—the one you paid so you could take me out of Whitehorse?"

"Sure, I remember."

"Well, he was here. And get this, Adrik, he's the one who stole the sled. My guess is he's also the one who's been nosing around here these past months."

"Did he say what he wanted?"

"Yeah. He told me his partner had done him wrong. Said the sled and sled box were stolen along with his other sup- plies, and he wanted them back. That the box contained some papers—a claim. Adrik, he offered to make it worth my time if I helped him retrieve it."

"Did you let on that we had it?"

Jacob shook his head and picked up his rifle. "No."

"Well, that's good." Adrik looked toward the trees with a worried expression.

"I kind of doubt he'll come back tonight," Jacob said. "He seems more of a coward than I remember. I suggested he tell you about all this, but he wanted nothing to do with that."

Adrik turned back to face Jacob. "You did good, son. I'm proud of you."

Jacob warmed under his praise. Adrik had become a sur- rogate father to him, and he'd learned a great deal from the man. "So what do we do now?"

Adrik took one final glance back at the trees, then put his arm around Jacob and started for the house. "I think we'd better take another look at that sled box."

⊣ CHAPTER TWENTY-FOUR ⊢

THE SLED BOX, however, proved to be nothing special at all. It was five simple, thin pieces of pine, nailed together with a hinged top to complete it. Adrik had taken the top off, in order to make a bed and play area for Andy.

"I can't figure why this would get anyone too excited," Adrik said, shaking his head.

"It's this place that gots 'em all messed up," Gump threw in. "The darkness made men mad, and long hours of light do no better. The vinter leaves 'em cold and hungry for the gold and a decent meal—it's more than enough to make a man foolish."

"I quite agree," Adrik said, forgetting about the box.

"That's vhy I'm gettin' out. Yes, sir," Gump said, scratching his chest. "This place vants to kill me. I von't let it. I think ve got to make our choices based on vhat's best for our own bodies and mind."

"I don't blame you, Gump. I'm just not sure what Karen and I will do. I'm not sure what direction God would take us now."

And he wasn't at all convinced that the answer would easily present itself. Adrik had prayed and prayed for a sign—something to show him whether he should sell out with Gump and return to Dawson or Skagway or whether he should stay put.

"I guess we can all sleep on it," Karen suggested. "You didn't sleep, Adrik. Why don't you go back to bed?"

Adrik looked at the clock. "It's already ten. I'll just relieve Jacob early and let him have some extra rest. I need the time to think and pray on what's to be done. Gump is right. We're going to make our choices soon."

———

Karen woke up earlier than usual and lay in the bunk, listening to the sounds of the morning. Reluctantly she pushed back her covers and crawled over the edge of the bunk. She wouldn't be sorry to leave the cabin and its lack of amenities. Every day was a challenge—whether it was for lack of a proper bathroom or need of a bigger kitchen with running water. She had never worked so hard to accomplish so little.

Moving around the room as quietly as she could, Karen smiled gratefully when she saw Gump had already stoked the fire in the stove. She'd have a quick time of it putting the breakfast on with the stove already hot and ready to go.

"Karen!" Grace called from her bed. Her note of alarm brought Karen quickly.

"What's wrong?" She looked at her bleary-eyed friend and then to the lethargic baby in her arms.

"It's Andy. He's burning with fever!"

Nothing struck fear in the heart of a mother more than to see her child ill. Karen didn't have to have children of her own to realize this. She remembered only too well, fussing and fretting over Grace's bouts of illness—and Karen had only been her governess.

"Well, we can wash him in a lukewarm bath and see if that brings the fever down," Karen suggested.

Grace nodded, but worry obviously consumed her. "He will be all right, won't he? I mean, I know he's never seemed like that strong of a baby, but surely this is just something simple."

Karen wanted to encourage her friend. "Maybe it's just teething. I remember my sister telling me her children all ran high fevers while teething."

Grace seemed to relax a bit. "Yes, maybe so."

Karen went around the room gathering the things they'd need for the tepid bath. "You go ahead and get him ready. It shouldn't take too long to heat up a bit of water."

Grace began unfastening the gown Andy slept in. Karen could see that her friend's hands were shaking from nervousness. *Lord, please give her strength to face this,* Karen prayed. They'd all heard of someone down the line who'd lost a child or a loved one. Grace had already endured the loss of her husband—it seemed unusually cruel for her to be forced to deal with the loss of a baby, as well.

Karen chided herself for such dark thoughts. There was

no sense in imagining Andy dead and buried at this point, yet Karen couldn't help but worry over him. He was so precious. He offered them all the hope that one day—hopefully soon—things would work out for good and that they'd all be safely back to the places they longed to be. Karen wasn't exactly sure where that place would be for her and Adrik, but she prayed daily for God to show her.

Grace brought Andy to the tub and waited until Karen nodded her approval of the temperature. He didn't so much as stir when they placed him in the water, and that was when Karen began to worry in earnest. She remembered Aunt Doris teaching her to make a tea from the white ashes of hickory or maple wood. It was an alkaline tea that, when taken several times daily in weak portions, seemed to reduce the fever. The only trouble was, she had no opportunity to go scouting for hickory or maple trees. She didn't even know if they had such trees in the Yukon.

"Oh, Karen, he's really sick. What are we going to do?" Grace looked up at Karen, fear eating away her usually cheerful countenance.

"I don't know. I'll talk to Adrik while you keep running the water over his body."

As Karen grabbed up her shawl, she heard Leah call from behind her, wanting to know what was wrong. She didn't wait to explain the matter but instead exited the cabin in search of her husband.

"Adrik?" she called out in the morning light. "Adrik?" She circled the cabin and found him in the back near the cache.

"What are you doing out here so early?" he asked. "Couldn't bear to be away from me?" He grinned and casually rested his rifle on his shoulder.

"Andy's sick, Adrik. Really sick. He's running a high fever, and when we put him in a tub of water, he didn't even open his eyes. I'm afraid he may die if we don't get help."

Adrik's expression quickly changed. "I'll come with you, and we'll see what's to be done."

Just then Grace's scream filled the air. Adrik and Karen ran for the front of the cabin, just as Leah came running from inside. "Hurry," she cried, "Andy is shaking all over the place."

Adrik stepped ahead of Karen, but Karen dogged his heels into the cabin. There in the tub, while Grace held him, Andy jerked in a strange, spasmodic rhythm.

"He just started doing this," Grace said, tears streaming down her face. "Oh, Karen, help me. Help him!"

By this time, Gump and Jacob were up and watching. Finally, Andy's body stilled just as suddenly as the spasms had begun. Grace looked to her son and lifted him in her arms. "He's still breathing," she sobbed.

Karen went forward and gently took the baby from her friend. "Adrik, we must get him to a doctor."

"I agree. I'll get the dogs hitched to the ore cart. We'll use it to pack Grace and the baby in. It won't be a fast journey, but they certainly can't walk all the way."

"I want to come with you," Karen said, wrapping the baby in a towel.

"Me too!" Leah declared.

Adrik nodded. "Jacob, you and Gump stay here and don't worry about mining. Just keep an eye on things. I'll take them down to Gold Bottom. That's less than two miles. There's a doc who shares a claim with his brother. He ought to be able to help us."

But the doctor had already returned to Dawson, the brother told them when they arrived some time later. They were encouraged to travel on toward Dawson with the possibility of another doctor who had come north for gold, taking up residency somewhere to the west of Last Chance Creek.

Karen knew the distance was considerable, but there was really no other choice. Adrik pushed out, urging the dogs to pick up the pace. By the time they reached Last Chance, more than ten miles away, Karen was completely spent. She knew they'd have to rest for a time and was relieved when Adrik suggested the same.

Andy's fever remained high and he refused all attempts by Grace to nurse him. His lethargic state terrified the group. There was no sense to it.

Once the dogs had rested a few hours, Adrik woke Karen and Leah and told them they'd have to push on. Grace felt bad for being the only one to ride in the cart with Andy.

"There isn't room for all of us," Karen said, trying to reassure her, "and you need to keep Andy quiet. You'll also need your strength to deal with his illness."

"Karen, will you please pray?"

Karen nodded and smiled. "I already am."

They seemed to travel forever, but without a doctor to be found along the claims on Hunker Creek, they had no choice but to head on to the Klondike River and Dawson. The minutes seemed to drag by, and Karen thought she might very well collapse from the pace they kept. Adrik and the dogs seemed hardly winded, but Leah wasn't doing well. Finally Karen suggested that there might be enough room for Leah to sit with Grace in the cart, if both ladies swung their legs out over the sides. It was a rather improper display, but it worked and the proprieties were forgotten.

Karen tried to focus on praying while she walked and jogged to keep up with the cart. The path was impossible in some places, with mud and debris left behind after the swollen creeks had receded back to their banks. In other places, the path was well-worn and fairly easy to navigate, but Karen was getting more tired by the minute.

As they drew nearer civilization—although she used that term quite loosely—Karen was saddened by the state of the land. The once lush forests, full of pines and spruce and floored with thick vegetation, had been stripped of its glory. Denuded land was a stark reminder that gold came at a high price.

The natives of the area had been pushed out and away from the wealth of the rivers of gold. Karen felt bad for the way she'd seen the local natives treated. It was the same for the Tlingit and other tribes. The stampeders had come with a hunger for that which had never belonged to them. It didn't matter that a native had found the gold in the first place—it only mattered that others could come and take it away.

Karen knew her father would have hated the changes in the land. He would have mourned the passing of the beauty and would have been enraged at the treatment of the Indian people. He had loved his Tlingit brothers and sisters—had given his life in service to them. He wouldn't be pleased that Karen was a part of this maddening rush.

She wasn't pleased with herself. Seeing how people acted around her—how they fought each other for a slice of bread, how they murdered and stole from one another, all in order to have a little bit more than their neighbor. It was a sickness, a fever—every bit as deadly as Andy's.

God forgive us, Karen prayed. She knew her husband was considering what they should do for their future, but she was already coming to some of her own conclusions. She'd speak to Adrik as soon as the opportunity presented itself.

They arrived in Dawson in the late afternoon of the second day. Adrik quickly guided the team to the hospital. Karen was amazed at how dead the town seemed. There had once been people overflowing the streets and businesses, but things appeared oddly calm now. Only a few dozen souls ventured out as the group made their way through the town.

Adrik helped Grace from the cart, leaving Karen and Leah to see to each other. Karen didn't mind. She knew her husband was far more concerned for the deathly-ill baby. Karen and Leah joined hands as they followed Adrik and Grace into the hospital.

"Do you think he'll die?" Leah asked. Her tone suggested that she was near to tears.

"It's in God's hands," Karen said softly. "We've certainly done everything possible by bringing him here."

"What if the doctors can't help him?"

"I don't know," Karen said sadly. She knew Grace's entire life was caught up in that little boy. If he were to die, Grace would most likely follow him into the grave, a victim of a broken heart.

"He can't die, Karen. He just can't." Leah broke into sobs and buried her face against Karen.

Karen didn't know what to say to the child, for she felt the same way. Andrew had to live. He had to live so that Grace would have the strength to go on. He had to live so that Peter would come to them and take his family to the safety of their home far away. And that was really what Karen wanted for Grace, in spite of the pain it brought to think of being separated, perhaps forever.

The doctor refused to let anyone accompany Andy, save Grace. He directed the rest of the group to wait outside. Adrik appeared ready to argue with him, but Karen gently touched his arm and smiled.

"We can spend the time in prayer," she suggested.

And they did just that, waiting for hours on end to hear from the doctor as to what was wrong with the tiny boy. As time passed, Karen despaired of the news being good and finally excused herself from the group.

"I need to be alone for a few minutes. I shouldn't be long," she told Adrik. Walking out into the evening air, Karen marveled at the crisp, sweet scent—so different from the smells that permeated the hospital.

For several minutes she walked down the road, not at all certain where she was headed. She really had no place in particular to go, but she wanted to be away from the hospital so that she could clear her head.

"Father, we need a miracle," she prayed in a whisper. "Please heal Andy and give Grace the strength she needs to endure."

Mindless of her aching feet and sore muscles, Karen continued her walking prayer time. She had just about decided to head back to the hospital, when she spotted a woman who looked remarkably like Miranda Colton. From the distance Karen wasn't at all certain that it was Miranda, so she picked up her pace. A surge of hope coursed through her. Perhaps Miranda hadn't died.

Unable to keep up the rapid speed, Karen called out. "Miranda!"

The woman turned instantly, and then it was clear. It was Miranda! Karen hurried forward, calling her name again. "Miranda! Oh, it is you!"

Miranda put her hand to her mouth and looked as though she'd been robbed of her air.

Karen reached her and embraced her hard. "Oh, we thought you were dead."

"Is it really you?" Miranda asked softly. "I've looked so long and hard for you."

Karen pulled back and saw the tears in Miranda's eyes. "It's me. It's really me."

"We've been searching for you. We just now came back to town to gather supplies and were planning to head out again tomorrow," Miranda replied. "Did you see the flyer? Is that how you found me?"

"What flyer?" Karen questioned. "We, too, just arrived in town. Oh, Miranda, you don't know the situation at all. There's a problem. Grace needs you now, more than ever. She had her baby. It's a little boy and his name is Andrew."

"I know. I met up with Dr. Brummel. He apparently let her stay on with him for a time."

Karen nodded. "Yes. Yes, he did. Well, Andy is sick. He's at the hospital right now. You must come and help Grace stay strong. Oh, she'll be so happy to see you."

"But wait, we can't go without Peter," Miranda said, surprising Karen with her matter-of-fact statement.

"Peter is here?"

"Yes. He's been searching for Grace for months. He was beginning to think he'd never find them."

"So he knows about the baby?" Karen questioned.

"Yes. He knows. Come with me. I'll take you to him."

"Vell, I suggest five-hour shifts," Gump said as Jacob prepared to go out on watch.

"Five hours?"

"Ja, that would be enough time to sleep a bit and then be up to keep vatch."

Jacob nodded. "I think you're right. I'll wake you in five hours, then." He headed for the door, then realized he'd forgotten his rifle. "I guess it won't do me much good to go out on guard duty without a weapon."

"Ja, you might need it."

A knock sounded at the door. Gump and Jacob exchanged looks.

"Who could that be?" Jacob questioned. "You don't suppose they're back already."

"Nah, they vould just come in," Gump replied, moving to the door.

Jacob turned back to take up his gun as the urgent knock sounded again. Without picking up his rifle, he turned to see who it was as Gump opened the door.

In the blink of an eye, a gun fired straight into Gump's chest, sending the old man staggering backward. Jacob forgot what he was doing and rushed for the smoking barrel that was still stuck inside the door. The stranger cocked the rifle to fire again.

"What do you think you're doing?" Jacob cried out, grabbing the barrel.

Cec Blackabee was pulled into the cabin by the action.

The shock of his appearance caused Jacob to hesitate for just a moment. It was a moment that gave Cec the edge. Pushing Jacob backward, Cec tried to free his rifle from Jacob's hold. It did no good, however. Jacob wasn't about to let Cec have the upper hand.

The wiry man threw his weight onto Jacob, wrestling him to the ground, the gun wedged neatly between them.

"I figured if money wouldn't bring you over to my way of thinkin'," Cec growled as they fought, "fear might. I'd just as soon blow off your head as to look at you."

"You'll have to kill me before I'll let you get away with this," Jacob spat, pushing Cec off of him. Still holding on to the rifle, Jacob struggled to his feet, careful to keep the barrel pointed away from him.

The gun exploded again, the bullet narrowly missing Jacob's face. "I don't mind killin' you, boy. You've been nothin' but trouble to me. I ain't had much luck since I found you half drowned." Cec pushed Jacob off balance and struggled to cock the rifle one more time. Lowering the gun directly at Jacob, Cec smiled maliciously. "You ain't got a prayer, boy."

Before Cec could squeeze the trigger, Jacob heard someone yell.

"It's the Lindquist cabin!"

Cec turned his head just a bit, as if to ascertain where the voices were coming from. Jacob let his rage direct him. He flew across the distance to Cec and fought with all his might to wrench the gun from his hand.

Another shot fired, and by this time they could hear voices growing louder. Cec dropped his hold on the gun and darted through the smoky room and out the door before

Jacob could stop him. Standing there, the rifle in his hand, Jacob stared dumbly at the door, then turned to where Gump lay bleeding on the floor.

"Hold it right there!" a man's deep voice called out.

"Somebody grab him, he's killed the old man!" another man yelled.

Jacob turned just as two men grabbed hold of him, while a third firmly planted his fist in Jacob's face.

"Ride for the Mounties," one of the men commanded. "This boy just killed the old man."

"No doubt for his gold," someone muttered.

"No!" Jacob tried to yell, but the word came out very softly. "I didn't do it. There was someone else."

"I don't see no one else," the man replied. "Just you and the gun and the dead body. That's enough proof for me."

⫟CHAPTER TWENTY-FIVE⫠

GRACE COLTON SAT BESIDE the bed of her desperately ill son. She could find no reason in her mind or heart for why God would allow such a horrible thing to happen. Andy looked so small, so pale.

She touched him gently, stroking his cheek, so downy soft. She wondered how any mother ever found the strength to say good-bye to her child. Grace thought of her own mother and the boy she had lost. Grace had grown up without siblings—rather lonely and isolated. Her mother would rarely talk about her firstborn son, and Grace never really knew much about him, other than the devastating effect of his death.

He can't die, Lord, she prayed. *I can't bear the thought of losing him. He's my baby—my son. I've seen so much death and destruction—sorrow and pain. I just can't bear to see anymore.* She crumbled to her knees. *Please, God, hear my prayer. Please spare the life of my child.*

Grace sobbed into her hands. *Don't leave me here alone, God. Please don't leave me here alone.*

Someone touched her shoulder. At first Grace thought it was the doctor. Using the back of her sleeve, she dried her eyes and tried hard to square her shoulders. Getting to her feet with the man's help, Grace turned, only to realize the man was her husband.

"Peter." She spoke the name almost reverently. "Oh, Peter."

It had been well over a year since she'd seen him, but the time instantly fell away with the look of love in his expression. Grace thought perhaps it was a dream, or that she had gone mad, but either way, so long as he was there at her side, she didn't care.

She collapsed in his arms and buried her face against the once familiar chest. He smelled of fresh lye soap and hair tonic. As he tightened his hold on her, Grace thought she heard him draw a ragged breath. She pulled back just enough to see that he, too, was crying.

"I thought you were dead," he said.

Grace reached up her hand to touch his face. "Why would you think that?"

"Because the letter that came from the Mounted Police said it was you and not Miranda who fell overboard on Lake Laberge."

Grace shook her head. "How could that be?"

"I don't know, but I thank God you are safe and alive. You have no idea the hours I mourned your passing. The hours I pleaded with God for your return are too numerous to count. And now, here you are."

"It must have been a terrible shock to learn of Miranda," she said softly. She stroked his jaw, feeling the stubble of beard beneath her fingers. He looked so much older—he looked exhausted and spent. She feared he might even be sick. "I'm sorry about your sister."

"She's alive, Grace. There's no other way to tell you than to just come out with it. She's down the hall speaking with Karen at this very moment."

Grace let go of her husband, her voice catching in her throat. "She . . . she . . ."

Peter nodded, holding on to her shoulders. "She's alive. Apparently she washed up on the shore, and Indians found her. She was treated and cared for by an Englishman and his housekeeper. Her health was restored, and she came here to look for you and the others."

"I can't believe it. Oh, Peter, I think I need to sit down." Grace felt her vision blur and her head grow light. "I think I might very well faint."

Peter led her to a chair, but then instead of having her sit on it, he sat down himself and pulled her onto his lap. Cradling her there like a child, he held her tight. "You're as thin as a rail," he whispered, and then added, "I can't believe you're here and alive. I think of how things might have been—but I pushed it away, all because of my stubborn refusal to yield to God what was rightfully His."

Grace tried to clear her mind, but whenever she lifted her head the dizziness returned. She wanted to ask Peter a million questions but instead remained quiet. Perhaps this wasn't the time or place. For now, she could just be grateful he had come to her.

As if knowing what she needed to hear, however, Peter continued. "I cannot say the way was easy. Paxton continued to hound and plague me. I feared him more than I feared God or anyone else. He seemed to have a power to destroy my hope."

Grace nodded with a shudder, knowing only too well how Martin Paxton could be. She hoped she would never see the man again.

"In the course of my journey, God put me together with a great man named Jonas Campbell. Jonas helped me to see and understand what you'd been trying to tell me."

Grace raised up and looked at her husband. A flicker of hope warmed her heart as she met his loving gaze. "What are you saying?"

"I'm saying I'm sorry for the pain and misery I caused you—caused us. I'm saying I was wrong and that I hurt so many people because of that wrong attitude. I'm begging you to forgive me and take me back, because frankly, I don't know how to go on living without you." He paused and Grace thought he had never looked so handsome as he did in this vulnerable, apologetic state. "And I'm saying that I learned the truth of God for myself and gave my heart over to Christ."

"Oh, Peter," Grace whispered. She touched his face very gently and wiped away the tears that streamed down his cheeks. "God is so good. So faithful."

"Then you'll forgive me? Forgive me for all the ugly words, for the way I treated you?"

"I forgave you the moment they caused me pain. I love you, Peter. That didn't die in the wake of the battle, it was only bruised a bit."

She fought back her light-headedness to get to her feet. "Come here. I have someone you must meet."

Peter stood with her and went to the bed. "This is our son, Andrew. He's very sick and I don't know what the future holds in store for him. He was born last January here in Dawson."

"I know," Peter said, reaching out to touch their son. "Karen has told me all about him. He's beautiful, Grace. Thank you."

"The doctor isn't certain what's wrong. He fears it might be pneumonia or bronchitis. He says horrible things like, '*Such diseases are just stepping-stones to consumption.*' Imagine telling a mother that her child might well develop consumption. It seems most cruel."

"I'm sure he's not trying to be unreasonably macabre. Perhaps he's merely a realist. Maybe he just doesn't want you to have false hope. Maybe he doesn't know our hope is founded in God, and therefore is never false."

"I thought he might . . . might die . . . without you ever getting to see him," Grace said, stumbling on her words.

"He's a Colton. He's strong." Peter turned her in his arms. "But even if he isn't strong enough, God is. Oh, Grace, I see that now. I despaired during my search for you, feeling that maybe God was punishing me. For so long I believed you dead—your mother believes it, too."

"Oh, poor Mama!" Grace said, putting her hand to her mouth. The awfulness of the truth was settling in on her.

"We'll get a letter off to her as soon as we can," Peter promised. "There's so much more you don't know. Things that I must say, that you must know."

"What could possibly matter in light of all that you've already told me?"

Peter's expression grew very serious. "Paxton is dead. He's no longer a threat to us. He tried to make me believe you wanted a divorce. He knew things about our last fight that convinced me of his knowledge. But on the other hand, a part of me knew you would never give yourself over to him."

"He promised to return your company if I did," Grace said, shaking her head. The memory seemed as if it had taken place a million years ago.

"When I headed back to San Francisco after he told me you were dead, I found him on the same ship. There was an explosion and the ship went down. Paxton tried to leave me stranded on board, but instead, he was killed."

"Oh, the whole thing sounds just awful. Were you hurt?"

"Yes, but I healed eventually. Now Colton Shipping has been returned to the Coltons, and there is one more aspect of this story that you must know. You are a wealthy woman."

"What?" Grace could hardly believe she had understood him correctly. "For a moment I thought you said I was wealthy."

"I did," Peter said, reaching out to touch her face. "Your father protected most of his holdings by shifting everything into a trust for you. Paxton didn't find this out until your father was nearly bankrupt. When he realized he had been duped, he continued to threaten your father—promising to tell your mother and you about the affair. It's the reason Paxton suddenly showed up as your betrothed.

"When you ran away, your mother learned the truth, and Paxton was further frustrated to realize that she didn't care. She loved your father and stood by him, putting the past behind her. Realizing he'd been further thwarted, Paxton decided that the only way to get what he wanted was to go after you and force the marriage. He had documents forged to falsely proclaim his guardianship over you, then headed to Alaska once he knew where you were."

"It all makes sense now," Grace said. "But why didn't he follow me up here, if it was that important to him?"

"At first, he had no clue as to where you had gone. Then when he knew for sure you'd gone north, my guess is he was torn between whether to follow you himself or send someone after you. He was making a great deal of money in Skagway, plus he had Colton Shipping to think about. When the message came that you'd been killed, Paxton finally realized there was no hope of attaining what he'd worked so long and hard to have."

"That must have just about killed him," Grace said, glad that Paxton would have known the taste of defeat because of her. The man had been her family's undoing, and it made her feel better to know that he had been defeated.

"I'm glad he's dead," she said without thinking. "God forgive me if that is wrong, but the man was so horrible to me—to my loved ones. I feared that he'd find out about Andy and try to steal him away. I worried that he'd come here to Dawson and threaten our lives. I forgive him—I honestly do—but I'm glad it's over. I've had very little peace because of that man."

"You've had very little peace because of me as well, but I hope to remedy that. I'm not that same man, Grace. God has broken me, and I'm much better for it."

Grace wrapped her arms around Peter. "I love you so very much. I couldn't bear to lose you—again."

"You'll never lose me, darling," he whispered against her ear. "Never."

Just then Andy's faint cry could be heard. Grace nearly pushed Peter away at the sound. "Listen!"

She looked at her son and found his eyes open. His fussing was like music to her ears. Reaching out, Grace touched his forehead. The fever had broken—his skin was cool to her touch.

"Oh, Peter, he's better. This is the first time he's rallied since taking ill. Oh, thank you, God!"

Peter reached down to touch Andy's cheek. The baby began to cry a little harder at the appearance of this stranger. Grace quickly lifted her son, holding him tenderly to her breast. Andy immediately began rooting—seeming suddenly eager to nurse.

"I'd say he's hungry." Peter touched his head. "That must be a good sign."

"I'm sure it is. Oh, I'm sure it is!"

"I heard a baby's cry," Karen said, coming into the room. "Was it Andy? How is he doing?"

Miranda followed Karen and stood at the door, looking stunned. Grace felt as though she were in a dream. Karen moved beside Grace and reached out to touch Andy.

"The fever's gone," she announced.

Grace nodded. "I can scarcely believe what God has done." She felt the dizziness return to her head. "Would you please hold Andy for a moment? I'm feeling rather faint."

Karen quickly took the baby, while Peter took hold of Grace. Miranda came to her side and helped her to the chair.

"I thought you were dead," Grace whispered, tears falling anew. "I thought I'd lost my sister forever."

"I feared the same fate might well have happened to the rest of you," Miranda admitted. "I searched and searched but couldn't seem to make any headway. I couldn't find any of you. I found Crispin several months ago and he told me you were all well the last time he'd seen you. He died shortly after that, but he accepted Jesus as his Savior before he died."

"That's a great comfort," Grace said, remembering Crispin's gentle treatment of her while she labored to give birth to Andy. "I will always be fond of the man. He helped Leah deliver Andy, and for that I shall be eternally grateful. May he know peace now."

"I'm sure he does. His countenance was quite peaceful when he passed. I wish he could have been here to see us all reunited. I'm so happy, I can scarce take it in."

Grace embraced her sister-in-law with tears of joy, her heart overflowing with happiness. The lost was found and the prodigal had come home. The sick had been healed and the blessings of God's abundance flowed over them all like warm summer rain. All was right with the world once again.

"But I'm telling you, I didn't kill Gump," Jacob protested to the police officer. "He was a good friend. I wouldn't have done something like that. I had no reason."

The officer seemed unimpressed. "Did you kill Mr. Lindquist for his gold?"

"No!" Jacob declared, certain that if he spoke the truth they'd release him.

"So then did you kill him because of a disagreement?"

"I'm telling you, I didn't kill him."

The man looked at Jacob, his expression clearly betraying

his disbelief in Jacob's statement. "You say a man came to the door and shot Mr. Lindquist through the heart. After this, you wrestled the gun away from him and the man fled before anyone else could come to the scene."

"That's right. The man's name is Cec Blackabee. He admitted to stealing our sled and wanted to know if we had some of his other possessions. He figured to strong-arm his way in and take them by force."

"I see," the Mountie replied. "Then how is it that no one else saw the man leave the cabin? Upon hearing the shots fired, your neighbors came to investigate. No one saw another man leave the scene."

Jacob felt sickened by the events of the past few days. He had no idea how to make the truth any more clear. This man believed him to have murdered Gump. The poor old man was barely gone and they wanted to blame Jacob for the death.

"I'm telling you the truth," Jacob said, sitting back down on a bench in his cell. "I didn't kill Gump Lindquist. I didn't kill anybody."

———

Peter and Grace lay entwined in each other's arms that night. Sharing his bed with Grace for the first time in over a year, Peter marveled at how very right it felt. With her brown-black hair spread out upon the pillow, her chocolate-colored eyes wide, looking at him with evident adoration, Peter had never been happier.

"I thought I'd lost you forever," he whispered.

"I felt the same when you didn't come for me," Grace murmured.

"I was such a fool." He reached out and touched her cheek, then trailed his fingers down her neck. "I can't believe I risked letting you get away."

"We were both wrong—immature and inconsiderate."

"No. You were perfect," he said, shaking his head. "You only stood up for what you believed."

"Yes, but I belittled you at the same time," she admitted. "Not only that, I went behind your back to accomplish my will."

"Well, it's behind us now. We have each other and we have a son." Peter smiled at Grace's contented expression. "I can scarcely believe it."

"I know. I felt the same way for so long. When I was carrying Andy, it was like something out of a fairy tale. I couldn't believe I would really bear a child—hold him and see him as flesh and blood."

"The doctor sounded very confident of his recovery," Peter whispered, pressing his lips against the hollow of her neck.

"Yes," she half whispered, half moaned.

Peter didn't know if she was replying to his comment or his kiss. He decided not to question it and instead turned out the light.

—[CHAPTER TWENTY-SIX]—

SEPTEMBER CAME UPON Dawson with a threat of colder days to come. Miranda knew that her brother and sister-in-law were securing passage to return to California before the rivers froze and made travel a much greater risk. With Andy to think about, she knew they would take no chances.

Her heart ached at the thought of their leaving. She so enjoyed their company. Andy had regained his health, and they had taken up rooms on the floor above hers and Teddy's. It was wonderful having family so close after so many months of not knowing where they were or even if they were still alive.

Peter had seen to it that a letter was taken out in the first available mail packet. He'd included a note from Miranda to assure their parents that all was well. Miranda told her mother about Teddy and how very much in love she was with her Englishman. Still, she longed to see her mother and father—to know they were well and that her father had recovered from his heart attack.

Peter had told her about the recovery of the shipping firm. Miranda was certain that had to have been a boost to her father's health. He loved his ships and the sea, but most of all, he needed to know that his family was cared for.

Miranda looked at her reflection in the mirror. Brushing through her long brown hair, she couldn't help but think how the trip and all that had happened to her had changed her. She didn't even look like the same youthful girl she had once been. A married woman stood in her place now.

Turning to examine her figure, Miranda studied the flow of her quilted skirt. She had lost some weight, there was no denying that, but it was a pleasant sort of thing. Her waist appeared quite small, and her hips were pleasingly curved beneath the muted green-and-black print skirt. The pin-tucked white shirtwaist with its voluminous sleeves was another recent gift from Teddy. He loved to see her dressed up in pretty things and often spoke of the day when they would go to Europe together and he would buy her a wardrobe in Paris.

As if thinking of him had brought him to her, Teddy opened the door to their suite, wrestling a box marked FRAGILE.

"What's that?" Miranda questioned. She put down her brush, leaving her hair down, and turned to see what the contents might be.

"It's the shipment of herbs I ordered from England. I hope they were able to send everything." He acted giddy, like a child at Christmas.

Miranda crossed the room and pushed back the heavy green drapes in order to let in more light for better viewing. Teddy put the box on the table and pried off the top. He reached into the straw-packed box and began pulling jars and brown paper packages from within.

"Ah," he said, holding up a jar. "*Malva moschata*—musk mallow. This is a wonderful herb. It is used to reduce inflammation." He set the jar aside and unwrapped one of the packages. "This is *Pterocarpus santalinus* or red sandalwood—for treating fevers, inflammation, even scorpion stings. It comes to us all the way from India."

"How fascinating," Miranda said, catching Teddy's excitement. "What else is in there?"

Teddy pulled out another bottle. Miranda could read the label for herself. "*Mandragora officinarum*."

Teddy nodded. "Mandrake. Very deadly if not used in the correct proportions. But very effective as an anesthetic for surgery if used properly. You can put a person to sleep quite effectively with this, but it must be handled correctly."

"How wonderful that God gave us so many needful things in the form of wild flowers and other vegetation. These herbs will be so very beneficial to the doctors up here."

"That is the idea. One doctor told me how hard it was to get shipments on a regular basis. I offered to see what I could do, and here we are. I say, not a bad catch."

Miranda laughed. "I should say not."

Teddy finished arranging the bottles and packages on the table, then set the crate aside. "I'll package up some of these and have you take them over to the hospital."

Miranda smiled. He was such a generous man. He had so much to offer and plenty of material wealth to share. Teddy

Davenport was, in her estimation, a rare and wonderful find in a world of selfishness, greed, and ambition.

"What are you smiling at?" Teddy questioned as he looked up and caught her expression.

"I was just thinking nice thoughts about you, that's all."

He cocked his head to one side and raised a brow. "Oh, and what might those thoughts include?"

"I was thinking of how generous you are—what a wonderful giving man you are, and how so many people have benefited from your kindness."

"I'm doing no less than most would if they had the means."

"You and I both know that isn't true," Miranda replied. "This place is full of people who have gold dust a plenty, so much that it dusts their hair and sticks under their nails. They don't care about anyone but themselves. They think only of the gold."

Teddy pulled on his glasses and shrugged. "I suppose you are correct. There is a sickness among many of the souls here. Gambling and drinking thrive as the men seek to lose themselves and their past. Greed causes a man to do things he might never consider otherwise."

"I know that well enough." Miranda took a seat at the table and adjusted her quilted skirt. She was grateful for the warmth as September had turned cold and rainy. Today the sun had dawned bright and the skies were clear, but there was a taste of rain in the air, and Miranda knew that by evening they very well might be forced to endure yet another damp night.

"Oh, I nearly forgot. We're having dinner with your brother and sister-in-law this evening. Karen has agreed to keep the baby, so it will be just the four of us."

"I thought Adrik had said they had to return to the claim. He is upset they've already stayed so long in Dawson. If it weren't for those two sick sled dogs, I know they would have headed back to the claim the moment Andy recovered."

"Yes, Karen said he was quite upset at the delay of time. Apparently Mr. Lindquist desires to leave the Yukon and will need to pack out his things and reach Dawson in time to catch a steamer south." He continued looking over his herbs as he spoke. "I believe they plan to leave in the morning. They hope to reach the claim in a couple of days."

"Have they decided what they're going to do? I mean, are they staying through the winter?" Miranda asked hopefully.

"I don't believe so. When I spoke to Adrik he implied that they might be on the same steamer Mr. Lindquist would take south. Apparently there is some thought of their return-ing to Dyea. It seems Adrik has some distant relationship to the Tlingit Indians."

"Well, I shall be sorry to see them go," Miranda admitted. She tried to keep the worry from her voice, but in truth, she couldn't help but wonder how life would be once her friends returned to their various homes.

She lifted her face and found Teddy studying her. "Do you regret marrying me?" he asked.

The question completely stunned her. "Not at all. Why would you ever ask such a thing?"

He put down the bottle he'd been toying with and came to where she was sitting. Kneeling beside her, Teddy took hold of her hand. "I'm quite capable of dealing with the truth. If you are having regrets, I believe we should discuss it."

"My regrets have nothing to do with you," Miranda said, reaching out with her free hand. She gently touched Teddy's cheek. "I love you. I'm very happy to be your wife."

His worried expression seemed to relax just a bit. "But I hear a kind of longing in your voice."

Miranda smiled. "Oh, Teddy. You truly have learned to listen and to care. It blesses my heart in a way that I can never quite explain. No, the longing I have is simply one to see my mother and father. I know my brother will journey home and they will all be reunited. I suppose I miss them more than I realized. Seeing Peter and Grace, and knowing they will be a part of that life—well, I can't help but be reminded of my past."

"It's probably good we're having this discussion," Teddy said. "I had wondered what you would like to do with our future."

"Whatever you want is fine with me. My life is with you, and I'm not sorry for that. I want to help you with your book, if you desire to continue working with it. I want to see your homeland and to know the things that were precious to you as a child. As long as you are by my side, I don't care where we go or what we do. I only desire that we serve God as we do it."

"I am in complete agreement with that. The book, while important to me, is no longer my first priority. You are."

Miranda shook her head. "No, don't put me there. Put God there. If God is your priority, then I know I will be cared for."

"Of course, He is above all," Teddy agreed. "I just wanted you to know that I desire to make you happy.

"Oh, but you have, Teddy. You have." Miranda slid from

the chair and knelt beside her husband. Embracing him tenderly, she kissed him gently upon the lips. "Since we're here," she murmured, "perhaps it would be most fitting if we were to pray together for guidance."

—————

"I suppose," Peter Colton began, "it shall be a long time before we see you again." He had shared a luxurious dinner of baked chicken and wild rice with his wife and sister and brother-in-law. Although a cold rain pelted the glass of the hotel dining room in a steady pulsating beat, he felt warmer and more content than he had in months. Maybe even years.

Teddy spoke up before Miranda could answer. "It might well be sooner than you think. Miranda and I have agreed that a trip to spend time with your mother and father would be good for both of us. I have work to complete here, but it's nothing that can't wait."

"Truly?" Grace questioned, leaning forward. "Will you travel with us?"

"No," Miranda said, looking with an endearing expression toward her husband. "We need a bit more time. Most likely we'd go to California in the spring."

"Oh, how exciting," Grace said, reaching over to squeeze Peter's hand. "Isn't that wonderful!"

"It is good news," Peter agreed. He watched his sister, seeing in her a confidence and strength that he had not recognized before.

"That's not all," Miranda said, her voice charged with energy. "After California, we're going to travel across America and then on to England. Teddy wants to show me all the wonderful things about his homeland."

"It's amazing what God has done in just a short while," Peter declared. "I look at the man I was just two short years ago—even a year ago—and I'm overwhelmed. God's hand was on me even then, but I couldn't see the need for His guidance. I was certain I knew where I was headed and how to get there. It took Grace to show me where I was in error."

"And grace to bring you beyond those errors into forgiveness and new life," Teddy said.

Peter chuckled at his brother-in-law's play on words. "Exactly," he agreed. He turned to his sister. "You've picked a good man for yourself, Miranda. I could never have done as well for you." Miranda beamed under his praise, and Peter knew just how important his words were to her.

An hour later, Peter and Grace left Teddy and Miranda on the second floor of their hotel and walked to the third floor where Adrik and Karen were caring for their son.

Knocking on the door, Peter and Grace were met by Leah Barringer's animated smile. "Andy's been trying to walk again!" she exclaimed.

"How marvelous. He's so early at this," Grace said, taking her son in hand. Andy clapped his hands together, then smacked his hands up against his mother's face. "You'd never guess he'd been sick so recently."

"Was the doctor ever able to tell you what was wrong?" Karen asked.

"No," Grace replied, hugging her son close. "I suppose it was just one of those things that we shall never understand."

"I think I understand it well enough," Peter said, looking at his son in amazement. He still had a hard time believing he was a father. "Andy's illness brought you all back to Dawson and to me."

"True enough," Adrik admitted.

"So when are you heading back to your claim?" Peter asked.

Adrik looked to Karen then back to Peter and Grace. "Well, that's what we needed to tell you. We're leaving in the morning. We know you're heading home soon, but we just can't stay. It's already been two weeks, and I'm sure Gump and Jacob are just about beside themselves."

"I understand. It looks to me like this town is emptying out rather quickly."

Adrik nodded. "That's for sure. I'd say the heyday of gold in the Klondike is pretty much over. There will be those who stay on and make a living for themselves, but I don't think you'll see Dawson sporting a population of thirty or forty thousand ever again."

"The steamers on the Yukon reminded me of when we first came to Alaska," Grace admitted. "They were so full of people a person could scarcely walk the deck."

"They're all heading to Nome—that's where the most recent gold strikes have been found. And once again they're spinning stories of how a man can just pick the gold nuggets up off the ground. Never mind that they didn't find that story to be true in Dawson. They're just hungry for the gold."

"It's so sad," Karen spoke up. "So many people are struggling to find something they think will make them happy, and they don't even realize that what's missing in their life is Jesus."

Peter nodded. "That's true. I know that for myself." He smiled at Grace and hugged her close. "I'm going to miss our talks. You and Adrik have been good friends to us."

Karen moved closer and Peter saw her dab tears from her

eyes. He thought of how little he had cared for her when they'd first met. She was too independent, and he felt she poorly influenced Grace. Now he admired her very much and felt proud to call her his friend.

"You will always be welcome in our home," Peter said.

"And you in ours," Adrik replied.

Karen quickly agreed. "Oh yes. Do come back and see us. We plan to head to Dyea soon, but first we have to get Gump and Jacob and sell the claim."

"Jacob wants to get a job with your shipping company," Leah threw in.

"You tell him anytime he wants a job, it's his," Peter assured.

Andy began to fuss and Grace shifted him in her arms. "I think it's time we put this little fellow to bed."

"I suppose this is good-bye," Karen said, coming to embrace Grace. "I can hardly bear it, but I know it's for the best." They hugged each other tightly, causing Andy to howl in protest.

"Adrik, thank you. Thank you for caring for Grace when I was too blind and too selfish to do so myself." Peter looked to the big man and smiled. "God knew exactly who to send into my life and into the lives of my loved ones. I'm proud to call you friend."

"That goes the same for me," Adrik replied, clapping Peter on the back.

The day of Peter, Grace, and Andy's departure was a brilliant sunny autumn day. The crisp air felt exhilarating rather than cold, and Miranda was grateful for that as she prepared to bid her brother good-bye.

"I'm so glad you and Grace are back together," Miranda whispered as she hugged Peter's neck.

Peter pulled away and winked. "And I'm glad Teddy took you off my hands."

Miranda nudged him playfully. "You will have your hands plenty full with that boy of yours. Just look at him. He's all excited about the trip."

Their gazes went to the baby who squealed with delight at the sights and sounds of the steamer *City of Topeka*.

"He will no doubt run me ragged, but what a pleasure," Peter insisted.

Miranda felt her longing for home rise with every minute that passed. When the final boarding call was given, Miranda went to Grace and embraced both her and the baby. She tried not to cry, but the tears came just the same. "I shall miss you so very much."

Grace nodded, tears forming in her eyes as well. "I could never have made it without you. When I thought I'd lost you on the lake, my heart nearly stopped. You have been closer and dearer than any sister."

"Oh, I will come for a visit as soon as I can," Miranda promised. She kissed Grace's cheek, then turned to do the same for Andy. "You be a good baby," she admonished, rubbing his rosy cheek.

Teddy came up behind her and put his arm around her. "We shall journey to see you soon," he told Peter.

"You do that. I know Mother will want to meet the man who has so clearly captured Miranda's heart."

Miranda looked up to Teddy with her tear-filled eyes. "He

has done exactly that," she agreed. "He's taken my heart captive, as well as my mind." She looked to her brother. "I can speak more botanical Latin than a girl has a right to know."

They laughed and Teddy squeezed her close. "She makes a perfect assistant. But more than that, she makes a perfect wife."

"Then we are both truly blessed," Peter said, "for I feel the same about Grace."

Teddy and Miranda watched the trio board the steamer and waited until the ship had begun its journey up river. After they docked they would catch the railroad, now completed to Bennett, and be home within a matter of weeks instead of months.

"I know you will miss them, my dear," Teddy said, turning Miranda to face him, "but I promise you, I will take you home to your family. Do you trust me to do that?"

She nodded. "I trust you. I'm not unhappy, Teddy. Please understand that. I love you very dearly, and I am home wherever you are."

"Then I am doubly blessed, for I feel the same."

—| CHAPTER TWENTY-SEVEN |—

JACOB PACED THE confines of his cell while, outside, an icy rain pelted the town. He was worn and exhausted from his daily work on the city woodpile—punishment for all who were incarcerated. For over two weeks now he'd been jailed for something he didn't do. No one would listen to him—not the officer who brought his meals, not the commissioner in charge, not even God. At least that's how it felt to Jacob.

He tried to pray, but he felt his words were bound up in anger and resentment. *Why did you let this happen to me, God?* he couldn't help but ask. It became his focal question. *Why? I liked that old man and enjoyed working with him. I would never do him harm. So why am I now being accused of his murder?*

He hated the Yukon. He hated everything the Yukon stood for. The greed. The lies. The gold. He wished fervently that his father had never brought him and Leah north. What good had it done any of them? His father was dead. He was in jail. And now Leah was alone.

Once again, he'd failed his sister, and once again, God had failed him.

Why?

Pounding his fist against the wall, Jacob wanted to scream out that they were all mad. He felt as though the entire world had gone insane and only he remained knowing the real truth.

He let exhaustion overcome him as he stretched out on his cot to stare up at the ceiling. Daily he heard the Mounties speak of the vast numbers leaving Dawson. *The rats are deserting the ship*, he thought. *Leaving it for a more lucrative ship called Nome.* Jacob shook his head, failing to understand any of it.

Here he was, sixteen. He wouldn't be seventeen until January of the new century. Would he even live to see it? Would they proclaim him guilty and end his life for the murder of Gumption Lindquist?

"It's not fair," he muttered. "I thought when a person trusted God, if they did what they were supposed to, that God would keep them from harm—that bad things wouldn't happen to them. But I've had nothing but trouble."

The first few days after they'd taken him into custody, Jacob figured everything would be resolved in a matter of hours. He figured that somehow Adrik would get wind of his incarceration and come to his aid. He'd even asked the Mounties to look Adrik up at the hospital, but he guessed no one had ever seen fit to do that.

To say he was discouraged didn't begin to reveal the scope

of his emotions. The hopelessness that held Jacob captive seemed to breed other feelings that washed over him in waves. He was angry for the mistake—angry because no one believed him. He felt deeply grieved over Gump's death, sorry that Gump would never see his farm in Kansas and never know if his parents were still living.

Then there was the fear. Jacob hated being afraid most of all. What if no one ever came to his defense? What if the truth was never revealed and he remained in jail for the rest of his life?

He thought of Leah and worried about her incessantly. She was so young, just fourteen. What would become of her? He knew Karen loved her and would see to her upbringing, but Leah would have no family of her own. If they killed Jacob as punishment for Gump, Leah would be completely orphaned. The thoughts kept whirling through his mind.

Anger. Sorrow. Fear.

They were Jacob's cellmates—and they demanded their voice.

———

Adrik stared at the notice on the door to his cabin and shook his head. "This says that the property has been confiscated and quartered off by the Northwest Mounted Police."

"Why would they do that?" Karen questioned.

"I don't know."

"Where's Jacob and Mr. Gump?" Leah asked. She started to walk around to the backside of the cabin when one the Jones brothers hailed them.

"Ivankov, where have you been?"

"Jones," Adrik acknowledged and nodded. "We've been

to Dawson. Baby took sick. Didn't Jacob or Gump tell you?"

"They couldn't very well do that, now, could they?"

Adrik had no idea what the younger man was talking about. "Do you want to explain?"

"You don't know, do you?" The dark-haired man shoved his gloveless hands in his pockets. "That boy killed the old man."

"What?" Karen exclaimed, coming around Adrik to face the man. "What are you saying?"

"I'm saying the Mounties took Jacob off to Dawson. He shot old Lindquist right through the heart. They figure he was after his gold."

"No! Not Jacob!" Leah cried. She rushed into Karen's arms, looking up mournfully at Adrik. "Jacob wouldn't kill Mr. Gump—they were good friends."

"Well, the old man is dead, nevertheless. Mounties took him away and posted the notice on the cabin. We've been keepin' an eye on things ever since."

"I thank you for that," Adrik replied. "How long ago did all this happen?"

"Right after you headed out. I figured you might even learn about it while you were there. I'm supposin' the *Nugget* carried the story."

"I'm afraid," Adrik said, looking from Jones to the women, "we weren't paying much attention to the events around us. Well, we'll just have to gather our things and head back to town."

"Ain't suppose to go through the door—it's posted to stay out."

"I see that," Adrik said. "We got some things we can gather from the cache, but our gold is hidden in the cabin and I'm not leaving here without it."

Jones nodded. "Seein's how you're the old man's partner and all, I don't see no harm in you takin' your fair share. I'm sure no one will be the wiser for it. Sure ain't my business."

"I'll check in with the Mounties when I get to Dawson. Jacob's going to need some help in clearing his name," Adrik replied.

"I don't think you can clear the boy of something he did," Jones said turning to go. "I saw him myself—standing there with the rifle in his hands—looking all crazed. He said it were someone else, but I never did see nobody." He then ambled off toward his own claim, as if not wanting to know or say anything more on the subject.

Leah's sobs tore into Adrik's heart. "Don't worry, sweetheart," he said, reaching out to stroke her hair. "I'll see that this gets figured out. We'll get Jacob out of jail—you'll see."

"Why did this happen?" Leah asked tearfully. "Poor Mr. Gump, he was afraid this land would kill him, and now it has. And poor Jacob. He must be so afraid."

Adrik looked into his wife's eyes. He wished fervently that he knew what to say to comfort Leah, but nothing made sense. "I don't know."

In a numbed state of shock, the trio worked to pack out what things they didn't wish to leave behind. Adrik knew it would most likely cause problems with the police when they learned of his entry into the cabin, so he refused to let Karen or Leah go inside.

"Better it fall on me than you two," he told them. "Just tell me what you need for me to retrieve and I'll do my best to find it."

Adrik stepped into the cabin and stared at the darkened

shadows on the wall. He took enough time to light a lamp, dispelling the shadows, but to his horror, it revealed the bloody brown stain on the wooden floor. Gump had been so proud of that floor. He'd made it himself without much help from anyone else. He'd spent the winter months sanding it down to make it so smooth he could walk barefoot on it in the summer. Now his lifeblood stained the floor, forever marking it as a reminder of unfilled dreams.

Adrik felt his eyes mist. He'd loved Gump like a father, and now the old man was gone. Gone before he could take back his gold and surprise his family. Gone before he could see his mother and buy her the white leather, gold-trimmed Bible she'd always wanted. Gone.

"And that's what I plan to be as well," Adrik said, anger replacing his sorrow. "I'm taking my family and leaving this place. And if I never hear the word *gold* prior to stepping onto the golden streets of heaven, it'll be just fine by me."

Two hours later the cart was packed and the dogs were rested and ready to go again. Adrik knew if he never saw this land again, it would be perfectly fine with him. He longed for the simplicity of his life on the Alaskan coast.

They had what Adrik had been certain was several thousand dollars worth of dust and nuggets by now. As angry as the greed represented by the ore made Adrik, he knew he'd have to rely upon its bounty for a while longer. It was going to have to get them home and then some. They'd be able to buy the supplies they needed and the rest could be given away, as far as Adrik was concerned.

Adrik planned to send Gump's half to his family in Kansas, but first he'd have to convince the Mounties that he had a right to the gold. That might not be so easy to do in light of what had happened.

Karen wanted only her family Bible and a few sentimental trinkets she'd collected along the way. Leah asked Adrik to get Jacob's change of clothes and his winter boots, along with her things. He did this, wishing he'd been there for the boy when this tragedy had happened. There was no doubt in his mind of Jacob's innocence. What there was doubt about was who had been responsible.

"You two are going to ride," he said, lifting Leah into the cart. "I know it will be a tight fit, but we need to make good time. Jacob's already been all this time without us and he must be feeling pretty frantic by now. I've packed the gold under everything, but you should be comfortable enough. I put some blankets, along with our clothes, down as a cushion."

Karen and Leah nodded in understanding. "We'll be fine," Karen assured him. She let Adrik help her into the cart and smiled. "We've forgotten only one thing."

Adrik looked back to the cabin, then to Karen. "What?"

"Prayer."

Adrik knew she was right. He felt the warmth of God's presence even in her words. They hadn't thought to pray. They had waited until their fleshly needs were met—their criteria and agenda tended to—and then they had thought of prayer.

Adrik pulled off his hat, in spite of the fact that it had started to snow. Bowing his head, he started the prayer with an apology. "Lord, we're sorry for thinking of you last. We know it isn't the way we're supposed to be. We let ourselves get caught up in the moment. We saw the problem, instead of the answer-giver. Forgive us.

"And Father, we ask that you would be with Jacob just now. Sustain his faith, Lord. This has to be a terrifying time for him. He's probably confused and scared, and Lord, I just ask that you would strengthen him. Make your presence real in his life, and help us to help him. I don't believe for one minute that he killed Gumption. I don't know who would kill such a kind old man—but Lord, you know exactly who did the deed. Help us to find that man.

"Give us safe passage back to Dawson, and give us the strength and courage we'll need to deal with the days to come. In Jesus' name, Amen."

"Amen," Karen murmured with Leah.

Adrik dusted the snow from his hair and put his cap back on. He stood on the ledge at the back of the cart and took up the harness reins. Pulling the brake, he whistled to the dogs. They sprang to attention, eager for the run. Adrik gave the reins a snap. "Hike!"

Jacob had never been so happy to see anyone in his life as he was to see Adrik and Karen.

"Where's Leah? Is she all right?" he asked.

Karen and Adrik nodded in unison. "She's just fine," Karen said. "They wouldn't let her come back here, however."

"They almost wouldn't allow Karen back here, but we wore them down," Adrik said, giving the guard a playful nudge.

"You can have ten minutes," the guard said as he pointed them to a small wooden table. He then turned to Jacob.

"Don't even think of trying anything."

Jacob barely heard the man. He wanted only to hear Adrik tell him that he'd figured everything out and he would soon be set free. The trio sat down together while the guard watched on.

"You want to tell us what happened, son?" Adrik began.

"It was Cec Blackabee, Adrik. He showed up not long after you left. He didn't even give Gump a chance. Gump opened the door and Cec fired his rifle. He might have only meant to scare him, but Gump must have seen the gun, 'cause best I can figure, he tried to close the door and got the bullet in the chest."

"Then what happened, Jacob?" Karen asked softly. She reached out and touched his arm tenderly, motherly. He felt warmed by her presence.

"Gump fell over, and I charged for the man in the doorway. At first I didn't know it was Cec, 'cause he stood outside in the shadows. I grabbed hold of the rifle, but not before he had a chance to cock it again. The gun went off as we wrestled. Finally, he pushed me back and cocked it again, and aimed it right for me. It was then that we heard someone coming. The distraction gave me a chance to try again to take the rifle from Cec.

"When Cec heard the neighbors coming, he ran. When everyone else showed up, there I was holding the gun, and they all presumed the worst."

"What about Gump? Was he already dead?"

Jacob looked at the table remembering the horrible sight of Gump's bloody shirt, his pale, wrinkled face, his eyes glazed over, but open. "They told me he died pretty much instantly. The bullet went right through his heart."

"This is ridiculous," Karen proclaimed. "If you told them this, why aren't they listening? Why is he still sitting here in jail?" she asked Adrik.

"There were no witnesses who saw Cec leave," Jacob said.

"No one?"

Jacob shook his head. "Everyone focused on me. I was the only one they thought about. Cec was able to slip away without any trouble."

"I don't understand, son," Adrik said very softly. "Why would Cec Blackabee want to kill Gump?"

Jacob shrugged. It was a mystery to him as well. It was one thing to be a thief and cheat, but another to be a murderer. He'd known Cec to be underhanded at nearly every turn, but he didn't seem like a murderer.

"I know he said something about scaring me into helping him. I suppose he figured if I wouldn't help him for the money, I would do it if he threatened my life."

"Look, we're going to see this thing through until you're proven innocent and set free."

"I'd like to believe that." Adrik's words sounded good to Jacob, but promises weren't going to turn the key on his cell.

"You must believe, Jacob. God has a plan for you, and I am certain it isn't to leave you to rot away in a Yukon prison," Karen told him. Her gaze met his and refused to let him go.

Jacob appreciated her strength. He thought it might well be his imagination, but he already felt more hopeful. It seemed just seeing them here, sharing his plight and knowing the circumstances, helped him to bear his burden.

"We're going to leave now," Adrik told Jacob. "I'm going

to have a talk with the commissioner to see what can be done. Keep praying."

"I'm trying, but God doesn't appear to be listening."

Adrik grinned. "That guard over there doesn't appear to be listening either, but I know he is. And I know God is listening as well. You have to trust that, Jacob. Faith in times of plenty and peace isn't really faith. It takes a trial like this to build faith that moves mountains. Just trust Him, Jacob."

Jacob heard Adrik's words and took them deep into his heart. A tiny flame sparked to life, spreading hope and courage throughout his weary limbs. "I'll try," Jacob said, knowing the alternative was unthinkable.

Jacob tried to sleep that night, but his mind came back to the words Adrik had given him. The counsel was wise, he knew that full well, but it was also hard to believe. Jacob felt done in. Trust and faith came hard in the shadow of a noose.

"I'm trying, Lord," he whispered. "I don't know if that's enough or not. I guess if it's not enough, then I need you to forgive me. And if it is enough, then I need you to help me. Either way," he said, closing his eyes, "I need you."

"I don't care how many witnesses saw Jacob standing there with the gun after the shooting had already been done. I'm asking, did anyone see Jacob pull the trigger?"

The Mountie sitting across the desk from Adrik and Karen did not appear interested in their questions. "Sir, that's really not a matter I can answer."

"I believe, based on my knowledge of the boy and the relationship he had with the old man, that it would be impossible for Jacob Barringer to have killed Gump Lindquist," Adrik declared.

"That's all well and fine, but you must remember, we have a situation here that doesn't always allow for the normal way of things. The gold rush has brought out the savage beast in many men."

Adrik stared at the man's balding head and then looked past him to the window. Outside snow was falling, reminding Adrik that the time was quickly passing and soon they'd be facing winter once again.

"I know who killed Gump," Adrik finally stated. He looked back to the Mountie. He sat so completely regal in his stately uniform. The look on his face was fixed, almost stoic. He was a soldier through and through. "A man named Cec Blackabee killed him. Jacob was there and witnessed the entire thing."

"Why would this man, whom no one saw, with the exception of Mr. Barringer, want to kill Mr. Lindquist?"

"For months we've been dealing with a thief and sneak," Adrik replied. "We had a sled stolen and evidence of other attempts to break in. Then one night a commotion arose while Jacob was on guard duty. Cec Blackabee had come to ask Jacob to help him. It seems his partner ran off with his property, including the deed to a claim and a map. He asked about these things and admitted to having stolen our sled. He said the sled was taken from him by his wayward partner."

"Not only that," Karen piped up, "but a strange man appeared at our door some time back when the men were gone. He made me feel most uncomfortable and appeared to be up to no good."

"Was this the same man who stole the sled and supposedly killed Mr. Lindquist?"

"No," Karen said shaking her head. "I'm sure it wasn't. Jacob was there that night. He would have recognized Cec Blackabee if he'd been the man. I'm suggesting that Mr. Blackabee may have a partner."

"This is all very interesting, but it doesn't prove Mr. Barringer's innocence. I have eye witnesses——"

"Who saw the boy holding the rifle," Adrik interjected. "But no one saw him commit the murder."

"I wish I could help you. I will be happy to check into this matter more thoroughly, but the truth is, you're going to have to have evidence to confirm the story—evidence that will stand up in a court of law. Otherwise, I'm afraid the judge will deal most harshly with this young man."

"Meaning exactly what?" Karen asked.

"Meaning if he's found guilty, he'll most likely be hanged."

⊣ CHAPTER TWENTY-EIGHT ⊢

"ARE THEY GOING TO kill my brother?" Leah asked, her voice quavering.

Karen looked up from the dining table. "We can't even think that way," she said. "Surely, God won't let him be punished for something he didn't do."

"Innocent people get blamed for things all the time. You said so yourself," Leah replied.

Adrik turned to her. "You can't let this kind of thinking rule your heart. It isn't fair that Jacob is having to endure this. Nor is it fair that you have to endure this heartache."

"It also wasn't fair that Mr. Gump had to die," Leah interrupted. "Nothing about this place seems fair. People hurt each other and cheat each other—and all because of the gold."

"No," Adrik said. "It isn't the gold, it's the sin of greed.

The gold is just a metallic rock that lays there and does nothing. It has no thoughts or feelings, it simply exists."

"The wealth assigned it comes from human decisions," Karen added.

"Well, it's still not fair."

Adrik nodded. "You're sure right on that point. It's not fair."

"But then we should be able to do something about it!" Leah declared, pushing away her bread pudding.

"Sweetheart," Adrik began, "there is much in life that isn't fair—never has been, never will be. Innocence is lost, trust is betrayed, and love is misused. It's been happening that way since the beginning of time."

"It's sure been happening since the beginning of my time," Leah muttered.

"Leah, do you believe God is singling you out for trials? Look at Karen," Adrik replied. "She lost her mother and father. She left a good life in Chicago where she had plenty of everything she needed. She lost her aunt in a fire. And she got saddled with me." He grinned as he added the latter statement.

Leah couldn't help but smile as Karen interjected, "Yes, and he's been a troublesome burden ever since." She playfully nudged Adrik. "He's not at all easy to live with."

Leah enjoyed their playful spirit. It reminded her of her mother and father. Still, she also remembered times when her mother's heartbroken cries nearly broke her heart. "It's just so hard," Leah finally replied, sobering again.

Adrik gently touched her cheek. "I know it is. Jesus never said it wouldn't be. In fact, He told us life would be difficult. He told us we would have troubles, but that we could be of good cheer because He has already overcome the world and all the problems it could ever bring. That's in the gospel of John, sixteenth chapter. So you see, it isn't fair. And life is hard. But it's nothing new. Every person in the world has to deal with the same sort of thing at one time or another."

"They don't all end up in jail fearing for their lives," Leah protested.

"Maybe not the kind of jail your brother is in, but there are all kinds of ways to be imprisoned and all manner of dealings that threaten our very lives." Adrik squeezed her hand and smiled. "But Jesus is bigger than all of this. He's already seen it. Already dealt with it. It's as though when we have to go through it, we can rest in Him 'cause He already knows the direction to take to get us through in one piece."

"But Jesus could have kept the bad from happening," Leah said and tears came to her eyes. "He could have kept Jacob from being blamed for killing Mr. Gump. He could have kept Mr. Gump alive."

"Without a doubt," Adrik said, nodding. "And that really bothers you, doesn't it?"

Leah swallowed hard. "Yes. It hurts me to think of God just standing there letting Jacob get hauled away for something he didn't do. It makes me want to die inside when I think that things might keep going wrong—that God might keep standing back, doing nothing, while they decide to hang my brother."

It was Karen's turn to talk. "Do you trust God, Leah?"

The girl shrugged. "I thought I did. I sure want to trust Him."

"Sometimes the only thing we can do is accept that He knows best—that He has a plan and is just and loving."

"And sovereign," Adrik added.

"What does that mean?"

"Sovereign means that God is the absolute, highest authority. He's the final word on everything. He's the one in charge of how things will be. No matter what—no matter how it looks or feels. It means trusting that He's in control even when things seem very much out of control."

"That's really hard," Leah said. She lowered her head and wiped her tears. "My mama used to say that same thing. She told me when she was dying that God's ways were sometimes hard for us to understand, but that we have to keep on believing in Him—we have to have faith that He will take care of us."

She looked up to Karen and Adrik. "She said that was what being a Christian was all about."

"It sounds like your mother was a very wise woman," Adrik said softly, then added, "I'm figuring you're a lot like her. Maybe even more than you know."

———

Jacob sat at the same wooden table where he'd visited with Adrik and Karen only two days before. Now, however, instead of his friends, an American lawyer sat opposite him.

"Your friends have put me on retainer to see to your needs," the man said, adjusting his eyeglasses. "My name is Calvin Kinkade. I'm originally from Oregon, but I found it lucrative to journey north." He paused and, after fussing a bit more with his glasses, looked at the paper he'd brought with him.

"I'm afraid that there isn't much here to help me." He looked directly at Jacob, his eyes peering over the top rims of the silver-framed spectacles. "Unless we can produce a witness or this Mr. Blackabee, I'm not sure we'll be able to convince anyone of your innocence."

"I thought they were supposed to prove my guilt," Jacob said rather snidely. He wasn't feeling at all good about the fact that Adrik had brought a lawyer in on the situation. That had to mean that things didn't look good—that they were in desperate need of legal help.

"Yes, well, given the fact that so many people saw you standing over the dead man, gun in hand, I believe they feel they have sufficient proof of your guilt."

"That's what I figured. So why is Adrik wasting his hard-earned money by hiring you?"

The man was nonplussed. "I'm afraid I don't understand. Do you not see the need for legal representation?"

Jacob knew his anger would soon speak for him, so he took a deep breath and tried to calm his nerves. "I didn't kill Gump. He was a good friend, and the last thing I wanted to see was his death. I don't much care anymore what anyone believes. You aren't going to solve this case by sitting here picking at my brain. You need to be out there," Jacob pointed to the window. "Cec Blackabee is out there, and it doesn't much matter to him who ends up dead if it means that he gets what he wants."

"Yes, well, I suppose I can speak to your guardian on the details of this and see what is to be done."

When Jacob said nothing more, the man got to his feet. "I have arranged for you to have a visitor. Mr. Ivankov felt it was most important." The lawyer nodded to the guard, who in turn opened the door.

Leah Barringer ran across the room and threw herself

into Jacob's arms. "Oh, I thought they'd never let me in here," she cried.

"I can't believe they did," Jacob replied, holding her away from him enough to get a good look. "Are you all right?"

"I'm fine, but you look terrible."

He laughed. It felt good to laugh. "I'm fine. I'm working hard, but it's not too bad."

"Working? What are you doing?"

"I'm cutting wood for the city. That's how they keep the prisoners busy around here, and sometimes it's how they sentence guilty folks. They end up cutting wood for so many weeks or months."

"How awful," Leah said, glancing down to see the irons on Jacob's ankles. "Are they afraid you'll run away?"

Jacob shrugged, trying to keep things light. He could see the fear in Leah's expression and wanted to put her mind at ease. "They do this to everyone when they bring them out of their cell."

"Oh," Leah said, seeming to calm with his response.

"I'll give you two a moment alone," Mr. Kinkade said, then went to speak with the guard.

"Leah, I want you to promise me that no matter what happens, you'll stay with Karen and Adrik and grow up sensible."

"I promise. But what about you?"

"It doesn't much matter at this point. I can't free myself. I can't leave the jail and go find Cec. If I could, I would."

"Adrik's looking for him," Leah replied. "He'll find him."

Jacob reached out and pushed one of his sister's braids back over her shoulder. She was growing up so fast, she hardly resembled the youngster she once had been. Soon she'd have beaus and then a husband and children. He wanted a better life for her. Better than their mother had known. Better than they had known.

"I'm sure if anyone can find Cec, Adrik's the man. Just don't go getting your hopes up. Cec may be far from here by now."

"You have to have faith, Jacob." Leah's expression grew quite serious. "We have to trust God, even though it seems like He doesn't care. He's always out there—watching us and dealing with us. He hasn't left us, even if we don't understand why these things are going on."

"Sounds like you've thought this through," Jacob said.

"I have. I wasn't very happy when this all started, but while I'm still not happy with the way things are, I know God is in control of everything."

Leah's words were exactly what Jacob needed. He needed to know she believed in him—trusted him and loved him. But he also needed to hear her declare her faith. Somehow, for whatever reason, he felt as if he were sustained because of her faith.

"Karen and I have been praying. We know God has everything in His hand. He sees us and loves us, and He's not going to let you be falsely charged."

It warmed Jacob's heart to know that without even having to ask, Leah knew he wasn't capable of murdering Gump. He hugged her close. "Thank you. Thank you for coming here and thank you for believing in me."

Leah stepped back. "How could I not?" She smiled. "I have to go now, but just you wait. You'll see. We'll find that horrible Mr. Blackabee, and you'll be set free." She hugged him tight. "I love you, Jacob."

Her words broke through the wall Jacob had put around his heart. Holding her close, he countered her words with his own declaration. "I love you, too."

Long after she'd gone and Jacob was back to work on the woodpile, her words stayed with him. They gave him a rhythm to work with. "You'll be—set free. You'll be—set free." He lifted the axe and brought it down in an imagined beat. Then a verse from the Bible came to him. *Ye shall know the truth, and the truth shall make you free.*

"They'll know the truth," Jacob said bringing the ax down hard. "and I will be set free."

───────

"I think trying to find Cec Blackabee will be rather like hunting for the proverbial needle in a haystack," Karen declared as she, Leah, and Adrik sat keeping company with Miranda and Teddy.

The night had grown late, but while Teddy would have just as soon gone to bed, he knew his new friends needed to discuss their strategies. He wanted to help as best he could, but nothing seemed reasonable.

"The man could well be back down toward Whitehorse by now," Teddy reasoned.

"I thought of that already," Adrik declared. "I gave his description to the Mounties and told them all about Cec's saloon in Whitehorse. Someone there is bound to know him and should be able to keep an eye open for him. But I really don't think he would have left this area. He desperately wants those missing papers. They mean a lot of money to him—at least that's how I figure it."

"And you say," Teddy began, "that the man figured them

to be on the sled I sold to you?"

"That was his way of thinking. Why he figures that, I can't really say. He told Jacob that his partner had robbed him. He said the sled and sled box were a part of that thievery and that the sled box contained his documents."

"I say, why wouldn't the partner just keep the documents? Better yet, why not sell them to some poor unsuspecting fool."

"Well, as best as Jacob and I could figure out, the papers were hidden and the man wouldn't necessarily have known he had them."

"I see. Well, that does change things a bit."

"But if the man stole the sled, wouldn't he have found what he was looking for?" Miranda questioned.

"Well, apparently he thought the papers would be in the sled box," Adrik said. "But we'd taken the sled box inside and made a baby bed for Andy. It was a pretty nice box, simple, but nice. We put a well-worn crate in the sled for carrying supplies and tools. Cec probably didn't pay any attention when he took the sled. Once he got away and realized the box wasn't the same one, he had to figure on a way to get the box back."

"Well, now we have to figure a way to get Cec back," Karen said. "And we've got to do it soon."

—{ CHAPTER TWENTY-NINE }—

MIRANDA CURLED UP against Teddy's warm body and sighed. It was so very nice to have a husband to sleep alongside, especially when the weather turned cold. Her mind raced with thoughts. Even though she knew she'd be better off to fall asleep, she couldn't stop thinking about poor Jacob Barringer. She wished fervently there was something she could do for the boy, but she knew that, besides praying, she had no means with which to help him.

It seemed so little, and yet, she knew prayer was the ultimate weapon of a Christian warrior. She thought of all the times when she'd been truly afraid, and then remembered how God had soothed and calmed her. She prayed He would do that now for Jacob.

I'm sure he's not guilty, she thought. *He's too sweet a boy. He just couldn't have killed anyone.*

Miranda was just about to drift off to sleep when her attention was caught by a noise coming from the other room. Since marrying Teddy, they'd turned the other room into a large sitting room and work area. Teddy's tables and shelves consumed one end of the room, while the other end was used to receive guests.

The creaking sounded again, and this time Miranda sat straight up. She noticed a light threading through the space at the bottom of the door.

Slipping from the bed and pulling on her robe, she thought only to crack the door a bit to look out into the sitting room, but when she touched the knob, Miranda was no longer convinced she was doing the best thing.

She started to turn back when the sound of glass breaking caught her attention. Without thinking, Miranda threw open the door, hoping to scare the burglar into making a run for it.

"Teddy, wake up! We're being robbed!" she screamed. Stepping into the sitting room, she screamed again. "Teddy, there's a man in here!"

And indeed there was. The man quickly covered the distance that separated him from Miranda and clamped his hand over her mouth.

"Shut up. Do you want to wake up the whole hotel?"

She would have told him that she had exactly that in mind, but his foul-smelling hand made it impossible. Struggling against the man, Miranda tried to free herself. She pushed against him with all her strength, but it was to no avail. He held her fast in a steel-like grip.

That was how Teddy found them. Miranda saw his expression change from one of confusion, to anger.

"Let her go!" he declared, charging forth with uncharacteristic boldness.

"Stay back, mister. I've got a knife and I ain't afraid to use it."

Teddy halted at this news. "Please don't hurt her. You can take whatever you want. Just let her go."

"Look, mister, I don't know who you are, but you have my property and I want it back," the man said, pulling Miranda backward. The man turned her toward the work tables. "Where is it?"

"I don't know what you're talking about," Teddy said, moving very slowly to cross the room in front of them. "Please just let her go and tell me what this is about."

The man suddenly grabbed hold of Miranda's wrist and yanked her around, throwing her off-balance. She landed at his feet in a resounding thud.

She looked up at the wiry man. He was older than she'd expected. From his grip on her, Miranda had presumed him to be young. Instead, his face was weathered and wrinkled and his black hair was liberally sprinkled with gray, especially at the temples. He had a scar along his jaw, just under his chin. She might never have noticed it had she not been sitting at his feet.

"Please, tell me what you're looking for," Teddy said.

"You bought a sled from my partner. He stole it from me and also took some other things that didn't belong to him, including a sled box. I want it back."

"I don't have them," Teddy said. "I sold them."

Miranda realized that this had to be Cec Blackabee. She tried to scoot away from the man, but he stomped his muddy boot down on her robe. The foul odor told her mud wasn't the only thing he'd collected along the way.

"Stay put," he ordered. He turned back to Teddy. "I know you sold them. I followed the man you sold 'em to."

Miranda looked to her husband and realized by his expression that he, too, knew the truth of who this man was. He silenced her with the tiniest shake of his head.

"If you know this, then you know also that I do not have what you're looking for," Teddy declared.

"I think you're wrong, mister. I reclaimed that sled of mine—took it back from the man you sold it to. The sled box with my things was missin'."

"I'm sorry. What does this have to do with me? I sold the man both the sled and the sled box."

"I saw the sled box. It weren't the same one you were sold."

Miranda saw Teddy stiffen at this. "How would you know what the man sold me? You weren't there. He could have disposed of the item you're speaking of."

Cec nodded. "I suppose he could have, but I don't think he did. I think you've got it."

Teddy's expression changed at this. "Describe the box."

Cec shrugged. "It was about two foot deep and about a foot and a half wide. It was made out of good wood and painted white."

Teddy nodded. "Yes, I do remember it." He looked to Miranda as if to apologize.

She saw the misery in his expression and wished she could somehow comfort him. "Where is it, Teddy?" she asked softly.

"Back at the cabin."

"Where?" Cec questioned.

"A cabin I use that's out south of Dawson."

"Take me there."

Teddy shook his head. "It's a three-day trip and I have no transportation. The weather is bad, and we'd no doubt have a difficult time of it."

"I don't care. I can get us some horses," Cec said, scratching his chin. "The lady'll have to ride double with me."

"I say, why not just leave her here," Teddy suggested. "She can't help in this—she doesn't even know about the box."

Cec shook his head. "I don't think so. The minute you and me head out, she'd be over there telling it all to the Mounties."

"What if I gave you my word?" Miranda questioned. "I promise to stay right here in the hotel." She knew she could keep that promise and still go to Adrik for help.

"You must think me a fool," Cec answered. "Now you're both wearin' on my patience. Let's go."

"Look, we have to put on our street clothes. It's much too cold to travel in nightclothes," Miranda declared.

The man looked at her for a moment then turned his gaze to Teddy. He studied Teddy for several seconds. Miranda couldn't imagine what he must be thinking. The hard set of his jaw told her that he wasn't at all pleased with the delay, but he understood the logic of her statement. They couldn't very well go parading out into the night dressed as they were. If nothing else, the very sight of them would be sure to attract unwanted attention.

"All right. You go first," he finally told Miranda. "Get your clothes on—and no funny business or I'll cut him to ribbons. He can show us the way in pain, just as sure as he can without it."

Miranda nodded. "I promise I won't do anything but get dressed."

"We will need a few supplies," Teddy told Cec as Miranda got to her feet. "If you don't mind, I'll collect some of these herbs to take along. They're good for tea and medicines. You never know, the snow could come upon us, and we could find ourselves in grave danger."

"Take 'em if you like," Cec said without concern.

Miranda paused at the door, fixing her gaze on Teddy. She couldn't imagine why he wanted to take his herbs. Trembling, she reached for the door.

Once inside their bedroom, Miranda hurried to dress. She felt a foreboding creep over her. What if Cec killed them after he got what he wanted? She glanced at the hall door and thought about running to Adrik for help. They were just two doors down.

But if I don't hurry, Cec might hurt Teddy, and I could never forgive myself if that happened.

Miranda tried to figure out how best to dress. She knew it would be cold and possibly rainy. She layered her body in a variety of woolen stockings, petticoats, and even a pair of boy's trousers she'd used on the hike north. Finally, she topped the outfit with a heavy wool skirt and long-sleeved blouse. Her hands shook so badly that she had difficulty buttoning the blouse.

" 'The Lord is my light and my salvation; whom shall I fear? The Lord is the strength of my life; of whom shall I be afraid?' " She murmured the verse from Psalms, praying it would give her comfort and calm her nervousness.

Haphazardly, she knotted her hair at the nape of her neck, then took up a jacket and pulled it on over her blouse.

Glancing around the room, she quickly retrieved her coat and gloves. She hurried back into the workroom to find Teddy bundling up the last of the things he wanted to take.

"I'm ready," she said in shaky voice.

Teddy crossed the room and handed her the bundle. "I shall be only a moment."

True to his word, Teddy reappeared within minutes. Miranda could see that he, too, had dressed in his warmest clothes. "All right, let us be about this, then," he said, looking harshly at Cec. "I would like to appeal once more to your sense of decency. Please allow my wife to stay here."

"Get movin'," Cec said, pointing them to the door. "I got me a gun as well as a knife, and I'll use either one." He patted his pocket as if to emphasize the presence of his weapons.

Miranda opened the door and peered into the hall, hoping perhaps someone would be taking a middle-of-the-night stroll. The hall was empty, however, and the hotel was silent.

Cec grabbed hold of Miranda's elbow. "You go first, mister. That way if you try anything funny, I'll see it. I'll also have your woman."

Teddy's gaze met Miranda's once again. She saw the love he held for her in his expression. She knew he would die for her if necessary. He nodded slowly and headed out into the hall.

Miranda felt her courage giving way. She realized her only chance to alert someone would be to raise a ruckus in the hall. But what if no one heard her? She would only manage to irritate Cec and maybe even cause them to be killed. She saw Karen and Adrik's room door as they moved down the hall. If only Adrik could know what was happening. She made a quick decision.

"Ow!" she cried, and fell against the door to Adrik and Karen's room. Her impact made a terrible noise.

"What's wrong with you, fool woman?" Cec growled low. He yanked her back upright.

"I just twisted my ankle," Miranda offered apologetically.

Teddy turned, looking fearful. "What's wrong?" he asked quietly.

"Your woman took a wrong step," Cec replied, then grabbing Miranda, he thrust her forward again. "Don't let it happen again, missy."

"I'm sorry," Miranda said, not meaning it at all.

———

Adrik couldn't imagine who was coming to call in the middle of the night. He threw back the covers, disturbing Karen's sleep.

"What's wrong?" she asked groggily.

"I don't know—probably nothing more than a drunk wandering down the hall to his room," Adrik replied. "Go back to sleep." He went to the door. Throwing it open, he started to protest the interruption but found no one there.

It was just as he'd suspected. Probably nothing more than someone staggering down the hall in a state of inebriation. As he started to close the door, however, something came over him, and he paused. Stepping forward, he looked toward Teddy and Miranda's room. No one was there and the door was closed. He shrugged and glanced down the hall in the opposite direction.

He caught only the briefest glimpse of a woman and man, but he was almost certain it was Miranda, and he was even more certain that the man with her was Cec Blackabee.

─┤ CHAPTER THIRTY ├─

ONCE THEY WERE outside, Cec Blackabee led Miranda and Teddy around behind the hotel and down the alleyway. From out of the shadows, a thin, tall man appeared.

"You get it?" he asked.

Cec tightened his hold on Miranda and pulled her closer. "No. We've got to head out to his cabin to get it, Mitch."

"Where's that?"

"Three days out. You got the horses?"

"Yeah, but I don't got no three days worth of supplies," the thin man answered.

Cec growled, then turned to Teddy. "You got any supplies for the road?"

Teddy shook his head. Miranda hoped it would persuade Cec to forget about the journey.

"We'll just have to steal 'em," Cec told his partner.

The man shrugged. "Guess we can break into the dry goods store. Nobody is gonna be there at this hour."

"I wish you wouldn't," Teddy said. "It's bad enough what you're doing with us, but if you continue adding to your illegal activities—"

"I don't want to hear it," Cec told him, moving closer to Teddy. "I've killed when it was necessary. Stealing ain't that much of a bother for me."

Miranda couldn't see well in the dark, but she could sense the tension in Teddy. She longed to assure him that everything would be all right—that God would protect them—but she wasn't all that convinced herself. Her faith felt terribly immature at the moment. It was easy to quote the Bible verse that God was her light and salvation—that He was her strength. But putting it into practice was very difficult.

Cec and the man called Mitch conversed in low whispers for a minute or two before pushing Miranda and Teddy in a direction away from the hotel. Miranda struggled to keep from tripping over her skirts as Cec forced her to move faster and faster. When they reached the end of the alley, Mitch disappeared momentarily, then just as quickly reappeared with three horses.

Miranda knew horses were at a premium in this country. No doubt they'd been brought north on one of the summer steamers, but now that the weather was turning colder she wondered how convenient it would be to keep them. Poor beasts. They would no doubt suffer as most animals did in the frozen north.

"Get up there," Cec commanded Miranda.

She looked to the horse and back to Cec. In the darkness

she knew he couldn't see her confusion, so she spoke. "How?"

"What do you mean, how?"

"I mean, I don't know how to mount the horse. I've not ridden a horse before."

"Well, if that don't beat all," Cec said. "Put your foot in my hand and take hold of the horn. Pull yourself up and over and I'll boost you up there at the same time."

Miranda had no idea whether she was doing it right or not, but she put her boot foot in Cec's folded hands and grabbed hold of the saddle as best she could. Pulling herself up, she nearly flew over the other side of the horse as Cec gave a mighty push.

He grabbed hold of her leg and steadied her, as Miranda fought to balance herself atop the horse. Once she was settled, Cec took up the reins from Mitch. Pulling something from his pocket, he motioned to Teddy. "Walk ahead of the horse. I'll be right behind you. We'll go to the end of the block and around the dry goods store."

Miranda gripped the horn of the saddle for all she was worth. Terrified beyond words, she could only pray in silence.

Once they'd arrived at their destination, Cec surprised Miranda by handing her not only the reins to her horse, but the other two as well. "I've got a gun on your husband. He's coming with me and Mitch. If you know what's good for you, you'll keep quiet and hold these horses right here."

"But I don't know anything about horses," Miranda protested.

"Keep your voice down," Cec demanded. "Ain't nothing for you to know. Just sit still and hold the reins. If the animal starts moving around, pull back on the reins. He'll stop quick enough."

Miranda trembled as she took up the reins in one hand and clung desperately to the saddle horn with the other. She feared for Teddy's life, anxious that he might try to do something foolish in order to keep her from having to make the journey.

It seemed to take forever for the men to break into the back of the store and return, arms laden with supplies. Miranda knew in truth it was only minutes, but her heart was pounding like a kettledrum and her rapid, shallow breathing made her light-headed. She tried to calm herself—to pray—to focus on anything other than what was happening.

Cec hoisted himself up behind her and pulled her back against him. Taking the other horses' reins from her, he tossed them to Mitch. "You go ahead and lead the way, mister," he said as Mitch handed reins over to Teddy. "Just remember, I've got your woman back here. Any stupid moves and I'll cut her."

"Don't hurt her. I'm not going to do anything other than what you direct me to do."

"Keep it that way," Cec demanded.

Teddy knew the way to the cabin, even in the dark, but what had him worried was where they might take refuge along the way. There were a few claim cabins here and there, but his own place was well away from most of the hubbub of the gold rush. Not that there hadn't been folks trying to find gold on the property around his place. But so far, he'd not heard of any great finds.

God was faithful to provide, in spite of Teddy's worries.

By nightfall the next day, they'd managed to find an abandoned cabin on Baker Creek. The second night, they found a lean-to off the Indian River. Both nights Cec kept Teddy from Miranda, reminding him as they went to sleep for a few hours that he had the knife close at hand, should Teddy try anything at all.

The third day out it started to snow, and the snow quickly built into blizzardlike conditions. Teddy feared he'd never be able to make his way to the right path, but God was faithful, even in that. The snow lightened and the winds calmed, and as quickly as the blizzard had threatened, it departed. Teddy silently praised God for the blessing.

Glancing over his shoulder, however, he could see that Miranda was nearly done in. He felt bad for her, knowing how sore and stiff she must be from the ride. The first night she'd barely been able to walk when they'd dismounted, and by morning she was so stiff that Cec had to lift her to the saddle. Teddy resented the man touching Miranda, yet there wasn't anything to be done about it. He had a plan, but it would have to wait until they were in the cabin.

"There it is!" Teddy called back to the men. "That cabin tucked in the trees over there." He urged his horse forward, grateful the journey had come to an end. But even as he thanked God for a safe trip, Teddy began to fear what the men would do to him and Miranda once they had what they wanted.

Jumping from the horse, Teddy didn't concern himself with the others. He had a plan, and in order for it to work, he had to make certain that things came together. Rushing into the cabin, he went immediately to the stove, took up kindling and matches, and started a fire. He no sooner had that going when Cec came into the cabin, pushing Miranda ahead of him.

"What do you think you're doing?" Cec bellowed.

"I'm getting a fire going. She's half frozen," Teddy said, pointing to his wife. "I'm half frozen. I think some tea would do us all good." He added small sticks to the fire and watched as the flames greedily claimed the offering. Next he put in split strips of dried logs left over from the previous winter.

Miranda sunk onto the small bed and rubbed her arms vigorously. Teddy worried about her health, fearing the cold and continuous riding would be her undoing. Checking the fire again, Teddy was satisfied that it was going strong. He added a few more pieces of wood, then took up a bucket and, without waiting for Cec to comment, went out of the cabin.

Since it hadn't been cold for too long, he figured the creek would still be free flowing, but if not, there was the snow. Breaking through a thin crust of ice, Teddy filled the bucket and hurried back to the cabin. He hated to think of Miranda alone with Cec and Mitch. The two were the lowest kind of scum, and Teddy could only pray that God would deliver them before Cec could hurt them.

"Here's the water," Teddy said, entering the cabin as though they were all good friends.

"Look, I don't care about the water," Cec said angrily. "I want that box."

"I understand," Teddy declared, "but the tea is important." He poured the water into a pan and put it on top of the stove. Then, pulling a bundle from his coat, Teddy unwrapped the herbs he'd brought along with him.

"I ain't standing around while you play host," Cec declared.

Teddy measured out a portion of mandrake root and sprinkled it into the water. He could only pray that the amount was sufficient.

"I said, I want that box," Cec said, coming forward to take hold of Teddy's arm. "Let your woman fix tea, if that's what you want, but you get that box for me."

Teddy nodded. "Very well. Miranda, would you finish preparing the *Mandragora officinarum* tea?"

Miranda's brows raised in surprise, and Teddy knew instantly that she understood what he'd done. She nodded, getting to her feet slowly.

"Now, where is my box?"

"I believe," Teddy said, glancing around the room, "that I must have locked it in the cache outside. Let me check the other room, however. No sense in going back outside if the box is in the other room."

"Get to it, then."

Teddy saw Miranda take her place at the stove. She picked up the small bottle and studied the label as if to assure herself that she'd heard him right. "Darling, feel free to offer our guests tea after it has a chance to boil a minute."

Miranda nodded in understanding.

Teddy checked the bedroom knowing full well the box wouldn't be found there. He was buying time. Time to let the mandrake tea get hot. Time to see both men rendered unconscious.

Teddy made a pretense of digging through things, pushing blankets and boxes aside. Cec looked into the room about the time Teddy decided he'd done as much as he could. "It's not here," he declared. "Guess we'll have to take the ladder and climb to the cache."

"Hurry up! I've waited long enough."

"I'll only be a minute," Teddy said, seeing that Miranda was preparing to pour the tea. He took up a ladder that was stored by the front door. It was a simple homemade contraption that Little Charley had put together for him when he'd built the cache. "You go ahead and have some tea."

"I don't want tea," Cec fairly roared. "I want that box and I want it now. Mitch, you stay with the girl. I'm going with him."

Miranda was just handing Mitch a mug of tea when Cec made this announcement. Teddy saw her worried look. He knew she was thinking the same thing he was. If Cec went with him, then he'd return to find his partner unconscious and there would no doubt be a problem. Instead of worrying about it, however, Teddy ushered Cec quickly out the door. Mandrake worked fast, and if the man fell unconscious, Teddy wanted Cec completely removed from the scene.

—❙CHAPTER THIRTY-ONE❙—

MIRANDA WATCHED in wonder as Mitch slumped to the table. She felt a sense of relief as he appeared to sink into a deep sleep. She looked at the tea and smiled. Teddy had thought of everything. What a brilliant scheme.

Looking to the door, however, she frowned. Cec Blackabee would return with Teddy and see the man sleeping and know that something was up. She wondered what she could do. Perhaps she could drag the man to the back room and hide him. But though the man was thin, Miranda could clearly see that wouldn't work. She was tired and hungry from their journey. Cec hadn't figured it important to feed her much or see to it that she rested. Now, with complete exhaustion washing over her, Miranda knew she could easily fall asleep without the aid of the mandrake tea.

Still, sleep wasn't an option at this point. She had to

think, and think fast. The cache wasn't that far away, and once Teddy retrieved the box, Cec would march him back into the cabin, and then he would see Mitch and demand answers.

Spying the cast-iron skillet, Miranda decided her course of action. She picked up the skillet and went to stand beside the door. When Teddy came back, he'd no doubt be in the lead. She would wait until he passed by her, and then she'd club Cec over the head.

The thought turned her stomach. Miranda tried not to think of the graphic scene of Cec's head wounded by her hand. She cringed. Could she really hit him? Her hand began to tremble. *God, please help me.*

The door opened and Miranda held her breath. She raised the skillet over her head and closed her eyes for a split second. Letting her breath out slowly, she waited.

"Move!"

She heard the demand but startled at the sound of her husband's voice. She waited and stared in wonder as Cec Blackabee entered the room first. He carried the white box in front of him and Teddy followed. Then to her surprise, Adrik Ivankov came in behind them both.

"Thank you, Father," she whispered.

All three men turned to see her standing, poised and ready to strike. Smiling, she lowered the skillet. "I thought maybe I could hit him over the head," she explained to her husband.

Teddy went to the table where Mitch had passed out. He felt his neck and nodded. "He's still alive. At the rate Mr. Blackabee was rushing me, I couldn't be sure that I'd put in the right amount of mandrake."

"Look here," Cec said in protest, "I got a lot at stake here."

"So does Jacob Barringer," Adrik said without feeling.

"That's right," Miranda threw in. "You're letting a boy take the blame for a murder you committed."

"Nobody can prove I did it," Cec said smiling. "Now maybe if you were to let me take my box and go . . ."

Teddy shook his head. "Put the box down." He went to the back room and returned with rope. "Adrik, would you mind doing the honors? I'm afraid my knot tying isn't all it should be."

Miranda watched the big, burly man smile. "I'd be pleased to help out." He took up the rope and fairly knocked the box from Cec's hands. "Thought he told you to put that down."

"You both can be rich if you help me," Cec said, even as Adrik bound his hands.

"What's in that box that makes you willing to kill?" Teddy questioned. He lifted the white box and looked it over. Miranda edged closer to see if there was anything special about the piece. Teddy looked up and caught her gaze. "Are you all right?" he asked softly.

"I will be," she assured him. Her heart swelled with love for her husband. He'd been so brave and bold. She would never have imagined the quiet, mild-mannered botanist she loved would dream up serving mandrake tea.

"We're taking you back to Dawson and letting the law sort this out," Adrik told Cec as he finished tying him to the chair.

"I'm tellin' you, if you'd just listen to me," Cec demanded, "you could be rich."

Adrik shook his head. "I don't want to be rich. I want Jacob Barringer out of jail."

"Well, he ain't never gonna get that way if you take me in," Cec said snidely. "I'll tell 'em all how I saw him kill that old man."

"You'll do nothing of the kind," Adrik said. "You'll tell them the truth or I'll beat you senseless."

"Go ahead. Beat me. That will only help my case."

"Why do you need this box to be rich?" Teddy questioned.

Miranda stayed close to his side, fearful that Cec might yet break loose or that Mitch might awaken. She didn't want to be anywhere near either man should they find it within their own strength to gain the upper hand.

"Look, you let me go," Cec tried to dicker, "and I'll give you half the claim. Mitch ain't much good to me anyway. I have a claim on Bonanza Creek."

"Those are some of the richest claims in the territory," Adrik said matter-of-factly. "Where in the world did you get a claim like that?"

"I had a partner," Cec replied. "He went north while I stayed in Whitehorse. We figured I could keep sellin' whiskey while he went up and scouted us out a claim. He found one, but we needed to sell the saloon in order to finish paying the owner of the claim his askin' price."

"So you paid him off, received the deed, and your partner decided he wanted the claim for himself? Is that it?" Adrik asked.

"That's about the sum of it," Cec declared. "Only thing is, I hid the papers and the map. He didn't know where, but he thought he did. He knew it had something to do with the sled and so he stole off in the middle of the night and took the sled with him. He tried to take the dogs, but he never had learned how to hitch 'em to the sled, so they got away from him."

"So the man who showed up here to sell me the sled," Teddy interjected, "was your partner?"

"That's right."

"So what does the sled box have to do with this?" Adrik asked.

"That's where I hid the papers. He didn't know it, though. He figured, like I said, that they were hidden somewhere on the sled, but he couldn't figure it out. I had a secret compartment on the box, a false bottom where I hid the papers. When he robbed me of the sled, he robbed me of everything."

Teddy examined the box and, to Miranda's surprise, quickly figured out the puzzle of the box and opened a panel in the side. Tipping the box sideways, Teddy spilled out several pieces of paper. Miranda quickly retrieved them and handed them to her husband.

"It's a deed, all right," Teddy replied. He handed the paper to Adrik. "I don't know too much about such things, but since you have a claim of your own, maybe you can tell if this is the real thing or not."

"Looks real enough," Adrik said, studying the paper.

"This looks like a bill of sale," Teddy said, handing Adrik yet another piece of paper. He unfolded the final piece of paper and held it up. "This is the map."

"See, I weren't lyin'."

"Well, perhaps that's the only one of the commandments you haven't broken yet," Adrik said, "but I doubt it."

Cec spit on the floor. "Look, if you want that boy of yours to go free, then you're gonna have to do business with me. Mitch was out in the woods waiting for me the night the old man died. I'll tell the law it were him and not Jacob who killed the Swede." He looked hopefully to Miranda and then to Teddy. "That way we'll all be happy."

"I don't imagine Mitch would be too happy," Teddy countered.

"And then you'd be breaking the commandment about lying," Adrik added, "and I know how that would just about break your heart."

"I ain't gonna rot in a jail. Not when this claim on the Bonanza is worth fifty thousand if it's worth a dime."

The front door, which had been left partially open after Adrik had passed through, now opened in full. Two Northwest Mounted Police officers entered looking for all the world as if they materialized out of thin air.

Adrik turned to the men. "Have you heard enough?"

"Indeed we have. We'll take the prisoner into custody for the murder of Gumption Lindquist, as well as the kidnapping of Thomas and Miranda Davenport."

Adrik chuckled. "Ah, I'm sure there are quite a few more charges you can figure out to pin on him. Just remember, lying isn't one of them."

"I have my serious doubts about that," the sergeant said.

"Well, to tell you the truth, I have my doubts as well," Adrik admitted.

Relieved at the Mounties' appearance, Miranda longed for the horrid man to be taken from their cabin. She wasn't at all pleased when her husband suggested the hour was too late to start back for Dawson.

"You're welcome to keep him in the back room. There are no windows and only one entry."

The Mountie nodded. "I believe it would be prudent." He motioned for his subordinate to take Cec in hand.

"You ain't gonna pin that murder on me," Cec declared. "They'll hang Jacob for sure now."

Adrik crossed his arms and stared hard at the older man. Miranda saw his eyes narrow. He opened his mouth to say something, then turned and walked out the door. Miranda looked to Teddy. "I'd like to go talk to him." Teddy nodded.

Miranda slipped away from her husband even as Cec continued with his protests—cursing them all for their stupidity. Following Adrik outside, she was relieved to see that the snow had stopped completely and the sun was out.

"Adrik," she called after him. He had walked away from the house, but paused and turned.

"Sorry, I just had to get some air," he said as she joined him.

"I can well understand. I've been in his company for three days now and feel like the only thing I want is a bath. The man is as bad as they come. He doesn't care about anything but himself."

"He'd have let Jacob die."

Miranda shuddered. "Yes, he no doubt would have."

"I can abide a lot of things, Miranda, but that isn't one of 'em."

"I know."

Adrik pushed his hat back. "I've seen enough corruption

and evil to last me a lifetime. Here we are on the verge of new century, and it seems the entire world is so wrapped up in itself that most folks can't even see what's right or wrong."

"Teddy told me that many people believe the end of the world will come on the last day of the year."

"I've heard the same," Adrik replied. "They get all excited about dates on a calendar rather than focusing on what's real and true. And that includes folks in the church as well as those who aren't." He paused and shook his head. "I just don't get it. Makes me sorry I ever came north."

"I'm not sorry I came north," Miranda replied. "I might never have met Teddy. But I am sorry for the greed and the sins of the men who are driven by that greed. I rejoice in the Lord, however, that He made a way for Jacob to be found innocent without having to wait for a long trial. I'm sure he's miserable enough in jail."

"He is. His faith's been really shaken. Leah's, too. But I think they'll come out of the fire proven as gold. They're good folk and their hearts are right."

"Karen's done well with them, as have you. I know Jacob spoke to me of how much he admired you. You've become his only father figure. Do you mind taking on a ready-made family?"

Adrik grinned. "I hadn't figured to even marry, to tell you the truth. Didn't figure I'd find a woman up to the challenge. Karen proved me wrong on that. So I guess I can handle being father to a couple of orphaned kids. Especially when they're as great as Jacob and Leah."

"I'm glad. I wondered what would become of them since it's pretty certain their father never made it past the avalanche."

"I'll offer them both a home for as long as they want it."

Miranda smiled. "On the coast of Alaska?"

"Yes, ma'am. Back where I belong," Adrik replied enthusiastically. He looked to the cabin and then to Miranda. "You're good medicine. You've got me thinking back on what's important and right in my life, instead of what's wrong. Teddy's a lucky man. You're going to do him proud."

"Thank you," Miranda said, feeling suddenly embarrassed by his praise. "How about we go back now and figure what we can put together for dinner."

Adrik nodded. "The Mounties and I brought a few provisions. I couldn't rustle up much since we were struggling to keep pace with you, but what I have is yours."

Miranda looped her arm through his and pulled him forward. The big man kept an even gait with her steps, neither saying another word. *It is good to have friends like this*, Miranda thought. She knew no matter where the future took them, she'd always be able to count on Adrik Ivankov. He was just that kind of person.

Later that night, Miranda stepped out for a walk with her husband. The air was cold but not uncomfortably so. They walked hand in hand for a time without speaking a single word. Finally, Miranda looked up to catch Teddy watching her.

"What are you thinking about?" she asked.

"I was just remembering when you were brought to my cabin. You were so lifeless, I was sure you were already dead. Nellie was the only one who believed you'd make it. The men who brought you wouldn't even stick around for a meal, they were so certain you would die while they were there. And being very superstitious people, they didn't want to deal with your spirit being unleashed. Especially since it would be a most troubled spirit from having died so tragically."

"It was that bad, eh?"

Teddy nodded. "Gravely so. You were so very sick. With each passing day and no response from you, I felt confident that all I could do was pray for you to pass easily into God's awaiting arms." He stopped walking and pulled her into his embrace. "I'm so very glad He didn't take you then. I cannot imagine my life without you in it."

"I spent so many months angry that God would allow such a thing to happen to me. I imagined my grieving parents and friends and just thought what a horribly cruel joke it was to play on them," Miranda admitted. "Now, with that time behind me, I see how God took the bad and made it come together for good. He gave me you and he brought my brother back together with Grace. He was worried about leaving me here alone—about my being stranded and penniless. That's what brought him up here."

"Your brother is a good man," Teddy said, gently tracing Miranda's jaw with his thumb.

"He's changed a good deal—for the better, I'm happy to say. He never would have picked you to be my husband—not with the way he used to think and evaluate the potential suitors in my life."

Teddy dropped his hold and stepped away feigning hurt. "You mean I wouldn't have been good enough for you?"

Miranda laughed and the sound was lyrical and light-hearted. How good it was to be happy. To laugh again and have everything come together in proper order.

"To the way Peter Colton used to think, no one was good enough for me," she said, still smiling. "But he changed his thinking and suddenly realized I knew what was best for myself all along."

"And what was that?"

"You," she replied, stepping forward to wrap her arms around his neck. "Only you, Thomas Edward Davenport."

—[CHAPTER THIRTY-TWO]—

JACOB HEARD THE COMMISSIONER say he was free to go, but the words barely registered. His soul soared on wings—the wings of freedom. Leah jumped into his arms, laughing in her excitement.

"Did you hear that! You're free! I told you God would work it all out. I told you He wouldn't let us down."

"Yes, you told me," Jacob said, chuckling. Leah's laughter was contagious.

"We've been after this man for a long time," the commissioner said, leaning back in his chair. "Of course, we had no idea that the man who killed the true owner of the Bonanza claim and the man who killed Mr. Lindquist were one and the same."

Jacob loosened Leah's hold on him and sobered. "So he killed more than Gump?"

"Indeed he did. Mr. Blackabee killed the rightful owner of this deed." The man held up the paper as if for evidence to his statement. "We had witnesses to the crime, but no one knew the killer by name. We even had a drawing made up. See here?" He pulled a paper from his drawer. The likeness was very much like that of Cec Blackabee.

Adrik stepped forward. "We'd like to leave Dawson as soon as possible. How long before this can be cleared up? What with Jacob being a witness to Gump's killing, and all."

"It shouldn't be more than a matter of weeks at the most," the commissioner declared. "We'll do what we can to see the matter resolved in an expeditious manner. We have Mr. Barringer's written statement, as well as the statement of the Mounties who overheard Mr. Blackabee's confession. With the other charges against Blackabee, Jacob's testimony may well not be needed. Cecil Blackabee will most likely be hanged."

Jacob shuddered. It could just as easily have been him they were talking about. In spite of the way Cec had left him to take the blame for Gump's death, Jacob pitied the man. After all, he had saved Jacob's life. His mind protested too much concern, however, as Jacob knew Cec would have let him die in order to save his own neck.

Adrik and Karen led the way outside, with Jacob and Leah following close behind. Jacob drew in a deep breath as soon as his feet hit the muddy street. Freedom. How very precious it was. He had taken for granted the privilege and joy of just being able to come and go as he pleased.

Thank you, God, he prayed silently as they made their way to the Dawson Lucky Day Hotel. *I feel so blessed that you have delivered me from jail—from the possibility of death.*

362

"Peter Colton said to tell you that you could have a job with his shipping company whenever you were ready," Leah told Jacob.

Leah's news was just an added bonus to the day. "That's good to hear."

"What's this all about?" Karen questioned. "Are you making plans behind our backs, again?" She smiled and winked, making it clear she wasn't serious.

"I think I'm going to have to make some plans sooner or later," Jacob said, quite serious. "I'll be seventeen in January. I ought to find a decent job. I kind of figured if I got work with Peter, I could learn some kind of trade."

"That's good thinking, Jacob," Adrik said, slowing his pace to allow Jacob to pull up even with them. "Peter would make a good teacher. He'd be fair and honest, and those are traits you don't always see in your authorities on earth."

Jacob knew this to be true. He'd always admired the way Peter worked with Grace and Karen when the tent store had been a part of their lives. He didn't understand what had happened between Peter and Grace in their marriage, but he figured it wasn't his concern. He'd prayed for them both, however, as he had come to care about Grace as if she were family.

The foursome came to a stop on Second Avenue, as if the spot were some previously agreed upon destination. Adrik and Karen looked at Jacob as if searching for answers to unspoken questions. Jacob felt the need to continue.

"I want something better than what my pa had. He was a dreamer. Everything was always better one town over or at the next discovery of gold." He pointed down the deserted street. "You couldn't move along this street last year this time without running into someone or having to get out of somebody's way. Now it's almost worse off than when it started. That's always the way it seems to be. I've seen dozens of towns just like it. Leah has, too."

Leah nodded, as if to confirm his statement. Jacob reached over and gave one of her braids a playful tug. "I want something better. Something that offers more security to my family." He grew rather sheepish and added, "And someday I want a family—a wife and children. But I want to give them a home where they can live and know that every day there will be food on the table and a roof over their heads. I don't want them to worry about having to pack up their few belongings and head off to some new discovery of prosperity."

"Sounds like you've given this a lot of thought," Adrik said. "It also sounds like very wise planning."

"I figure it fits with what God wants for me, as well."

"Then God will point the way, Jacob," Adrik assured. "You can be guaranteed He'll show you the right direction."

———

October brought more snow and the promise of a cold and tiresome winter. Already there was less and less sunlight. Karen looked out the window of their hotel room and wondered how soon they would be able to leave. She was anxious to be settled in Dyea. Especially now.

She put her hand to her abdomen and marveled at the knowledge that she was to have a child. She hadn't told Adrik yet. She'd been waiting for a special moment. The baby, best as she could figure, would be born in May. It seemed a perfect month for a new life to come into the world. Even in the frozen north, new life could be found in May.

Karen thought of her mother and father and wished they could have lived to see her married to Adrik. They both had held him in such high regard, and Adrik had loved them even before Karen was a part of his life. Surely they looked down from heaven, happy for the union and proud of the choice she'd made.

She hoped they'd also be proud of her desire to pick up where they left off. After long hours of discussion with her husband, Karen felt confident that they were being called into ministry work with the Tlingit Indians. She particularly wanted to work with the children—teaching them everything she could so that they might be better equipped if and when they wanted to be a part of the White world.

"Well, it's settled," Adrik said, coming through the adjoining door to their sitting room. "Jacob is free to leave. The government released him."

Karen looked at Adrik and saw the joy in his face. He had been so worried about Jacob. He loved him as much as a man could love a son, and this warmed her heart. She knew he would be a good father.

"You look very pleased to hear the news," he said, sitting down to pull off his boots.

"I am. I'm also very pleased about the love you've shown Jacob and Leah. You have been so very good to both of them in the absence of their real father."

"They're easy to care about. Easy to love," he said, putting his boots aside. He pulled out his pocket watch and checked the time. "I didn't realize it was getting so late. The commissioner kept me even after announcing the news. He kept talking about the changes in the area."

Karen smiled. "It's no bother. I was too excited to sleep."

"I can well imagine. Waiting for this news has stretched our patience. But now that we have it, we can go back to Dyea and build us a cabin. Or, from the sounds of it, take one that's been deserted. I guess Dyea is hardly more than a few folks keepin' company these days. Skagway's suffering, too. I feel bad for the folks who poured so much time and effort, not to mention money, into building up those towns."

Karen nodded and unfastened the tie on her robe. "So do you think we can leave Dawson right away?" She slipped out of the robe and carefully draped it across the end of the bed. Turning down the covers, she waited for Adrik's answer, but none came.

She paused and looked back to see what had suddenly silenced him. "What's wrong?"

"Nothing," he said, getting to his feet. "I was just watching you. You are the most beautiful woman in the world. I still can't believe how blessed I am. I couldn't be any happier."

"Don't count on that," she murmured, getting into the bed. Her strawberry blond curls spilled out across the pillow as she leaned back. She watched her husband, memorizing each detail—his broad, strong shoulders, trim waist, and thick, muscular legs. He was a powerful man of great physical stamina. She wondered if they had sons if they would take after him. She smiled again at the thought of the child. How very blessed she was. God had given her the desires of her heart—so much more precious than rivers of gold or mountains that glittered with ore. A child!

Adrik quickly finished undressing and picked up the Bible on the stand beside the bed. It was their habit to read from the Word every night before retiring. He slid under the covers and eased back against the headboard of their bed.

"I have a request for tonight's reading," Karen said. She thought this the perfect way to break her news. "Read from the Psalms. Specifically Psalm 127."

"All right," he said, turning the lamp up a bit before flipping through the well-worn pages.

"Psalm 127," he began. " 'Except the Lord build the house, they labour in vain that build it: Except the Lord keep the city, the watchman waketh but in vain.' "

He smiled over at her and Karen reached out to tenderly touch his bearded face. He continued reading. " 'It is vain for you to rise up early, to sit up late, to eat the bread of sorrows: for so he giveth his beloved sleep.' "

Adrik grinned. "Now I see why you wanted me to read this. You're hoping I'll be quiet and let you go to sleep."

Karen giggled. "Not at all. I quite like being in your company Mr. Ivankov."

Adrik turned back to the Bible. " 'Lo, children are an heritage of the Lord: and the fruit of the womb is his reward. As arrows are in the hand of a mighty man; so are children of the youth. Happy is the man that hath his quiver full of them: they shall not be ashamed, but they shall speak with the enemies in the gate.' "

He looked at her quizzically. "That's it. It's a mighty short psalm."

"Yes, but it says quite a bit." She reached over and took the Bible from him and put it on the stand on her side of the bed.

" 'Except the Lord build the house, they labour in vain that build it,' " he murmured as Karen snuggled closer. "That's good counsel."

"Yes," she said. She reached over and took hold of his hand. Drawing it over to her stomach, she added, " 'Lo, children are an heritage of the Lord: and the fruit of the womb is his reward.' "

Adrik said nothing. Karen heard his breathing quicken, but still he said nothing. She looked at him and saw the disbelief in his expression. Smiling, she pressed closer and kissed his lips very tenderly. "We're going to have a baby."

"I can't believe it," he finally managed to say. "A baby." The wonder of it all was written in his face as his expression changed from shock to acceptance.

"Yes, a baby," Karen said excitedly. "The doctor believes it will come sometime in May."

Adrik pulled her close, nearly knocking the wind from her as he squeezed her tight. As if realizing his strength, he quickly released her. "I didn't hurt you, did I?"

"No, silly. You just surprised me."

"I surprised you? You just about gave me heart failure with your little surprise."

Karen frowned. "You aren't pleased?" She hadn't even thought he might not want to have children right away.

"Of course I'm pleased," he said, sounding hurt that she would even suggest such a possibility.

Relief coursed through her body, and she settled down in his arms once more. "I'm glad you're pleased. I'm so excited I can hardly bear it. It's too wondrous."

He drew her to him more gently this time. Stroking her long hair, he studied her face for a moment. "I'm so very blessed."

She nodded, "We're so very blessed."

The next morning Adrik woke up before Karen. He watched her sleep for a long time, completely amazed at the news she'd given him the night before. He was going to be a father. The news was not what he had anticipated, and yet it was so completely perfect. He couldn't imagine her not being pregnant—it seemed so right, so completely of God.

He had thought for a long time into the night about their future. About the plans he should make. He would get them back down to Dyea before the hard winter set in. He had friends there. Family too. He would see to it that they had a good home in which to raise their new child.

For as long as he could remember, Adrik had longed for a family of his own. He hadn't figured any woman in her right mind would want to live the way he did, dealing with the people who were so very dear to him. He figured marriage would probably not be something he'd be blessed with. But God had proven him wrong. And now, God had given him a child.

Karen stirred and opened her eyes. She looked up sleepily and batted her eyelids several times as if trying to clear the haze.

"Good morning, love," he whispered, leaning down to kiss her.

"Morning." She yawned and shrugged her shoulders. "How did you sleep?"

"Like a man who'd just been told he's going to be a father."

She smiled. "That well, huh?"

"I just started thinking of all the things we'd have to do and sleep became an impossible task."

Karen stretched and sat up. Adrik pulled her back against

him, relishing the way she felt in his arms. "So what is it that you figure we need to do?" she asked.

"Well, first off, we need to get back to Dyea," he began. "I want to secure a good place to live for the winter and make sure it's big enough for all of us. I don't know how much longer Jacob will be with us, but we'll plan for him as well."

"What else?"

"Well, we need to figure out what all you'll need for the baby. I can make the cradle myself, but we'll need to get some materials so you and Leah can start sewing up all those little doodads babies always need. We'll send a letter to Peter, and he can bring a load up the next time he comes to Skagway."

"That sounds wise. I'm glad you have this all figured out."

Adrik laughed. "I haven't had much of anything figured out since the day I first met you. But to tell you honestly, it doesn't matter. I'm enjoying myself immensely."

Laughing, Karen wriggled out of his arms and pulled on her robe. "You enjoy yourself far too much," she teased.

"Well, I figure—"

The knock at the door interrupted his thoughts. Karen tied her sash and went to the door while Adrik jumped from the bed and pulled on his jeans.

"Who is it?" she called.

"Miranda."

Karen glanced at Adrik. He nodded, then hurried to pull a shirt on over his long underwear.

Karen opened the door. "Good morning, Miranda. We slept a bit late. Hope you'll pardon our appearance."

"I'm sorry. I hadn't intended to bother you this early, but a man is downstairs waiting to talk to Adrik. I told Teddy I'd come and get him."

Adrik was surprised by the news. "I'll get my boots on and be right down. Any idea what the man wants?"

"He said he could offer you transportation to White-horse."

Adrik looked to Karen and laughed. "Well, God is certainly keeping us on the right path. That's a good start south. We'll be home before you know it."

———

"We're going to miss you terribly," Miranda said as Karen and Adrik told them the news of their departure later that night. They stood in the hotel lobby close to the fireplace in order to ward off the October chill.

"We certainly will," Teddy added. "You've been more than good friends. You've been a generous and loving family to both of us."

"We feel the same about you," Karen assured. "Don't forget your promise to look us up on your way to San Francisco."

"Since we probably won't be able to go until May or June, perhaps we'll get a chance to see the baby, as well," Miranda said excitedly. "I still can't believe the news. It's just so wonderful."

Karen looked to Adrik and laughed. "It is wonderful. I can't tell you how happy we are."

"May will take forever to get here," Miranda said mournfully. She looked to Teddy and forced a smile. She didn't want him to think her too sad so she quickly added, "At least, I'm sure you'll feel that way. Waiting for good things is always hard, especially when it involves a baby."

"And waiting with patience has never been easy for me," Karen replied. "I have very little in that area to draw from."

"Well, this child will come in God's timing and His alone," Teddy replied.

"Say, where are Leah and Jacob?" Miranda questioned. "Do they know about the baby?"

"They do indeed," Karen answered. "As for their whereabouts, they're upstairs packing. They're very anxious to leave Dawson. They're ready to begin anew and settle down to a different kind of life."

"Oh, we shall miss you so," Miranda said, hugging Karen and then Adrik. "You both mean the world to me. I'm so grateful you allowed me to come north with you."

"Despite the fact we lost you in the lake?" Adrik jokingly asked.

"Especially for losing me in the lake," Miranda replied, then went to Teddy's side. "I might never have found my true love, otherwise. You shouldn't feel guilty at all, but rather rejoice for having played a part in God's plan to put Teddy and me together."

"That's definitely one way of looking at it," Adrik replied.

"It's the best way of looking at it." Miranda's words gave her the strength to say good-bye to yet another group of loved ones. She wasn't left comfortless or without love. She reminded herself of her blessings and looked up to catch Teddy's loving gaze. Yes, she thought, it was the best way to look at the events of her life over the last couple of years.

One event had been built upon another, and each had brought her to the place she was now.

Miranda would see all her loved ones again one day, and for now, she had her Teddy—her beloved Teddy.

⫣ C H A P T E R   T H I R T Y - T H R E E ⫠

33

CHRISTMAS 1899 PASSED with much joy in the Colton household. San Francisco was a far cry from the cold of the Yukon, and the spirit of celebration was upon the whole family.

Andy, now nearly a year old, was the apple of his grandparents' eyes. Walking with awkward baby steps, he delighted the family to no end. Still too small for the rocking horse his Grandfather Ephraim had given him for Christmas, Andy was content to merely slap his palms against the wooden seat and chatter, "Horsy. Horsy."

"There's news from Teddy and Miranda," Peter said, unfolding a letter. "Actually, the news is from Teddy. He intends to surprise Miranda with a visit much sooner than planned. He's discussed lecturing here in San Francisco on the botanical wonders of the Yukon. Apparently there's a great deal of interest, and he's decided to approach an American publisher in regard to his book."

"How marvelous," Grace declared.

Abigail Colton nodded enthusiastically. "Oh, I long to see Miranda."

"Mother Colton, it won't be long," Grace assured. "She'll be here before you know it."

"Indeed," Peter replied. "Teddy plans to leave the Yukon shortly after the first of January. Apparently his native friends have agreed to help them."

"Oh, that's just days away," Abigail said, looking to Ephraim with great joy. "How long will it take them to get here?"

"Well, it depends on the weather. Teddy wants to arrange passage out of Skagway by the thirtieth of January. He worries that he might be delayed on the trail, but if that happens, they'll merely wait it out. I'll pick them up in Skagway. I'm planning to arrive there on *Merry Maid* the twenty-fifth of January. I'll be delivering supplies to the town anyway, as well as making a delivery to Karen and Adrik Ivankov in Dyea."

"Will Grace and Andy go, too?" his mother asked with concern in her tone.

"No, they'll stay here as the weather will probably be threatening. But I'm sure we'll make many more trips to the north."

"What of transporting gold miners to Nome?" Ephraim asked.

"We're already devoting *Summer Song* to that purpose," Peter explained. "I meant to discuss it with you last week. I've been using *Summer Song* for the past couple of months to take men and supplies into Nome. The biggest problem is that Norton Sound freezes solid. We end up having to harbor out deep and then transport folks and supplies across the ice. It isn't something I'm really comfortable with."

"I can well understand. What if the ice melts?"

Peter smiled at his mother. "They tell me it freezes many feet thick, but still, there's no sense in risking life and limb. The passage is long and risky, but the profits are good due to the tremendous need for supplies. I've received an order requesting I bring as many work dogs as possible, along with any fresh fruit I can find. I'll probably take *Merry Maid* up that way once the weather is better." He refolded the letter and put it into his pocket, adding, "Of course, we must get the Davenports here first."

"It will be so good to have Miranda home. Does Teddy say how long they can stay?" Grace questioned.

"No, but I'm sure if he's to lecture, it might well turn into a lengthy visit."

"Oh, I hope so," Grace said smiling. "I know it would do us all good to be a complete family again."

———

Miranda waited in the lobby of the Fairview Hotel. The elegance and grandeur of the once popular hotel had faded with the diminishing numbers of people still residing in Dawson. But it didn't matter. The citizens of the town had decided a New Year's Eve party was in order, and it had been a most entertaining and rewarding evening.

Miranda and Teddy had dressed in their finest clothes. Miranda wore a salmon-colored satin gown that was trimmed with black jets and lace. The full cut of the muttonchop sleeves were inset with ebony lace, which the dressmaker had assured Miranda had been handmade in Paris.

Teddy, ever the refined Englishman, sported the latest fashion—a black Prince Albert–styled frock coat with satin lapels and gray striped trousers. Miranda thought him the most handsome man at the party. He moved with such grace that Miranda felt almost clumsy alongside him. But it wasn't long before he had her dancing comfortably in his arms. He was as gentle and tender a teacher on the dance floor as he had been in training her in botanical research.

"Here we are," Teddy said, coming from the cloakroom with Miranda's cape and his own coat. He put the fur-lined cape around her shoulders before donning his coat. "I'm certain the weather is quite frigid."

"Then I shall have to walk very close to you in order to stay warm," Miranda teased.

"You shall walk very close to me anyway," Teddy replied. "I wouldn't have it any other way." He pulled her near and held her close. "Did you enjoy yourself this evening?"

"Very much," she answered, looking up into his face. "I enjoy myself wherever you are."

Walking from the hotel, they left behind the gentle strains of a Strauss waltz. Miranda had enjoyed the music even more than the dancing. She had missed the concerts she and her mother had attended on occasion in San Francisco. The thought had never even entered her mind until coming here tonight.

Fact was, she tried hard not to think of San Francisco at all. Even though her family could not consider themselves as wealthy, Miranda had enjoyed many cultural programs that had given her great pleasure. Those things were few and far between in Dawson. It wasn't for a lack of trying, however.

In its heyday, Dawson's Opera House and Palace Theatres were acceptable places of entertainment, but it wasn't the same. Miranda felt as though she were stuck at the end of the earth, with no hope of ever rejoining civilization.

She knew part of her depression was the lack of light. The winter months were very difficult to endure—especially for one who treasured the sunlight so very much. Then there was the cold and the snow. Miranda felt she'd endured enough of both to last her a lifetime.

"What are you thinking about?" Teddy whispered against her ear.

Miranda smiled. Teddy made it all bearable. She was so glad for his company—his love. "I'm just thinking how fortunate I am that God brought us together. You've given me so much."

"It helps that my holdings are vast," Teddy said laughing.

"No, not the material things," Miranda replied. "I know I shall most likely never want for those, but I'm speaking of your love and tenderness. I love being with you—learning from you. I feel as though a whole new world has been opened up to me."

"As do I. I know my focus for years was on one thing alone: the botanical book that would fulfill my father's dream. But it doesn't fulfill my dreams. You do that."

Miranda reached across Teddy's waist and took hold of his arm. Pulling it to her, she gently kissed his gloved hand. "And you do that for me. I adore you, you know."

"I hadn't guessed."

He paused outside their hotel and lowered his lips to hers. "Happy New Year, Mrs. Davenport."

Miranda forgot about the cold as her heart raced,

warming her blood. "Perhaps," she whispered against his mouth, "we should go upstairs."

He pulled back grinning. "You are a bold one, Mrs. Davenport."

She giggled. "I wasn't implying anything improper. I'm merely confident that we will freeze to death if we wait out here much longer."

Teddy laughed and opened the door. "After you, my dearest wife."

They went directly to their room, ignoring the revelry of other hotel guests who were celebrating the new century. Miranda thought it all such a wonder that they should find themselves in the year 1900. What would the years to come bring? Would there be new wonders and innovations to bless them in their daily existence? Or would there be wars and tragedy? No doubt there would be both, and only a faith in God would help them endure the passage of time.

Once they'd reached their room, Teddy helped Miranda with her cloak, then saw to his own things. Shedding his frock coat to reveal a snug, white waistcoat and starched shirt, Teddy then pulled the gray silk ascot from around his throat.

Miranda watched as he put his things very carefully aside, then pulled his glasses from his pocket. She frowned. Usually this was the signal that he intended to work, but it was well past midnight, and she had not figured him to even be interested in such matters.

"Where are you going?" she asked as he walked from their bedroom into the sitting room and work area.

"I have something I need to tend to," he said.

Miranda dispensed with her handbag and gloves and followed her husband into the other room. "Teddy, it's very late. Couldn't it wait until morning?"

"No, I'm afraid that will be too late."

"Too late? What in the world could possibly be so important that it can't wait until morning?"

He opened his journal and motioned her to come to his side. "Come see for yourself."

She did and noted the calendar he had created for the month of January. The thirtieth was circled. "What's this all about? What is so important about the thirtieth of January?"

Teddy smiled secretively. "Well, that's what cannot wait."

"But that's thirty days away," she protested. "What happens on the thirtieth?"

"That's the day we catch a boat out of Skagway bound for California. In fact, if all goes well, it will be your brother's ship *Merry Maid*."

Miranda stared at her husband in disbelief. "What are you saying?"

Teddy closed the journal and reached out to take her in his arms. "I'm saying that we're leaving Dawson tomorrow. Little Charley and his friends are coming to take us south by dog sled. Are you up for the trip?"

Miranda felt tears come to her eyes. Teddy's words were just too wonderful. "Do you mean it?"

"Absolutely. Can you be ready?"

"Of course I can," Miranda declared. She wrapped her arms around her husband's neck in girlish anticipation. "Oh, Teddy, this is the best news you could have ever given me. When did you decide to do this?"

"Your brother and I spoke before he departed Dawson. I told him I would write to him to confirm the date, but I was certain the plans we set into motion would work well for us."

"But what of your work?"

"I'll take it with me. There's no need to remain here. I've exhausted the area in my searching, and I've an opportunity to take what I've learned and present it in lecture form for various universities and lecture halls."

"That's marvelous. Why didn't you tell me sooner?"

"I wanted to surprise you. I figured I owed it to you. You've been so very good to endure the departure of your friends and family. You've not complained about being left behind in this dying town, and I knew it would do us both good."

"When I first met you," Miranda said, lovingly touching her husband's face, "I thought you were the most self-centered man in the universe. You were buried deep in your work, and you scarcely even noticed that I was alive."

"I'd never had reason to think of anything else. My work had become my life, and even my faith suffered for it. But no more. I've learned the importance of listening with my heart, as well as my ears. I've learned that God doesn't desire us to live in isolated little shells, thinking of nothing and no one but ourselves. He longs for us to reach out—to share His love and to make mankind our greater concern.

"I started that journey from isolation when I met you, and the rewards have been most amazing. There isn't a river of gold I would trade for the love I have with you or the friendships I've made through you. I had no idea what was missing in my life, until you came along."

"I knew what was missing," Miranda said softly. "I just didn't know where to find it. But God did." She melted against him, longing only for his touch.

"I suppose," Teddy said, his voice husky with desire, "that we should get a good night's sleep. Little Charley will be here for us around ten o'clock."

"I'm not sleepy," Miranda whispered against his ear.

"Me either," Teddy replied. He pulled away enough that Miranda could clearly see his face. "Do you want to help me pack my samples? Or you could log the information for each one in the journal."

She took hold of his hand and pulled him gently toward the bedroom. "I think I'm more tired than I realized."

He chuckled and followed her without hesitation. "Ah, Mrs. Davenport. How am I ever to get my work done with you to distract me?"

Miranda laughed and closed the door to their room. "I'm sure you'll figure it out in the years to come. After all, I intend for us to have several score of years together. That's a lot of time for figuring."

"Or loving," he whispered.

She nodded. "Especially loving."